THEY RODE TOWARD THEIR DESTINY
WITH ALL THE MIGHT OF STEAM
AND STEEL . . . AND DESIRE

Ted Henderson—A frontier fighter who had lived all his life with danger, now called upon to perform one last patriotic duty—so treacherous, so risky that he must choose between his country and his heart.

Yellow Crow—A Sioux warrior chief obsessed with killing the half-breed renegade Long Walker . . . and heading toward a rendezvous in the darkest places of the soul.

Judy Hubbard—A pioneer woman with a past filled with shame, but a courage so magnificent that brutality and terror could not turn her from protecting those she loved.

Chin Lu—A Chinese stranger who bore the brand of the lion, his superb fighting skills would become implements of death to the lawless . . . or his own destruction.

Little Fern—An Indian princess who surrendered her heart to the foreigner she called Man-Who-Walks-Like-Shadow . . . but he had given his to vengeance.

Bear Fallon—A stone-cold killer whose orders were to stop the Union Pacific railway, but to do it meant stopping one man—Ted Henderson.

D0377353

WINNING THE WEST
Book III

UNION PACIFIC

Donald Clayton Porter

 ™

Created by the producers of
Wagons West, Stagecoach,
Badge, and White Indian.

Book Creations Inc., Canaan, NY · Lyle Kenyon Engel, Founder

BANTAM BOOKS
TORONTO · NEW YORK · LONDON · SYDNEY · AUCKLAND

UNION PACIFIC

A Bantam Book / published by arrangement with
Book Creations, Inc.

Bantam edition / April 1988

Produced by Book Creations, Inc.
Lyle Kenyon Engel, Founder

ISBN 0-553-26708-6

Published simultaneously in the United States and Canada

Bantam Books are published by Bantam Books, a division of
Bantam Doubleday Dell Publishing Group, Inc. Its trademark,
consisting of the words "Bantam Books" and the portrayal of
a rooster, is Registered in U.S. Patent and Trademark Office
and in other countries. Marca Registrada. Bantam Books, 666
Fifth Avenue, New York, New York 10103.

PRINTED IN THE UNITED STATES OF AMERICA

KR   0 9 8 7 6 5 4 3 2 1

UNION
PACIFIC

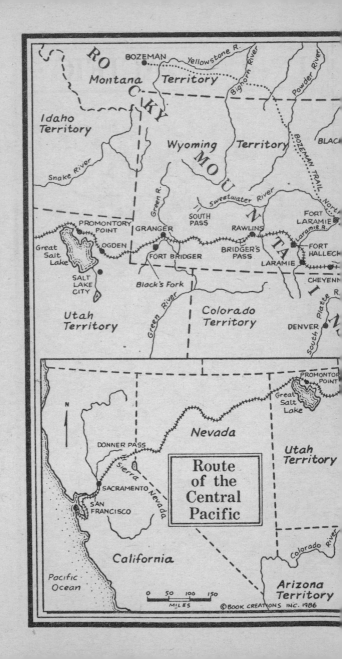

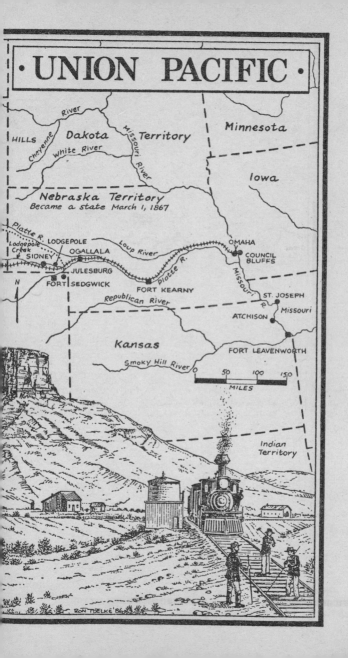

One

The Indian warrior-chief Long Walker snorted in disgust. The sound was heard easily above the chant of the nearby medicine man and the sweep of the mild autumn wind over the Nebraska tall-grass prairie. At Long Walker's side a swarthy Ute, Two Thorns, turned to face the warrior-chief.

"Long Walker does not believe in the magic of the medicine rope?" Two Thorns asked, noting the flash of anger in Long Walker's blue eyes. The color of the expressive eyes reflected Long Walker's half-white ancestry.

The part-Seminole who had risen to high rank among the Sioux glared back at Two Thorns. Long Walker's bare torso bore fresh scars, and his partly withered left arm was the result of his recent encounter with white soldiers. Yet Long Walker still commanded more than two hundred warriors who had scorned all peace treaties to carry on the battle against the whites.

Ribbons of muscle rippled along Long Walker's chest as he gestured with his good right hand toward the small gathering of Indians clustered around the medicine man, who continued to chant as he stood over a coil of thick rope.

"They are children," he snorted. "They think the medicine rope will capture the iron horse—the thing the white man calls a locomotive—and they do not see the real enemy."

Long Walker pointed toward the thin twin ribbons of metal glinting in the midday sun alongside the Platte River, barely a rifle shot away. "There is the enemy," he said bitterly, "an arrow of iron piercing the heart of Indian land. It is this iron arrow that must be broken. The white man calls it a railroad. Long Walker calls it the red man's grave."

Two Thorns's eyes narrowed in thought as the incantations of the medicine man continued to rise and fall from within the circle of rapt braves. "But would not the capture of

1

one of the iron horses be strong medicine to the Indian?" he asked. "Could not the white man's entire herd of the beasts that make dark smoke be captured?"

Long Walker abruptly turned away as though drawn into a sudden and deep meditation. But his action was to prevent Two Thorns from seeing the quick gleam of satisfaction in the chief's blue eyes. The swarthy Ute had finally raised the point toward which Long Walker had been leading him patiently.

"What Two Thorns says is true," Long Walker said after a long pause. "The capture of an iron horse would be great medicine. But consider this: Would not the killing of an iron horse be even stronger medicine? Would a leader able to kill the iron horse not be hailed as the greatest chief and hunter of the Plains? Would not the tribes rally behind such a powerful leader to stop the metal rails and to drive the white man from the Indian lands?"

Two Thorns pondered the idea briefly, then nodded. "It is true. Among all the tribes the metal arrows are hated. If they cross the hunting grounds the buffalo will run away. More white men will follow the tracks of the iron horse. A man who could kill such a beast would boast such magic that all red men would rush to the power of his shield. Reservations would empty and warriors by the thousands would again take up the lance."

And, Long Walker thought to himself, *I will be that man.* Only he among the Plains warriors understood how a railroad worked. Captured by white soldiers at the age of thirteen from a Seminole raiding party, he had been spared because of his blue eyes, the result of a marriage between a Seminole chieftain and a captive white woman. Living with whites, the part-Seminole had decided to learn from them what he could. He attended their schools and learned their ways. Before being dispatched to the Plains as an agent of the Confederacy during the recently ended war, Long Walker had studied the new locomotives.

Inwardly he sighed in contentment. Always an Indian at heart, he had dreamed of a red nation dominating the center of the continent with himself at its head. He had come to the Plains on foot, walking all the way from the East and earning the name Long Walker. Soon he had dropped his association with the Confederates and had led the Sioux in a war against the white man. He had been defeated in that war, and his dream had been dashed. But now it was within reach once again.

The medicine man's incantations stopped. Long Walker turned his attention back to the circle of braves, watching as the holy man sprinkled a few grains of sacred sand over the coils of a thick rope made of twisted buffalo skin. Long Walker knew the medicine man's plan would fail. And then he, Long Walker, would succeed. He would make a small miracle at first, then a larger one. And soon his ranks would be swollen by thousands of Indians, enough to drive the hated white man from the Plains forever.

A short time later, Long Walker and Two Thorns lay side by side, peering over the crest of a low, grassy hill toward the railroad tracks below. The trap had been set. The medicine rope stretched across the tracks, and at each end two burly braves waited patiently for the approach of the iron horse.

The locomotive came slowly, with a mournful whistle. Long Walker noted with satisfaction it was a small engine, pulling a few carloads of supplies to rails' end beyond Fort Kearny. When the time came, his own target would be much bigger.

The locomotive neared the sacred medicine rope. Just before it touched the rope, the four burly braves leapt to their feet, yanking the rope tight across the tracks to trip the iron horse and bring it to a halt.

The locomotive slammed into the rope. The impact jerked the lead brave on Long Walker's side beneath the front wheels. The three other Indians went tumbling, their palms bleeding as the medicine rope ripped through their hands. With a derisive toot of the whistle the train chugged past, laughter coming from the engineer's window. The train vanished around a bend as the concealed Indians gathered about the mangled remains of their ill-fated comrade. The medicine rope lay neatly severed into three sections where it had dropped to the rails beneath the wheels of the locomotive.

Long Walker held up both arms until a hush settled over the distraught group of Indians. Slowly, he knelt beside the mangled mess that had been a strong and healthy Indian brave only moments before. He poked a forefinger into the gore. With theatrical gestures he streaked his cheeks and forehead with the blood of the dead man. He beckoned Two Thorns to his side and repeated the streaking procedure on the Ute's face.

Then he turned to face the group of now-curious braves.

"Brothers, listen," he called in a strong voice. "The powers of the iron horse have been seen. They are greater than even those of our beloved medicine man. But Long Walker has had a vision. He knows now how to kill the iron horse!"

A mutter of excitement rippled through the small gathering. "Once, when he was defeated by the long knives at Fort Kearny, Long Walker feared his medicine was lost. Now he knows that the spirits were only saving him for this far greater test." He touched the shoulder of the blood-streaked and wide-eyed Two Thorns. "With only this man—Long Walker's brother in the eyes of the spirits—Long Walker shall kill the beast with but a single holy bullet from his rifle!"

He grasped the carbine that had been leaning against his side and hoisted the Henry repeater high overhead. "This, the greatest of all hunts, shall end tomorrow when the sun stands there!" He pointed the rifle toward the midafternoon sky.

"How does Long Walker know an iron horse will pass at that time?" a young Arapaho asked curiously.

"The spirits have said so in a vision," Long Walker replied calmly. A message from the spirit world meant something to these superstitious, almost childlike warriors, he thought wryly. It would impress them a great deal less to learn that Long Walker had merely observed the strict schedules of the supply trains.

"Two Thorns and Long Walker shall return to this very spot when the white maiden of the night rides the skies," Long Walker said. "Then, under her soft light, they will perform the magic. Only the two of them are to use this magic. The rest may return when the sun is straight overhead. No other red man must appear before then. When the iron horse draws near, Long Walker's medicine bullet will bring it to its knees. This the spirits have spoken. Now go. Leave Two Thorns and Long Walker to work their magic!"

Long Walker stood by the visibly shaken Two Thorns until the small band had gathered the remains of the fallen brave and disappeared toward the north. Then the two Indians retrieved their ponies and located a dry wash a half-mile south of the railroad. Here they could camp, unseen by the infrequent patrols from Fort Kearny.

Two Thorns finally spoke, breaking a long silence. "Two

Thorns does not question Long Walker's medicine, but why did the spirits choose but a junior warrior to help in such magic?"

"Two Thorns fought well in the battle at Fort Kearny," Long Walker replied solemnly. "Two Thorns stood by Long Walker, sharing his strength with Long Walker, when he was injured in the fight." The blue-eyed Indian saw no reason to give credit to the considerable surgical skill of the Cheyenne medicine men who had ultimately attended his wounds. "For this, Two Thorns is honored and rewarded by the spirits." Long Walker stared intently into the Ute's eyes. "However, the spirits say Two Thorns must never reveal how this magic is to be done," he added ominously. "If Two Thorns speaks of such things, the spirits shall rot his tongue."

Two Thorns shuddered at the thought and promptly pledged his eternal silence.

Leaving the Ute in camp, Long Walker made his way back to the railroad on foot. He soon found what he needed. At one point where the rails joined, a hurried workman had not tightened the bolts on the fishplate, the heavy iron clamp that connected one piece of rail to another. With considerable effort, Long Walker was able to remove the bolts. Tossing the disconnected fishplate aside, he returned to camp to await nightfall.

Then, returning to the rails, the two Indians carefully tended small fires on several cross ties throughout the chill October night. Shortly before dawn, the blazes had eaten through the cross ties that held the rails firm. One of the rails lay several inches out of line with the one to which it had been connected. Long Walker was satisfied. He knew no train was expected until midafternoon. It would be a supply train of one locomotive and several cars, if the white railroad men stuck to their usual routine.

At the appointed time Indians began gathering. Long Walker noted with interest that their numbers had increased by perhaps a dozen. It was good. The more eyes that saw his magic, the more tongues would talk.

The Indians waited patiently until a smudge of black smoke marked the approach of the supply train. Long Walker raised a hand, silencing the group. He made a great show of deliberately emptying his repeating rifle, then selected a single cartridge at random from his ammunition pouch. He touched the blunt lead slug of the cartridge to the dried blood on his own face, then to that of Two Thorns.

"The time has come," he intoned. "The medicine bullet is ready." Dramatically, he opened the action of the Henry rifle and dropped in the single cartridge. "No whites are to be killed by Indians when the iron horse dies," he cautioned. "Today the iron horse is the target. Later all braves shall move against the white eyes. Now it is time to hide and to wait for the iron horse."

Long Walker took up a position slightly in front and to the side of the spot where he and Two Thorns had separated the rails. He lined the sights of the Henry on the approaching locomotive.

When the front wheels of the locomotive were only a few feet from the severed rails, Long Walker fired. He heard the *splat* of the bullet as the slug tapped harmlessly at the front of the locomotive. At first nothing happened. Then, slowly, the locomotive began to tilt as its wheels slipped from the rails into the prairie soil. Ponderously, and with a screech of metal, the locomotive tipped still farther and then fell with a great crash upon its side. The machine gouged a huge chunk from the prairie. Over the noise of the derailment came the agonized scream of the engineer as raw steam and fire blasted through the overturned cabin.

For a moment the stunned Indians could only stare at such magic. Then, from the rear of the ranks, came the single cry, "The iron horse is dead! Long Walker has killed it!"

Long Walker cut short the growing cheer with a wave of his rifle. "Go now—and quickly!" he called. "The great beast is dead. That is all the spirits meant to happen today. Ride hard! Tell all the tribes of this great day and what has happened! Call to those who are unhappy on the reservation, those who are not content to be the white man's pets. Soon the red man will be great once more! All the iron horses and all the whites will be killed! This is a day of great medicine for the red man!"

Long Walker watched in silence as the braves—Cheyenne, Sioux, Ute, and Arapaho—sprinted toward their ponies. They were the seeds that would sprout into his new army.

He gestured to Two Thorns and they rode at an easy trot through grass that brushed against their horses' knees.

"What now, Long Walker?" Two Thorns asked, a touch of awe in his voice. "When does another iron horse die?"

"Much patience is needed. In the camps of the strongest chiefs, even those of Big Nose and Sitting Bull, many warriors ache to take up the lance against the hated iron horses. Those who are not squaws at heart will join together and become strong enough for a great kill—one that will prove the red man's medicine for all time."

Long Walker confidently stroked the barrel of his Henry carbine. "Soon the spirits shall tell Long Walker of a certain iron horse. In the wagons it pulls will be many important people in the white man's world, people who are responsible for the violation of Indian lands. This iron horse shall be killed, and the scalps of white chiefs shall dangle from the red man's belt and lance."

Long Walker's inner rage grew as he talked, and he raised his carbine and shook the weapon in challenge. "The whites will be swept from the buffalo land. At Long Walker's waist will hang the scalps of his most powerful enemies—the Cheyenne traitor Yellow Crow and his blood brother, Ted Henderson. Then Long Walker's life shall be complete!" he vowed.

Two Thorns shook his head in silent wonder. All tribes knew of the feud between Long Walker and the lean but strong Cheyenne who had climbed to the rank of peace chief of his own large band and in the process had helped lay low Long Walker's earlier dream of greatness. Each man had taken the blood oath. It would be interesting to see which warrior the spirits favored. So far the strongest medicine seemed to have been on the Cheyenne's side. But the former chief of long knives, Ted Henderson, who had escaped both Indian lance and white man's bullet through many wars and for many moons, might be an even tougher bite of buffalo hump.

Ted Henderson sipped halfheartedly at the lukewarm coffee in its delicate porcelain cup and idly wondered if he looked as uncomfortable as he felt. The White House, he decided, was considerably less inviting than a friendly council fire to a longtime plainsman, a man who had begun his career as a rider for the Pony Express and had risen to the position of colonel, in command of army troops stationed at Fort Laramie in Wyoming Territory. But one did not ignore a summons from the President of the United States, even if the message did mean an interruption of a well-earned vacation.

He ran a calloused finger under the high, stiff collar of his new shirt. Unlike the familiar soft and supple buckskin he preferred, the shirt felt as if it were trying to choke him, a hangman's noose of civilization. The dress shirt had not been designed to fit a man whose neck and shoulders testified to years of physical exertion and untold hours in the saddle. In his mid-thirties, Ted Henderson was a fine, rugged figure of a man.

"More coffee, Mr. Henderson?"

The question jarred Ted from his musing. He glanced up at the slender, bookish-looking personal secretary to the President and shook his head. "No, thanks," he replied, surrendering the porcelain cup.

The President's secretary closed an eye in a knowing wink. "Not very good, is it?" he asked wryly.

Ted could not conceal a slight grin. "It doesn't have quite the kick of cavalry coffee on a cold morning," he said. "Mind if I prowl around the office a bit?"

"Not at all. I'm sorry you're having to wait, sir."

Ted heaved himself from the overstuffed chair and stretched his muscles as best he could without ripping his suit. He watched as the man placed the used cup and saucer on a nearby tray and returned to his desk. Ted knew the man was not what he appeared to be. The finely boned hands boasted scars about the knuckles and the tip of the right thumb was thickly calloused from constantly cocking the hammer of a single-action handgun on a practice firing range. Ted made a mental wager with himself that a large-caliber pistol was within easy reach of the slender bodyguard.

He was once more conscious of feeling only half dressed. For the first time in years he carried no weapon, and he felt strangely out of balance without its reassuring weight.

Ted strode to a nearby window, idly watching the hacks and pedestrians scurry about the streets around the White House. Late afternoon sunlight streamed through the glass panes, casting a golden glow of autumn across the rich wood and leather interior of the waiting room. Outside, splashes of fiery red, rich yellow, green, and orange mingled in the October streets of Washington.

In his mind's eye Ted saw that same sun touch the snowcapped peaks of his beloved Rocky Mountains. For an instant he could almost taste the clear high-country air and hear the distant bugling of an elk, the restful murmur of leaves among the trees.

Ted was not ashamed to admit he was homesick. Washington was a beautiful city. But it was a city, and therein lay its fault.

At first the trip to Washington had seemed like a good idea, a change of scenery and climate from the scorching heat and howling blizzards of the mountains and Great Plains. But the bustle of humanity in Washington had soon closed in on Ted.

True, Taylor and Vi Elkins were superb hosts as well as being good friends whom the Hendersons had first met as residents of Fort Laramie. Vi's letter of invitation had sparkled with the appeal of the nation's capital. Ted admitted the trip had provided some high points. And his wife, Wilma, had glowed with excitement and the delight of new sights and sounds as they drifted from one spot or activity to another.

But Wild Bill, the Hendersons' son, who had recently passed his fourth birthday, seemed to have more of his father in him. The boy rapidly had become bored with having to dress up almost every day, and he had taken to fretting about the condition of his pony back in Laramie.

Ted did not blame the boy.

"The President will be with you shortly, Mr. Henderson," the secretary said, interrupting Ted's reverie. "If you will follow me, please?"

"Certainly, thank you," Ted said. "I must admit I'm still both stunned and mystified at this summons. I have no earthly idea why President Johnson would want to see an old ex-horse soldier like myself."

"I suspect you will find out in short order, sir," the secretary said, swinging open a heavy door leading to a corner office. "President Johnson seldom wastes time in getting to the point. Incidentally, sir, this room used to be the favorite study of President Lincoln." The secretary's voice had dropped in respect to the late President. "President Lincoln had a great deal of respect for you, Mr. Henderson."

"He was a great man," Ted said quietly. Next to his family, Ted's most prized possession was the small statue of the Pony Express rider that was displayed on his mantel at home, and beside it a framed letter of congratulations signed *Abraham Lincoln.*

Ted heard the door close softly as the secretary left the

room. For a moment he studied the plain but sturdy desk from which a lanky lawyer had directed the course of a nation in its most agonized years. A man who still had somehow found the time to write personal letters to small girls and colonels of cavalry. Here, too, he felt the sense of loss, yet it was not so sharp as it had been a few days before when Ted stood before Ford's Theatre.

He turned at the sound of a door opening, preparing to greet the President. Instead, Ted found himself facing a small man with dark beard, cigar, and a glint in his eyes—General Ulysses S. Grant, whose Union forces finally had brought an end to the tragedy of the great war between North and South.

Automatically, Ted snapped a sharp salute to the general. Grant casually returned the gesture, a hint of a smile deepening the lines around his eyes. "Old habits die hard, don't they, Colonel?"

Ted flushed slightly. "Yes, sir, I guess they do. After so many years in uniform I suppose I'm not quite accustomed to being a civilian yet."

Grant extended a hand and Ted sensed firmly controlled power in the grip. "Pleasure to meet you face-to-face, Colonel Henderson. From what I've heard and read, I expected you to be eleven feet tall and picking your teeth with a buffalo thigh bone," Grant said. "Incidentally, President Johnson got ambushed by some red-eared senator and sent me along to keep you company for a minute or two. We're supposed to tell each other lies about the war or some such until he shakes loose."

Ted was about to reply when the door swung open and President Andrew Johnson strode forcefully into the study, a sheaf of papers clutched in one hand.

"President Johnson, may I present Ted Henderson," Grant said, fishing in his tunic pocket for a fresh cigar.

Over the handshake, Ted briefly studied the President's face. A hint of inner tension lurked in the piercing black eyes. Ted appreciated the tremendous pressures that had fallen on the shoulders of the Southerner who had been catapulted into the nation's highest office after the assassination of President Lincoln.

"It's an honor to meet you, Mr. President," Ted said.

"The feeling is mutual, sir," Johnson said brusquely.

"Please have a seat, Colonel—I should say 'Mister,' I suppose—Henderson."

Ted eased himself into a straight-backed wooden chair.

"Any chance we can talk you into taking back your command at Fort Laramie?" the President asked.

Ted shook his head. "No, Mr. President. No offense to the military or to General Grant—and especially to the men of the Third Cavalry Regiment—but I've had all the uniform time I can handle."

Johnson grunted, then glanced at Grant. "Well, there you have it, General. I promised I would ask."

Grant sighed. "Pity. It's hard to find good help these days."

For an instant Ted thought the President almost smiled, but the fleeting expression was gone from the intense black eyes as they shifted back in his direction.

"Glad we caught you before you wound up your vacation here," Johnson said to Ted. "We need a good man for a special job. Your friend Taylor Elkins, whose judgment I value, says you might be the man."

Ted's eyes narrowed. Had Taylor, a former Union secret agent now working as national news editor for the *Washington Globe*, used this "vacation" as bait to lure the Hendersons to Washington for other purposes? Ted made a mental note to have a talk with his friend about the matter later.

Johnson waved the sheaf of papers in his hand. "General Grant here says the same. He picked your name from among a half-dozen possible candidates. Your record seems to back up their faith in you. And President Lincoln's files contained several complimentary references to you and your work on the frontier."

Ted felt the color rise in his cheeks at the unexpected compliments. "I'm afraid I get too much credit, sir," he said. "The men I've worked with deserve it more."

Johnson waved away Ted's protest by thumping the papers onto the top of the desk. "We might as well get on to the point of your being here, Mr. Henderson," he said. "This nation has two major projects that must be completed as quickly as possible. One is the rebuilding of the South. That's a job for politicians like me. The other has grabbed the imagination of the American people like nothing since the Revolution itself."

Johnson paced to a window and stared out for a moment.

Then he turned to face Ted. "Are you familiar with our plans to build a railroad across the entire continent?"

"In general terms, sir," Ted replied with a nod. "It is a rather prominent topic of conversation, as you implied."

Johnson's gaze locked onto Ted's. "We want you to help us build that railroad."

For a moment Ted sat, stunned, and stared at the President. "But, sir," he finally stammered, "why me? I'm no railroad man—"

"We have railroad men," Grant cut in. "Experienced builders, surveyors, track crews—the works. Track is being laid eastward from Sacramento by the Central Pacific and west out of Omaha by the Union Pacific." Grant flipped ash from the cigar and squinted through the gray smoke. "And, already, the Union Pacific has problems. That's where you come in—we hope. We need a man on the scene at railhead. A man with special qualifications."

"We have reason to suspect there have been deliberate acts of sabotage against the Union Pacific," President Johnson explained. "But we don't know who is behind them or why. There have been Indian troubles as well. We've ordered cavalry protection for the track crews, but except for your old unit—the Third—we have few experienced soldiers along the route."

The President stalked back to his desk and perched on a corner, dangerously near an inkwell. "There's also the severe weather, even though autumn has been kind to the Plains so far this year. There's some tricky terrain. Fights among the construction crews. In short, Mr. Henderson, you can pick any one of many problems."

Johnson hefted the sheaf of papers and waved them in Ted's direction. "What we propose—with the knowledge and consent of the construction engineers and top railroad executives—is to place an agent of our own at rails' end. His official title will be general field superintendent and chief of scouts, and he will have substantial powers and authority to act on his own. So you see, Mr. Henderson, a very certain type of man is needed."

The President riffled a thumb through the stack of papers. "Your qualifications are exactly what we want. You are already a legend on the frontier, a man whose name commands respect. An experienced Indian fighter with a capacity for leadership that you displayed more than adequately during your military career. And finally, no one has a better working knowledge of the climate and terrain. In fact, the route of the Union Pacific across the Plains and through the Rockies will be almost the same trails you rode with the Pony Express."

Johnson glanced as if in anger at the ticking clock on the mantel above the small fireplace, then extended a hand. Ted rose, holding back a score of questions, and took the President's hand.

"General Grant will fill you in on the details," Johnson said. "I can't order you to take the job—or I would. All I ask is that you consider it with care. Now, gentlemen, if you will excuse me, I must go and tweak the noses of a couple of congressmen who are trying to pull a fast one on my Southern constituents." The President sighed. "I wonder if this blasted war will ever end—even though the shooting has stopped."

With that, Andrew Johnson strode from the study. The door banged shut behind him.

Ted stood silently for a moment, his mind still trying to grasp the proposal the President had outlined.

"Sit down, Colonel," Grant said, breaking the brief silence. "This may take a spell. I'll answer your questions when I can and send for the answers when I can't." Grant stabbed his cigar out in a fragment of a cannonball. "Ted, I don't think anyone has to tell you how important this railroad across the country will be. What you and your fellow riders of the Pony Express did for the nation's communications before the telegraph, the railroad will do for the nation now."

Quickly, the general highlighted the commercial value of the railroad. Goods that had to be freighted to seaports and then sent by ship around the Cape could be moved by rail from coast to coast in less than a week. The valuable China trade could be expanded, with great benefit to the entire nation. Finally, agricultural products from the fertile Missouri Valley and points east, and precious metals from the nation's midsection, could be transported hundreds of miles in only a matter of hours.

"As a military man," Grant added, "I'm sure you appreciate the value of a railroad as a tactical weapon in and of itself." The general heaved himself from the chair and began pacing the small room. "I learned a lot about railroads in the

Civil War," Grant said. "With rails it is possible to move men vast distances in only a few hours or days, with arms and supplies to back them up. It could mean the end to those long, tough field campaigns we both know so well."

Ted frowned. "Since the South is unlikely to ever secede again, I assume your comments are directed toward war with the Indians," he said bitterly.

Grant sighed heavily. He stopped pacing and turned to face Ted. "I know how you sympathize with the Indians. How you resigned an important military rank and command to work for peace between the red man and the white—and did a magnificent job of it. But wouldn't we be deceiving ourselves if we believed there would never be another outbreak of Indian warfare? Also, the Plains Indians respect you. Perhaps you, with help from Colonel Abel Hubbard and the Third Regiment—I understand you trained young Hubbard well—could keep a small spark or two from turning into a prairie fire."

Ted returned Grant's level gaze. "The President mentioned Indian troubles now going on, General. Just how extensive have these difficulties been?"

Grant waved a hand as if to dismiss the problem. "Just a few small bands of outlaw bucks. The major tribes are observing the peace you helped hammer out at Fort Laramie."

"General," Ted said bluntly, "the peace we have with the major tribes is shaky at best. This railroad could very well prove to be more than your small spark or two."

Ted rose and walked to the window, trying to control his growing sense of anger and frustration. "The rails will cross Indian lands, just as the Overland Trail did. The movement of the buffalo herds will be interrupted. Perhaps the government sees the red man as a savage, sir, but he isn't stupid. If the railroad poses a threat to the hunting grounds of chiefs of the stature of Sitting Bull and Big Nose . . ." His voice trailed away. There was no need to complete the comment.

"It's out of our hands now, Ted," Grant said quietly. "The railroad will be built with or without your help or mine. There is national pride at stake. And a great deal of money from both the government and the railroad companies. Millions upon millions of dollars, all riding on the success or failure of one of the most magnificent engineering feats in this country's history."

Grant's hand rested on Ted's shoulder. "Besides, we

don't believe the Indian problem to be that severe," the general said. "Your personal challenge will be more in the line of busting your backside to see that track is laid without incident and as rapidly as possible.

"All we ask, Colonel, is that you think about it. Talk it over with your wife and friends here in Washington. Then let us know. The government wants you at railhead, Ted. Hell, *I* want you at railhead. But we don't want you to go in thinking we are using you."

Grant's voice brightened a bit. "I doubt it will be a factor in your decision, but since the job likely will be dangerous as well as physically and mentally difficult, you will be highly paid for your services. You have to think of your future, you know. There will come a day when you'll be an old war-horse and won't be able to work for your beans and sourdough."

Ted had to choke back a sharp retort. He wanted to snap that the money was not worth it. Then he realized he was overreacting to Grant's words. The general had simply called Ted's own fears into the open. Besides, he had to consider the money. The Hendersons were not rich, but they were comfortable by frontier standards. Still, he had a wife and child to support. The ranch they co-owned in Wyoming was doing well under the management of his former comrade in arms, Kevin O'Reilly, and Kevin's Navajo wife, Wind Flower. But the ranch was not yet a going concern. A couple of bad years could put them out of business.

Also, Ted had to admit he was not growing younger. The frontier toughened a man, but it also aged him in a hurry. The once-dark hair that had escaped many an Indian's scalping knife was now streaked with gray.

"I'll think it over, General," he said quietly.

"Good, good!" Grant said in obvious relief. "My personal hack is at your disposal to take you back to where you're staying."

As Ted stepped into the simple black buggy a few minutes later, he noticed the sun had dropped near the horizon. General Grant's driver, a dour, middle-aged man, clucked the bay buggy horse into motion before Ted had a chance to speak. Apparently the driver had his instructions on where to deliver the passenger.

Ted mulled over the proposition, trying to put it into perspective. Keeping a bunch of raw cavalry recruits in line was one thing. Handling a group of hardened construction men who loved brawls and dedicated drinking was a different matter.

Still, some of Grant's enthusiasm for the project had rubbed off. The railroad would be built anyway. And there was the money to consider, security for the future.

Ted felt the muscles in his legs begin to ache from lack of exercise. The Elkinses' home was only a short distance away. He called to the driver and the buggy eased to a stop.

"Ain't my place to say, I reckon," the driver growled as Ted dismounted, "but if I was you, I'd stay right there in that buggy seat. This here's a good neighborhood, sure enough. Prime target for footpads, it is." The driver spat a stream of snuff juice over one of the wheels.

"Footpads?" Ted asked.

"Yup. Sneak up behind you, whop you on the noggin, take your money if you look like you got any." The man patted his coat pocket. "Got me one of Colonel Colt's equalizers here. Little persuader for Washington toughs."

Ted glanced about the wide street. Stately homes overlooking manicured grounds glowed in the half-light of dusk. He recalled that Taylor Elkins had complained about the growing crime rate in the nation's capital. With the war recently ended and the country not yet recovered economically, many ruffians had drifted into Washington. Still, the need for physical exercise and the calm, tranquil appearance of the street exerted their pull on Ted.

"Looks peaceful enough to me," he said.

The driver shrugged. "Suit yourself." With that he flicked the buggy whip lightly over the bay's haunch, and the horse's hooves clopped off into the distance.

Ted unbuttoned the high, confining collar and the top fastener on the tight shirt, flexing his shoulders in relief. For the first time all day he was able to draw a deep breath.

He swung into a long, ground-covering stride. He still wore his comfortable cavalry boots. Not even Wilma, let alone the President, could get him into a pair of town shoes.

As he passed a high hedge alongside a massive home, Ted was absorbed in the subject of the railroad. He almost did not hear the shuffling sound behind him. But the faint warning finally registered. He spun about to face two chunky men in ragged, soiled clothes. Their unshaven faces bore half-mocking smiles. One of the men tapped a small club against the palm of a broad hand.

Ted did not speak. He merely shifted his weight forward slightly, placing the bulk of his one-hundred-seventy pounds over the balls of his feet. He blinked casually at the pair standing barely a stride away.

"Out fer a little stroll, bud?" one of the men asked, his small eyes glittering above a nose that had been broken more than once. Ted thought the man looked like the kind of person who would enjoy beating up people.

"Think we got us a live one, Chick," the man said. "Way he's dressed he oughta be carryin' a good poke."

Ted deliberately raised both hands to a level near his shirt pockets, palms out as though to ward off the two by pleading. "I don't want any trouble with you gentlemen," he said quietly.

The answer was a hefty swing of the club held in the fist of the man with the broken nose. Ted danced back, letting the club whistle in front of his belt buckle, then lunged forward. One previously open hand had folded into a fist. It landed with a sharp *crack* on his assailant's forehead. The man's head snapped back. Ted followed the blow with a sidestep and a quick, chopping motion of his open left hand. The dense muscles along the little finger side of Ted's hard palm crunched into the thug's exposed Adam's apple. Cartilage crumpled beneath the blow. The man tried to cry out but only managed an agonized wheeze. Ted ripped a hard right fist into the man's gut. The club clattered to the cobblestones.

The other man, momentarily taken by surprise at the effectiveness and violence of the unexpected counterattack, finally tried to get into action. He jabbed a hand into the side pocket of his trousers. Ted stepped forward, pinned the man's hand in his pocket with a firm grip, and in the same motion drove a knee into the thug's groin. He collapsed with a strangled scream. Ted helped him on his way down by cracking an elbow into the back of his neck. The attacker's forehead thumped on the stone. He did not move.

A shrill whistle sliced through the evening air. Seconds later a uniformed policeman was at Ted's side, nightstick gripped casually in a big hand as he surveyed the scene.

"Problem here, sir?" the officer asked.

"Ask these gentlemen," Ted said with a shrug. "I don't have a problem."

"What happened, sir?"

"They bit the wrong dog," Ted replied, and briefly recounted the incident.

The policeman studied the two men lying on the ground. "We've been looking for these two for quite some time, sir," he said. "They're wanted for burglary, assault, robbery, rape, and I think I can find other charges. Sleeping in the street, perhaps," he added with a wink. "Would you like to press charges as well? Attempted assault, maybe?"

"I think not," Ted said. "I don't plan to be in Washington long enough to testify against them, and it sounds as if you have plenty of ammunition as it is."

As the officer quickly manacled the two prisoners, Ted realized he had enjoyed the brief conflict. It had loosened his muscles and set the blood to pumping again. "Think you will have any trouble with them, officer?" he asked.

The policeman shook his head sadly. "I doubt it, unfortunately. I'd like nothing better than to put more knots on their heads. But it looks as if you gave them enough headaches to keep them quiet." He produced a stub of a pencil and a notebook. "If you don't mind, sir, I will need your name. For the arrest record."

"Ted Henderson. Fort Laramie, Wyoming Territory."

The officer scribbled a line or two, then glanced at Ted. "Mr. Henderson, there's a small reward out for these two. It's yours."

Ted waved away the suggestion and noticed for the first time a trickle of blood from a scraped knuckle on his right hand. "I don't need that kind of money. Perhaps you could find a good charity? I'm rather fond of children."

The policeman grinned. "I believe that can be arranged, sir. By the way, if you have no criminal record and might be looking for employment, the police department could use another good man."

"No, thanks," Ted replied. "I've already been offered one job today. I must admit, though, that your offer sounds more promising." He sucked at the damaged knuckle for a moment. "My wife is going to give me fits for this," he said ruefully.

Declining the policeman's offer of an escort home, Ted touched his hat brim and strode away, feeling the spring come back into his step as he massaged his bruised knuckles. Who would have believed a man was safer on the Western frontier than in the nation's capital? he thought.

Moments later he turned onto the walk leading to the towering columns that bracketed a carved oak front door. The two-story white home boasted a bay window, its heavy drapes drawn aside to catch the fading light of the evening. Ted paused, once again admiring the Elkinses' home. In Washington it might be just another big house, he thought, but in Laramie it would be a mansion. Only Vi and Taylor lived in the sprawling structure, and Ted thought of the times he had shared quarters with two full companies of soldiers in billets half its size. It seemed too much house for only two people, but the couple who lived there had earned their creature comforts. Especially Vi, who had known more than enough poverty and grief and who had worked hard all her life.

The door suddenly swung open and Wilma Henderson peered into the semidarkness. Gaslights in the foyer behind framed her dark hair and full but firm figure that was the envy of women many years younger. Ted felt his heart leap. Although they had been apart only a few hours, he still had the soldier's gut reaction to a safe return home. Especially to Wilma.

"Ted! Is that you?" Wilma called.

Suddenly a smaller figure appeared and sprinted to Ted's side.

"Hi, Dad," Wild Bill said as Ted rumpled his son's hair in greeting. "Did you see the President?"

"Yes, son. I saw him."

"What's he look like?" Bill asked.

Wilma greeted Ted with a brief but warm hug. She smelled of soap and rose water. Ted was careful to keep his right hand and its scratched knuckle clear of her white dress. He kissed her lightly, then turned back to his son.

The boy grimaced his disapproval at all the kissing going on. "Tell me about the President!" he repeated.

"He looks like a worried man, Bill," Ted replied, describing President Johnson as they entered the house. He included the harried look in the President's eyes. "He has a tough job, son," Ted concluded.

Bill walked in silence for a couple of strides, his brows bunched in thought. "I don't think I want to be a President," he finally said. "I bet he never gets to ride his pony, even."

As they stepped into the full light of the foyer, Wilma gasped. Ted knew she had noticed the blood on his hand.

"Ted! What happened?" She held his hand in a delicate but strong palm, studying the cut.

"Good question," Taylor Elkins added from the doorway to the drawing room. "You didn't slug the President, I hope?"

Ted grinned at his host. The crow's feet around Taylor's hazel eyes hinted at his wry sense of humor. He was in his early forties, with touches of gray in thick brown hair. "Just had a little set-to with a couple of toughs down the street," Ted said. "Guess they thought a man with a new suit on should have something worth taking."

Vi Elkins joined the group as Ted recounted the incident with the thieves, minimizing his own part in the action as much as possible. Wild Bill listened to his father with rapt attention as Wilma led Ted to a chair and began cleaning the cut.

"Ted Henderson," Wilma scolded, "I can't let you out of my sight for an hour without your getting into some scrap like a schoolboy at recess. Between you and your son, I'm turning gray before my time. At least it's nothing but a scratch. Lord knows I've patched up worse on you."

"You gonna spank him for fighting, like you do me, Mamma?" Bill asked seriously.

Wilma could not hide a smile at her son's question. "Not this time," she said. "He didn't start it. You still have to learn when to fight and when not to."

Taylor's eyes reflected his concern. "I'm glad they jumped the wrong man," he said emphatically. "Ted, you have my permission to go for more walks—anytime you want. Maybe you could thin out a few more of these thieves and toughs around here. I worry about Vi when I'm not around."

Ted chuckled. "I've seen Vi in action. Any thugs who break in here might find more than they bargained for." Beneath her calm and composed exterior, Ted knew Vi carried a toughness born of her hard times on the Western frontier. Yet she seemed to have aged very little since the time he had met her years ago when they both worked for the Pony Express, Vi and her first husband having run one of the numerous way stations along the route, where riders could get a meal and change their horses.

Though she was only in her late thirties, Vi had been

twice widowed, both times at the hands of Confederate agents. The Hendersons' son was named in honor of her second husband, Colonel "Wild Bill" Robinson, the commander of the Third Regiment who had been both friend and teacher to Ted and Wilma before a rifle bullet sent him to a grave beneath a piñon tree in a remote pass in the New Mexico mountains. The shared agony of that occasion and others had forged Ted, Wilma, and Vi into an extended family. Taylor Elkins had been quickly accepted into that unit.

"The only problem with having a little money is that someone else is always trying to take it away from you," Taylor complained.

Ted caught Wilma's grin at Taylor's reference to "a little money." In addition to his earnings as a journalist—and a good one at that—Taylor had received a considerable sum in payment for his services as a secret agent for the Union during the war. In the past few months he had also sold two books that promised to be highly successful. Even the *Globe*'s competition had given them glowing reviews.

"Dinner's ready, if anyone is interested," Vi announced.

Ted knew the meal would be delicious. He had been eating Vi's cooking off and on from the time she had run the Pony Express station in Ted's territory. Between that remote and dangerous outpost and the Elkinses' modern kitchen in Washington, Vi also had managed the Laramie Hotel, where the Hendersons had often eaten. There was no question of Vi's artistry at the stove.

Ted was not disappointed. On the dining room table was his favorite meal, a hearty pot roast, flanked by a variety of vegetables and freshly baked sourdough bread. Ted's nose told him a deep-dish apple cobbler waited beneath the nearby silver warming tray. A bowl of fruit added a splash of color to the table, over which a cut glass chandelier sparkled its reflections of the gaslights.

"Now I know I've been set up," Ted said as he held a chair for Wilma. "Taylor, did you lure us to Washington just to give the President and General Grant a shot at me?"

Taylor smiled wryly. "Let's talk about it after dinner. Right now I'd like to turn my attention to something more important, like one of those roasted potatoes, if you please?"

When the meal was finished, Ted pushed back his plate and moaned in mock misery. "If you can spare a basket, Vi, I'd like to take what's left back to Laramie. It was delicious."

Wilma cast one last, longing look at the apple cobbler. "It isn't fair," she said mournfully. "Vi can eat anything and not gain an ounce. I can put a spoon in a cobbler and it doesn't go to my stomach. It goes straight to my hips."

The group moved into Taylor's book-lined study, a large room stuffed with heavy, comfortable furniture. A desk piled with pages of Taylor's flowing script testified to the new book he was writing.

Ted declined his host's offer of brandy but accepted a cup of hot spiced tea. Vi and Bill began to construct a fort from a stack of dominoes on a low table nearby as Ted and Wilma waited for Taylor to begin speaking.

"In answer to your earlier question, Ted, we didn't invite you here for a government work detail," he said. "You were already on your way when President Johnson and General Grant recruited me back into my old role as an agent for the Union government. Incidentally, Grant is being groomed to succeed Johnson in the White House, at least according to the gossip around town."

Ted waited patiently as Taylor swirled the brandy in his snifter, staring at the rich dark liquid. "I can't seem to say no when a President asks me to do something, Ted. Once a spy always a spy, I suppose. Anyway, when we decided we needed a good man at railhead to keep an eye on things, your name naturally came to mind."

Taylor started to outline his own role in the investigation when Ted interrupted with an upraised palm. "I haven't decided whether or not to climb onto this wagon. Perhaps you shouldn't be telling me any trade secrets at the moment."

The older man snorted in derision. "If I can't trust you, Ted Henderson, I'm no judge of character. In my business, if you can't read people you might as well buy an anvil and hammer and take up blacksmithing." He drained the last of his brandy and returned the empty glass to a silver tray.

"Briefly, I'm to use my social and professional contacts in Washington to try to find out who is responsible for the railroad's troubles and what they are planning to do," Taylor continued. "Vi has become one of Washington's more popular hostesses. She's likely to pick up some valuable information from the society crowd here. After a few glasses of port, some of the wives around town tend to let things slip."

"Not to mention," Vi interrupted, "they're trying to get my famous journalist husband into a strange bed."

Taylor winked at Ted. "When you've got steak at home, who wants bacon at some hash house? I must admit, though, some of that bacon does look awful tasty—" He yelped as a domino sailed past his ear. "But believe me, dear, I'm not hungry."

Vi blushed furiously and muttered something about "incorrigible husbands."

Taylor turned back to Ted. "So how about it? Ready to help build a railroad, even though someone doesn't want it finished and we don't know who or why?"

"I've promised to think about it, and I will. More than that I'm just not ready to say," Ted replied with a grin.

An hour later Wilma and Ted were curled up next to each other in bed, a faint light from the street lamps filtering in through the white lace curtains. Neither Wilma nor Ted could sleep.

"I know what's really troubling you, Ted," she said. "It's your fear for the Indians. And especially for Yellow Crow."

Ted sighed. "Woman, sometimes it's scary how you can read my mind. And you're right as usual. There is a chance this railroad would put me on a bitter trail with the Indians. I still have nightmares about the fight where I almost killed Yellow Crow in the canyon skirmish. I couldn't stand to face that again, Wilma."

"I know, dear," she said softly. "The last few years have been difficult for you and your blood brother."

Ted propped his head on an elbow and looked down at her.

"Heaven knows I've no desire to see you in danger again, Colonel Henderson," Wilma said. "I've patched enough bullet and arrow holes in you already to last a lifetime. But I think you should take this job."

She placed a finger on his lips to silence his protest. "What better place could you be to help avoid any armed conflicts with the major tribes than at rails' end? We both know that Yellow Crow will do his best to keep the peace among the Cheyenne. He'll need your help, Ted. Help Yellow Crow salvage some of the Indians' pride and culture."

"Woman, you aren't playing fair," Ted said softly. "But we could use the money." His hand seemed to move of its own will, stroking her shoulder, gliding down to her narrow waist, and coming to rest on the firm fullness of her hip. "Are you recruiting for the government, too?" he asked.

"Nope," she whispered, her normally husky voice dropping even more. "Just watching out for my own. You aren't the only one who has a deep feeling for Yellow Crow or the only one who suffers when trouble plagues the two of you. You know you would be miserable if something went wrong and you weren't there. You would spend the rest of your life chastising yourself."

In the pale light, Wilma studied her husband's face intently. "There's something else," she added, "and you might as well admit it. You're not ready for a rocking chair and a shade tree. You've been an active man all your life. Without a new challenge you would fall apart like a snowman under a July sun. I'm not going to let that happen to you."

Ted playfully smacked her hip. "Trying to get me out of the house and out from underfoot, eh?" He laughed and snuggled closer to her warm body. "Okay. I guess the battle is lost, and maybe I'm glad to lose. I admit I'm getting itchy again. But I do have some reservations. I'm not sure I can handle the job, controlling the track gangs and all."

She pulled him closer and pressed her body against his. "Colonel Henderson, you can handle anything—even your disgracefully wanton and totally shameless wife—if you work at it."

"Woman, you have the strangest definition of work," Ted whispered just before their lips met.

Garth Pfister shifted his considerable bulk in the overstuffed chair, shuffling the papers on his desk as he waited for a visitor. The fading light of the New York afternoon probed with small success at the dirt-smudged window overlooking the waterfront.

The knock at the door was sudden, loud, and startling. Pfister's heart began pounding as he glanced up to see the dark outline of a blocky figure framed in the opaque glass of the door. He relaxed a bit.

"Come in, Fallon," he called. He used both arms to push his overweight body upright. The door opened, revealing the lettering on the glass.

SOUTHERN OVERLAND COMPANY
G. PFISTER, CHAIRMAN

The man who entered almost had to turn sideways to get his massive shoulders through the door.

Pfister waddled forward, a hand extended in greeting. "Good to see you again, Jack."

"You sent for me, Garth?" Fallon's voice still carried a slight brogue from his Irish ancestry.

"We have a job for you if you're available. Have a seat."

Jack Fallon, who stood an inch under six feet and carried two hundred and sixty pounds of heavy muscle on a big-boned frame, eased himself into a sturdy wooden chair. Pfister knew the man had earned his nickname "Bear" both by accident of heritage and by deliberate action. The October air was nippy, yet Fallon wore no jacket. A blanket of red hair spilled through the opened collar of his flannel shirt and matted his bare forearms thickly. According to legend on the New York waterfront, he had been the only man to have gone three full minutes with a traveling show's trained wrestling bear. Damn near pinned the beast, too, the story went.

Pfister could believe it.

Bear Fallon gestured over his shoulder toward the door. "New company, Garth?"

The chairman of the Southern Overland nodded. "We'll get to that in a minute, Bear." Pfister lumbered back to his own chair and settled into it with a sigh, slightly winded from the exertion of walking a few steps.

Pfister removed his heavy spectacles and began polishing them with a silk handkerchief as he squinted at Fallon. The two men respected each other. For all his muscle, Bear Fallon could think on his feet. The heavy brows, pierced by scars from bareknuckle brawls, framed alert eyes. His mind was surprisingly quick to grasp situations and understand what they meant. It was a trait that had brought him from the sweating stevedore ranks on the waterfront to the job of troubleshooter for some of the nation's most powerful and ruthless men.

Above his flab, Garth Pfister boasted a mind that held a sixth sense for making money, along with a calculating ruthlessness to take his share of it. Together the two men made a formidable team.

"Bear, have you ever been out West?" Pfister asked, replacing his spectacles.

"Depends on where you mean. Been to Saint Jo a couple of times, 'Frisco some."

"Want to see the rest of it?" Pfister inquired.

Bear Fallon shrugged, an impressive motion. "Not much out there to see. But a man's got to be somewhere, and if the money's good . . ." Fallon's voice trailed away meaningfully.

"On this one, Fallon, you can just about name your own price, not that you wouldn't anyway. Let's just say you could become extremely comfortable, perhaps downright wealthy, if you get the job done." Pfister nodded toward the door. "The story's a bit detailed, so be patient. Southern Overland is a new company, as you noticed. It's just a dummy corporation, existing on paper only."

Fallon's bushy eyebrows bunched in obvious interest. He knew when Pfister set up a new company big money was not far behind. Along with a few heads to knock, usually.

"Our sole purpose," Pfister continued, "is to funnel money from several sources—primarily shipowners and freighting people—into one project. These funds must be acquired and distributed quietly, for reasons that will soon become clear. But our project is in trouble at the moment. I told the other board members you would come high, but that you would be worth it." The chair groaned as Pfister shifted his weight. "Bear, our objective is to stop this transcontinental railroad."

Bear Fallon shook his massive head. "No way, Garth. Might slow her down some, but you can't stop her."

Excitement danced in Pfister's deep-set eyes. "Precisely. That is the conclusion of the board. When those rails span the United States, some of our directors—our contributing companies—are going to lose money. Lots of it. Shipping around the Horn will be hurt bad. Overland freight firms will lose those lucrative cross-country contracts. They won't go under, but they'll feel the pinch. Which is why we've modified our objective somewhat: not to stop but to delay the construction of the railroad as much as possible."

Fallon reached into a shirt pocket, produced a sack of tobacco and papers, and began rolling a smoke. "Any of the big boys playing?"

"Not of the scope of Butterfield or the Leavenworth and Pike's Peak people," Pfister said. "But the men involved own a lot of short-haul, interconnected lines on the freight end. And every connection hikes the price of the goods—and the profits—even if the same company owns both lines in the operation."

Fallon licked the edge of the paper, folded and smoothed it, then expertly twisted the end and lit it. "I know most of the tricks involved in screwing the public, Garth. You don't have to draw a picture. But you don't seem too worried, and your ship business looks shaky with a railroad cutting across the country."

"I've found a way to turn this to our advantage," Pfister explained, folding his hands over his belly. "The railroads have one weakness. Both the Central Pacific and the Union Pacific depend mostly on government money to finance construction. And they're paid by the mile, in blocks of a hundred miles or so of finished track. They're headed for a case of the money shorts, Bear. We want to make their cash problem worse."

"So how does the Southern Overland stick a thumb in that pie?"

Pfister grinned. "When the railroad gets in a financial bind, Southern Overland just happens to buy up some blocks of stock or make a repay-on-demand loan. Just enough to keep them going. If the railroad runs into enough construction delays to miss a number of payment deadlines, we will wind up controlling a goodly chunk of railroad stock. And at the right time, we call in the loans—when we know they can't pay. We take stock in lieu of cash. In the end, Southern Overland will own itself a railroad bought for pennies on the dollar and built for us by the government to boot!"

Fallon squinted around the smoke curling from his cigarette. "And in the meantime," he said, "every day the railroad is delayed puts another day's income in the pockets of the shippers and freighters?"

"We can't lose," Pfister gloated. "For now, we control a major share of the shipping and freighting business. When the railroad is finished we will own controlling stock in that, too. Then we turn our ships to exploiting the China trade. We charge damn near any price we want to move freight by rail. I tell you, Fallon, there's no limit to the amount of money we can grab!"

Fallon dropped his cigarette to the floor and crushed it beneath a heel. "You mentioned something about trouble?"

Pfister sighed. "That's where you come in, Bear. We couldn't find you at first, so we put another man on the Union Pacific railhead. He's supposed to be slowing things down, but he isn't getting the job done. The Union Pacific is laying over a mile of track a day! That's unacceptable, so he's got to go as soon as you've worked your way into position to take over his spot as leader of the rail gang. You're smart enough to figure a number of ways to delay construction. You've worked on railroads in the East, so you know the business."

Pfister paused for a moment, then chuckled. "Best of all, you're as ruthless as any of us. A man to get the job done without letting his conscience get in the way. And you like money." Pfister leaned forward, propping his elbows on the desk. "When you're through, you'll own a piece of a railroad. Not bad for an Irishman who used to work eighteen hours a day for room, board, and rum, eh?"

Fallon pondered the proposition. He knew that anyone who bucked Pfister usually wound up in the Hudson River. And the job sounded pretty good.

"Okay," Fallon said. "You've hired yourself a railroad man. But what about the Central Pacific? You got a man there, too?"

Pfister nodded. "So far, he hasn't had to do all that much. The weather and the Sierra Mountains are doing his work for him. It's the Union Pacific, with all that flat prairie, that's our number one target."

"This man of yours at the Union Pacific railhead. What's he going to think of it?"

"He will be told of your arrival, of course," Pfister said. "He will think you're being sent along just to help him out. I expect you to come up with a way to remove him as soon as you've set yourself up as next in line for his job."

Fallon folded one big hand across the other, cracking the knuckles. "That can be arranged."

"One word of caution, Bear," Pfister said solemnly. "We've always been up front with each other. If you fail, as this man has, you will be called back here to answer to me." Pfister's eyes narrowed maliciously. "I don't think either of us wants that to happen."

Fallon calmly stared at the fat man. "Nope," he said, "but I don't figure to mess it up."

"Good. How soon can you be on your way?" Pfister asked.

Bear Fallon scratched the dense stubble on his chin, calculating. "Two, maybe three days," he said. "I got a contract to finish here. Railroad's end out West might be a healthier place to be for a spell. Could get a little touchy for me in New York."

Pfister nodded vigorously. "I'll have everything ready when you are." He fished in a desk drawer and pulled out a thick sheaf of currency, which he tossed to Fallon. "Traveling money and initial expenses," Pfister said, "plus a hefty advance on the contract. You need more, you'll know how to get in touch. A packet of instructions will be waiting for you at the Omaha terminal of the Union Pacific. Read them and destroy them. Then size up the job and name your final price. Now, how about a drink?"

Fallon nodded.

Pfister produced a pair of water glasses. "Some good Irish whiskey?"

"Nope," Fallon replied, accenting his brogue. "Me ancestors upon the Emerald Isle never learned to squeeze out a good whiskey. I might have me a wee dram of rye, me friend."

Pfister laughed. "I just happen to have your favorite brand right here." From a cabinet behind the desk he produced a bottle. He filled one glass almost to the rim and handed it to Fallon, then poured an ounce or two into his own glass. While Pfister sipped at his drink, Fallon raised his glass and drained it without stopping for breath.

The chairman shook his head in amazement. He had heard that Fallon could drink any man under the table and not even stagger when the bottles were empty.

Fallon waved off a refill. "Got some work to do. Then we can start to steal us a railroad." He rose, waved a farewell, and walked out of the small office. Pfister realized with a start he had not heard a board creak as Bear Fallon left.

Deciding to keep a close watch on the New York papers for the next few days, the chairman of Southern Overland did not have to wait long. The following morning a headline blared from the first page of the *New York News*:

NEW YORK JUDGE GUNNED DOWN;
NO SUSPECTS IN VILE MURDER

A second headline added, above the full-column story:

WIFE, CHILDREN FOUND WITH
THROATS SLASHED IN HOME;
OFFICERS SAY KILLER SLEW
FAMILY FIRST, WAITED FOR
VICTIM'S TRAGIC RETURN HOME

Pfister smiled to himself. The murder had all the earmarks of a Bear Fallon contract. He suspected Fallon would be going west very soon.

Ted Henderson eased himself into a chair at General Grant's gesture. Grant cocked an eyebrow. "Well, Colonel? What is your decision?"

"Unless you've changed your mind, General, I suppose you have hired yourself a railroad man."

Grant sighed. "Good. But then, I expected as much. Arrangements have been made for your return trip, with an open date for departure. How soon do you wish to leave?"

"In a couple of days, sir. How did you know I would accept?"

"I pride myself on being a good judge of men, Ted," Grant said quietly. "If I didn't have that capacity, General Lee would have eaten my troops for breakfast." He grinned ruefully. "He damn near did, anyway."

Grant shuffled through a stack of messages on his desk and located one. "This might be of interest to you. It came in late yesterday. A band of Indians have managed to derail one of the Union Pacific supply trains. The engineer died in the wreck. Surprisingly, the Indians did not attack after the derailment. But one of our employees, a former soldier at Fort Kearny, recognized the leader of the band, a Sioux named Long Walker."

"Long Walker! Damn!" Ted exclaimed involuntarily. The year before, Long Walker had abducted the Hendersons' son, Bill, and cost the lives of several good men in the rescue that followed. And he was the sworn enemy of Yellow Crow as well.

"You know this Indian, Colonel?" Grant asked in surprise.

Ted nodded grimly. Any doubts he might have had about taking the railroad job were silenced. He knew he would have paid for a chance to even the tally with Long Walker.

"Surely one lone Indian chief and a small band of braves

couldn't be much of a problem?" Grant asked, puzzled by Ted's strong reaction to Long Walker's name.

"Don't underestimate this Indian, General," Ted said in a voice tight with hate. "That half-breed is intelligent. He's a fearless warrior and a fine leader, a former agent for the Confederacy, and a force to be reckoned with on the frontier. If Long Walker has set his mind to bedeviling the railroad, this Indian problem is anything but simple."

Grant eyed the tip of an unlighted cigar, twirling it between his fingers. "I gather from the tone of your voice that you and this Indian don't like each other."

"That, sir, is an understatement of some magnitude." As briefly as possible Ted told Grant of Long Walker's activities on the Plains. "I had hoped," he concluded, "that we had seen the last of him. And I promise you, General, that if I get him in my sights, at least one problem at railhead will be solved."

Grant nodded solemnly, then scratched a match and touched it to the tip of the cigar. "Now I'm sure I have the right man for the job," he said. "Just watch your hair out there."

Two

The low, throaty growl from the mongrel dog at Wind Flower's side drew her attention from the midday meal she was preparing. The stiff hairs along the animal's powerful neck and shoulders bristled a warning.

"Quiet, Toby," Wind Flower said in her native Navajo tongue as she wiped her fingers on her apron. The dog stopped growling but remained ready to attack if his mistress were threatened. He was one of the best warning systems around, and a valued companion to a pregnant wife on an isolated Wyoming ranch. Knowing the animal rarely sounded a warning by mistake, Wind Flower lifted the old .36 caliber navy revolver from the countertop nearby and checked the loads. She walked to the window, tucking the pistol into the waistband of her skirt beneath the apron. The unborn child squirmed as if in protest.

"Shush, little one," she muttered softly, "the gun is not aimed at you."

From the window she saw what had drawn Toby's attention, though the figure was still far away. A slightly stooped man led a stocky horse, which seemed to be favoring a front leg, to the stream that ran beside the ranch house and southward through the meadow beyond the front door. The horse dipped its muzzle into the stream and drank for what seemed to be a long time. Then the man tugged gently at the reins to signal the animal that it had had enough for the moment. He stood and looked at the ranch house as if debating whether or not to approach, then led the horse forward.

As he neared, Wind Flower saw the man was Mexican. A wide-brimmed, flat-crowned hat shaded his features, and he walked with a slight shuffle as though age bore heavily on his shoulders. Like the horse, the man limped slightly.

Wind Flower remained unconcerned for her own safety,

though she was alone at the moment. Her husband, Kevin O'Reilly, had ridden to the north side of the ranch the O'Reillys owned with Ted and Wilma Henderson to check on the distribution of bulls among the cows in their growing herd. In his absence she had the dog and the navy revolver. They had served her well in the past and if necessary would do so again. She went outside with Toby at her heels.

The Mexican stopped a few feet from the front porch and courteously removed the hat from his head. His face was streaked with sweat despite the mild autumn air. The face was deeply lined by the years. The soft brown eyes, however, showed no effects of aging. They remained alert and, Wind Flower thought, kind. The Mexican bowed his head slightly in greeting.

"*Buenos días, señora,*" he said smiling.

"*Buenos días.*" Wind Flower hesitated for a moment, searching for the polite phrasing of a tongue she had not used in some time. "*Habla usted inglés?*"

"Yes, señora." The answer came in a deep, rich voice almost free of accent. "I speak English."

"Good. I fear that while my people once spoke fluent Spanish, my own grasp of the language has slipped. Have you traveled far?" Wind Flower asked.

"Yes. I do not wish to be a bother, but I thought it best to tell you I have watered my horse in your stream. Is this all right?"

Wind Flower nodded and smiled. "The water is free to all thirsty animals and people," she said. "Your horse—is he injured?"

The Mexican's weathered hand gently stroked the neck of the compact, well-mannered bay. "He seems to have hurt a shoulder muscle by stepping in a badger hole. He is a good horse. We have been long together. I do not ride until he is once more well."

Wind Flower studied the horse with a knowing eye. "He is too fine an animal to risk further injury," she said. "Welcome to the Henderson-O'Reilly Ranch. Have you eaten?"

The Mexican hesitated for an instant. Wind Flower was afraid she might have accidentally insulted him. "Yes," he finally replied, "but it was so long ago that my stomach must think my teeth have been turned out to pasture like an old horse."

"My husband will return soon. You must have a meal with us. There is plenty. I am called Wind Flower."

The Mexican inclined his head. "Valdez Cabrillo, at your service, señora. Thank you for your kind invitation, but I will not eat unless I may work in return." He studied her briefly. "Wind Flower. It is a fitting name for one of such beauty. You are the daughter of the Navajo chief Gallegos?"

"Yes," Wind Flower said, surprised. "You knew my father?"

"Only by the stories. All in New Mexico know of the courage of the great chief. And of his daughter Wind Flower and her big Irishman, the soldier who fought the Navajo yet followed on the Long Walk in search of the woman he loved. How finally they were married in a Navajo ceremony and moved north to make a home."

Wind Flower smiled gently. "The stories probably have grown in the telling. Each of us merely did what he had to do." She waved toward the back of the house. "Kevin will be back within the hour. In the meantime, there is a spare stall in the barn and some grain. I am sure you wish to care for your horse. In a small tin by the saddle rack is a mixture of bear grease and crushed herbs. It is smelly, but I have had some success at doctoring horses with it. Use what you need."

The Mexican bowed once more. "*Gracias*. You are most understanding. I do not doubt the mixture will work. The granddaughter of a great medicine man knows much of such remedies."

Valdez Cabrillo gathered the reins and led his horse toward the barn. His equipment was meager and worn, but well tended. The stalk of the broad saddle horn bore deep burns, apparently left by the cowhide braided *reata* now tied loosely to the saddle by a leather thong. The man himself walked as one unaccustomed to being out of the saddle, his limp exaggerated by high-heeled boots. There was a distinct bulge in the left pocket of his *chaparajos*—or chaps. Wind Flower was sure it would be a revolver.

She turned to her work, removing her own handgun from beneath the apron. From time to time she glanced out the back window of the kitchen and could see into the barn through the open barn door. Valdez's hands seemed gentle and expert as he unsaddled the bay, dipped his fingers in her herb mixture, and massaged the animal's damaged shoulder. He fed the bay a modest portion of grain. Finding a pitchfork and makeshift rake, he quickly and efficiently cleaned the barn stalls.

Only then did he attend to his own needs. He drew a bucket of water from the well in the backyard and drank deeply from a gourd dipper. He poured the remainder of the water into a shallow basin beside the back door and washed thoroughly, then took a carefully folded bandanna from a pocket of his leather vest and dried himself.

With the meal almost ready and coffee steaming in a pot—and knowing that no Western man entered a house without an invitation—Wind Flower opened the back door and called, "Come in, please."

Toby met the visitor with a rumbling growl but quickly calmed at Wind Flower's sharp command. Valdez Cabrillo sat at the table and sipped a cup of coffee gratefully. Much to Wind Flower's amazement, he began to idly scratch Toby's ears. The mongrel seldom allowed anyone but herself, Kevin, or visiting children to touch him. But the dog's chin rested trustingly on Valdez's knee.

"You are a *vaquero*, a cowboy, Señor Cabrillo?"

Valdez nodded. Wind Flower thought she saw a quick flash of pain in his brown eyes. "I do not wish to boast," he said, "but in my younger days I was one of the best vaqueros." Then his eyes brightened. "You have the makings of a fine ranch here. On my way, I passed some of your livestock. Fine cattle and good solid horses."

The conversation was interrupted by Kevin's arrival. Wind Flower met him at the corral gate with a warm embrace. "We have a visitor, Kevin."

Well over six feet tall, rawboned and muscled, Kevin had to lean forward to hug his much smaller wife. "I saw the bay in the stall," he said. "Fine animal. Also, someone mucked out the barn. Is this visitor a saddle tramp?"

Wind Flower shook her head. "A vaquero who seems a bit down on his luck. I think he is a good man. And Toby likes him."

Kevin looked surprised, then grinned. The flash of white teeth gave an almost boyish look to his face. "If the two of you like him," he said, "he must be all right. Your instinct for people is good—after all, you married me. And if that mongrel dog likes him, this vaquero must be nice."

Within minutes Kevin and Valdez were on a first-name basis and discussing the vagaries of cattle raising. Wind Flower noticed Valdez ate sparingly despite his obvious hunger. Perhaps, she thought, that was one reason he remained so trim and fit-looking despite his years.

"Valdez," Kevin said, "you are welcome to stay here as long as you wish. Or if you have some place in mind to go, I will lend you a horse and care for yours until you return."

"That is a most gracious offer, Kevin. But I have nothing to provide in return." The aged Mexican suddenly turned to Wind Flower and smiled. "When is the little one due?"

Wind Flower unconsciously stroked her swelling abdomen. "In the time of the deep snows," she said.

"It is good," Valdez commented. "Such a fine young couple should have children. I was so blessed once. . . ." His voice trailed away. No one pursued the point since it was obviously a painful subject for Valdez.

Suddenly Kevin stopped with his fork in midair. "Valdez, I'm almost embarrassed to suggest this. I could use some help on the ranch if you are interested. I couldn't pay much, because we have put most of our money back into the operation. Wind Flower has been my right hand and a fine helper, but as her time nears I would rather keep her out of the saddle."

Valdez's eyes were downcast. "I *am* in search of work, Kevin. I do not require much, a place to sleep, a bit of food, some grain for my horse. But I am an old man. Perhaps I cannot do the work you need done."

Kevin grinned. "Valdez Cabrillo, I expect that you have forgotten more about horses and cattle than I will ever know. Knowledge is more efficient than youth, I've learned—the hard way."

Valdez finally looked up, a twinkle in his dark eyes. "Perhaps the saints guided my horse's hoof to the badger hole to bring me here," he said. "When do we begin?"

Kevin pushed his chair back and stood. "This afternoon, if you like. I have to push some cattle down from the high country. The weather has been kind, but it may fall apart any minute. I'd sure hate to lose some fine cows to a sudden blizzard."

A few minutes later Wind Flower stood on the front porch and watched her husband and Valdez ride away at an easy trot. She stroked her stomach. "Valdez Cabrillo," she whispered, "you say you have nothing to give. I think, perhaps, you are wrong. When the little one arrives it will have a good grandfather figure."

The steady *clack-clack-clack* of the passenger car wheels over rail joints had worked its metallic lullaby on Wild Bill Henderson. Now a seasoned traveler, the boy napped in his seat between his parents as the Union Pacific train clanked its way across the rolling prairie.

The youngster's initial excitement at going home had worn off after a couple of days in the confines of first one passenger coach and then another on the long trip from Washington City to St. Joseph, Missouri. On the trip east, Bill had dashed from passenger to passenger and from window to window, jabbering in delight as new scenery flashed by faster than even his pony could run. Now, however, he had resigned himself to the relative boredom of being moved from one point to another with no effort on his part.

Bill had regained some of his animation at St. Joseph when they had left the rail car for the more dramatic trip upriver on a flatbed steamer. Shortly after they boarded the craft Bill had found a new friend in the helmsman, and soon was peering earnestly into the murky Missouri River, watching for floating logs or sandbars waiting to trap "his" boat.

Ted thought the riverboat, piled high with railroad supplies and goods needed on the frontier, seemed to move sluggishly. He had not envied the captain his job of steering the ungainly craft through the treacherous channels.

In the twin cities of Council Bluffs, Iowa, and Omaha, Nebraska, boomtowns on opposite sides of the river, Ted felt it necessary to retrieve his repeating rifle and handgun from the family's baggage. Both towns were riding the crest of an economic wave generated by construction of the Union Pacific. They were awash with burly railroad laborers, both black and white, poverty-stricken Indians reduced to begging, well-dressed businessmen, armed frontiersmen, a few soldiers, and more than a few unsavory types.

Ted had not relaxed until the train to rails' end had put miles between itself and the Missouri River. Nevertheless, he kept the Henry .44 caliber rimfire rifle and heavy .45 Colt Dragoon revolver close at hand.

Ted stared thoughtfully at his young son, who was snoring slightly as he leaned against his mother's shoulder.

"I don't think he realizes we have crossed more than half

a continent in only a few days," Wilma said. "I wonder if he will ever be impressed with the enormous amount of time and effort that went into a trip like this in the days before railroads?"

Ted sighed and shook his head, remembering the West of his younger days when the call of the frontier had first surged strongly in his blood. "I don't know. Maybe trains will make things too easy."

He glanced out the window as the wheels clattered above a tributary of the Platte River, which ran near the tracks. Ted grimaced. There was not a mature tree of any size to be seen for miles. Where once stately cottonwoods and oaks had fed on the prairie storm runoff there was only empty space. The rivers and creeks had been stripped of trees to feed the railroad's insatiable appetite for wood for ties, power, and trestles. The passing of the trees seemed even more symbolic of the changing times than the smoke-belching, powerful locomotive, Ted mused silently.

The coach windows were closed against the November chill, and the air inside the coach had become smoky and stuffy. From time to time a passenger would crack open a window for a moment. The cold fresh air was a welcome tonic to Ted. He was eager to be out in it once more, free and astride one of his horses. The restlessness because of forced inactivity once more nagged at Ted's muscles as the endless, rolling grasslands of Nebraska flowed past the windows.

"If you will excuse me, Wilma, I have to stretch my legs again," he said, easing himself from his seat. He walked along the aisle, studying the passengers. There were a few in business suits, but most of the riders wore rough frontier clothing. Several seats were occupied by soldiers heading for a new assignment or returning to duty after a brief leave. There were few women, and Bill was the only child on the train. The rest of the passengers were laborers headed for rails' end, a rather coarse lot whose command of the English language seemed confined to swear words. Many of the male travelers carried weapons and looked as if they knew how to use them.

Ted knew in the next car there would be fewer guns and less swearing. The plush car carried wealthy people and some railroad officials hoping to persuade the affluent travelers to invest in the railroad. The Hendersons had been offered seats in the elegant car, but Ted and Wilma had politely declined.

They had had their fill of small talk with the wealthy and powerful during the trip to Washington.

Ted paused beside a seat occupied by an aging scout, a thin, angular man with a flowing, snow-white mustache and wearing square wire-rimmed spectacles. An ancient muzzle-loading long rifle leaned in the crook of the man's arm.

"Well, Cap, how do you like travel by rail?" Ted asked.

The old-timer, whom they had met on the riverboat, tugged at an end of his mustache and shook his head. "Had my druthers, I druther be on hossback. Man can't see nothin' all boxed up like a coon before a hound-dog hunt." Cap waved a gnarled hand toward the window. "Seen sumpin' back a ways, Ted. Telegraph wire down. Ain't so sure what it means, but I don't like it. Iffin a man don't stay a tad twitchy he don't stay healthy long out here. Ain't seen no feathers, but this here's Sioux country sure 'nuff."

"How far back, Cap?" Ted asked, suddenly concerned.

The scout shrugged. "Who can tell on a damn train? Maybe quarter-mile."

Ted's sixth sense began to stir. The Indians feared the talking wires that brought soldiers. If they were up to mischief, their first act usually was to sever the telegraph lines. Most of the major tribes were now in winter camp, but this was renegade country—Long Walker's country.

"See anything else, Cap?"

"Nope. Might do well to keep an eye out, though. I got me a feelin' they's Injuns about. Maybe out huntin' a iron hoss—well, lookie here!" The scout pointed toward a low hill coming into view as the train rounded a gentle curve along the Platte River. A slight cloud of dust floated above the hill a mile away. "If that ain't antelope or buff'lo, we're in for a scrap," Cap said.

Ted knew instinctively the old scout was right. The train would be a tempting target. In addition to the passenger cars, there were several cars loaded with goods for the frontier trade, along with construction supplies. Ted nodded to the aging scout and hurried back to Wilma.

"Could be trouble ahead, dear," he said quietly. He lifted the flap of the cavalry holster at his belt and handed the Dragoon to Wilma. "Just in case," he said. "Cap thinks he smells Sioux, and I'm inclined to agree with him. I'm going to inform the crew. If anything should happen, get Bill down on the floor under the window. The wood is thicker there and it should stop any bullets or arrows. You get down with him, too."

Wilma glanced at the sleeping boy, then calmly nodded, taking the heavy handgun.

Ted found the brakeman examining a door latch inside the plush car ahead. The trainman listened intently as Ted told him of the potential trouble.

"I'll get word to the engineer to slow her down and watch close for torn-up track," the brakeman said. "We lost a supply train not far from here a few days back. I don't intend to let any savage hurt my train."

By the time Ted had returned to his own seat and plucked his rifle from the overhead rack, the speed of the locomotive had slowed perceptibly.

Suddenly the train jarred to a halt with a lurching jolt and a screech of metal. Wilma instinctively braced herself against the back of the seat before her and wrapped her free arm around Bill. The boy's eyes popped open at the jolt and the sudden bedlam among the passengers.

"What is it, Mamma? What happened?" he asked.

One woman who had been tossed from her seat sat dazed and wide-eyed, bleeding from a slight cut on her forehead. Ted grasped her shoulder and pushed her to safety between the seats as a rifle ball shattered a window nearby. A man yelped as flying glass sprayed over his face.

"Indian attack!" Ted yelled above the din. "Women to the floor! Every man with a gun, get ready!"

He slid into a window seat, tried to open the glass, and found it stuck. He smashed the glass with the butt of his Henry rifle and glanced quickly at Wilma, across the car and a couple of rows behind him. She was calmly checking the caps on the Dragoon.

The first line of Indians swept into view over a small rise, quirting their ponies toward the stopped train as a second group of warriors fired over their heads. Arrows and lead slugs ripped through the windows and thinner wood panels of the railroad car.

Ted swung his rifle, lined the sights with care, and squeezed off a shot. The slug knocked an Indian pony down, but the Sioux rolled free of the screaming animal and rose to one knee, leveling a handgun toward the window. Ted's second shot caught the Sioux in the chest.

Before the blast of Ted's second shot had settled, other

men in the car began firing. The handful of soldiers had grabbed carbines and were picking their targets with care. Less experienced shooters were banging away with revolvers at the Indian charge, doing little damage but making a lot of smoke and noise.

Cap sighted down the long barrel of his muzzle-loader and squeezed off a shot. A brave seemed suspended in midair as the .50 caliber rifle ball struck home. The Indian's pony ran on, leaving the hapless brave to drop limply to the ground. Cap grunted and reached for his powder horn.

Suddenly one passenger stiffened and then slumped. The blood welled from the back of the man's neck as he slid from the seat.

A mounted Indian whose pony bore the markings of the Cheyenne Dog Soldiers came within a few feet of Ted, an arrow at full draw in a powerful bow. Ted shot quickly, catching the brave in the hip. The arrow went high, quivering as it lodged in the top of the window frame.

The firing from both sides became an almost constant roar. Through the swirl of gunsmoke and dust from the charging ponies, Ted saw the initial wave of braves sweep past, veering their mounts to dash alongside the train. Several of the Indians were down, and the riderless ponies added to the confusion. Most of the damage had come from Cap's old muzzle-loader, from Ted's repeater, and from the soldiers' carbines.

Abruptly, an uneasy silence settled over the scene.

"We whupped 'em off, boys!" someone yelled.

"Don't count on it!" Ted yelled back. "Get ready! They'll be coming again!"

The words were hardly out of his mouth when withering fire from the crest of the low ridge raked the railroad cars, forcing Ted to duck below the window as he thumbed fresh cartridges into the loading port of the Henry. He glanced over his shoulder. Wilma had crouched down, shielding her son's body with her own, Ted's handgun still firmly in her grasp.

The Indian tactics for the second assault soon became clear. As their companions fired steadily, keeping the passengers pinned down in the cars, a number of braves raced ponies close to the sides of the train. The gunshots from the ridge abruptly stopped as the mounted Indians hurtled past, firing arrows and bullets into the cars at close range. Wood splinters nicked Ted's cheek at one near miss. The Indian who had fired the shot was gone before Ted could shoot back.

Something thumped onto the roof overhead. Ted caught a glimpse of a blazing pine-pitch torch as it slid from the slightly rounded top of the rail car to the ground outside.

"They're trying to fire the roof!" he yelled. "Aim for the Indians carrying torches!" He leaned from the window, momentarily exposing himself to the Indians' fire, and snapped a shot that tumbled a torchbearer from his racing pony.

As the civilians struggled to reload handguns, the soldiers kept up a steady and measured fire with their new breech-loading cartridge rifles or repeating Henrys and Spencers. One of the younger troopers, temporarily blinded in one eye by blood flowing from a scalp wound, calmly shifted his carbine to the other shoulder and knocked a Ute from his pony with a well-placed shot.

Ted and Cap picked up the rhythm of the Indian attack at about the same time, letting the braves race by the windows without returning fire. Then, as the horsemen kneed ponies away from the tracks to circle and race back, Ted's Henry or Cap's long rifle cracked. The result was usually another riderless pony. The Indians were paying a high price for their display of horsemanship.

Ted squeezed the trigger and the firing pin dropped on an empty chamber. He crouched to reload, realizing he was down to his last half-dozen cartridges. He glanced in Wilma's direction. She was staring intently at the roof near the back of the car.

Suddenly Ted heard the scuff of moccasins on the roof. At least one Indian, possibly more, had managed to scale the car. If they were able to set fire to the coach, the passengers inside would soon be at their mercy.

The thought was interrupted by the blast of the heavy handgun in Wilma's fist. The lead ball, nearly a half-inch in diameter, ripped through the wood of the roof. Wilma fired again, the muzzle blast almost deafening in the confines of the car. There was a strangled scream from above and a Sioux tumbled from the roof, his groin a mass of blood. Wilma emptied the revolver at the ceiling and Ted heard the braves scrambling to get clear of the car. They hit the ground running, and four were cut down in a hail of gunfire.

The attackers seemed to be wavering, Ted thought, their firing becoming less intense. Then the appearance of a man on horseback caught his attention. Squinting through the smoke and swirling dust, Ted felt his heart leap as he recognized the Indian. It was Long Walker!

He forced himself to concentrate only on the one horseman. He realized the range was almost four hundred yards, pushing the Henry .44 to its limits. Ted raised the muzzle and touched off two shots as fast as he could.

Both shots missed, though the second shot kicked dust beneath the belly of Long Walker's pony. Long Walker wheeled his horse just as Cap's long rifle boomed. The pony stumbled, then regained its footing, and the leader of the raiding party rode from sight beyond the ridge.

Cursing his own bad luck and Long Walker's fortune, Ted turned to call to Wilma—and panic struck him.

In the window directly above the crouching Bill, a painted Ute face had appeared—along with a brown hand gripping a revolver pointed straight at Wilma!

"Wilma! Watch out!" Ted shouted.

As he cried the warning, Ted tried to swing his rifle around. But the front sight of the weapon snagged in the cloth back of a seat. The split-second delay sent a surge of agony through Ted as he realized he would be too late.

Suddenly, Wild Bill glanced up at the brown fist and the pistol above his head. The boy, though wide-eyed with fear, did not hesitate. He shoved his small body up, grabbed the pistol barrel, and pushed it down. His strength, slight though it was, pinned the Indian's gun to the wall for an instant.

That was all the time Cap needed. At Ted's cry he had turned, his hand stabbing toward his belt. A flash of metal split the smoky air in the rail car. Cap's knife buried itself to the hilt in the Indian's neck. The Ute's convulsion tripped the hammer of the pistol, but the slug dug a harmless track along the wall.

Bill dropped back to the floor, the handgun clattering alongside him. Then the Ute was gone. Ted ran to their side, wrapping thankful and protective arms around his wife and son. Slowly it dawned on Ted that the firing had stopped. Through the window he could see the Indians in full retreat toward the north.

Cap made his way to the Hendersons and stood for a moment watching the Indians flee.

"Reckon them redskins chomped into a bigger biscuit

than they could chew," the old scout said. He peered through his spectacles at Bill. "You all right, son?"

Bill, badly shaken but putting up a brave front, could only nod.

"Good. You done fine, boy." Cap tugged at his silver mustache. "Be many a wailin' squaw in that camp tonight."

"Cap," Ted said, "that's one I owe you."

The old scout waved a hand. "Don't owe me nothin', Ted Henderson. Your young'un here gets the credit." The old-timer sighed. "Ain't throwed a knife in many a moon. Wonder is I hit the Injun at all, let alone where I was aimin'."

The arrival of the brakeman, worriedly checking his passengers, interrupted the conversation.

"Thanks to your warning, Mr. Henderson, we came out of this in pretty good shape," the shaken brakeman said. "The engineer spotted the break in the rails just in time to stop. If he hadn't slowed down . . ." The brakeman shook his head.

"How about casualties?" Ted asked.

"One man dead here, sir, and two wounded. Only one minor scratch in the car up front."

Cap, who had worked his way up one side and down the other looking out the windows, returned to the group with a young corporal in tow.

"Thanks to the work of these here sojer boys, looks like we took a fair plug outta that bunch," Cap said. " 'Bout fifteen dead Injuns. Prob'ly that many more is a-hurtin' some now."

The young noncom, who looked barely old enough to shave, held out a hand to Ted. "Corporal Bauer, sir. My squad is en route to Fort Bridger as replacements."

Ted shook the young man's hand firmly. "My compliments to your squad, Corporal Bauer. That was some nice shooting. My bet is the Indians weren't counting on that much firepower on this train. Looks like we will be keeping each other company as far as Fort Laramie, and the additional guns will be welcome indeed."

"All right, you Union Pacific men!" the brakeman yelled above the muttered conversations. "Fall to and let's get the rail fixed! Looks like you're going to work sooner than you expected." The brakeman swung the rear door open, leading the burly work crew outside.

"Be back in a shake," Cap said, heading for the door. "Gotta get my knife back. That's the best Arkansas toothpick

I ever had." He paused and glanced at Bill. "Young'un, that's your Injun out there. You want his ears to remember 'im by?"

Bill, still putting on a brave front, silently shook his head. The old scout nodded and slipped out the door.

For the first time Wilma noticed Bill was cradling his right hand against his body. "Bill! Are you hurt?" she cried.

Reluctantly, the child held out his hand. The pistol discharge had left a nasty powder burn across his palm and little finger.

The young corporal scurried away to get the first aid kit his squad carried as Wilma examined the burn. It was painful but not deep. Ted clasped his son's arm. "It's all right to cry when you hurt, Bill," he said softly. "And you saved your mother's life."

"I didn't think," Bill said, his voice quavering. "I just done it."

"Did it," Wilma corrected gently. "Even a brave warrior like you shouldn't scalp the English language. And I'll bet you did that just to get out of doing your chores for a few days," she added teasingly.

Despite the pain, Bill grinned.

As Wilma cleaned and dressed the burn, Ted fished around beneath the seats until he found the weapon dropped by the dying Ute. It was a .36 caliber Dance, a percussion handgun used mostly by the Confederacy during the war. He showed the gun to Bill.

"In a few years, son, this will be yours. In the meantime, I'll keep it for you," he said tucking it into his own waistband.

Shortly after Wilma finished tying off Bill's small bandage, the track crew climbed back on board sweating with exertion in spite of the November chill. Within moments the train began moving once again. The smoke was soon whisked from the car as the cool autumn air flowed through shattered windows. The passengers reached for jackets or blankets, but no one complained. They were still alive.

The sun was near the western horizon when the train chuffed to a halt at a switching station near rails' end.

For the Hendersons and the soldiers, the cluster of tents that made up the terminal was a welcome sight. A long stage ride still lay before them, but leaving the train meant they were nearing home.

Cap stepped down from the car, his bedroll under one

arm and the long rifle cradled in the other. The old scout had a chew of tobacco stuffed in one cheek.

He turned to Wilma and Ted. "Iffin you young folks don't mind none and you got room, I'd be obliged to tag along till I can find me a hoss for sale."

"We would be delighted, Cap," Wilma said. "I'll bet the stage driver can find room for everyone."

Ted hastened to agree. The old frontiersman would be the equal of any three men if trouble came along, and Ted liked him. Cap was the last of a rare breed, he thought sadly.

"Where's the little Ute grabber?" Cap asked, peering through the spectacles perched high on the bridge of his nose.

Wilma waved toward the small cluster of soldiers a short distance away. "He went to help Corporal Bauer unload."

Cap nodded. "Gonna be a good hand, that'un. Kinda took me a shine to him. How old he be?"

"Almost four and a half," Wilma replied.

Cap snorted. "Big for his age. Had 'im figured for a couple years longer in the tooth than that. Scrapper, ain't he?"

The temporary rail terminal was buzzing with activity. Eastbound passengers arriving on the stage stared in awe at the marks left by the Indian attack and quizzed westbound travelers for details. Ted made his way amid the bustle to the telegrapher's office and wired ahead to Fort Laramie, letting Abel Hubbard know they were on schedule.

As he helped the stage driver hitch up a fresh team, Ted noticed a work train chuffing in reverse from rails' end a couple of miles ahead. The string of flatcars carried a score of husky workmen who would transfer the railroad equipment from the newly arrived cars to the smaller train for the return trip.

The loaded stage sat heavy on its thoroughbraces as they prepared to move out. Wilma and Bill shared the cramped interior of the coach with four of Corporal Bauer's troopers. The corporal rode shotgun alongside the driver while Ted, Cap, and two other soldiers scrounged space atop the stage, surrounded by baggage that would not fit in the stuffed boot.

"Y'all set?" the driver called, then clucked the six-horse hitch into motion. "Gonna be an uncomfortable ride," he said. "We're overloaded, but this old coach is a tough 'un.

We'll pick up a cavalry escort from Fort Sedgwick a few hours out. Many guns as we got now, might not need 'em."

The stage road veered a short distance north of the railroad's path along the Platte. Soon after leaving the terminal, Ted heard the sounds of railroad builders at work, the faint sounds of lilting Irish songs punctuated by the clang of hammer on metal. As the sounds gradually faded into the distance, the stage passed a large herd of grazing cattle, apparently the meat supply for the rail crews. Ted knew that before many more weeks had passed he would return to the railroad work site and be part of that commotion.

At midafternoon of the first day, the stage picked up an escort—a band of Indians riding a trail parallel to the coach's course.

Cap dismissed them with a single glance. "Sioux, all right," he said. "But they don't appear to be lookin' for trouble. Expect they done heard 'bout how we punched some holes in that other bunch's medicine shirts."

To Ted the hours seemed to drag as familiar landmarks came into view, then fell behind the jolting, lurching stage.

Twenty miles from Fort Laramie on a bend of the North Platte River, a final cavalry escort party relieved the soldiers from Fort Sedgwick. Ted was delighted to see that the detail was led by Corporal Carl Keller, one of the original Henderson's Scouts and a longtime friend. The escort detail led three saddled horses—Ted's own favorite gelding, Wild Bill's paint pony, and Wilma's bay mare which meant an end to the cramped conditions on the stage.

Also among the escort party was Ellen, the full-blooded Arapaho girl adopted by German-born Carl Keller and his wife, Anna. Ellen was Bill's self-appointed big sister.

As Keller and the Hendersons exchanged warm greetings Ellen thoroughly embarrassed Bill with an enthusiastic hug. However, Ted noted a gleam of delight in Bill's eyes. Soon the two youngsters were jabbering away in their own language, a curious mixture of English, Arapaho, Sioux, and Cheyenne with an occasional Ute phrase thrown in. The chatter continued as Bill spotted his saddled pony and walked quickly to the animal, hugging the pinto's neck in greeting.

After introducing Cap and Corporal Keller, Ted mounted his horse and drew Keller aside. "Any word of Yellow Crow?" he asked.

The corporal nodded, idly scratching a chin stubbled

with tough, graying whiskers. "He's 'bout recovered from gettin' shot up down on the South Platte in the Black Kettle massacre. So far he's been able to keep the young bucks in his band on the reservation. Reckon he'll have his hands full at that for a spell."

"If anyone can keep the reins tight on the Cheyenne, Yellow Crow can," Ted said. He sighed wistfully. "He and I were supposed to take Bill on a fall hunt this year. But it didn't work out."

The two friends watched as Bill swung aboard his pony. Forking the Mexican-style saddle that was a scaled-down version of the one ridden by his father, the boy was soon putting the pony through his paces. Using only his voice and knees, Bill took the willing pony through sharp turns, quick stops, and sudden accelerations.

"Yellow Crow may be goin' on his own hunt, Ted," Keller said softly. "He's still carryin' that Spencer cartridge left over from the run-in we had with ol' Long Walker. Took the blood oath on it. Was I a bettin' man, I wouldn't put a wood nickel on Long Walker."

Wilma mounted her bay mare, having slipped behind a clump of brush to change into a split riding skirt. She always rode astride and held a grudge against the man who designed the sidesaddle. "Dignity be damned," she had once said, "if an Indian's after me, I want to be able to handle my horse." Ted knew from experience that she could handle a horse quite well. Better than most men, in fact.

At the stage driver's cry, "Time's a-wastin', folks!" the travelers moved out again on the final leg of their trip home.

The trip into Fort Laramie was uneventful. As the caravan made its way through the streets of the growing community outside the walls of the fort itself, Ted realized Fort Laramie was changing rapidly. The whiskey mills and bawdy houses had grown in number and all seemed to be doing a booming business. He nodded here and there at familiar faces, occasionally exchanging brief words of greeting as they rode down the main street of the settlement. At the same time, Ted noted the number of strangers, gamblers and drifters, who had moved in. Some of them appeared to be railroad workers, who Keller said had found the Union Pacific too demanding and were looking for easier—and possibly illegal—employment. A scattering of prospectors loitered about, many of them with faces darkened in anger at finding the

Bozeman Trail to the Black Hills closed to white traffic. There was a tension in the air, a barely suppressed violence, that made Ted uneasy.

The atmosphere seemed to have its effect on Wilma as well. As they rode through the gates into the parade ground of the fort, she touched his arm.

"Darling, I have to say it's good to be home again," she said with a slight frown. "But somehow, it doesn't seem the same. It's as though we've been gone for a year instead of just a couple of months."

Ted was pleasantly surprised to find both Abel Hubbard and Major David Wills on the post. Abel, a few years Ted's junior, had assumed command at Fort Laramie following Ted's resignation. David Wills was only a couple of years out of West Point, but he had been one of Ted's more apt students. He had proved his ability to lead men on the frontier and was second in command to Abel.

As Wilma and Bill went to oversee the unloading of their belongings, Ted followed Abel and David into the cramped quarters that served as the command post of Fort Laramie and a wide swath of the Wyoming, Nebraska, and Dakota territories. Both men seemed different to Ted than they had the last time he had seen them. Abel, Ted thought, must simply be tired. The lieutenant colonel's handsome face looked haggard, and his broad shoulders and stocky frame appeared to droop more than usual. Ted could sympathize with him. The Laramie command was not for anyone weak of body or spirit. Meanwhile, Wills, slighter of build than Abel but with erect military bearing, seemed slightly depressed, almost preoccupied. It was unlike the optimistic, energetic young officer to wear a gloomy expression. Idly, Ted wondered what Wills's problem might be.

Inside the command post, Ted reached for his own cup, still resting in its niche above the stove, and helped himself to some coffee. As he sipped the strong brew, he watched Abel scan the packet of documents Ted had brought from General Grant.

Abel returned the papers to their pouch and looked up, his dark brows wrinkled in concern. "That's a tall order, Ted. I'll give the Union Pacific all the help I can, of course. But I don't have enough men for full-time support and still keep things in line here. We're undermanned, like all the other forts in the West." He smiled wryly. "As one of our better-known generals recently said, it's difficult to surround three Indians with one soldier."

Ted nodded solemnly. "No one is more familiar with the situation than I am. The Third Cavalry has always had more to do than any two regiments can handle. Just give us what help you can spare. What is the status with the Indians at the moment?"

"So far the major tribes are quiet," Abel replied with a shrug. "We've had a few isolated instances of young bucks leaving reservation grounds and stealing a horse or a few cows. Nothing really serious. The peace chiefs have kept their people in line. Yellow Crow and Big Nose are helping us patrol the Bozeman Trail, turning back miners and prospectors who slip by our troops. No major incidents there as yet, but it could blow up at any time. All the big Indian raids have been to the east, out in Long Walker's territory. I've chased him a time or two, but he's smart and slippery."

Abel leaned back in his chair, made a steeple of his fingertips, and peered over them at Ted, obviously worried. "I don't know if the peace will last after the railroad crosses the Plains," he said.

"I don't want those rails much either, Abel," Ted said. "But they're coming nonetheless."

The somber discussion was interrupted by a solid rap on the office door. At Abel's call the door swung open and a huge black man stepped into the office, one leg dragging a bit. A grin flashed on his broad face. "Heard you were back in town, Colonel," Sergeant Major Albert Jonas said.

Ted's hand disappeared into a massive black fist. A smile of genuine pleasure spread across his own face.

"How are you, Albert?"

The sergeant major's eyes twinkled. "Healing. Not as fast as I want but quicker than I deserve. Colonel Hubbard decided to keep me around. Reckon he needed a desk soldier underfoot."

Ted chuckled. Regardless of what Albert Jonas said, Ted knew there were few if any sergeant majors in the U.S. Army more efficient. And he knew he never would be able to repay the man who had almost forfeited his own life so the others could escape when Bill and Ellen were rescued from Long Walker's camp. All hope for his survival had been lost, but somehow Albert had managed to slip past the Indians and stagger back to Fort Laramie—literally just in time for his own funeral.

"Sergeant," Abel said, "consider yourself relieved from desk duty tonight. We're planning a little welcome home dinner for Ted and Wilma. You and that pretty woman you married are invited." He turned to Ted. "You'll be wanting to help Wilma, I expect, and David and I have a mess of paperwork to do. We'll chew on this railroad bone a bite at a time."

"Fair enough," Ted said, plucking his hat from the nearby rack. Before joining Wilma at the house where they were staying in the fort, he went in search of the old scout.

He located Cap at the livery stable, busy rubbing down a big sorrel gelding. Cap declined Ted's invitation to dinner.

"Fancy table ain't no place for me," he said. "I got manners like a timber wolf. Figgered on tappin' a jug and bunkin' out with them sojer boys." The old-timer stroked the sorrel's shoulder. A puckered wound dimpled the animal's muscles.

"Me an' ol' Ouch here found each other a tad after I got to Laramie," Cap explained. "Sojer boy found him wanderin' on the prairie, still saddled. Had an arrow in his shoulder. Was blood on the saddle. Don't take no educated man to figger what happened. Anyhow, he's sound now, and a hoss what's been bit by a Injun arrow's better'n any watchdog for a man what wants to keep his hair. Kin smell a redskin a mile off."

Cap sighed. "Be on my way in a couple days, son. This here country's gettin' too crowded. Gotta find me some elbow room. Maybe Idaho. Ol' Jim Bridger tol' me he liked that country." Cap spat a stream of tobacco juice. "I'm gettin' on in years. Figger me an' ol' Ouch will spend what time I got left out in the Almighty's best work. You bein' a family man and all, I don't reckon you'd care to tag along?"

"I'd like nothing better, Cap," Ted said sincerely, "and thanks for the invitation. But I can't."

"Figgered as much," Cap said. "Leastways, I'll miss seein' some hurtful things you'll be around to see, Ted Henderson. I'll be gone before the West is."

The old scout's words haunted Ted until the dinner party began at the Laramie Hotel. He had expected a fine meal, but the rich table left him in awe. Judy Hubbard, Abel's blond wife, had taken over the hotel when Vi and Taylor Elkins moved to Washington. Then Judy had scored something of a coup, talking Sally Jonas, Albert's wife, into selling her seamstress shop and joining her in operating the hotel. The two women made a good combination.

Judy and Sally left the running of the hotel to their well-trained staff and joined the dinner party. Judy was dazzling in a deep blue gown that highlighted her long blond hair and expressive blue eyes. Sally Jonas was just as fetching in a rich gold dress that dramatized the cream-coffee color of her skin and gold-flecked brown eyes. Ted noted with satisfaction that Wilma was certainly not outshone by either of the younger women.

The usually solemn Abel gradually relaxed and joined in the banter, with Albert Jonas's wry sense of humor setting the tone. David Wills, however, remained reserved. His brown eyes constantly shifted about the crowded dining room as though looking for a specific face.

Wills's search appeared to be in vain. By the meal's end he seemed more downcast than before. The young officer excused himself early and walked toward the bar. He had consumed three whiskeys already, and Ted was concerned about the major since he knew from personal experience what liquor could do to a man. David Wills had too much potential to travel that road.

Ted forced himself to put his concern aside. He was a civilian now, and any problem Wills had was Abel Hubbard's responsibility.

When they returned to their house afterward, stuffed with prime elk steaks and with Bill sent off, protesting, to bed, Wilma eased herself onto a small loveseat at Ted's side.

"I'm glad we decided it would be best for Bill and me to winter at the ranch while you're away," she said. "From some of the characters I've seen and some of the talk at the table tonight, I think I'll feel safer at the ranch than in Laramie. You know, Judy told me she actually has had to start keeping a loaded shotgun close at hand."

Ted felt his wife shudder slightly despite the warmth of their quarters. "Ted, how can a town change so quickly? Laramie has been rough at times, but until now it never seemed so—so threatening."

"I wish I had an answer, darling," Ted said softly. "I guess we have to put it down to so-called progress. I know how you feel. I would personally be more at ease in the middle of the Sioux nation than on the streets of Laramie now."

Abruptly Wilma's tone brightened. "It doesn't matter. We will be happier at the ranch anyway. Wind Flower will be needing help soon. And Bill can pitch in with some of the small chores. He needs to start learning how a ranch works. After all, it will be partly his one day."

Her violet eyes were soft, almost misty, as she stroked the back of his hand. "The ranch is really home to us. It will be so nice to return to it again," she said, reaching out for Ted.

Ted pulled his horse to a stop atop the ridge overlooking their ranch, and studied the scene below. The solidly built ranch house overlooked a wide meadow, nestled in a valley between mountain ranges. Behind the house a small horse herd grazed, half-grown colts frolicking in the deep grass that even in its dry winter stage remained rich enough to maintain stock well until spring came again.

Once, years before, during the time he had been a rider for the Pony Express, the ranch had held terrors for Ted. The nightmare of his first wife and child being brutally butchered by white men who tried to make the massacre appear to be the work of Indians died hard. The grisly discovery had sent Ted crawling into a bottle, and he suspected he would have been there yet, but the dark-haired woman at his side had pulled him from his bog of grief and whiskey. She had also cleaned up the house and redecorated it to remove all signs of the tragedy. Now Ted saw their home as a fine working ranch, a healthy place for a young boy to grow into manhood.

He turned to Wilma and smiled. "From the looks of the place, Kevin and Wind Flower are leading us straight to prosperity," he said.

A small figure emerged from the house and waved vigorously in their direction. Wind Flower, at least, was home. Ted nudged his horse into motion.

It was a joyous homecoming. Wilma and Wind Flower embraced, and Ted took the Navajo woman's dainty hand in his own. "Wind Flower," he said solemnly, "if I did not already have a fine squaw and if your husband were not as big as the side of a barn, I would be sorely tempted to challenge him for the right to tie ponies before your lodge."

A shy grin creased Wind Flower's fine-boned face. "If I

did not have Kevin," she replied, "Ted Henderson's ponies might have to learn to understand Navajo."

Ted smiled and began unloading their belongings.

Kevin rode up as they finished unloading the wagon. The big Irishman greeted Ted with a whoop and a crushing handshake and affectionately cuffed young Bill on the shoulder. Then he yelped in mock pain as a small fist returned the blow—about halfway up Kevin's ribs, which was as high as young Bill could reach.

Kevin led Ted on a quick tour of improvements he had made since Ted's last visit. A new room had been added to the house, largely to accommodate the occasional guest. Wilma and Bill would be quite comfortable there. Additional stalls had been built and the barn enlarged. New corrals made of sturdy pine poles had gone up, and alongside the barn was a newly built shelter—a lean-to of thick logs, carefully chinked against the coming winter, still oozing sap from the green wood.

"Hired a hand," Kevin explained. "Best man with a horse I've ever seen. He can look at a cow and tell what she's thinking. And, Ted, he can do things with that rawhide rope I still can't believe."

Ted nodded in satisfaction. "It's good there will be another man around the place. Plus, Carl Keller and some of the other Scouts will be dropping by from time to time, along with any patrols sent in this direction. That should help discourage any Indian problems."

Kevin laughed heartily. "The tribes in the hills around here have no intention of raiding this ranch. Wind Flower has become widely known as 'Medicine Woman.' The Indians bring their sick or injured to her for treatment. I seriously doubt they will try anything that might harm their very special physician. Also, I took your advice, Ted, and stocked some beef steers just for the needy Indians. When times are tough, they do not hesitate to come to us for help. So far they have been nothing but honorable. I've even become friends with some of the senior warriors among the Arapaho and other tribes around."

Valdez Cabrillo arrived moments later. The man certainly lived up to Kevin's enthusiastic appraisal, Ted thought as he took the Mexican's leathery hand. Behind the gentle eyes and courtly manner Ted sensed a quiet but competent toughness.

Valdez greeted Wilma with a respectful bow and then offered a hand to Bill as one grown-up to another, forever sealing a friendship in the process.

"*Hola, amigo pequeño!*" Valdez said.

A slight frown crossed Bill's face as he sought the meaning of the strange language. Then he recalled a commonly used word.

"*Amigo* means friend?" he asked.

"Yes, Señor Bill."

"And *pequeño?*" the boy asked.

"Little. Or small."

Ted and Wilma watched arm-in-arm as Valdez and Bill went to tend the horses. "There he goes again," Wilma sighed, a touch of pride in her voice, "learning another language. Sometimes when he gets excited I have to make him stop and translate from one of the Indian dialects that I don't understand well. Now I guess I'll have to add Spanish to that."

The visit was entirely too brief to suit Ted. But then any visit shorter than forty years was going to be too little, he thought.

He reined his horse to a stop at the top of the rise for a final look back. Each parting seemed to get more painful. He raised his hand in a last wave, swallowed the lump in his throat, and kneed the dun back onto the long trail toward the Union Pacific railhead.

"Ted Henderson," he grumbled aloud, "you're getting too old and too accustomed to family life to be riding off again." He noticed that the ears of the dun gelding were laid back in his direction along the muscular neck. Ted realized he must have spoken aloud, and the horse probably was wondering from the rider's tone if he had done something wrong. Ted reassured the animal with a pat on the neck.

"Just grousing to myself, Buck," he said. He tugged the heavy greatcoat closer against the bite of the late-December morning. "And we'll be sharing New Year's Eve somewhere between here and the Union Pacific railhead. You're not my idea of the best company to welcome in the year eighteen sixty-seven with, but you'll do. And what the hell," he said, settling back into the saddle. "Maybe I can work in an occasional visit in the next year or two."

The compact dun, satisfied it was not in danger of catching a spur in the ribs, settled into a slow and easy trot that covered ground quickly.

The Cheyenne warrior eased his battle-scarred body from the back of the palomino gelding. He knelt and studied the tracks, each as big as the palm of his own hand, in the soft sand along the creeks. They were only moments old.

Yellow Crow stood and sniffed the breeze that blew from the dense tangle of wild plum thicket a few yards ahead. The odor was faint but distinct in his nostrils. A musky hint of fur and carrion.

The Cheyenne grunted in satisfaction. The great timber wolf had taken refuge in the thicket. He could almost sense the animal's pain and desperation, its body slashed in the fierce battle that had left three Cheyenne dogs dead near camp, its muscles torn by an ill-aimed shot from a young and inexperienced warrior's rifle. Finally, tortured and exhausted from the relentless pursuit of the man on horseback, it had chosen to make its final stand.

The palomino's nostrils flared as the horse tested the breeze. Its ears pointed toward the thicket. Yellow Crow stroked the gelding's neck in reassurance.

"Do not fear, yellow horse," he said softly. "It is not necessary that you carry Yellow Crow any closer. You have done your job."

Yellow Crow looped the hackamore reins around the horse's neck. If anything happened and the horse had to flee, the reins would not tangle in a bush or about its forefeet.

He left the Spencer repeating rifle in its saddle sheath. This was a job to be done the old way. The wounded beast deserved that dignity. Yellow Crow nocked an arrow onto the twisted sinew string of the powerful Osage orange bow. It was a shorter bow than most of his tribesmen carried, and its power was such that few men could draw it to full arc. In Yellow Crow's hands it seemed a toy.

The Cheyenne stood silently for a moment, facing the thicket. The wolf had chosen the ground for the last battle well.

"Great wolf, hear Yellow Crow," the warrior called softly. "It is not in anger but in sadness that Yellow Crow comes. We are much alike—once brothers of the forest in a land of plenty for the sharing. But now your spirit is bitter. You take more than your share and kill for the joy of the slaughter.

Thus brother must face brother, and one shall not see the new day dawn."

Yellow Crow moved soundlessly into the edge of the thicket. He paused there to watch and listen, his senses tuned to the slightest movement, sound, or smell. A ground squirrel chirred in anger from the edge of its burrow and a jay squawked raucously from a branch close by. The wolf's smell grew stronger.

A few more cautious steps brought Yellow Crow to the edge of a clearing scarcely larger than his own lodge. Brush rustled on the far side of the clearing. The ground squirrel stopped its chatter. In the shadows of the thicket a pair of yellow eyes gleamed. For a moment the Cheyenne and the timber wolf stared into each other's eyes.

Then, with a growl of rage, a mass of fur and muscle the size of a small pony burst from its lair and charged, fangs bared. Yellow Crow snapped the bow to full draw and released the arrow as the wolf left its feet in a lunge toward the Cheyenne's throat. The knife-edged broadpoint sliced into the animal's chest. The beast jerked in midleap as the arrow drove home.

Yellow Crow ducked aside, deftly escaping the slashing teeth. The huge gray body fell heavily into the sand of the clearing. The wolf tried to rise. It twisted its muzzle to snap at the fire in its chest. Then it sank to the ground, its powerful chin resting on sinewy forelegs.

The Cheyenne approached the downed wolf with caution until he was sure the beast was dead. He knelt at the wolf's side and touched the silver-tipped mane of the neck.

"May you find peace and good hunting in the next world," he whispered, then stood. He would not take the wolf's pelt. The animal had been touched by bad medicine. The evil spirit that had driven it might yet live in the coarse hair. One did not so tempt the spirits as to bring into one's lodge such a pelt.

Yellow Crow walked slowly back to his palomino. The horse snuffled a quiet greeting, then nudged its soft muzzle into Yellow Crow's side. The Cheyenne stroked the horse's gaunt flanks. "The chase was long and hard, old friend," Yellow Crow said. "You have seen many such chases and many summers. Yellow Crow and his faithful horse have shared long miles and many battles. When next the grass turns green you will see no more saddles. For the rest of your days you need only to graze and grow fat. This you have earned many times over."

Yellow Crow swung into the saddle easily. He had grown to like the white man's saddle during his days as a rider with the Pony Express, finding it more comfortable and functional than the traditional Cheyenne trappings.

The stalk of the wolf had carried him far from his own band to less than a day's ride from Fort Laramie. For a moment he was tempted to knee the gelding toward the settlement, where he had many friends. And many days had passed since he had seen his godson. He shrugged off the impulse. There was too much to be done among his own people. Yellow Crow had not sought the rank of peace chief, but he had not shunned his responsibility when it was urged upon him.

He turned the palomino back toward the Cheyenne reservation, toward the Blackfoot woman who had become his wife. A slight smile tugged at the corners of his mouth. He had been pleased when Talking Bird had chosen him instead of the freedom to return to her own people when he had purchased the dark-eyed captive from another Cheyenne warrior. Yellow Crow was still young enough to begin a family, to have a son, to complete the circle of life.

He held the horse to a slow, easy walk. Despite his dislike for the actual killing of the wolf, Yellow Crow had enjoyed the hunt. For a time it was as it had been in the old days. When life was simple, when dangers were known by the color of their fur or the striping of their war paint.

Topping a rocky hill, Yellow Crow abruptly reined the palomino to a halt. A half-dozen riders were a short distance away. They were Arapaho, and they carried war shields but no paint. Nonetheless, Yellow Crow slipped the Spencer from its saddle sheath, checked to make sure a cartridge was chambered, and then casually rested the barrel of his rifle across the crook of an elbow where it could be used quickly if needed. He waited, face impassive, as the Arapaho neared. They were all young men and he knew none of them by name.

One of the braves raised a hand in greeting. Yellow Crow did the same, but he did not relax. He had found it best not to trust the Arapaho.

"Arapaho warriors travel far from their homelands," Yellow Crow said.

"They are bound for the tall grass near the great river," the leader of the group said. "There they join many others, to kill the iron horses that cross the Indian lands." The Arapaho's voice brightened in animation. "A great chief there has much medicine. The spirits have shown him how to kill the iron horse. Warriors of many tribes go there."

Yellow Crow frowned. "The warrior speaks of the blue-eyed one? The warrior named Long Walker?"

The Arapaho nodded. "Even now, those who have seen Long Walker perform this magic ride to visit each tribe—"

"Do these men of vision travel to the Cheyenne camp of the peace chief Yellow Crow?"

The Arapaho frowned at the interruption, then spat in contempt. "It is said that the Cheyenne of Yellow Crow's band are but squaws. And that their peace chief has lost his courage and now turns tail at the first sign of danger."

Yellow Crow gazed calmly into the young warrior's eyes. "This is Yellow Crow of the Cheyenne," he said quietly. "It is an easy matter to settle the question of Yellow Crow's courage."

He let the challenge lie. Anger flashed in the young Arapaho's eyes, and for an instant Yellow Crow thought the challenge would be met. Then another member of the band whispered something to his leader. The angry one's expression abruptly changed to caution, perhaps a little fear. The Arapaho shrugged.

"There is no time," he said lamely.

Yellow Crow nodded. "Another day, perhaps." He would grant the Arapaho his lame attempt to save face. "In the meantime, answer Yellow Crow's question. Do the warriors who have seen this great power of Long Walker's go to Yellow Crow's village?"

"Yes."

"Then Yellow Crow will go and challenge them," the Cheyenne said angrily. "When the Arapaho see this great medicine chief Long Walker, give him a message. Tell him he is never to send anyone to the land of the Cheyenne. Further, tell him that one day his bones shall lie scattered on the prairie and his scalp shall ride at Yellow Crow's belt!"

The Arapaho, taken aback at the sudden heat of Yellow Crow's words, merely nodded.

"The young warriors are not of Yellow Crow's tribe and this is not Cheyenne land," Yellow Crow said. "If either were the case they would be forbidden to continue. But Yellow

Crow's authority does not extend to the Arapaho, whose chiefs lack vision. He asks the warriors to turn back, for nothing but grief shall come of this trip."

The Arapaho did not reply. Instead, he set his eyes on the eastern horizon and brutally kicked his pony into motion. The others followed.

As the small band gradually faded from view, Yellow Crow replaced his rifle in its scabbard. His fingers touched the soft deerskin pouch hanging by a sturdy rawhide thong about his neck. In the pouch was a single cartridge for the Spencer rifle. Yellow Crow was saving it for Long Walker.

The Cheyenne kneed his tired palomino into motion, checking the inner urge to hurry back to his village. No representative of the hated Long Walker was worth the death of a fine horse. Soon, he thought bitterly, there would be much death. It rode the blue-eyed Indian's path, a vulture of darkness.

Three

Ted Henderson knelt in the knee-high dry grass that still crackled with the morning's heavy frost and studied the fresh tracks in the prairie soil. The crushed blades told their story as clearly as a telegraph message to the veteran frontiersman's eyes.

Ten mounted Indians had been there less than a half-hour before. The riders had halted, their mounts milling about. Then abruptly the trail changed direction. The unshod pony tracks fell into the pattern of horses moving at a brisk trot.

Ted casually plucked a stem of the dormant grass and chewed on the crisp stalk, pondering the situation. He had elected to travel alone through the vast land north of the Platte River to rails' end of the Union Pacific. It would be his last chance to enjoy solitude for many months.

He had sensed this particular band of Indians was up to no good when he had first crossed their tracks at dawn. The band was too small for a hunting party, yet too large to be a scouting group. At intervals a single rider had left the main group and ridden to the top of a ridge or rolling hill. Obviously they were looking for something.

They must have found it, he thought. Their tracks led toward the Platte.

Ted stood, slipped out of the heavy greatcoat, and shuddered briefly in the sharp cold of the early January morning. The coat tended to get in the way when action was needed. He slipped the garment under the saddle thongs that held his bedroll in place, then took his Henry from the scabbard. He stepped into the saddle and nudged his horse into a fast lope.

"Might be a wild-goose chase, Buck," he said quietly to his horse, "but there's only one way to find out." He glanced down from time to time, making sure he was still on the

Indians' trail. It was an easy task. The band had made no effort to hide its tracks.

For just over a mile Ted rode cautiously, his eyes constantly scanning the land ahead. Following Indians was one thing. Finding them unexpectedly was another.

The sharp crack of a rifle shot from up ahead jarred him into action. He put spurs to the dun and cocked the rifle in the same motion. A second, flatter report, possibly a handgun, sounded. The horse was running flat out when Ted heard the sound of a ragged volley of gunshots.

The dun was blowing hard when Ted pulled the animal to a stop just below the crest of the shallow canyon gouged out by the Platte River. He stepped from the saddle, rifle in hand, before the horse completely stopped, and sprinted to the edge of the low bluff above the river.

Ted understood the situation with a quick glance. In a U-shaped depression a hundred yards downriver, three men huddled behind the body of a downed horse as bullets kicked sand around them. Halfway between Ted and the trapped men were the Indians he had been following.

The braves, six Sioux and four Ute, had their backs to him. There was no lookout peering in his direction. Instantly Ted swung the carbine to his shoulder and lined the V-shaped rear notch and front sights on the back of the nearest Indian. The Henry jumped against his shoulder. The brave jerked as the slug ripped into him, then shuddered and lay still in the scrub brush.

Ted swung the rifle muzzle toward another Indian and squeezed off two quick shots. The startled Indians glanced over their shoulders, then scrambled for cover at the sight of the smoke from Ted's rifle. Ted ducked behind the rocks as slugs from the Indians' rifles plowed into the ridge. He crawled back out of sight, then sprinted a few steps to his right and wormed his way to the top of the bank once more. His fourth shot staggered a stocky Ute.

Another Indian yelped as a pistol round from the direction of the trapped men struck too close for comfort. One of the remaining Sioux bolted for his horse and Ted levered two quick shots at the running Indian. Both missed. The Sioux reached his pony, swung aboard, and raced his mount across the riverbed.

The other Indians, caught in a cross fire from Ted's rifle

and the handguns of their intended victims, broke off the attack and scrambled for their horses.

Ted lined his sights on one young brave, then lowered his rifle. The Indians' ambush had failed; Ted had no taste for unnecessary bloodshed.

He watched as a mounted Sioux raced toward a downed comrade, leaned over, and scooped his wounded companion onto his pony's rump. The rescue maneuver never failed to fascinate Ted, though he had seen it done many times. As horsemen few tribes could match the Sioux, and no white man could even come close.

Feeding fresh cartridges into the Henry, Ted waited until he was positive the Indians had no intention of circling back to strike again. Then he retrieved his horse, quieting the nervous gelding with a calm word, and rode slowly toward the three men below.

"Anyone hurt?" he called as he neared the trio.

A young red-haired man with a neatly trimmed beard was the first to reply. "Aside from being scared out of ten years' growth, I don't believe anyone is injured," he said in a clipped New England accent. "Where are your companions?" he asked.

The question puzzled Ted for a moment until he realized the red-haired man must have thought there had been more than one man on the riverbank.

"I'm them, I suppose," Ted replied wryly.

The man blinked in surprise. "Sounded like a whole patrol out there. But, mister, I don't remember when I have been more delighted to see one man." He started to hold out a hand, then realized he was still gripping a pistol. He smiled sheepishly as he stowed the weapon in his waistband.

"I'm Jeff Quarles, surveyor for the Union Pacific."

"Ted Henderson. Glad I could help."

Quarles nodded toward his two companions. "Jerry Leach and Ray Flemmons. Flemmons is the ugly one. We're new on the job. Only our fourth day out, and it was nearly our last. Will they be back?"

"Not that bunch," Ted said, shaking his head. "They're Sioux and Ute, and it's bad medicine when one of them gets shot on a raid. If they were Apache, we'd still be in a mess of trouble." Ted glanced around. "Where are your other horses?"

"Took off at the first shot," Flemmons grumbled. "Damn Injun knocked the rod right out of my hand. Thought there for a while ol' Satan and me were gonna meet up quicker than I'd planned. I'm obliged to you, Henderson."

Leach, obviously the youngest of the three, stared about wide-eyed. "How—how many did—we get?"

"Two dead and a couple more wounded," Ted said matter-of-factly. "Leave the dead where they lie. The Indians will come back after a while for the bodies. I'm going to take a look. Sometimes a dead Indian can tell you more than a live one."

Reluctantly he turned to the dreaded but necessary task of examining the results of his work. The first Indian he had shot still lay facedown, a small dark circle marking the entrance of the rifle slug. Ted slipped a hand under a shoulder and rolled the man over. His slug had passed through a rib, mangled the Indian's heart, and left a large, bloody exit hole.

A glance at the brave's face confirmed what Ted had suspected earlier. A long scar began above one eyebrow, crossed a broken nose, and furrowed along a bronze cheekbone to near the jawline. Ted instantly recognized the mark of a cavalry saber. The dead Indian was called Hook, known to have been one of Long Walker's first recruits. The Brule Sioux had become a subchief of the outlaw band, one of Long Walker's most valued lieutenants. No one knew how many white scalps Hook had taken, but it had been a goodly number.

At least that bullet did not go to waste, Ted thought.

He did not recognize the other Indian. Markings on the man's clothing identified him as a member of the Santee Sioux tribe.

Ted left the two bodies as they lay, glancing at the large black birds already circling overhead. He shivered, but not because of the cold. "Hook," he said solemnly, "it looks as if your buzzards are coming home to roost."

He made his way back to the survey team. "Hope you gentlemen don't mind walking," he said. "My horse won't carry double, let alone four. We can take turns riding and walking. That should save some wear and tear on your feet."

"Mr. Henderson," Jeff Quarles said with a smile, "after today I don't think I'll ever again complain about having to walk anywhere."

Jerry Leach scuffed a toe nervously in the dirt. "Reckon we could get moving pretty quick? I'd just as soon not be here if those red devils should decide to come back."

The sun had almost reached its perch on the western horizon when Ted led his footsore, weary, and cold charges toward rails' end. They had covered almost fifteen miles in a little over half a day. Not bad for white men, Ted thought, even if it would not impress a Cheyenne or a Crow. It was amazing how raw fear could increase a man's stamina.

He watched as a lone horseman from rails' end galloped toward them on a rawboned and sturdy bay. Before the rider had skidded the big horse to a stop, Ted knew who he was. The description of Jack Casement, known as "General Jack" for his considerable exploits during the war, could hardly apply to anyone else. He was a small, wiry man with bushy beard, black hat, a bullwhip draped across the saddle, and an expression that hinted at his bulldog nature.

Casement nodded to Ted, then turned to Jeff Quarles. "Troubles?"

Ted detected the genuine concern behind the gruff question.

"Yes, sir, General Jack," Quarles said. "If it hadn't been for the timely appearance of this man here, I think it doubtful any of us would be needing haircuts in the future."

Quarles briefly recounted the ambush of the survey team and Ted's role in routing the Indians. "General Jack Casement," he concluded, "may I introduce Ted Henderson?"

"Been expecting you, Henderson," Casement said as he extended a hand, "but not exactly under these circumstances."

The construction chief's hand was thickly calloused and his grip was surprisingly strong for a man of such slight build. Ted decided Jack Casement probably would not hesitate to pick up a spike maul and give a man twice his size a run for the money in a day's hard labor.

"Welcome to rails' end of the Union Pacific, Ted," Casement said. "Looks like you went on the payroll a little sooner than expected." Casement glanced again at the survey crew. "Are you boys sure you're all right? You look like curdled milk."

Leach, who had been quiet almost to the point of seeming timid during the long, grueling walk, suddenly smiled. "Sir," he said, "I'm tired, hungry, thirsty, dirty, my feet are blistered, and I'm still half scared to death. And I never felt better in my life."

Casement grinned broadly. "Getting away from the Sioux will do that to a man," he said. Abruptly his tone changed.

"Dammit! You were supposed to have an army escort! This is going to get some blue backside chewed out, but good!"

"I wouldn't be too tough on the army, sir," Ted said quietly. "They don't have many men and they have a lot of miles to cover. Maybe they did send out a patrol and just missed connections. It's a big country out there."

Casement sighed and shrugged. "I suppose you're right, Henderson. Well, let's get these boys to the feed trough and have a bite ourselves. Then we'll swap a few lies and get better acquainted."

A few minutes later in Casement's railroad car office and quarters, Ted looked down in disbelief at the plate set before him by a cook's helper. The platter-sized container was almost overflowing with two thick steaks, a heaping mound of fried potatoes, and what appeared to be a full dipper of red beans. An oversized cup of coffee steamed at the side of his plate and a tall mound of biscuits waited on a nearby tray with a brick-sized block of yellow butter.

"Something wrong, Ted?" Jack Casement asked.

Ted shook his head in awe. "General, I've lived for a whole week on less than this," he said.

Casement's soft laugh was full of amusement. "Takes a heap of food to keep a railroad hand going," he explained. "Some of the boys here will eat twice that much at a setting. A man who swings a pick, shovel, or spike maul, or spends all day hefting iron around, works up a pretty fair appetite." Casement waved his fork. "Don't worry, you don't have to eat it all."

Ted gave it his best try. He was ravenous, but it seemed he had hardly made a dent in the pile of food when his stomach began to protest. He reluctantly put down his fork and rubbed his belly. "You have a good cook on your staff, sir."

Casement plucked an ivory toothpick from a pocket and tucked the sharp end into his mouth. "Standard railroad worker's fare," he said casually. "Sometimes I take my meals with the men, just to make sure the quality and the quantity stay up to measure."

He leaned back in his chair and worried at a piece of steak with the toothpick. "Know anything about building railroads?" he asked Ted.

"No, sir."

"Call me Jack. We'll give you the tour of the operation

tomorrow. You may not realize it, Ted, but you and some friends of yours from a few years back gave us an idea how to build a railroad in a hurry."

Casement walked to a cabinet and produced a bottle. "Whiskey?" he asked. Ted shook his head. Casement poured a small quantity into a glass and brought it back to the table.

"When we accepted this contract, we knew we had to come up with a new approach to railroad building," he said. "As you mentioned earlier, it's a big country out there. Long ways between towns. So we knew we had to come up with a self-contained 'town' that would support the demands of hundreds of workers and animals." Casement sipped gingerly at the whiskey and made a face. "Got to get a better bourbon," he said. "At any rate, we found the planning already had been done—by the Pony Express."

"What?" Ted was incredulous.

"Think about it for a moment. Each of the one hundred sixty-three relay stations of the Pony Express was self-sufficient. Each contained a storehouse of food and other supplies, sleeping quarters, kitchen facilities, spare arms and ammunition, blacksmithing equipment, a water source for men and animals—all the essentials. What we did was simply to put those facilities onto rails. This construction train is merely one huge Pony Express way station. As the tracks move westward, the station simply rolls along behind the construction crew."

Casement grinned. "We're laying over a mile of track a day—and it's no accident," he said, plucking the ivory toothpick from his mouth and slipping it back into its case. "Speaking of accidents," he went on somberly, "I hope you will have more success in getting to the root of our troubles than I have had. On top of that, there's the Indian problem. We've lost a survey crew and a tie-cutting crew already this week."

"I'll do my best, Jack."

Casement smiled shrewdly. "We checked you out pretty thoroughly, and you've got a reputation for getting things done. If it's trouble you like, we've got it like a skunk's got stink." Casement waved a hand toward a curtained compartment along one side of the railroad car. "You can bunk out here for a couple of nights. My brother Dan's gone back to Omaha to twist some ears over a late shipment of rails. He should be back in a few days."

"I'm looking forward to meeting him," Ted said.

"Not much difference in us except between the ears," Jack Casement said with a grin. "Dan's the one with the brains. All I do is ride around and yell a lot."

He stood and pulled at the bell rope. In a moment a cook's helper came to clear the table.

Later, as they settled in for the night, Casement delivered a warning. "Ted, only three people—myself, Dan, and you—know the real reason you're here. I'll introduce you around as the new general superintendent and chief scout, but you'll be on your own with the men." Casement puffed out the lantern.

"You can be sure there'll be some who won't like you for one reason or another. We have good workers, because those who don't work don't last long. But they're an odd mix: Irishmen, war veterans from both sides, a goodly number of Negroes, and some poor Southern boys, wanting to see new and different things. Some of those groups don't like each other very much. And most of them don't like outsiders at all."

Ted heard sheets rustle as Casement slipped into his own bunk. "Get a good night's sleep, Ted," the railroad man said. "It may be the last one you get for a while."

"Shut up, Quarles," Bear Fallon growled from his bunk in the workers' sleeping car. "We've heard just about all we want on this hotshot hero of yours."

Quarles protested weakly, then fell silent. Fallon was a bit disappointed. He had hoped the red-haired surveyor would fuss back. Fallon was in a bad mood, and he felt the need to stomp something.

He settled back on the soft mattress that covered the wooden bunk. This Henderson fellow was an unexpected development and Bear Fallon did not like unknowns. Also he was beginning to work up a healthy dislike for Ted Henderson. Quarles's yammering about the set-to with the Indians had impressed a number of the rail workers. In the few weeks Fallon had been at rails' end, he had established his own following. Those who did not follow willingly he had bullied into line, establishing himself as the cock of the walk. Now this Henderson was threatening Fallon's place just on the basis of some kid's ravings.

Already Bear Fallon had planned several moves to delay the Union Pacific. He would have to set them aside for a time, until he knew how the wind blew with this Henderson fellow. Fallon felt in his duffel bag and located a thin cigar and a match. He fired the smoke, the sudden flare of the match bringing a startled yelp from somewhere in the blackness of the sleeping car. He took a deep drag on the cigar.

"Stow it, Fallon!" someone called. "That thing stinks!"

"You don't like it, I'll stick it in your ear!" Fallon shot back. The voice stopped protesting. All the men in the car knew Bear Fallon did not make idle threats.

After a few moments Fallon stabbed the cigar out on the wooden floor beside his bunk. *We'll see just how much guts this Henderson has*, he thought. A good hard shove or two should either goad Henderson into a fistfight, in which case he would be laid up for a long time, or else cause him to back down and be branded yellow by the railroaders. Either way, Henderson had to be put in his place. And it might as well be soon. In fact, tomorrow would be a good time to start.

The gray dawn came slowly to the Union Pacific's railhead. Leaden skies and a slight but bitter breeze hinted at an end to the unseasonable mildness of the winter.

Ted stood beside General Jack Casement and watched with interest as the night wrangler eased the Casement horse herd into a makeshift corral, a circle of ropes held loosely in the hands of teamsters and drovers getting ready for the day's work.

Ted hugged his coat against the cold and noted with some curiosity that a sizable crowd had gathered. Here and there he caught sly or amused glances in his direction.

"Catch old Double-Be for me," Casement called to the day wrangler who would watch over the horses until nightfall. "Put a loop on old Hellbender for Mr. Henderson here."

The day wrangler grinned and winked at the construction chief. Then he turned to the horse herd, shaking a small loop into his rope. A figure-eight swing and a flick of the wrist sent the noose gently around the neck of a big black. Casement slipped the bit in the animal's mouth. The wrangler returned to the herd and a moment later led a wide-eyed, snorting sorrel up to Ted. Ted looked the horse over briefly.

"Hellbender, eh?" he said casually. "Sounds like I may be in for some fun."

The horse laid back its ears and tried to fight the bit, but Ted jammed a thumb in the corner of the sorrel's mouth and forced the jaws open. As he swung the saddle into place Ted was aware that the crowd had grown, and the night wrangler had not yet left for chow and a bunk, though his shift had officially ended.

The day wrangler stood and watched, rope in hand. Ted tugged the cinch tight. The rear skirts of the saddle lacked a handspan of touching the sorrel's hide. Hellbender was humped up like a raw bronc.

"Five dollars says the new scout'll stay on!" a voice called from the gathering crowd. It was the young surveyor, Jeff Quarles. Ted glanced at him and smiled.

"You might want to save your money, Jeff," Ted said. "Old Hellbender here may be more than I can handle."

Ted slipped out of his heavy jacket, unbuckled his gunbelt, and pulled the Henry from the saddle scabbard. He handed the equipment to Jack Casement. "No sense getting a new coat and a pair of good guns dirty," he said.

The betting rose to a fever pitch. Then a loud, challenging voice lifted above the general babble. "I got fifty on Hellbender!"

Silence suddenly fell over the crowd. Ted turned to face the man who offered the big bet. He was a huge man with massive shoulders and a tuft of hair showing at the throat above a cloth jacket. The face was broad and dark, almost menacing, Ted thought. He decided he did not like the man, and he had learned to trust his instincts in such matters. He also realized the huge man had no takers. Apparently no one else had fifty dollars to spare.

"I'll cover the fifty," Ted said lightly. "I hate to take money from a total stranger; what's the name?"

"Fallon. Bear Fallon."

Ted merely nodded. "Ted Henderson." Neither man offered a hand.

Then Ted turned away, focusing his full concentration on the horse. He took a short rein, then abruptly jerked back on the bit as he mounted. The unexpected sharp pull set the horse back slightly on his haunches, giving Ted the split second he needed to pick up the offside stirrup and turn his toes out. He dropped some slack into the reins.

Hellbender squalled and exploded into a high, twisting jump and a powerful kick that snapped his rider's head back. The sorrel hit the ground and whirled, a short, choppy jump to the right. Ted felt his foot slip in the stirrup and rammed a cavalry spur into the cinch. After two bone-jarring jumps, and with the man still on his back, Hellbender began pitching. But Ted had the elusive rhythm of the horse's jumps. Timing his moves with the sorrel's leaps, he raked his spurs across Hellbender's shoulders with each jump. The horse's enthusiasm for the game began to fade rapidly.

After a few last, halfhearted hops, Hellbender gave up and stood docilely as Ted leaned forward and patted the horse's neck. The ears that had been laid back in anger perked forward as Ted reined the sorrel toward the watching crowd. He pulled Hellbender to a stop in front of Bear Fallon.

The big man's face was livid. For an instant Ted thought he was going to charge like a mad bull. But Fallon stabbed a ham-sized fist into his pants pocket, counted out the fifty from a hefty roll of bills, and tossed the currency into the dirt.

"Hand them to me, Fallon," Ted said in a quiet but icy tone. "You made your bet. Now pay up like a gentleman."

"Yeah, Bear," a voice from the crowd chided. "You sure missed the bet that time."

The veins on Fallon's neck bulged in growing rage. But he picked the bills from the ground and thrust them at Ted. Ted took the money, folded it, and tucked it into his shirt pocket.

"All right, boys! Fun's over! Let's get to work!" At General Jack's bellowed orders the crowd quickly dissolved.

The day wrangler strode to Ted's side. "Looks like you know your way around a bronc, Ted Henderson. I lost five on you." The deeply tanned wrangler held out a hand. "Friends call me Gus. Nice ride." The man's voice dropped to a near whisper. "You best watch that big 'un," he warned. "Bear Fallon don't like to be showed up. He'll be layin' for you. I seen what he done to a couple guys. Warn't purty."

"Thanks, Gus. I'll keep that in mind. Sorry about your five."

"Hell," Gus said, "it was worth twice that much."

Ted reined Hellbender alongside Casement's black. "Testing me out already, Jack?"

The construction chief chuckled. "Just trying to make it easy for you," he replied dryly. "They might not all remember your name right away—but they'll remember the man who rode Hellbender to a standstill. It's never been done before."

"It almost didn't get done this time. I'm going to have sore spots in places I didn't even know I had spots. And how'd you know I could ride this idiot sorrel?" Ted asked.

"I didn't," Casement said. "But it was worth a try. Besides, it wasn't my tail in the saddle. Now, let's go build us a railroad."

The rhythmic speed and efficiency with which the Union Pacific rail crew put down the twin ribbons of metal with little machinery other than their own strong backs left Ted shaking his head in wonder. He also found himself learning a new language as Casement explained the operation.

The assault on the prairie had begun in earnest with the earlier passage of the grading crews. Following the path marked by survey teams, the graders were several miles to the west of rails' end. Their picks, shovels, and mule-drawn scoops had raised and leveled a rail bed, a surprisingly smooth surface upon which the rail gang worked its muscular magic.

The lilting lyrics of an off-color Irish pub song were punctuated by the rasp of shovels and clang of mauls on spikes and the sharp barks of foreman Sean Grady.

The track-laying crew worked in pairs, one man on each side of the track. In the forefront were the joint-tie men. Armed with shovels, measuring tools, picks, and tamping devices, the joint-tie men carefully bedded a heavy square cross tie every fourteen feet. Men called fillers followed, bedding ties between those laid by the joint-tie men.

The rails, each twenty-eight feet long and weighing about seven hundred pounds, were carried aboard a flatbed car called a truck. Attending the truck were the iron men, five on each side. Once the ties were bedded, and at the cry, "Away she goes!" the iron men slid two rails from the truck and carried them forward. At the call "Down!" the husky rail handlers seemed to simply drop the rails. But the metal strips fell into place on the ties with a precision that testified to the long practice and close coordination of the crew.

Men known as head spikers gauged the width between the ribbons and, with a couple of brisk strokes, rammed spikes home with heavy mauls.

Among the head spikers was Bear Fallon, who cast a dark glare toward Ted as the two horsemen rode past. Ted's gaze met Fallon's and he saw the fiery anger in the Irishman's eyes. Ted shrugged off the emotion, turning back to the work of the rail crew.

He marveled at the dexterity of the spike peddlers, who were usually smaller and more agile than the spikers and iron men. Their job was to place the spikes in the ground for the hammers of the head spikers, who drove home six of the oversized nails per tie, then moved on to repeat the process.

As the head spikers moved on, the track liners took their place. Wielding crowbars, the liners put the track into perfect position. Completing the connections were the back spikers, who drove home the remaining spikes to secure metal to wood firmly. Finally came the screwers, who bolted the heavy iron fishplate connector into place at each joint between the rails.

The almost hypnotic pace of the work crew so fascinated Ted that he was surprised by the foreman's call for the noon break. Ted noted with a start that the rail crews had laid a good three-quarters of a mile of track in only half a day!

Casement nodded toward the newly laid rails. "Good morning for work," he said. "Cold enough that a man wants to keep at it to stay warm. It's the summer heat that saps a man." Casement glanced toward the gray sky. "Don't know how much longer the good weather will hold, but it looks like we'll make over a mile and a half by quitting time today. Well, what's your impression of our operation?"

Ted could only shake his head in wonder. "I've never seen anything quite like it." He nodded toward the laborers making their way toward the meal car. "Those fellows really earn their pay. By comparison, I almost feel like I'm stealing my wages."

Casement glanced sharply at Ted. "You'll earn yours, too, never fear. I saw the way Fallon looked at you back there. You're going to have trouble with him."

Ted shrugged. "If it happens, it'll be because he started it. From the looks of him, he just might finish it, too. What do you know about him, Jack?"

"Not much, really. He's a good, experienced worker. Sean Grady says he's one of the best spikers he's ever seen, and that Fallon could be foreman material. So far he's caused no serious trouble."

"Let's hope it stays that way," Ted said.

It did not. The showdown came that very evening.

The laborers were filing back toward the work train for a meal and bed when Ted rode in from an afternoon scouting foray. He was satisfied with his tour. There had been no fresh signs of Long Walker's bunch in the ridges and hills to the north of the Platte River.

A commotion a hundred yards away drew Ted's attention and he spurred Hellbender into a trot.

A circle of workmen surrounded a pair of figures in the dirt along the railroad tracks. Ted saw at a glance one of the men was Bear Fallon. The second was a considerably smaller man. As Ted neared the scene he saw Fallon lash out with a big fist, sending the other man skidding on his back in the dirt.

Ted reined in as Fallon lunged forward, kicking a heavy work boot into the downed man's ribs. Sean Grady, the foreman, was standing nearby, making no move to break up the fracas.

The shouts of excitement abruptly died. Fallon grabbed a broken pick handle and towered over the man on the ground, poised to smash in the man's head with the makeshift club.

Ted slipped his Henry from the saddle scabbard, pointed the muzzle toward the sky, and fired. The sudden blast sent railroad men scurrying aside and set the sorrel to dancing between Ted's knees.

"Hold it, Fallon!" Ted yelled, his voice cracking like a whip as the echoes of his rifle shot faded. He suddenly realized that the man on the ground was Jeff Quarles. The red-bearded surveyor was holding his ribs where Fallon had kicked him, and he was moaning in pain.

The huge Irishman, face flushed in rage, slowly turned to face Ted, still holding the pick handle. "You dealing yourself in on this hand, scout?" Fallon snarled.

"If need be," Ted said calmly. "Put the pick handle down." He kept the muzzle of his Henry lined squarely on Fallon's shirt front.

The Irishman slowly lowered the club, then tossed it aside.

"You," Ted said to a worker at the edge of the group, "help Quarles to his feet and get him to the surgeon. Now, what's going on here?"

"Your little redheaded buddy got to running off at the

mouth," Fallon said maliciously. "I had to teach him a few manners."

Ted sighed in resignation. He wanted nothing more than to turn and ride away from the confrontation. But he knew he could not.

"Don't play games with me, Fallon," Ted said. "Both of us know it's me you want. You don't have to go beating up on my friends to get that."

Fallon snorted in contempt. "You're real brave when you got a gun in your hand, scout man. Some day I'm going to call you out, man to man."

Ted glanced at Gus, the day wrangler, who was standing nearby. "What day is it?" he asked casually.

Gus's brow puckered in thought. "Let's see, now—I was hung over like a possum in a tree three days ago . . ." He counted to three on his fingers. "Reckon that makes this about Wednesday."

"Then this is as good a day as any, Fallon," Ted said, swinging down from his horse and handing Gus the reins. "I don't know what's stuck in your craw, but we might as well get this thing settled."

A sudden flash of triumph shone in Fallon's eyes.

Ted studied the man facing him across the small circle. He knew Fallon's sheer size and brute strength would be the major factor in the fight. As Fallon slipped out of his light jacket, Ted saw the Irishman's biceps were almost as big as Ted's thighs. The knuckles of the massive hands were mostly scar tissue.

Ted realized he was in for no ordinary scrap. He was outweighed by some eighty pounds, and Fallon would be in excellent physical condition from constantly swinging a spike maul. The only question was the big man's speed. *Well, you've got yourself in a hell of a mess this time, Henderson,* he thought.

He swallowed a touch of fear, then forced his muscles to relax. His strategy was simple. His only chance to survive, perhaps even to beat the snarling Irishman, was to counterpunch, to rely on his own agility and knowledge.

"Any time you're ready, Fallon," he said quietly.

The burly Irishman took a cautious step forward, a sneer twisting his lips. For a brief moment the two men circled cautiously, testing, looking for an opening.

Then, with a speed that caught Ted by surprise, Fallon

lunged forward and lashed out with a huge fist. Ted threw up an arm and ducked but only partially avoided the blow. Fallon's fist crashed into his temple, sending him sprawling in the dirt. His vision blurred momentarily. Through the haze he saw a work shoe aimed at his head. Ted stabbed out, half blind, and rolled as the foot descended. He heard the solid *thump* of Fallon's heel beside his ear, then his own fist closed over the coarse cloth of a pants leg.

Ted shoved against the leg with all his strength and pushed Fallon off balance. The big man staggered long enough for Ted to roll to his feet and shake his head, clearing his vision. The next few seconds, he knew, would be crucial.

Fallon regained his footing and charged toward his opponent, his arms outstretched to grapple with the smaller man. Ted ducked beneath the clutching arms, stepped aside, and rammed Fallon in the belly with a right hook that carried all the strength he could muster. Fallon merely grunted. He quickly turned and snapped a quick left at Ted's chin. The blow whistled just beneath Ted's jaw, barely nicking his throat.

Ted countered with his own left jab. His fist cracked against Fallon's bushy eyebrow, but Fallon barely blinked, then jabbed a wicked right to Ted's ribs. A sharp pain lanced through Ted's side. He raised his right forearm, deflecting Fallon's left jab, and drove his left fist viciously into Fallon's belly. This time a sharp gasp burst from Fallon's lips.

Ted danced aside, unwilling to be drawn into a slugging contest with the big Irishman. As Fallon charged, Ted grabbed the man's wrist, ducked low, twisted, and pulled sharply. The combination of Fallon's momentum and Ted's grip sent the big man flying over Ted's hip. Fallon hit the ground with a solid *whomp*, momentarily stunned. Ted pounded a quick left and a hard right into Fallon's face. It was like hitting a stone, but the blows opened a small cut on the big man's forehead.

Then Fallon reached out a huge paw and swept Ted's feet from under him, causing him to fall heavily at Fallon's side. Ted dodged a kick, rolled out of range, and got to his feet. Fallon was on him with the quickness of a fox, his fists flying.

Ted managed to block most of the blows. But one landed solidly on his chest. Before he could recover, Fallon had wrapped his massive arms around Ted's lower back in a bear hug.

Ted knew he had but a split second to escape the grip. One quick yank of those powerful muscles would pop his spine in two. With his free right hand Ted rammed a thumb deep behind Fallon's ear, in the tender spot where jawbone touched earlobe. Fallon yelped in pain, releasing the grip for an instant.

That was the opening Ted needed. With all the strength he could muster, he slammed a knee into Fallon's groin. The big man's mouth opened in a silent scream. Ted slashed a quick combination of lefts and rights into the cut on Fallon's face, turning the nick into a large gash. Blood streamed into Fallon's eyes.

The two combatants stood, chests heaving, and glared at each other for a moment.

"Gotta—give you—some credit, scout," Fallon wheezed. "You—lasted longer'n most."

Then the big man launched himself at Ted in a low dive. A solid shoulder sent Ted tumbling, and Fallon was on him, flailing away with his heavy fists. Ted felt his remaining strength begin to fade as he tried with only partial success to avoid the blows.

Then somehow he managed to trap Fallon's right wrist between his own neck and shoulder. Ted quickly twisted to his right and slammed a left hand into the back of Fallon's extended elbow with a blow that would have shattered a lesser man's elbow. But the leverage forced the big body clear, and Ted took the opportunity to escape.

His own vision misty with fatigue, Ted staggered to his feet. Fallon heaved himself up and stood, weaving and gasping for breath. One eye was rapidly swelling shut. Ted realized the man was unaccustomed to fights that took more than a few seconds. His stamina was going. The knowledge gave Ted a new spurt of strength.

Methodically, he began to hammer away at Fallon, concentrating on the man's midsection, willing to take an occasional blow in order to deal out two or more of his own. He lost all sense of time. Two minutes—or an hour—could have passed for all he knew. He drove himself with pure determination, willing leaden arms and quivering legs to continue past the limits of fatigue and pain.

At last he got his one clear shot. Fallon dropped his

guard, and a whistling right from Ted cracked onto the side of his jaw.

Fallon went down. The Irishman lay in the dirt for a moment as Ted struggled to pull air into his aching chest. Then Fallon tried to rise. Ted let him make it to one knee, then slashed the edge of his hand against the side of Fallon's neck. The railroad man fell once more.

Exhausted, Ted dropped to one knee—and saw in disbelief that Fallon was once again trying to get to his feet!

"Dammit—Fallon," Ted gasped, "stay—down. It's over!"

Fallon, the air whistling through his battered mouth, struggled to get his feet beneath him. As he tried to heave his battered body erect, Ted measured the big man carefully. Then, with the last of his strength, he hit Fallon in the jaw.

Ted knew it was not much of a blow. He did not have much left. But it was enough. Fallon flopped forward and lay still—unconscious.

A murmur of astonishment swelled among the railroad laborers. Then the exhausted Ted felt hands lifting him to his feet. A few feet away, Bear Fallon's cronies gathered about the form of their beaten leader.

Fallon stirred, fought his way back to consciousness, and glared through swollen eyes at Ted. The blood-smeared and battered face twitched. Finally, the Irishman was able to form words. "Damn you—scout—I'll have—your hide on a rack—for this! Next time—I'll stomp you—like a bug."

Ted made no effort to reply. He let the friendly hands lead him away toward the work train.

"Whoo-ee," a voice at his side said. "That was one helluva scrap! Wisht I coulda sold tickets." Gus cackled with delight. "You know, Henderson, Fallon ain't a-gonna forgit this. He warn't blowin' smoke just now. You keep a eye peeled for that feller."

Ted tried to nod through the stabs of pain in his head. He felt the blood trickle from the cuts inside his lip, spilling a warm, salty taste into his mouth. As they neared the car that contained the surgeon's office, Ted realized that even as bad as he felt then, it would be even worse tomorrow.

"My—my horse," he muttered. The words sounded odd to his own ears, as though spoken by a stranger.

"He's bein' took care of," Gus assured him. "You just try to keep a'standin' till we get to the doc."

*   *   *

The next morning Ted made it out of his cot in Jack Casement's quarters on the third try, and immediately wondered if he had made a mistake. Every muscle and joint of his body screamed its outrage and the coppery taste in his mouth almost made him gag. He stumbled to the washbasin and peered into the mirror.

The face that looked back at him was one he had never seen before. One eye was shut. His swollen lips were twisted into a grimace. Cuts and bruises covered most of his features. Gently, he probed at his teeth with his tongue, then sighed with relief. The teeth were all there, still firm in their sockets.

Ted's arms felt as if they weighed a ton as he gingerly washed his face. The cold water helped some, but he decided against shaving. There wasn't a spot of undamaged skin left for the razor. The cut inside his lip shot pain each time he moved his mouth, and Ted realized he would be eating beans one at a time until the cut healed and the swelling went down.

The simple act of getting dressed left him panting with exhaustion.

He was nursing a cup of coffee, trying to sip the steaming liquid and hold it down over waves of nausea, when Jack Casement entered the car. A wisp of cold air edged inside as Casement closed the door. "How you feel this morning, Ted?"

"Like I just got run over by one of your locomotives," Ted mumbled, wincing at the effort of talking.

Casement chuckled. "If it's any consolation, Bear Fallon feels at least as bad—or worse—than you do. He lost a tooth, along with a lot of pride." The construction chief clapped Ted on a sore shoulder. "Why don't you take a day off? You've had a busy couple of days at railhead."

Ted shook his head. "No. I've got to do my day's work. I'll not give Fallon the satisfaction of knowing I'm in bed. And the men will be waiting to see if I show up."

"Okay," Casement said, sipping at a cup of coffee, "but you may regret it before the day's through. Fallon tried to duck out today. I told him to get his butt on the end of a maul and earn his pay. By the way, the doc says you don't have anything broken."

Ted had to grin, even though it cost him another stab of pain. "I can't believe he didn't miss something. You sure he didn't say I didn't have anything that *wasn't* broken?"

Casement chuckled, then drained his coffee and stood. "Got to get the boys on the road," he said. "You sure you're up to riding?"

Ted struggled into his greatcoat and followed Casement to the horse herd, ignoring the glances that were cast in his direction. He had Gus catch the gentle dun horse he had originally ridden from his ranch. Saddling up in his condition required a lot of effort.

"Go easy with me today, Buck," he said quietly to the horse. "I'm hurting."

As he and Casement rode past the line of laborers trudging to rails' end, Ted's gaze met Fallon's for an instant. The look in the Irishman's one opened eye would have chipped stone, Ted thought.

Bear Fallon glowered at the receding figure. *I underestimated you this time, scout,* he thought. *I won't make that mistake again. Next time it'll be different.* Fallon knew he was in for a long, rough day. But as soon as he healed a bit, he had some ambitious plans. *This railroad is going to lose some time—and a foreman as well,* he thought, staring at Sean Grady's broad back.

Jack Casement glanced at the lowering sky and tugged his black coat tighter against the breeze. He turned to Ted.

"Hope we make some good time today," Casement said. "Don't know when we're going to lose this good weather. We're overdue for a blizzard now. At least I don't have the Central Pacific's problems," he added with a sigh. "I'll bet the snow is thirty feet deep in the high Sierras about now."

Far to the west, on a crest of the Sierra Mountains in California, the contractor for the Central Pacific Railroad pulled his prized buffalo-skin coat tight against the frigid blast of howling wind. He shook a fist toward the sky and cursed the weather with a fluency that would have left a mule skinner shaking his head in awe.

Slipping on the hard-packed, ice-coated snow underfoot, Charlie Crocker struggled up the slope and entered a cavern carved into the massive snowbank. Inside the ice cave the air seemed warmer. He knew it was a deceptive warmth, created by the absence of wind. He figured the temperature probably hovered around twenty or thirty degrees below in the cavern.

Crocker paused once more to marvel at the work force

that he headed. Squads of Chinese coolies labored in the ice tunnel, small yellow men in quilted coats and high-topped, moccasin-type boots, with cone-shaped hats held in place by strings beneath their chins. At the end of the tunnel was a rare sight—bare earth. It yielded grudgingly before the persistent picks of the coolies. Yet, shovelful by shovelful, the Sierras crumbled into wheelbarrows, to be trundled by hand back to the entrance. Millions of years of rock formations were becoming the grade along which the Central Pacific's locomotives would run.

Crocker was a big Irishman, carrying well over two hundred pounds on his large-boned frame. He was satisfied with what he saw. The work was slow, but it was going. He still did not know how these small, stooped men did it. Few among them would weigh half as much as he did, yet the amount of earth they rearranged in a day's time under miserable weather conditions almost boggled the mind of even veteran railroad observers.

"Charlie Crocker," he muttered to himself as he walked to his office, "you may be a damn fool for taking this construction contract, but by God you did one thing right by hiring these coolies."

Outside the small frame building that served as his office, Crocker shucked off the big coat, shook the snow and ice from it, and went inside. He draped the coat on a nail and moved to the rough pine desk to fill out his daily reports, rubbing his hands briskly to restore the circulation.

He had been at work for some time, carefully calculating the progress of the rail bed and predicting when the coolies would break through on the east slope of the Sierras, when a touch of cold air tickled the back of his neck.

Crocker looked up in surprise. He had not heard the door open or close, or heard a footstep. Yet a slender man with skin the color of fine yellow parchment stood before him. The Chinese held a battered cloth hat in his hands. Despite the horrendous cold outside, he wore only a light quilted jacket. He was somewhat taller than most of the coolies, perhaps five feet seven, with sloping shoulders and fine-boned hands. He wore his dark hair straight, almost to his shoulders, rather than in the traditional pigtail the majority of the Chinese coolies fancied.

"Please forgive the intrusion," the Chinaman said in

fluent English, his voice polite and quiet. "I do not wish to disturb, but I was told I might find Charlie Crocker here?"

Curiosity buried the quick flash of anger that Crocker had felt at the interruption. "I'm Crocker," he said brusquely. "You want work, boy?"

The Chinese shook his head apologetically. "I do not seek work. I seek only information. I am told that you might help, if you wish to do so."

Under ordinary circumstances the quick-tempered Crocker might have summarily booted the man from his office. But something about him intrigued the railroad builder. He was the same color as the others, yet somehow different. The brown eyes were gentle, respectful, and patient, and an air of calm seemed to hover about him.

Crocker tossed his pencil aside. "If it's knowledge you're looking for, you probably came to the wrong man," Crocker said. "But I'll help if I can."

"Thank you," the Chinaman replied, inclining his head slightly. "I am Chin-Lu. I search for a woman."

"You'll find precious few women in this camp, Chin-Lu," Crocker said wryly. "A few of the workers bring their wives along, but not many. What is so important about this woman that you come all the way out here in winter?"

"She is my sister," Chin-Lu said. "She was married to one who worked on your railroad. His name was Kai Ton. Some months back I received a letter from her. There had been an explosion and her husband was killed. I have come from China to take her home. Do you know of her whereabouts?"

· Crocker sighed. "I'm afraid not. The Chinese are great workers, but I know only a handful by name. I have seen a few women. Can you describe her for me?"

"She is a dainty woman of great beauty, with long black hair. She is called Ling-Tse. About her neck she wears a medallion." Chin-Lu reached into a small pouch at his side and produced an ornament on a gold chain. "It is much the same as this one." He handed it to Crocker.

The Irishman studied the talisman. It was made of jade, in the shape of a crescent. Then he shook his head, handing the medallion back to Chin-Lu. "I'm sorry. I don't remember having seen it. And I don't recall her husband. There have been so many accidents and so many men killed on this project. . . ."

Crocker studied the impassive face before him as Chin-Lu returned the necklace to its pouch. "I'm sorry about your brother-in-law. And I hope you find your sister. If you wish, you may ask among the workers. Perhaps they will remember something."

Chin-Lu bowed slightly. "Thank you, Mr. Crocker. Your kindness will not be forgotten."

Before Crocker could reply, the Chinaman was gone. The departure had been so silent and so fluid that very little warmth leaked from the shelter.

Outside, Chin-Lu stood for a moment, his face turned to the biting wind that knifed through his meager jacket. Then he reached up with his right hand and touched the cloth above the lion-head scar burned into the flesh of his left shoulder. From it he drew warmth and the reminder from his teachers that cold was but a state of mind. The chill left his bones, fled through the skin of his lithe body, and flowed from the fingertips.

Comfortable once again, Chin-Lu plucked his small bundle of belongings from the ground and made his way toward the long line of his countrymen nibbling away tenaciously at the great mountain range. Somewhere among them, he knew, was one who knew of his sister. He had only to find that person.

Throughout the day, Chin-Lu moved among the workers. He was not discouraged despite the frequent shaking of heads.

That evening, when he had made his own spare meal and was preparing for nightfall, a wizened Chinese elder with a scraggly beard cautiously approached Chin-Lu's resting place.

"It is said that a man named Chin-Lu seeks the woman known as Ling-Tse," the old one said quietly. "Perhaps I may help on your search."

The elder squatted beside Chin-Lu. "After the death of her husband, Ling-Tse knew not what to do. She had but little money from her husband's wages. One afternoon some men came. It was in the summer, and Ling-Tse had gone to bathe in a stream. They took her away. This I saw, and am ashamed, for I did not try to stop them. I am but an old man, and they were many."

Chin-Lu merely nodded. "Your decision was wise, elder. Your death would have helped no one. Do you know where they took Ling-Tse?"

"No," the old one replied. "But I did recognize one of the men. He is among those employed by a man called Quan Krai. Quan Krai is from Canton in the home country, but in San Francisco he operates a shop that deals in Chinese herbs and spices. That, however, is not his primary business."

Pain showed deep in the old man's eyes. "I curse myself for bringing you this news, Chin-Lu. It is known that Quan Krai is a dealer in flesh—in women."

Chin-Lu's face did not show the agony that pierced his spirit at the old man's words. "Then I will take the work train back to San Francisco and find this Quan Krai. From him I shall learn the whereabouts of my sister," he said calmly.

"When you find him, Chin-Lu, be of caution," the elder warned. "He is a leader in the Order of the Ox, a secret society of the Tong. It is said that always he has with him a guard, a large Korean who has great skill with the short sword. Quan Krai will not receive you. He will not speak to you of your sister."

Chin-Lu calmly looked into the old man's eyes. "He will speak," he said softly. "Thank you, elder, for telling me of this. No one shall know my source, for the Tong's reach is long. And do not bear the weight of your guilt into a new day. My sister's fate was not of your doing."

The old man nodded, then shuffled away toward his own group. Chin-Lu once again stroked the lion-head scar on his shoulder. Tonight he would rest. With the new dawn he would be on his way to San Francisco—to find this man named Quan Krai.

The evening fog had begun to thicken over the bustling San Francisco streets, casting halos around the lanterns in the Chinese district.

Inside a richly decorated office in the rear of an unobtrusive shop, Quan Krai finished off the last of his jasmine tea with a contented sigh. Business had been good, and the supper had been one of his favorites, chicken breast strips delicately fried with almonds and mushrooms on a bed of rice. Quan Krai was a contented man.

He waved a chubby hand toward the big Korean standing impassively near the table. The Korean, who stood almost six feet tall and weighed nearly two hundred pounds, barked an order toward a bead curtain leading to another room. The curtains parted and a young Chinese girl scurried in and began clearing the plates from Quan Krai's meal.

In her nervous haste to comply, the wide-eyed girl accidentally dropped a fine porcelain saucer. The small dish shattered on the hardwood floor. At Quan Krai's nod, the Korean stepped forward and rammed a fist into the girl's stomach. The girl crumpled to the floor with a cry of pain. She lay sobbing, gasping for breath.

"Get this one on the next boat to New Orleans," Quan Krai said with barely a glance at the small form writhing on the floor. "Perhaps she will be more careful with Madam Touffant's customers than she is with my needs."

The Korean grasped the girl's hair, hauled her to her feet, and shoved her toward the beaded curtain.

"Get this mess cleaned up and bring me some rice wine," Quan Krai said to the Korean as the girl stumbled through the glass beads into the other room.

The Korean moved toward a cabinet inlaid in mother-of-pearl, his back momentarily turned to his employer.

"You are Quan Krai?"

The soft voice from the corner of the room startled the portly Chinese. He twisted in his seat behind the expansive desk. The intruder stood relaxed against the wall, a slender, barefoot Chinese man stripped to the waist, a bright green sash tied about his hips. "How did you get in here?" Quan Krai demanded.

"It is of no matter. I am here. I seek the man called Quan Krai."

"And what do you wish of Quan Krai?" The Korean had spun around and stood poised, one hand on the haft of a short sword at his belt.

Quan Krai waved a hand, a signal not to kill the intruder.

"I seek a woman," the man said softly.

Quan Krai chuckled. "Most men who come here do," he said.

"I seek a specific woman," the slender man explained. "Her name is Ling-Tse. I am Chin-Lu. Ling-Tse is my sister. Your men took her from the mountain stream last summer."

The sneer on Quan Krai's lips suddenly faded in alarm. The name had meant nothing—there had been so many women—but the sight of the lion image branded on the intruder's shoulder suddenly registered. Men who wore the mark were much to be feared.

"Kill him!" Quan Krai shouted.

The Korean sprang into action, whirling the short sword as he lunged toward Chin-Lu. The blade flashed out—and struck only empty air. Suddenly the bodyguard screamed in agony as the edge of Chin-Lu's hand sliced into the back of his knife wrist, shattering the bones. The blade dropped harmlessly to the floor. Then the Korean gave a strangled gasp as Chin-Lu's hand sliced at his neck. Blood spurted from the big man's lips as he raised a hand halfway to his throat. He moaned and slumped to the floor, his larynx crushed.

For an instant Quan Krai sat stunned. The death of his bodyguard had been so quick he had not even seen the blows. In panic, Quan Krai stabbed a hand into the desk drawer at his side. His fingers closed on the butt of the pistol hidden there.

The intruder rammed a knee into the desk drawer, slamming it on Quan Krai's hand. An agonized cry from Quan Krai filled the room as the delicate bones of his hand crumpled. The color drained from his face.

Chin-Lu's knee kept the horrible pressure on the desk drawer. "Now," he said softly, "we shall continue our discussion. Where is Ling-Tse?"

"My—my hand—" Quan Krai sobbed, his face contorted in agony.

"Your hand is not my concern," Chin-Lu said. "I seek only information. Perhaps you shall live, perhaps not, when I have received this information. I do not ask you again. Where is Ling-Tse?"

Quan Krai shook his head. His breath whistled through clenched teeth. "I—do not—know. Must check records—" With his free hand Quan Krai waved weakly toward the mother-of-pearl inlaid cabinet. In the cabinet was a short, sharp dagger, if he could only reach it. He cried out again as the pressure against his hand eased, then pulled his hand free. Across the back the edge of the desk had left a deep pressure cut. The crushed bones had twisted the fingers.

"Check your records, Quan Krai," Chin-Lu said softly. "I must know of Ling-Tse's fate."

Quan Krai heaved himself erect and almost fainted at the pain from his shattered hand. Cradling it against his ample midsection, he stumbled to the cabinet and awkwardly opened the doors. He glanced at Chin-Lu. The slender man with the lion's brand had followed, and was within arm's reach.

The flesh peddler reached into the cabinet, pulled out a ribbon-tied scroll, and dropped it to the floor. Cold sweat of desperation ran down his forehead into his eyes as his fingers closed on the handle of the two-edged dagger. He knew he had only one chance.

As quickly as he could move, Quan Krai spun, slashing toward Chin-Lu with the razor-sharp knife. The blade passed within a fraction of an inch of Chin-Lu's midsection. Quan Krai cried out as he felt a crushing grip on his wrist. His collarbone popped beneath a single sharp chop. Then a thumb slid onto the back of his knife hand, fingers wrapped around the inside of his wrist. Slowly and steadily, the point of the knife neared Quan Krai's throat. He was helpless against the controlled power of the brutal wristlock. The point of the weapon touched the side of his throat and left a sharp sting against the skin.

The terrified pounding of his own heart was loud in Quan Krai's ears. A single shove against the wristlock would drive the dagger deep into his neck.

"Wait—please," Quan Krai begged. "I—remember now." His eyes were bulging, and the smell of urine was overpowering. "The one—you seek. She wore—crescent."

"Yes." Chin-Lu's voice held a deadly calm that was even more frightening than the point of the dagger.

"She—was sold—to man who—plans woman-house—for workers on—railroad." Quan Krai's voice came in ragged, gasping bursts. "Look for—her at town called—Omaha. Nebraska—"

"Quan Krai tells the truth?"

The dealer in flesh tried to nod, but the motion only dug the point of the dagger deeper into his skin. "Now—you go. You—promised."

Chin-Lu sighed. "I said perhaps you might live. The Order of the Lion does not idly take a life. But no more shall the innocent suffer at Quan Krai's hands for coins. This is forbidden by the Lion and the laws of man."

Quan Krai's last sight was that of a calm, almost apologetic face. Then an icy pain lanced through his neck. He slumped to his knees, his own hand still clutching the haft of the dagger sunk deep into his throat.

Chin-Lu watched as the flesh merchant's lifeblood flowed past the imbedded knife. "Many outrages are now avenged," he said quietly. "Quan Krai forfeited his right to live with his violations of the flesh."

As Chin-Lu stepped through the curtain of glass beads, he saw a wide-eyed girl with her hand to her mouth in terror. She raised a palm as if to ward off this new demon.

"Be still, young one," Chin-Lu said. "Are you injured?"

The girl shook her head.

"You must leave this place," Chin-Lu said, "for the Tong will be searching for someone to punish. Their ways are severe. Do you have friends or family nearby?"

Slowly the girl regained her composure. "No," she replied. "But anywhere would be better than this place. Here I am reminded that my body and my spirit have been soiled."

Chin-Lu gently took her elbow. "You must remember that the soiling was not of your own will," he said. "You shall come with me. At the dock now is a sailing vessel. Its captain is an honorable man known personally to me. Quickly, now. Gather your things and let us leave this place of evil."

She hesitated. "But I have no money. . . ."

Chin-Lu moved to the opened cabinet and soon located a thick sheaf of American currency and a pouch of rare gems of considerable value. He handed the riches to her. "Consider these as your legacy from the estate of the late Quan Krai. You have earned them, and more."

The girl's eyes misted as she took the money and jewels. "But what of you?" she asked.

"I have some funds. Enough. Now we must leave quickly."

Chin-Lu donned the shirt and shoes he had removed before going in to see Quan Krai, as the girl hastily tied her belongings into a small bundle. Chin-Lu glanced at the high, narrow window through which he had entered the building unseen. He gestured toward the opening. "Can you squeeze through that?"

She studied the window for a moment, then nodded.

Chin-Lu hoisted her bundle and his own blanket roll, leapt, and grasped the windowsill with his fingers. He dropped the two bundles softly into the alley beyond, then held out his hands to his companion.

A moment later they stood in the alley, breathing the cool night air, then began the long trek toward the docks.

"I will arrange for your passage to China," Chin-Lu said as they walked. "Once there, you will go to the Forbidden City. I will give you a document that will guarantee your acceptance. There, in the Imperial Palace, you will be afforded sanctuary and protection."

The girl gasped. "The Imperial Palace? No one of my low birth has ever been there."

He smiled at her. "Then you will be the first," he said calmly. "I am well known there. Once I was a member of the Imperial Guard."

"But—the lion brand on your shoulder. Are you not a priest?"

"Once, yes. But no longer." He did not explain the statement, and she dared not ask. She could only wonder at her sudden deliverance and good fortune.

Within two hours' time, the girl's passage had been arranged on a ship that was to sail at noon of the next day. As Chin-Lu turned to go he felt her light touch on his shoulder.

"I am forever in your debt," she said. "But what of you, Chin-Lu? Where will you go?"

"I go in search of my sister. But first I must make my way back to the railroad camp of Charlie Crocker in the mountains. He will have maps and much knowledge. I must find out how to reach this place called Omaha in the land named Nebraska."

Somehow, Charlie Crocker knew without looking up why the sudden touch of icy wind had fluttered the flame of his oil lamp.

"Did you find her, Chin-Lu?" he asked, still scribbling in his daybook.

"No. But I found where she might be."

Crocker put down the pencil and leaned back in his wooden chair, the joints of the chair screeching in protest. He looked at the slender Chinaman standing before him. "Why did you come back here?"

"I do not wish to intrude yet again," Chin-Lu said, holding the brim of his bedraggled felt hat in his fingers. "But while I know the name of the place, I do not know where it is. If you would be so kind as to spare a moment, I would ask your help."

"Shoot," Crocker said.

Chin-Lu hesitated in momentary confusion. Crocker smiled. "Sorry," he said. "That's just an American phrase that means go ahead, or continue."

The puzzled expression left Chin-Lu's eyes. "I see. Ling-

Tse is in the land called Nebraska. At a place called Omaha. I know little of your country. If you would be so kind, I would know the way. Then I may continue my search."

Charlie Crocker's lips pursed in a silent whistle. "You mean to tell me you are going more than halfway across a continent?"

Chin-Lu merely nodded. "It is my desire."

"Chin-Lu, it's not my place to tell a man what to do. But let me warn you—crossing the mountains, the desert, and the plains between here and Nebraska Territory is no Sunday stroll. Just crossing the Sierras at this time of year can be fatal. Then, should you get that far, there's the Indians—"

"I have no quarrel with the Indians," Chin-Lu said, as though the subject were closed.

"That won't make any difference to some angry brave wearing war paint and looking for a stray scalp to pluck." Crocker waved the stubborn man toward a chair. "Coffee?" he asked.

Chin-Lu shook his head. "I drink only water. Sometimes tea, but thank you."

"If you're determined to go on with this foolishness, Chin-Lu, I can't stand in your way. What can I do to help?" Crocker asked.

Within a few minutes, he had spread a map of the United States on his cluttered desk. The map displayed the planned route of the Central Pacific and the Union Pacific, generally following the Overland Trail. As Chin-Lu studied the map, Crocker described as best he could some of the main features and landmarks along the way. "I have no map to spare, I'm sorry," he said in conclusion.

"It is not needed," Chin-Lu said casually. "I have seen your map. I will remember. I am grateful for your help." He turned toward the door.

"Wait," Crocker called. "If you plan to survive, let me give you some advice. Wait until spring. Work for me on the railroad until then. Don't try to fight the mountains in the middle of winter!"

"It is not necessary to fight nature," Chin-Lu replied. "It is necessary only to respect. The oak tree fights the gale and it tumbles. The willow bends and survives."

Crocker shrugged in exasperation. "Very well. But at least do one thing—try to travel with groups. Army patrols. Railroad engineers, teamsters, drovers. Anyone going in your direction. In numbers there is strength, and strength is frequently needed on the American frontier."

Chin-Lu nodded politely. "This I will do. Your words are wise." He picked up his light blanket roll. "Now, Mr. Crocker, if you would be so kind as to point out the direction in which I might find this place called Donner Pass?"

"Chin-Lu—aw, what the hell. Your funeral. You have a horse?" Crocker said, struggling into his own heavy coat.

"No," Chin-Lu replied. "I walk. Small steps soon become large distances."

Outside, the contractor pointed through the swirling snow toward a distant break in the rugged mountain peaks. "Donner Pass," he said with a sigh. "On the other side—if you make it—you should find someone headed east."

Chin-Lu bowed politely. "Thank you, Mr. Crocker. You have been most generous of your time and knowledge. I am in your debt."

With that the lean figure began to move away. Through the swirling snowflakes, Crocker could only shake his head in admiration. "Somehow, Chin-Lu, I have a feeling you'll survive."

Four

The first heavy snowfall of the winter of 1866–67 finally came, catching the Union Pacific in Nebraska Territory. The thick, wet flakes were as big as the tip of a man's thumb, yet there was little wind. The flakes drifted straight down, piling high on any exposed surface and restricting visibility to no more than a few yards.

Still, the rails continued to be laid. Shovel crews out in front of the track layers cleared the roadbed. The thump of iron on cross ties and the clang of spike mauls rang out, muffled by the onslaught of snow. Though water carriers kept their pails covered, they frequently had to break a thin sheet of ice to ladle out the contents.

Bear Fallon paused in his mechanical swinging of the maul to sip from a water carrier's dipper. Then he looked long and hard into the man's eyes.

"Everything set?"

"Yes, Bear. At the noon break." The water carrier, one of Fallon's group of followers, glanced about nervously. "Just give the sign when you pass the iron truck."

Fallon nodded. "Don't mess it up," he warned. "If something goes wrong you don't get paid and I don't get to be foreman. In that case, I don't think you'll want to stick around the railhead long, Birch."

The threat was not lost on the man. "Nothing's gonna go wrong, Bear," he whined. Then, as Fallon reached for his maul, Birch shuffled away through the storm. Fallon quickly covered the few steps to his work station. Between strokes of the maul, he glanced at foreman Sean Grady, barking orders to the rail crew. "Enjoy yourself while you can, Grady," Fallon muttered ominously. "It's a damn fine day for an accident."

At Grady's sharp whistle signaling the noon meal break,

Fallon dallied until the Union Pacific crew foreman came alongside. "Sean," Fallon said softly, "let's lay back a bit. Let the others go on ahead. I have an idea that could slow this railroad by a month and make us a nice bonus from the folks back East. I want to kick the idea around with you."

Grady nodded. "I've been racking my brains trying to come up with something, Bear," the foreman said. "I'm sure glad they sent you along."

The two soon fell behind the other workers who hurried toward the warmth of the dining car and a hearty meal. Fallon was careful to keep Grady between himself and the rail bed as they trudged along, talking quietly.

Some fifty yards from rails' end the two men had to skid down the bank of a narrow creek. The fill that had leveled the roadbed stood a dozen feet above their heads. And on the fill sat the rail truck, piled high with iron. Earlier, Birch and a few other of Fallon's men had restacked the pile of rails, so that all it would take was a slight nudge of one of the rails to send the pile toppling over.

Fallon glanced up. The tons of metal were almost straight overhead. He reached up and casually removed his hat. The sudden screech of sliding rails pierced the air. "Watch out below!" came a cry from the rail car. Fallon suddenly lurched into Grady, sending the foreman's body skidding to the snow-covered creekbed, then hurled himself to the side.

Grady's frantic scream ended as a dozen iron rails crunched onto his downed body. He died instantly, crushed and mangled beneath two tons of steel.

Fallon himself narrowly escaped despite his careful planning. A length of rail brushed the back of his leg, not making contact with flesh but still sending his heart into a skid. He stumbled and went down deliberately, then dragged himself to his knees.

"Iron down!" Fallon screamed as the few lagging rail workers turned at the clatter of metal. "Sean's hit! Get crowbars and the doctor!"

As a handful of men scrambled down the creek bank to the site of the iron fall, Fallon smiled in grim satisfaction. The man on the truck who had touched off the metal avalanche would get his pay as promised. Soon, Bear Fallon would be foreman—and the Union Pacific was *really* due to catch hell then.

General Jack Casement was among the first to reach the

scene, his black horse floundering through the knee-deep snow.

"What the hell happened?" Casement demanded.

Gasping and feigning shock, Fallon glanced at the man on horseback. "Don't know why—but the rails fell off the truck. Sean slipped—couldn't get out of the way. Is he—okay?"

A workman peering into the tangle of iron rails slowly shook his head. "He isn't okay, General Jack. One of the rails is halfway through his head. Popped his brains out like a ripe melon." The ashen-faced worker suddenly turned away and was noisily sick.

Casement dismounted and probed among the rails, helping workmen armed with crowbars remove the iron from the mess that had been his foreman. The railroad physician came running. "Might as well have the carpenter start putting a coffin together," he said after taking one look. "There's nothing I can do for this man."

Casement, his features contorted in dark anger, snapped, "I'll expect a full investigation and a complete report. Find Ted Henderson. I want him to look into this."

A few hours later Sean Grady was buried on the Nebraska plains near Ogallala, within twenty yards of the creek where his life had ended. Jack Casement read from the Book of Psalms in the brief ceremony, then signaled the pick and shovel men to begin filling the grave. As the burial party dispersed, Casement motioned for Ted to follow. He turned toward his combination office and living quarters in the rail car.

"Well, what do you make of it, Ted?" Casement asked as they settled in for a warming cup of coffee.

"It's hard to say for sure, Jack, but I'm not all that inclined to believe this was an accident."

Casement lifted an eyebrow.

"I've watched your men work, Jack, and they're not the sort to make a mistake stacking the rails. Plus, that was too much dead weight, piled solidly, to suddenly shift for no apparent reason. The snow couldn't possibly have caused a slide. I can't be sure, though, and I'll make no firm accusations without names—and proof."

Casement sighed. "It's just one more of those strange 'accidents' that have been nibbling at the Union Pacific for months," he said. "Fortunately, most of them have not been fatal. What puzzles me is that I had begun to suspect that

Sean Grady himself might have been behind some of the mishaps. I must have been wrong. At any rate, I've got to find a new foreman now."

Casement downed the last of his coffee and refilled the cup. Ted shook off the pot waved in his direction. "I guess Bear Fallon would be the logical choice," Casement said without enthusiasm. "He has his own followers, and is enough of a bully that the rest of the workers would stay in line from fear of getting stomped on."

A sudden thought struck Ted. "Jack," he said, "I've got a wild idea. Maybe a totally insane one. Both of us have reservations about Fallon. Mine are probably tainted with personal dislike, but you don't sound too enthusiastic about having him as foreman."

Casement shook his head. "I'm not. But where else can I find a man to handle this lot?"

"Would you settle for a big Irishman—almost as big as Bear Fallon—a man we can both trust from topknot to bootheel? Who can brawl and drink with the best of them and keep us informed of any suspicious activities at the same time?"

Casement's eyes showed his curiosity. "And just where will we find such a man?"

Ted hesitated for a moment. "I don't know if he will even consider it," he said. "The man I have in mind is my partner in the ranch—Kevin O'Reilly. They don't come any more honest."

Briefly, Ted recounted his experiences with O'Reilly. "I've trusted that big Irishman with my life before, Jack," he concluded. "I wouldn't hesitate to do it again."

Casement swirled the coffee in his cup, pondering the proposal. "What does he know about railroading?"

"Not much, as far as I know," Ted said with a sigh. "But he learns quick."

"And the ranch?"

"Kevin has hired a man, a vaquero who is a top hand with cattle and horses. In his last letter, Kevin was complaining that Valdez Cabrillo did so much work he left little for Kevin himself to do. And Wilma is there. She's a good hand when it's necessary."

"Can we get him?" Casement asked.

"There's one way to find out. I can telegraph Fort Laramie and have one of the scouts deliver a message to Kevin. In this weather it will take a few days to reach him and a few more to get a reply. And then he will have to make the trip—if he agrees. You see, his wife is due to have a baby any day now."

Jack Casement thumped his coffee cup onto the table. "Do it, Ted. We can get by for a while without a foreman." He stood and walked to the window, watching the heavy snow float down. "In this weather we won't be laying rails very fast, anyway."

Ted pushed his chair back and reached for his coat. "I'll get the message off right away," he said. He paused with his hand on the door latch. "Jack, Bear Fallon isn't going to like this—not one bit. He thought he had the job wrapped up."

Jack Casement's eyes narrowed. "I don't give a tinker's damn what Fallon likes," he snapped. "As far as I know, I still run this railroad!"

Dawn was breaking at the Henderson-O'Reilly ranch when the first stab of pain hit Wind Flower. It was little more than a cramp, of the sort for which Indian women were banished from their lodges until the bleeding stopped. But the second pain a few minutes later had more authority.

Wind Flower gasped at the unexpected power of the contraction. She leaned forward, propping herself with one hand against the window from which she had been watching the snow grow deeper by the moment.

"Wind Flower—what is it?" Kevin O'Reilly asked anxiously as he entered their house after tending to the livestock in the barn. "Are you ill?"

The Navajo woman smiled softly. "No, Kevin, I am not ill. I think it is time."

Kevin was at her side instantly. For one of the few times in his life, the usually self-confident man was bewildered and frightened. "What can I do?" he asked plaintively.

Wind Flower squared her shoulders. "Get Wilma," she said. "Do not worry, Kevin. Nature has looked after such things for many centuries, since the earth and its creatures were but babes themselves."

As the door closed behind her husband, a violent contraction almost sent Wind Flower to her knees. She stroked her tightly stretched abdomen. "Whew," she breathed, "little one, you do not play gentle games with your mother."

The door opened, and Wilma put her arm around the

younger woman's shoulders. Wind Flower glanced up, drawing comfort from the warmth and confidence in Wilma's eyes. "It is time?" Wilma asked.

At Wind Flower's nod, Wilma led her toward the bedroom. "Are the pains strong?"

"Yes. Very strong," Wind Flower said as she eased herself onto the bed.

Wilma turned from her friend. "Kevin, your presence is not needed in here," she said firmly.

"But—but what do I do?" the father-to-be asked hopelessly.

Wilma smiled reassuringly. "Just stay out of the way, and keep Wild Bill with you. There are things you men call woman's work and this is the ultimate task in that category." She placed a comforting hand on Kevin's huge arm. "Believe me, you would only be in the way—and what will happen in here is not pretty to watch. Now, begone with you."

Wilma went to the stove and heated a tub of water until it was near the warmth of a mother's body. She carried the tub into the bedroom, poked the small blaze in the fireplace back into life, and put the container where it would remain warm.

A low moan came from the bed. "Everything is going to be fine, Wind Flower," Wilma said, wiping the woman's sweat-beaded forehead with a clean cloth. "It will be over soon."

As she scrubbed her hands, Wilma silently offered thanks that she had learned about delivering babies while helping Dr. Mason, the post surgeon in Fort Laramie. Helping bring new lives into the world had been one of her most rewarding experiences.

Placing her hand on the young woman's abdomen, Wilma felt the strong, regular contractions beneath her fingertips.

"Wind Flower, dear," she said softly, "you must try to ignore the pain and remember to push when the little one begins to come from his lodge." Then she settled down to wait, listening to the ticking of the mantel clock nearby, and offering encouragement to her friend.

At midmorning Wind Flower suddenly gasped and clutched the supporting poles of the bed's headboard. She arched her back. "Wilma—it—is here."

Wilma folded back the light blanket and quickly realized Wind Flower was right. The final stages of labor had begun.

Wilma kept talking in a quiet, encouraging tone, telling Wind Flower when to push and when to relax and breathe deeply.

Wilma's heart suddenly sank. As the baby began to appear Wilma realized it was not the child's head that was showing. Somehow the baby had turned. Both mother and child were in grave danger!

"Wind Flower," she said urgently, "we have a small problem. For a moment or so you *must not push!* Fight the contractions! Stop them for just a short time."

She heard Wind Flower's breathing change from short, gasping pants to a deeper, steadier rhythm. Wilma knew what she had to do. Once she had assisted Dr. Mason in just such a difficult situation.

Gently, she eased her hand into the birth canal. Her probing fingers soon discovered the problem. The child had only partly turned, leading with its shoulder instead of its head. She felt Wind Flower's next contraction building and fought back a surge of panic. Another strong push could break the baby's neck!

"Wind Flower, help me," Wilma urged, forcing her voice to remain calm. "Do not let the push happen!" Gradually she felt the muscles relax. Quickly but gently, Wilma pushed against the small unborn shoulder, turning the baby, and sighed in relief as the child's head slipped into position. Fortunately the umbilical cord had not wrapped around the baby's neck.

"Now, Wind Flower!" she whispered. "Push hard!"

Moments later it was all over. Wilma held the small bundle in her hands and listened to the welcome sound of a new voice crying its lungs into action. She smiled down at Wind Flower. "You have a fine, healthy son, little mother. Now rest."

Wilma quickly washed the small body in warm water, dried it with soft cloths, and wrapped it in a warm Navajo patterned blanket Wind Flower had made for the occasion. She handed the baby to the new mother.

"He is beautiful," Wind Flower said as she gazed lovingly at her son. She looked up at Wilma, gratitude and love shining in her eyes. "I thank you for my son's life—and my own."

"You did the work, Wind Flower," Wilma said, feeling herself begin to tremble now that the crisis had passed.

A few minutes later she went to the door and called

Kevin. The big Irishman bolted toward her in one quick motion. "We have a son, Kevin," Wind Flower said. She turned down the blanket covering the child, which was nursing at her breast. Kevin grinned broadly and gently kissed his wife on the forehead as Wilma made her way from the room.

Valdez Cabrillo greeted her with a question and a welcome cup of tea. Wilma smiled, contented. "No," she said quietly, "there were no major problems." She had no desire to tell anyone of the near disaster, or of her own part in warding it off. She felt both satisfied and lonely. If only she could share this time with Ted, she thought.

Wind Flower's recovery was so swift it made Wilma shake her head in wonder. Within a week's time, the Navajo woman was bustling about as energetically as ever. What to name their new son had been the subject of some discussion between Wind Flower and Kevin, Wind Flower suggesting Patrick, and Kevin favoring Swift Deer. Finally it was decided to give the child both names in honor of his dual heritage but to call him Patrick until he grew older and could decide for himself which name he preferred. In the meantime, little Patrick was a source of delight not only to his proud parents but to Valdez and Wild Bill as well.

"Mamma," Bill said one morning as he rocked the child in the cradle Kevin had made, "am I going to have a little brother or sister some time?"

Wilma sighed. The boy had voiced her own wishes.

"Perhaps, Bill," she replied quietly. *But we've got to get your father home first,* she thought.

Just then Kevin glanced out the window.

"Rider coming," he said in surprise, squinting into the glare of early sun reflecting on the snow. "Looks like Carl Keller. Wonder what brings him out this way in this weather?"

Keller wasted little time before answering Kevin's question. Not even removing his coat, the scout produced a telegraph message from a pocket. "This came for you, Kevin. Telegraph man said it was important, so I just rode on out with it. Hey, what's this?" he asked, spotting the new baby. Soon Patrick was cradled in Keller's trail-hardened but gentle hands.

Kevin scanned the message, then glanced at Wilma. "It's from Ted," he said. "He sends you and Bill his love—and he wants me to go work on the railroad."

Keller glanced up in surprise. "A man told me once

never to rush an Irishman," the scout said, "but I reckon as to how I should wait for an answer."

Throughout the rest of the day, Kevin paced the floor. Ted needed him, but he had a new son to raise. The ranch would be safe in Valdez's capable hands, and Keller insisted the veterans of Henderson's Scouts would take turns keeping watch over the place. And the prospect of a new, high-paying job was exciting and the possible adventure was equally appealing.

It was Wind Flower who calmly settled the issue. "Ted Henderson needs you. He and Wilma have done so much for us that it is only fair to repay their kindness. Your son and I will be here when you return. Your presence will be missed, but you will return before long." She nuzzled his shoulder. "And when you return, we shall make a little sister. Children should come in pairs."

Carl Keller rode out the next morning, bearing a simple message from Kevin. "I can stand it if you can. Be there as soon as possible."

February of 1867 was doing no favors for the Union Pacific, Ted thought wearily as he unsaddled the sorrel horse Hellbender. It seemed odd that such a relatively mild winter on the Plains could cause such difficulty.

The daytime sun held enough warmth to turn the top layer of snow into slush, a mixture of ice, water, and snow that grew heavy on the shovels of laborers struggling to clear the roadbed. At night the cold returned, changing the slush to sheets and chunks of ice that yielded only reluctantly to the picks of the workers and left footing treacherous for everyone.

General Jack Casement, who could be one of the most affable of men, drove his workers unmercifully, shouting and growling as the rails slowly inched forward. Despite the Union Pacific crews' earlier rate of laying a mile or more of rail per day, their pace slowed to a mere crawl. A quarter-mile a day under such conditions was considered excellent.

The telegram from Kevin O'Reilly accepting the job of foreman momentarily brightened Ted's spirits, and he eagerly anticipated the big Irishman's arrival. In the meantime there were long, hazardous hours in the saddle, squinting against the constant glare of sun on snow. But there was no sign of Indian activity. Ted had even been called into duty to help with the Casement horse and cattle herds. The animals tended to scatter as they pawed away the half-frozen snow to get at the grass beneath.

Ted was delighted the Casement nerd of Durham short-horn cattle remained in good shape during the winter. If the Durhams could survive on the prairies, the cattle on the Henderson-O'Reilly ranch, with its protective mountain ranges easing the wind, should be in fine shape.

He rubbed the sorrel down before turning it loose, feeling a measure of pride in Hellbender's docile attitude. Since the first day's set-to, Hellbender had never again tried to pitch Ted.

On his way to his quarters on the construction train, Ted passed the darkly glowering bulk of Bear Fallon. Ted knew that the square, beefy Irishman would never rest until he had avenged the beating he had been given. The man's ill-concealed hatred of Ted had grown as the days passed and the job of foreman still remained unfilled.

When Kevin O'Reilly arrived there would be yet another confrontation with Fallon. Ted forced himself to shrug off his concern for his friend. He had enough to worry about without hunting more trouble.

He glanced up as a lone horseman approached in the growing dusk. His spirits soared as he recognized Kevin.

The towering Irishman dismounted, a wide grin creasing his face. "Help's here," Kevin said, gripping Ted's hand in a crushing greeting. "The only question now is, can you survive it?"

Ted cuffed his old friend playfully on the shoulder. "Are you a new father yet?"

"Yes sir. Pleased as a pup with a syrup biscuit. That little half-breed's going to be *muy hombre*. Takes after his mother, too, praise the Creator."

The two men cared for Kevin's mount, then started toward one of the sleeping cars. After depositing Kevin's blanket roll and saddlebags they strode toward Jack Casement's office. "Ready to learn about building a railroad?" Ted asked as they shuffled through the snow.

"Know some about it already," Kevin said with a grin. "I've been playing Sioux for a couple of days, lurking around, watching, and listening. Found me a man in Laramie who'd worked on some lines down South for the Confederates. Reckon I can handle it."

Jack Casement took an immediate liking to Kevin, welcoming him aboard the Union Pacific with a hefty slug of whiskey and a quick rundown of Kevin's duties. The wiry little railroad man was obviously pleased with Kevin's new knowledge. Casement appreciated a man who did a bit of homework before tackling a new job.

That night Casement called a rare assembly of rail workers in the dining car and introduced Kevin as the new rail gang foreman. Glancing at Bear Fallon, Ted saw the fury in the man's eyes. Surprisingly, Fallon made no effort to cause trouble, but Ted decided he would not bet on that being a permanent condition. Almost all the other men seemed ready to accept Kevin as foreman.

The next day Kevin gained even more converts. A bitter wind swept the prairie, felling one shovel worker with frostbitten feet. Kevin sent the man to the doctor, picked up the man's shovel, and took his place among the workers.

Riding off on yet another scout, Ted grinned as Kevin's voice soared in song over the work force with an exaggerated Irish brogue.

> Me pappy was a farmer
> And a whiskey-drinkin' man.
> Took half the Dublin constables
> Just to lock him in the can.
> Me sister was a sailor
> Or at least she told us so.
> And her purse was allus full o'coin
> From her labors down below.

The words faded in the distance as Ted rode from the railhead, but he knew the lyrics would get more earthy before Kevin finished the song. Ted could almost feel the spirits of the workers lift despite the cold and hard work.

That night after eating he found Kevin spinning a yarn to a group of workmen. He waited until the gathering exploded in laughter at the punch line, then motioned Kevin aside.

"So how did it go, Kevin?" he asked.

The Irishman grinned wryly. "I don't have a muscle that isn't torn and sore. I've got blisters on my hands, a pain in my head, and an ache in my back. But it went well. There's some good lads in this bunch. We'll get on. Provided, of course, I can make it out of the cot tomorrow," he added ruefully.

In a far corner of the dining car, Bear Fallon glared at the two men. *The time's coming, Henderson, when you and your pet will get your comeuppance. You're both dead men and don't know it. That foreman's job was mine by rights.* Fallon felt the fury gnawing at his gut, and he refilled his cup with potent rye whiskey. The burn of the liquor fueled the fires of his hatred. *I'll stop this railroad dead in its tracks first,* he thought blackly, *then you two are next.*

Leading Kevin outside, Ted once more warned his friend of possible trouble with Fallon. "Watch out for him, Kevin. He's not going to be any happier with you for taking the job he thought was his than he is with me for seeing that you got it."

"That's something we'll tussle with when the time comes," Kevin replied calmly as he glanced up at the sky. The stars twinkled brightly in the biting night air. "Reckon spring will ever come, Ted?"

Ted sighed. "It will. And then we'll have still more problems." He waved a hand toward the north. "Long Walker is somewhere out there. When the grass comes and the ponies are fat, I'm afraid we'll be up to our backsides in outlaw Sioux."

The mild March breeze bore a hint of the coming spring to the Chinese man in the battered hat who was perched amid the cargo of an aging wagon that jolted along the Overland Trail.

Chin-Lu was pleased with his journey thus far. Once he had broken through the Donner Pass and descended the eastern side of the Sierras, he had encountered little difficulty in finding company on his long trip. First had been the fur traders, then a series of military patrols, and an occasional ride with a teamster.

He glanced about, recognizing some landmarks from Charlie Crocker's description and committing others to memory. Most of them he was able to place on the map he carried in his mind from the one in Crocker's Central Pacific office. Chin-Lu was sure he was somewhere in the place called Wyoming. And beyond Wyoming was Nebraska.

He pondered the trio of teamsters with whom he was traveling. They seemed to be a coarse lot, and they had been drinking almost steadily since he had climbed aboard their supply wagon two days before. His instincts had warned him not to join them, but the urge to hurry to the place called Nebraska and his sister, Ling-Tse, had overcome his inner caution. The teamster who held the reins, a stocky man called Gaither, had invited him aboard, saying they were bound for a place called Fort Halleck.

The wagon lumbered to a halt alongside a stream in the foothills of majestic mountains before them. "Good spot to camp," Gaither called.

His two companions, one called by the strange name of Grits who slurred his words when he spoke, and the other named Monk, muttered agreement through an alcoholic haze. All three men were heavily armed, but Chin-Lu was not worried. He meant them no harm.

As he had done the previous night, Chin-Lu gathered firewood and brought water from the stream for the teamsters' camp.

"You a handy man to have around, China," Monk muttered. He was a portly man with a scraggly beard.

"It is small enough payment for your offer of transportation," Chin-Lu said with a slight bow. "You have been most kind."

Chin-Lu set about making his own camp a few yards distant from the teamsters'. He built a small fire, put some rice on to boil, and made his way to a hill nearby. There he sat, legs crossed, palms turned upward, and in his mind muttered the chant that would bring relaxation. The daily meditation brought Chin-Lu closer to nature and left him refreshed.

Though his eyes were closed and his thoughts calm, Chin-Lu distinctly heard the sounds that hovered about the camp: the drone of the teamsters' talk, the call of a hawk overhead, the mutter of water over stones. After a few moments, his spirit once more in harmony, he rose and made his way to the teamsters' camp.

"If you please, at the stream I noticed some wild onions. I would gather some for you. Their flavor is strong but sweet, and they help ward off illness," Chin-Lu said quietly.

"Now, that'd just be mighty white of you, China," the thin, stooped Grits said. Chin-Lu ignored the mocking tone in the man's voice. He bowed slightly, then strolled toward the stream.

The three teamsters sat for a moment, watching the slight figure until they were sure the Chinaman was out of earshot.

"Well, Gaither," Grits said, "whadda we do with ol' China yonder?"

"Yeah," Monk chimed in. "Been wonderin' that myself. Figger we'll top Bridger Pass tomorrow, then run toward the Black Hills and all that gold just a-layin' around." The pudgy Monk rubbed his hands in anticipation. "Gonna be some joke on them sojers, us takin' their supplies and sneakin' into gold country. Man, I can see that yeller metal now."

Gaither stared in Chin-Lu's direction for a long moment. "Reckon we got some choices," he finally said. "One thing's for sure. We can't let him loose. He might run tattlin' to Fort Halleck and we'd have them damn blue coats on us certain." He sighed. "That means we either knock him on the head and leave him, or take him with us."

"Dunno, Gaither," Monk said, scratching his ragged beard. "Reckon we best pop 'im on the noggin. Kinda makes me nervous, sneakin' around all quiet like, not sayin' nothin'. And all polite-like. Ain't like most Chinamen I knowed."

Grits snorted in derision. "Only China types you knowed, Monk, was female—and flat on their backs, too."

"You boys hand me that jug and shush up a minute," Gaither ordered. "I got me some thinkin' to do."

After a moment's silence, Gaither nodded. "Yep. Got her figgered out. Now this China, he says he's a-lookin' for his sister. We know it takes money to travel. And I seen him a-fingerin' some kinda necklace. Green stone, it was. Might be worth some money. Now, they's a heap of hard work to be done on a gold strike. What I'm thinkin' is this. Let's knock this'un on the noggin, take his money, wrap him up, and take him along. Be handy to have a coolie do all the heavy work for us now, wouldn't it?"

Monk nodded. "By golly, Gaither. I sometimes think you maybe got a brain under that hat after all. When we gonna do it?"

By the time Chin-Lu returned with a double handful of wild onions, his fate was sealed with the teamsters. "Thankee, China," Gaither said, holding out a hand for the washed and trimmed onions.

"It is my pleasure," Chin-Lu said.

"Have supper with us?"

"No, but thank you. I have my own food. Is there something more you need?" Chin-Lu asked.

At Gaither's shake of the head, Chin-Lu retired to his own small meal.

They were up and on the move again slightly after sunrise, Chin-Lu once more on the back of the wagon. By midafternoon they had reached the summit of Bridger's Pass. "Gotta let the horses blow," Gaither said. "Got a long trail ahead of us." He looked anxiously toward the north, where the fortune of the Black Hills waited. Then he glanced over his shoulder. Grits, astride his gray horse, had pulled alongside the rear wheel. His rifle rested across his saddle.

"Hey, China!" Gaither called.

Chin-Lu turned to see what the teamster wanted. He did not see Grits shift the rifle. Too late he heard the whistle of air, then the gun stock cracked into the back of his head. He pitched forward, unconscious, on the pile of goods in the wagon.

Eventually Chin-Lu struggled back to consciousness, aware of the pain in his head at each beat of his heart. He had no idea how long the blackness had held him. As his senses gradually returned, he remained with his eyes closed, unmoving. It was best, he thought, that the three teamsters still believed him unconscious. After listening to their conversation for a few minutes, he realized Gaither was in the wagon seat, driving the horses at a clip that seemed much too great for the condition of the trail. Grits rode at the right side of the wagon, Monk at the left.

Chin-Lu also became aware that he was bound hand and foot with a coarse, scratchy rope, apparently of grass. Cautiously he opened one eye just a fraction. From his place high atop the supplies in the wagon he could see the unfamiliar terrain. The mountains and valleys did not register on the map in his mind. He knew, however, that the sun, which should have been either before or behind them, now stood off to one side. The wagon had veered from its course and was headed north.

Chin-Lu closed his eye, feigning unconsciousness once more as the sound of the horse carrying Grits came closer.

"Damned if he ain't still out cold," Grits said in apparent satisfaction.

"Could be you done killed him, Grits," Gaither snapped from his post on the wagon seat. "You did, you gonna have to do his work when we get to the Black Hills and the gold. You two look sharp, now. We's ridin' into Cheyenne country. Them redskins don't like miners much."

Chin-Lu heard Grits working the lever action of his repeating rifle. "Let 'em come. I ain't afeared of no savages," Grits bragged.

"You best be," Gaither grumbled. "We ain't far from the Bozeman Trail—where we ain't supposed to be. We're coverin' as much ground as we can afore dark. From here on we travel by night and hide out by day."

Both the Bozeman Trail and the Black Hills were on the map in Chin-Lu's mind, so he had a rough idea where he was. His route to Ling-Tse fell farther behind with each turn of the wagon wheels. He would be patient. When the time came to strike, he would know.

Without visible movement, Chin-Lu carefully tested the bonds that held his feet and wrists. The white men had been careless. It would be a small matter to work the ropes free. He began alternately tensing and relaxing the muscles and tendons of his wrists. After only a few moments the bonds loosened slightly. It would be easy to form the snake's head with his hands and slip them from the ropes, then free his feet.

The sun gradually faded, giving way to the cold night air. The men had taken Chin-Lu's quilted jacket and he felt the chill. Deciding nothing more could be accomplished by pretending unconsciousness, Chin-Lu uttered a small moan.

"Well, lookie here," the bearded Monk said. "China ain't dead after all. Got a headache, coolie?"

Chin-Lu made no effort to reply. The effects of the blow were fading, and strength was flowing back into his muscles. He moaned again as if in severe pain, then struggled to sit erect.

"Why do you do this?" he asked plaintively. "I would have shared such small things as I have, had you but asked."

Monk chuckled in the growing darkness. "China, you got just one thing we want—a strong back. If we don't have no luck in the gold fields, we can allus sell a China-boy to some farmer or Injun trader. Good slaves bring high prices out here."

The wagon finally jolted to a stop well after sundown. Rough hands grabbed Chin-Lu and dragged him from the wagon. He let himself be dragged to a twisted tree stump, where Gaither dumped him to the ground. Chin-Lu leaned back against the rough bark of the dead tree.

The three teamsters ignored the slight Chinese as they went about making camp. They did not offer him water or food, but it did not matter. Chin-Lu drew nourishment from within when none was available from without. He contented himself with watching the full moon rise higher in the sky.

The opportunity he sought came as the trio sat around a small fire, noisily gulping down a quick supper. For the moment, their attentions were elsewhere. Chin-Lu made the snake with his hands and slipped free of the ropes. The knot of the bonds about his ankles yielded quickly to his agile fingers. He then stood, keeping his back to the tree.

Grits glanced in Chin-Lu's direction and his eyes widened in alarm. "China—"

At the single word, Chin-Lu launched himself toward the startled trio. He reached them with two quick, gliding steps.

Grits dropped his plate and grabbed for his rifle, attempting to rise. Chin-Lu's heel kick caught him in the stomach, tumbling the man backward. The rifle went flying.

Chin-Lu spun to his left, lashing out with his right foot. The spin-kick caught Monk as he tried to rise. The Chinese man's heel cracked solidly into Monk's skull. The man went down without a sound. Chin-Lu felt strong arms trying to wrap themselves about his upper body. He dropped fluidly to one knee, grasping the sleeve of Gaither's heavy coat, and tugged. Gaither went high over Chin-Lu's shoulder and slammed hard into the ground. The Chinese man cracked him sharply in the temple, a short, powerful backfist. Gaither's head snapped to the side. The stocky body lay still.

Grits staggered to his feet, a knife in his hand. Before he had a chance to bring it into play, Chin-Lu was upon him. The Chinese slapped the knife wrist aside, dodged a wild swing, and calmly drove the extended knuckle of his middle finger into the tender nerve complex below Grits's breastbone. The man sagged, gagging, and Chin-Lu ended the dispute with a quick, sharp jab to Grits's jaw.

Scarcely even breathing hard, Chin-Lu searched the wagon until he found what he wanted. Within moments the unconscious trio was bound securely.

A low moan indicated that one of the three was regaining consciousness as Chin-Lu retrieved his jacket and his blanket roll from the wagon. He knelt before the stirring Monk, who struggled against his bonds without fully realizing he had been tied up. Chin-Lu waited patiently until Monk had regained full consciousness and recognized his plight.

"China—what—you mean—to do?" Monk's eyes were wide with fear.

"I do nothing," Chin-Lu replied calmly. "I continue my journey to the land called Nebraska."

"My God—China, you can't—leave us like this!" Monk pleaded. "The Injuns—"

Chin-Lu shrugged his shoulders. "It is as you would have done to me had you not wished my labors. Do not worry. I will return to the path called the Overland Trail. There I will find soldiers. I will send them. They should arrive within two days. You will not die of starvation or thirst in so brief a time."

Chin-Lu paused at Grits's unconscious body. He probed the man's pockets until he found his crescent medallion. Then he lifted Grits's wallet and carefully counted out the exact amount of money the teamsters had taken from him.

Without looking back, Chin-Lu shouldered his few belongings and set out by the light of the full moon toward the Overland Trail.

The midmorning sun was warm and a mild breeze blew gently as he paused to drink from a clear, cold stream several hours later. When he had finished, he noticed a band of horsemen approaching. Stumbling along behind the half-dozen Indians were the three men Chin-Lu had subdued the night before. He studied the Indians as the group neared. They were unlike the other red men he had seen in his travels, the Diggers and Snakes of the California region.

These Indians rode sturdy ponies, sitting straight on their blanket saddles, and each man carried a weapon. Most of them cradled white man's carbines. Some had powerful short bows and a quiver of arrows slung across their backs. Chin-Lu felt no alarm, only a mild curiosity. Had they meant him harm, he already would have felt the sting of a bullet.

The lead Indian reined his horse to a stop before Chin-Lu, the dark eyes reflecting his own curiosity. Chin-Lu inclined his head politely in greeting. From the captives, a voice called, "We'll get you for this, China!" A sharp yank on the lead rope silenced the captive.

"You are called China?" the Indian who led the party asked in English.

"These three called me that," Chin-Lu replied. "China is the name of my homeland. I am known as Chin-Lu."

The Indian tilted his own head. "I am Deer Stalker of the Cheyenne," he said. "You are the one who defeated these three men without the use of arms?"

Chin-Lu nodded. Deer Stalker shook his head in wonder. "These trespassers into the land of the Cheyenne proved most eager to talk—at the point of a lance. We did not believe them, that a single man could disarm and capture three."

"It is an art I have been taught since I was but a child," Chin-Lu said simply. He nodded toward the trussed-up trio. "What will become of them?"

"They will be taken to Fort Laramie and turned over to the army. The white man is not allowed on the Bozeman Trail or in the Black Hills. We do not kill them this time. But if they again soil Cheyenne land with their presence, they will be killed."

The Indians were staring intently at Chin-Lu.

"Your skin is not red," Deer Stalker finally said, "yet your features are similar in some ways to those of the Cheyenne. You must be a great war chief in your own country—this China—if you defeat three men at the same time."

Deer Stalker turned to the others for a brief conversation in a tongue that was strange to Chin-Lu, then the Indian turned back to the Chinese. "We will divide our forces here," he said. "Four of my warriors will deliver the defilers of Cheyenne soil to the soldiers at Fort Laramie. You will come with Deer Stalker and Limps-on-Foot to the lodge of our chief. He will wish to know more of this strange warrior on our land."

Chin-Lu inclined his head in agreement. The Indian's tone had been neither an invitation nor a threat. It was simply a statement. But despite his yearning to return to the trail that led to his sister, Chin-Lu would not insult the Indian by arguing. He decided a few days' delay would harm no one—and he was curious to learn more of these obviously proud people who placed such great store on personal fighting ability.

"Do you ride?" Deer Stalker asked.

"Yes. I have ridden." Noting the ease with which the

Indians handled their half-broken mounts, he added, "But I do not ride as well as the people called the Cheyenne."

Deer Stalker motioned for one of the two saddled horses belonging to the captives to be brought forward. It was Grits's gelding. Chin-Lu was barely familiar with the American saddle, but he swung easily onto the gray's back.

As the four Indians rode past, leading the three captives, Monk glowered at Chin-Lu. "We won't forget this, coolie! Your day with the devil is a-comin'."

"I do not think that one likes you, man of yellow skin," Deer Stalker said.

"It is each man's choice to feel as his heart leads him," Chin-Lu replied calmly, reining the gray into step behind Deer Stalker. Limps-on-Foot positioned his animal behind Chin-Lu, and the small procession turned east and slightly north, toward what Chin-Lu assumed would be the Cheyenne village.

Five

The gentle southwest breeze carried the scent of an early spring to the blue-eyed Indian who sat atop a low, rocky hill overlooking the Nebraska grasslands. A wisp of smoke rose from the sacrificial fire on a flat stone near his feet.

Long Walker finally stirred, as though emerging from a trance, and slowly looked around the circle of red faces. His most trusted lieutenants stood a respectful distance away. One did not crowd a war chief when he made medicine.

Long Walker gazed confidently into each pair of questioning eyes. Then he raised his hands, palms upward. Small droplets of blood welled along the tracks the medicine knife had left on his forearms.

"Brothers, the spirits have spoken to Long Walker," the Seminole-turned-Sioux said. "Wakan-Tanka has sent the warm winds early and banished the snow. The red man has been warm in his lodge, his belly full through the time of the snows."

Long Walker paused briefly, savoring the respect from the warriors about him. "Now Wakan-Tanka has shown Long Walker a vision," he continued. "In this vision many strong ponies trotted into the red man's camp. They wore the brand of the white man's railroad. The Great Spirit has told Long Walker how this wonder shall occur. With only as many braves as he has fingers and toes, Long Walker will lead a raid on the white man's horse herd along the iron rails!"

A mutter of excitement swept the group. Only one voice was raised in caution. "The ponies are yet weak from the snows," the Ute Two Thorns said. "Should Long Walker not wait until the grass grows long and the ponies fatten?"

Long Walker raised a hand, silencing the murmur of protest at Two Thorns's apparent hesitancy. "The question is good," Long Walker said. "Wakan-Tanka has answered it in

112

Long Walker's vision. The white men will think as does Two Thorns. They will be caught asleep in their saddles by Long Walker's raiders. If the white man believes it is too soon for the Indian to strike, is this not the best time to attack?"

Bored with winter camp and anxious once more to smoke the war pipe, the warriors instantly agreed.

"Then it shall be," Long Walker said solemnly. Carefully he squeezed a fresh drop of blood from one of the small cuts on his arm. He collected the drop of blood on the tip of the ceremonial knife, then touched the knifepoint to the embers of the fire. "Those who would ride with Long Walker shall open their skins and add their blood to his upon the stone," Long Walker said. "With the second sunrise we shall raid the railroad pony herd. The white man feeds his horses grain during the snow time. They are strong. With these horses, the Indians will raid again and again, until their own ponies are fat. White settlers come behind the iron horses. They shall feel the lance and bullet of those who ride with Long Walker."

Long Walker noted with satisfaction that his words had fueled the smoldering war fever among the subchiefs. One by one they filed past, each nicking his skin with the medicine knife and adding a drop of blood to the embers of the fire.

When the last of his lieutenants had sworn the oath, Long Walker stood. "Go. Each warrior will select two of his best braves for this raid." He again raised his arms, this time as if to include the entire group in a magic circle. "Now begins the Season of Blood for the hated whites."

Ted Henderson stood above the mound of earth on the Nebraska plains and cursed with a quiet vengeance. The exhaustion of a long and mostly fruitless chase lay heavy in his heart as he stood over the grave of Gus, Casement's day wrangler.

Ted felt a hand on his shoulder. Dan Casement, General Jack's brother, still clutched the Bible from which he had read over the wrangler's grave. "Don't be so hard on yourself, Ted," Dan Casement said quietly. "It wasn't your fault. No one could have predicted this Indian raid—"

"Dammit, I should have," Ted snapped impatiently. "That's what I get paid for. I didn't do my job, and now a good man is dead. It didn't have to happen."

"Ted, you can't be everywhere at once. If anyone is to

blame, it's Jack and me. We should have hired some help for Gus. At least you got back part of the herd."

Ted snorted in disgust. "I wouldn't exactly call that a resounding success. Long Walker's rear guard just turned the slower animals loose when we got within firing distance. Now a friend is dead and we're short of mules and draft horses." He slapped his hat against his thigh to knock away the dust, then he tugged the hat brim down low over his eyes.

"Dan, I appreciate what you're trying to do. But making excuses for me won't bring Gus back. This is just the beginning. I know that Indian out there—well enough that I should never have let him sneak this raid past me." Ted sighed heavily. "There's nothing we can do now except try to guess where Long Walker will strike next. God knows he has plenty of targets."

He spun on a heel and strode away. A few yards from the group he stood silently, facing the north. *So now the game begins in earnest,* he thought. His hand drifted to the butt of the revolver at his belt. *I've got to climb inside that renegade's head.*

Meanwhile, Long Walker sat contented outside his lodge and listened to the celebration in the camp. The raid could not really be called a triumph. But they had stolen a few animals and killed a white man. They had not lost a single brave, and the minor victory had boosted the spirits of his men.

At a call from Two Thorns, Long Walker rose and strode to where the stolen horses grazed outside the circle of lodges. An expectant hush fell over the warriors as he approached. As war chief and raid leader, he had the choice of all prizes captured. Now he would savor a special moment.

He turned to the waiting braves. "Long Walker claims but one animal," he said. "Among the captured horses is one the color of deer hide, with a stripe along his back. This one Long Walker claims, for it is the mount of his sworn enemy. It will be a great joke on the white man Ted Henderson that Long Walker rides Ted Henderson's own horse into battle against him."

Long Walker waited until the ripple of amusement subsided. Then he raised a hand.

"Brothers, as the days grow longer, so shall the lines of brave red men who join to cast the whites from Indian land.

By the time the leaves turn in the fall, the scalps of many whites shall hang from Indian war lances!"

With the whoops of agreement ringing in his ears, Long Walker strode back toward his lodge. Capturing Ted Henderson's horse had been a stroke of good fortune, he thought. *Now, there is one more horse to claim—a palomino. And tied to its tail, the scalp of the Cheyenne coward, Yellow Crow.*

Paints-His-Horses winced as he stretched his right leg before him in the lodge of the peace chief Yellow Crow. The knee, shattered by a cavalryman's rifle ball many years before, seemed to pain him more with the passing of each season.

Once Paints-His-Horses had been a fearless warrior and a clever war chief. Now, feeling the weight of the years, his influence had been turned to peace. It was this quest that had brought him to the lodge of Yellow Crow.

"There is much anger among the young men of the Cheyenne, Yellow Crow," Paints-His-Horses said. "The iron arrows cross the prairie, and behind them flows a sea of white faces. Paints-His-Horses feels anger himself, yet the years have given him the wisdom to reason past his own heart. Peace *must* be preserved. The red man cannot win a war with the whites. Perhaps, if the red man is quick of mind, he might win a just agreement. . . ." The old man's voice trailed off.

"Yellow Crow has so counseled, not only in his own camp, but in the camps of other tribes as well," Yellow Crow said. "Yet he sees not the dawn of peace, but the storm clouds of war." The Cheyenne peace chief's voice tightened in anger. "A handful of red men threaten to sweep all the Indians into the storm. The blue-eyed Sioux, Long Walker, will lead everyone down the path to destruction."

Yellow Crow did not notice the concerned expression that crossed the face of his Blackfoot wife, Talking Bird, who stopped stirring the stewpot to glance in his direction. Yellow Crow's thoughts had been so turned toward the outlaw Sioux, and so blackly, that it seemed a wall had begun to rise between man and wife. Once Talking Bird had watched as two bull elk fought to establish a right to a herd of young cows. The battling elk had locked antlers, and both had died. The young cows were without a mate that season.

Talking Bird sighed inwardly. In so many respects her

husband and the Sioux called Long Walker were like those elk, and she was like the young cows. Try as she might, Talking Bird had been unable to turn Yellow Crow's mind from his obsession. Even when he was in the lodge, his thoughts were elsewhere, and the darkness fell across his face often. Once again she felt the fear of losing Yellow Crow—not to a war lance or a snake, but to the blackness of his own soul.

"What you say is true, Yellow Crow," Paints-His-Horses said solemnly. "Long Walker's raids could doom all. The whites will not long tolerate the raping and killing and burning, and Paints-His-Horses fears they will take vengeance upon all red men for the acts of one."

A sudden commotion outside cut through the conversation. Talking Bird glanced at Little Fern, the young woman who had accompanied her father to the meeting with Yellow Crow. Little Fern quickly moved to the opened flap of the lodge where she stood peering out for a moment. Then she turned, her soft brown eyes wide with wonder.

"Deer Stalker returns," she said in a soft and melodic voice. "He brings a stranger, one unlike any Little Fern has ever seen."

Yellow Crow rose in a single fluid motion. Paints-His-Horses remained seated, partly to favor his aching leg and partly because, as a guest, it was not proper to interfere in the greeting of new arrivals in the host's lodge.

Deer Stalker swung from his mount, greeting Yellow Crow with a respectful nod. He waved a hand toward a slender yellow man on a gray horse. The peace chief listened intently, studying the calm yellow face, as Deer Stalker told his story. Then Yellow Crow stepped alongside the man on the gray.

"Deer Stalker says you speak English."

"Yes. I am sorry to say I do not speak your tongue," Chin-Lu answered, inclining his head in a respectful greeting.

"What are you called, and what is your tribe?" Yellow Crow asked.

"I am called Chin-Lu. I am from a tribe in a place called China. It is far from here, across a great sea."

Yellow Crow nodded. "I have heard my white friends speak of such a place." He motioned with a hand. "You are welcome in the lodge of Yellow Crow of the Cheyenne."

Chin-Lu stepped from the saddle and followed Yellow

Crow into the buffalo-hide lodge held erect by poles—and for an instant Chin-Lu thought he had stepped back in time.

Across the small fire that burned in the center of the lodge stood a proud young woman with dark hair that tumbled about her shoulders. For a heartbeat Chin-Lu believed he was looking at the princess called Aikiota—the woman he secretly loved but knew he could never have. The brief thought shook him as nothing else had done in years. Then he realized there was a similarity of attitude and build, of haunting beauty. But this apparition did not wear the silks of the Imperial Palace. Her slender body was covered from neck to ankle in soft, supple deerskin. Her arms and shoulders seemed to be a lighter shade than the skin of other Indians he had seen, and in the warm brown eyes he saw a hint of tranquil streams and gardens.

"My brother in the way of peace, Paints-His-Horses," Yellow Crow said, introducing the newly arrived guest. "My wife, Talking Bird, and here, Little Fern, daughter of Paints-His-Horses."

Chin-Lu bowed politely to the women as their names were called. Little Fern gazed at him for a moment in open interest and curiosity, then turned her face aside shyly.

Chin-Lu found himself struggling to keep from staring at the Cheyenne maiden constantly. She was, he thought, the most beautiful woman he had seen since the princess at the palace.

At questions from Yellow Crow and Paints-His-Horses, Chin-Lu recounted his quest in search of his sister and the fight with the would-be prospectors. The honesty of the Cheyenne lodge came as a breath of fresh air to him. He could not help but wonder at the similarities between these people and himself. It was Paints-His-Horses who put words to Chin-Lu's thoughts. The aging peace chief muttered something in Cheyenne.

"Paints-His-Horses wonders," Yellow Crow translated to Chin-Lu. "You are not Indian, yet your features are similar. He finds this curious."

"Perhaps, in the distant past, we shared common ancestors," Chin-Lu replied. "I have noticed that many of the Cheyenne warriors carry bows. They are much like those of my own land." He nodded toward Yellow Crow's powerful Osage orange bow at its place of honor near his blankets.

"That is a fine bow," he said. "It will send its arrows true and far."

Yellow Crow's brows arched in curiosity. "You know of the bow?"

"I have been taught."

"Then try my bow," Yellow Crow said.

Chin-Lu nodded. "I would be most honored. But it is of such power, perhaps I cannot draw it."

Yellow Crow translated Chin-Lu's words as he reached for the bow and strung it, then picked up a quiver of arrows. Paints-His-Horses grunted in interest and struggled to his feet. Even the women followed as Yellow Crow led the visitor from the lodge.

Chin-Lu saw that a large number of the Cheyenne had gathered, obviously curious about the newcomer.

He accepted the bow from Yellow Crow, stroking the finely polished wood reverently. Then he selected an arrow from the quiver. Yellow Crow pointed toward a target, a chunk of wood the size of a man's head, some thirty yards distant.

Chin-Lu nocked the arrow and tested the power of the bow. Then, in one smooth motion, he drew the bow to full arc and loosed the arrow. Its point drove home, striking true in the center of the target.

A murmur of astonishment rippled through the watching Indians. That such a small man could draw Yellow Crow's bow at all was wonder enough. That he could so easily place the arrow in its target impressed even the best archers among them. Chin-Lu handed the weapon back to Yellow Crow, inclining his head. "It is a magnificent bow," he said. "I am greatly honored to have held it in my hands."

Paints-His-Horses said something that brought smiles to the faces of the warriors. "You have been paid a great compliment," Yellow Crow said to Chin-Lu. "Paints-His-Horses says he would not bet his best horse or blanket in a bow contest with the man Chin-Lu. And Paints-His-Horses is the best bowman of the Cheyenne."

Chin-Lu nodded in respect. "Tell the great chief," he said, "that such a contest shall never occur, for I have no horse to lose."

Friendly laughter followed Yellow Crow's translation. Then the Cheyenne peace chief placed a hand on Chin-Lu's shoulder. "You will stay with us as long as you wish. There is much we would learn from you."

At Yellow Crow's nod, several small boys raced toward the target, eager for the honor of retrieving the chief's arrow. As the group turned back to the lodge, Talking Bird fell into step with Little Fern.

"Talking Bird sees the way Little Fern looks at the strange yellow man," Talking Bird said. "Her eyes give away her thoughts."

Little Fern felt her skin warm as a shy smile touched her lips.

Later, Chin-Lu had an opportunity to speak with Talking Bird. "You speak English well," he said. "I would give a message to the woman Little Fern. I wish to apologize for staring at her. But she is of great beauty. Had I the Cheyenne words, I would tell her myself."

Talking Bird glanced toward the slender young woman preparing the evening meal. "I tell her your words, Chin-Lu. And now you start to learn Cheyenne. Then you will not need Talking Bird's tongue." The Blackfoot woman smiled at Chin-Lu. "One day," she said, "I think you will tie ponies before her lodge."

The remark puzzled Chin-Lu. It seemed of great significance, yet he had no ponies as gifts for the young Cheyenne woman. He had little opportunity to wonder over the matter, for soon he was concentrating on the difficult Cheyenne names for objects within the lodge, trying to form the words as Talking Bird spoke them. But from time to time his attention wandered, his gaze drifting toward Little Fern.

Over the next few days, Chin-Lu found himself drawn more and more deeply into the day-to-day life of the Cheyenne. They were an honest and open people, quick to laugh. They treated him with respect, as he treated them. Their lives were simple yet difficult. And he was beginning to be able to form a few sentences in broken Cheyenne that usually made the children laugh.

Each day seemed to bring a new gesture of acceptance to Chin-Lu from the Cheyenne. He was brought into the confidence of the peace chiefs, told of the long-standing feud between Long Walker and Yellow Crow, and of the threat of the renegade chief to the shaky peace. He learned that Yellow Crow had a blood brother among the whites, a man named Ted Henderson. At times his advice was asked, as though his words were highly valued, and he answered as best he could. With daily usage his command of the Cheyenne language grew rapidly.

By the time the moon had grown full once again, Chin-Lu knew he could grow to love this life and these people. It was a dangerous thought. His quest to find his sister remained unfinished. But he felt a growing tenderness toward Little Fern and that was a luxury he could not afford. Was she not the daughter of a great chief? he thought. Did that fact put her out of reach, as had been the case with the princess in the Imperial Palace? These were questions that Chin-Lu must have answered, once his search for his sister had ended.

On a mild spring morning, Chin-Lu stepped from the small lodge that had been erected for him, his blanket roll clutched under an arm. The time had come for him to move on.

He found Yellow Crow and Paints-His-Horses once more deep in discussion about the coming of the railroad and the Indian called Long Walker. Chin-Lu waited respectfully until Yellow Crow nodded a greeting.

"I must go," Chin-Lu said. "I have made a promise to my father. One must keep such vows. I regret that I have nothing with which to repay your kindness." He glanced at Little Fern, and for an instant Chin-Lu thought he saw a hint of pain in her soft brown eyes.

Yellow Crow nodded solemnly. "Vows once made must be kept," the Cheyenne said, grimly fingering the soft pouch that held the single rifle cartridge. "You owe the Cheyenne nothing. May the spirits guide you to your sister."

Paints-His-Horses struggled to his feet. "Paints-His-Horses and Little Fern are to leave within the week to return to their own band," the aged chief said. "Chin-Lu is welcome to travel with them. Their journey will take them near the road Chin-Lu seeks. Just beyond a place called Cactus Springs, where they will camp one night, Paints-His-Horses will show Chin-Lu the trail that leads to the road."

Chin-Lu was about to decline when he noted the surge of hope brighten Little Fern's features. He decided a few more days could do little harm. He inclined his head. "Chin-Lu would be most honored." At least, he thought, for a while longer he would have the welcomed company of the Cheyenne— and of Little Fern.

* * *

Ed Gaither banged an angry fist into the rough pine bar of the Laramie saloon. The establishment was in a run-down section of town, and its whiskey was raw and rank. But it was cheap, and since Gaither and his two friends had paid their fines for trespassing on the Bozeman Trail, they had little money left.

The fine had been bad enough. But when they had been slapped in the garrison stockade for two weeks, Gaither's rage had begun to build even more.

Monk Farler and Grits Smith were in a sour mood as well. The bad whiskey fueled the fires triggered when the Cheyenne had paraded them down Laramie's main street trussed up like a Christmas package. Monk already had stomped one man for a sarcastic comment on their lack of "Injun fightin' " abilities.

Gaither was down to his last few dollars, but at least there was a full bottle of whiskey on the bar before the three men.

"Dammit, Ed," Grits muttered, his Southern drawl slurred by whiskey, "we can't let them Injuns get away with this! I done worked me up a good temper, and only thing's gonna settle it down's a fresh scalp!"

Monk Farler growled his agreement. "Nobody treats me thataway. How 'bout it, Ed? Wanna go knock a few Injun noggins?"

Gaither downed a hefty slug of liquor. He stared groggily at his two companions. "Why the hell not? We'll teach them redskins a thing or two, might even find us a prime young squaw. Gawd knows ain't nothin' around here no better. Squaw's damn sight less expensive, too." Gaither turned to a bald man drinking with the teamsters. "How 'bout it, Curly? Wanna go on a scalp hunt?"

The bald man, halfway through his own bottle, grinned. "Been thinkin' that myself, Gaither. Might pick us up a few dollars, too. 'Fore I quit bustin' my butt on the good ol' Union Pacific I run acrost a man from down Colorado country what pays prime gold for Injun scalps. Don't matter none what tribe, neither."

The comment fanned the spark of enthusiasm still further. "You mean we gets paid for killin' Injuns?" Monk asked. "Hell, that's like payin' a man for drinkin' and whorin'. No work, all play, and pay to boot!"

"I know a few other boys, mostly ex-railroad men like me, who'd jump at the chance to go along," Curly said. "What d'ya say we split the scalp money even?"

Within an hour the quartet had grown to nearly a dozen armed, mounted—and mostly drunk—men. Grits, who had stolen the horse he rode, anxiously led the party at a long lope north from Fort Laramie. Whooping and yelling, the scalp hunters spurred toward Cheyenne land.

"Ain't gonna take us long, boys," Curly yelled. "Betcha by daylight tomorrow we done got us some scalps a-hangin'. Place up ahead called Cactus Springs. Any Injuns movin' likely camp there!" He slapped the saddle horn in exuberance. "Hot damn, if this don't beat railroadin' all to hell!"

Chin-Lu sat quietly on his blankets and listened to the sounds of Paints-His-Horses's group settling in for the night.

The place the chief had called Cactus Springs would remain long in Chin-Lu's memory. The gentle calls of night birds and whir of insect wings lent a cheerful peacefulness to the shallow valley. Water gushed from a low rock bluff and tumbled over stones in a soothing murmur. It was almost as if he were in a garden back in China, only the voices about him spoke Cheyenne, not Chinese. This would be his last night but one in the company of the Indians.

Chin-Lu glanced about the camp. Paints-His-Horses traveled with only one lodge for himself and Little Fern to sleep in. The half-dozen young braves accompanying the party slept in blankets under the stars, as did Chin-Lu.

The slender Little Fern stepped from the lodge and glanced about. Chin-Lu's heart leapt as she spotted him and walked in his direction.

He rose to his feet as the young woman approached. The moonlight left touches of silver on the black of her long hair. Her delicate features held a look of sadness in the gentle half-light of the rising moon.

"With the second sunrise will Chin-Lu go?" she asked quietly.

"Yes." Chin-Lu's skin tingled as she lightly touched his arm. "He must go. His sister is somewhere in this big land. He must find her."

"It is Little Fern's hope that Chin-Lu shall return safely. . . ." The Cheyenne maiden spoke softly before turning and walking quickly away.

Chin-Lu fought back the urge to call out. Instead the words formed in his mind. *One day soon, Little Fern, I shall return. One day I shall be worthy of a chief's daughter, and my ponies shall stand before your lodge.*

Now that he understood the gesture by which a Cheyenne proposed marriage, Chin-Lu felt no hesitation in mentally voicing the promise of tying ponies before Little Fern's lodge. With a heavy heart, he walked from the camp. At the edge of the little valley a hundred steps away, he found his place of meditation. It was alongside a cluster of small shrubs that rustled in the light breeze on the south side of the camp.

Chin-Lu began the chant that would calm his spirit. As the spell deepened he again became aware of how acute his senses had become. In the deep peace-state it was said one could hear the fall of a single leaf—

Abruptly a sound that was not in harmony with the night reached Chin-Lu's ears. It was the scrape of a hard-soled boot scuffing in sand. Someone who was not Indian watched over their camp. Slowly he opened his eyes and glanced about without moving his head or making a sound. A dozen strides away a shadow detached itself from a cluster of boulders. Somehow the shadow seemed familiar. Then Chin-Lu realized with a start the shadow was the thin and angular form of the man called Grits, who had attempted to take him prisoner!

Chin-Lu sat unmoving as the shadow figure disappeared from view, then silently got to his feet to follow. Such a man was always a threat, and he was not the type with enough courage to travel alone. Chin-Lu had covered barely fifty strides when he heard the muffled creak of saddle leather and the faint sound of horses' hooves moving away slowly. For a moment he thought of returning to the Indian camp to sound an alarm. Yet if there was no danger, there was no need to frighten Little Fern. He increased his pace to a trot but his passing left no sound.

For perhaps two miles he ran steadily, a whisper flitting across the grasslands. Then he slowed his pace as the murmur of voices reached his ears. Cautiously, one step at a time, Chin-Lu drew nearer the camp the thin man had led him to. Soon he was close enough to make out individual voices. He recognized the words of the man called Gaither, who had driven the wagon, and the voice of the one named Monk. The others were strangers to him.

Chin-Lu dropped to his belly in the tall grass and began working his way soundlessly toward the camp. There were about a dozen men in the group around a small campfire. They were a tough-looking bunch, heavily armed, and passing around bottles of whiskey.

"They's there, Gaither. Curly, you done called it on the nose—a band just a-sittin' at Cactus Springs. I make it six braves, an ol' man and a young squaw. And boy, she is some looker!" Grits cackled evilly and massaged his crotch.

A large bald man bobbed his head. "Told ya, Ed. Lessee, now—eight scalps gonna fetch us over three hunnerd. And we get to play with that squaw first." The bald one, Curly, rubbed his hands in glee. "Best of all, this feller in Colorado pays a hunnerd apiece for the tits off a young Injun woman," he continued. "Makes tobacco pouches outta 'em. Yes, sir, boys, we done hit us a gold mine."

Chin-Lu tensed at the bald one's words. His skin crawled at the mental image of what they planned to do to Little Fern. *But first*, he thought grimly, *they have to reach the Indian camp.*

The group began to lay its plans. Soon the moon would be high overhead. The raiders would strike then, while the Cheyenne camp still slept. There would be enough moonlight so that the men could make sure no Indian escaped. They would surround the camp, and charge at a signal. They were confident it would be over in a moment.

Chin-Lu glanced at the moon. With a sinking heart he realized there was not enough time to return and warn the others. He would have to stop this outrage himself before it could begin. He closed his ears to the talk of what the men would do to Little Fern and concentrated on the nearby terrain. The grass was tall enough to conceal a man on foot, if he kept low and was careful. He knew also that the white man tended always to follow a trail, where the going would be easier. A distant trail led toward Cactus Springs from the raiders' camp. Two hundred yards down that trail, they would pass along a shallow creek and between a jumble of boulders on one side and a heavy brush thicket on the other. It would be impossible for them to ride more than two abreast.

His decision made, Chin-Lu backed away silently from

the camp and turned toward the cluster of boulders in the near distance.

He climbed partway up the pile of rocks and found the spot he wanted. He glanced toward the sky. They would be coming soon. Chin-Lu waited, relaxed and calm. He had no firearms. But if his plan worked, he would not need them. If it did not, the sounds of the shots that took his life would alert the Cheyenne to danger. It would be a small price to pay for Little Fern's escape.

Chin-Lu saw the dark shapes of the horsemen as they neared the shallow creek. As he had suspected, they followed the well-defined trail rather than picking their way through the moonlight over unfamiliar ground.

The two raiders who led the group were only a few strides from Chin-Lu when the big one with the bald head turned in the saddle. His words came clearly through the night. "Hush up the yammerin', boys, them Injuns might be light sleepers. Keep quiet till we're all set."

The bald man turned back to study the trail ahead as he and Grits came alongside the rocks. Chin-Lu drew a long, slow breath, then launched himself in a feet-first dive from the boulder.

His booted heel cracked solidly into the neck of the bald one. The impact knocked the big man from the saddle. Chin-Lu dropped onto the man's back, slapping with his forearms to break his fall, then quickly rolled aside to escape the flashing hooves of panicked horses. The frightened animals whirled and kicked, clogging the narrow passage with their lunging, struggling bodies as they tried to turn around and escape the strange form among them.

Startled cries and curses came from the other riders, who were fighting to control mounts. Chin-Lu sprang forward as Grits tried to aim his rifle. The Chinese slapped the rifle barrel aside as fire flashed from the muzzle of the weapon. His fingers closed on a thin wrist. He yanked the lanky man from the saddle and, stepping in close to the lunging horse, whirled Grits to the ground. The edge of Chin-Lu's hand ripped into the bridge of Grits's nose, shattering bones as it sliced into the man's brain.

The bald one staggered groggily to his feet, one hand grabbing at his holster. He never got the handgun clear. Chin-Lu snapped a kick that landed solidly in Curly's groin.

The big man folded and fell forward with a soundless cry. Chin-Lu jumped high in the air, tucked his feet back, and landed with both knees slamming into Curly's ribs. The ribs crushed beneath his kneecaps. He leaned forward, grabbed the big man's chin, and placed the forearm of his free hand behind the man's neck. He gave a sudden, sharp yank. Curly died before his head struck the ground, his neck cleanly snapped.

Chin-Lu felt the crack of air alongside his ear as a bullet whipped past, the heavy blast of the handgun quickly following. He rolled clear and dived toward the cover of the thicket. The man with the pistol fired two wild shots and fought to control his dancing horse.

Chin-Lu's fingers closed on a jagged, flat rock the size of his palm. He waited as the gunman's horse whirled, then flicked his wrist in an underhand motion. The stone struck the horseman on the temple, sending his hat and pistol flying, and almost knocked him from his horse.

The rest of the riders panicked, wheeling horses back toward town. The man struck by the stone slumped over the saddle horn as his terrified horse raced to catch up with the others.

Chin-Lu stood for a moment in the moonlit trail then walked slowly to the two dead forms in the narrow trail.

The sound of hoofbeats came from behind him, but they were Indians, alerted by the sound of the shots.

The lead brave checked his horse for an instant, glancing at the two bodies in the trail, then at Chin-Lu. He shouted a command and the four Cheyenne took up the pursuit of the white men riding for the safety of Fort Laramie.

A moment later Paints-His-Horses rode up, carbine in hand and with his stiff right leg standing out from the horse.

Quietly, Chin-Lu told the chief what he had discovered and of the one-man ambush of the scalp hunters. Paints-His-Horses listened without interruption, then nodded.

"Wise-One-Above has sent a great warrior in a time of need," the chief said. "Come. Leave the chase to the young braves." Without further word, the old Cheyenne reined his horse toward the camp at Cactus Springs. Chin-Lu followed, his long, fluid stride keeping pace with the chief's pony.

Upon reaching camp, the aged chief swung from his pony and handed the hackamore reins to one of the two braves who had remained behind to guard Little Fern. Paints-

His-Horses waved off the warrior's question. "When the others return the story will be told," he said.

The four Cheyenne who had taken up the pursuit arrived as the first pale light of dawn streaked the eastern sky. They led the two horses that had been ridden by the dead men.

"Our ponies are not yet strong enough to catch the white man's horses—and they ran as if a demon were chasing them," the leader of the pursuit said as he dismounted.

Summoning Little Fern from the lodge and with the warriors gathered around, Paints-His-Horses recounted Chin-Lu's role in thwarting the planned raid. Chin-Lu respectfully kept his silence, though he believed the chief had given him more credit than was due.

One by one as the story ended, the warriors came forward and grasped Chin-Lu's forearm in the Cheyenne greeting of respect. Little Fern, though shaken by the tale of plotting and violence, looked into Chin-Lu's eyes with open warmth and gratitude. "It is not for the woman to speak at such times," she said, "but Little Fern's heart sings many songs in praise of a great warrior."

"Chin-Lu is not a great man," the Chinese replied quietly. "He is but a man. He did only what had to be done to keep Little Fern and the others safe."

Paints-His-Horses gestured for the two captured horses to be brought forward. One was a rangy bay, the other a small, powerfully built sorrel. The horses snorted nervously at the strange sights and smells of the Indian camp. Paints-His-Horses gathered the reins and solemnly handed them to Chin-Lu.

"Chin-Lu would give much honor if he would accept these ponies as a gift. They shall be the symbol of great friendship. The saving of the Cheyenne at the place called Cactus Springs is a story that will be told in many camps."

Chin-Lu accepted the reins with a gracious nod. "Chin-Lu accepts, because when he rides these horses, he shall remember his friends." He declined the offer of the rifles and pistols recovered from the bodies. "Chin-Lu has no use for firearms," he said. "He is unskilled in their use. He asks Paints-His-Horses to give them to the fine warriors guarding Little Fern."

The Cheyenne chief nodded in satisfaction. "It shall be

done." Then, to Chin-Lu's astonishment, the old man extended his hand as the braves had done. Over the Cheyenne grasp of salute, Paints-His-Horses said, "Though soon Chin-Lu will ride from this band, the hearts of the Cheyenne ride with the warrior of China."

Abruptly, the old man began issuing orders to break camp. "It is near the time of morning travel. Let us put this place behind us, in case the whites return."

The sun had barely cleared the horizon as the small band moved away from Cactus Springs. Chin-Lu found himself accorded the place of honor at the side of the great chief. They rode for a while in silence.

"Chin-Lu does not understand why a man would pay for the scalp—the death—of another human being," the Chinese said.

Paints-His-Horses sighed deeply. Chin-Lu thought he heard a tinge of pain in the slow exhalation. "It is a bad thing," Paints-His-Horses said. "But among both tribes, white and red, are bad men—just as there are men of good. All must try to keep this thought in their minds and hearts, and with the help of Wise-One-Above, be able to recognize the difference."

The next morning Chin-Lu rose in the small hours, a heaviness in his heart. The rest of the camp still slept as he gathered his small bundle of belongings and rolled it into his blankets. He had decided not to wait until dawn, for the pain of saying farewell to Little Fern would then be too great. Still, he had one last thing to do before heading down the faint trail the chief had pointed out to him the evening before.

Little Fern awoke in the hour before dawn, a strange dream clouding her mind. Her father already was awake. Paints-His-Horses sat on his blankets, looking tenderly at his daughter.

"Father," she said quietly, "Little Fern has need of your wisdom. In the night-visions came something she does not understand."

"If something troubles Little Fern she should speak," the old chief said.

"A shadow-man came to her in her sleep. The form was not clear, but as seen through a fog. It spoke in the white man's tongue, of which Little Fern knows but few words. Yet she seemed to understand." Little Fern shook her head in confusion, setting the strands of her long hair into motion.

"This sometimes happens in dreams, Little Fern. It is no cause for alarm," her father said, his voice soft and reassuring. "What did the shadow-man say to Little Fern?"

The girl's smooth brow creased as she tried to remember exactly. "The shadow-man said his spirit will protect Little Fern from harm. That the spirit was in the stone of green." Little Fern stirred beneath the warm robe that covered her and thrust a hand under the soft bundle that cradled her head. Her fingers touched a strange object.

She pulled the object from beneath her head and gasped in astonishment. It was a strange green stone, shaped like a half-moon, suspended from a chain of yellow metal. "It—it is the stone—the stone of which the dream man spoke," she said, her voice quavering. She held the strange stone up for her father to see.

Slowly, Paints-His-Horses rose to his feet and crossed the lodge to where his daughter sat. He peered closely at the stone. "It is as the dream man said," the old man said reassuringly. He reached out a weathered hand, took the necklace, and draped it over his daughter's neck. The green stone lay between her breasts. "It is a sign from the dream man. Wear it, daughter. It carries strong medicine from the dream man, to protect Little Fern from harm."

Ted Henderson stared in revulsion at the carnage strewn about the smoldering remains of the Overland Stage and the mutilated bodies of those who had ridden the ill-fated coach.

Only six hours before, the five bodies had been living, breathing human beings, departing the rails' end stage terminal where it intersected the Bozeman Trail. Ted had to force himself to examine the bodies. Even at the height of the Indian wars he had seldom seen such wanton savagery.

The attack had been swift and brutal, the coach and those aboard it riddled by gunshots and arrows. He felt a special pang of loss at the deaths of the elderly couple. They had spoken with him briefly of the planned reunion with their son and daughter-in-law at Fort Laramie. At least, he thought bitterly, the woman had been old—or her death would have been much more agonizing instead of mercifully swift.

He knelt to study the tracks that led away from the

scene. Seeing one particular set of hoofprints he swore bitterly. He would have known them anywhere. At the sound of hoofbeats and an approaching cloud of dust, Ted cocked his rifle, then lowered the weapon as he recognized members of the Third Regiment.

Major David Wills waved his patrol to a halt, surveyed the wreckage, then dismounted. "My God," he muttered, his face ashen. "We saw the smoke. . . ." His voice trailed away.

Ted nodded grimly. "So did I. Unless I've gone completely stale at reading sign, this was the work of Long Walker himself. And they hit the stage less than an hour after a patrol from Halleck had passed on this very road."

Wills turned to a trooper. "Form up a burial detail," he said. "Four men. The rest of you, check your weapons. We're going after the savages that did this. Colonel, are you coming?"

"I'd like nothing better—especially since one of those murdering bastards is riding my horse. They stole the dun in a raid on the railroad herd. But I've got big problems back at railhead." Ted touched his hat brim in salute to the young major. "David," he said, "Long Walker is deadly. Don't ride into any traps." He gathered the reins of Hellbender and toed the stirrup. "What's the latest report from Abel and the scouts?"

"Not good, sir," Wills replied. "Several small bands of young Cheyenne and Arapaho warriors have been spotted moving toward the east. Colonel Hubbard believes they're headed toward Long Walker's band."

Ted nodded grimly as he reined the sorrel back toward railhead, little more than an hour's ride distant.

When he arrived, he realized his own black mood was reflected in the faces of the sweat-soaked railroad workers he saw as he searched for Jack Casement. At rails' end he reined in at Kevin O'Reilly's side. The big Irishman raised an eyebrow in a silent question. Ted shook his head.

"Damn!" Kevin said sharply. "I'd like to get my hands on that blue-eyed half-breed."

"So would a lot of us," Ted said bitterly. "What's the situation here?"

"The men are surly," Kevin replied. "Two days past payday and still no coin. Dan Casement's headed back to Julesburg to see what the holdup is. General Jack's on the telegraph right now trying to get an answer. If these boys don't get paid soon, Ted, we'll have trouble. Big trouble, I'm afraid." The usually jocular Kevin had been forced to replace his usual songs and jokes with threats and irate shouts to get the crews to work.

Ted headed back toward the supply train. He found Jack Casement as the wiry little engineer stepped from the telegraph car.

"What's the word, Jack?" Ted asked.

Casement angrily yanked a cigar from his pocket and ripped the end off with his teeth. He spat the bit of tobacco onto the rail bed. "Payroll's on its way, but it'll be a couple more days," he grumbled. "Bosses back East said the government wasn't paying for the last hundred miles—something about a survey and mileage question. But some outfit bought up some stock, enough cash to meet a payroll."

Ted felt his brows narrow. "Who bought it?"

"Company I never heard of. Southern Overland. Out of New York."

Ted made a mental note of the name. It might be a perfectly legitimate transaction. If so, Taylor Elkins would know. If not, Elkins might want to find out more about the business deal.

Jack Casement swung aboard his horse and together the two men rode toward the track crew. Casement suddenly pulled his horse to a stop, glaring at a shovel man who was staring at a piece of paper he held in his hand.

"What the hell's that?" Casement demanded.

The shovel man looked up, startled. "Don't reckon as I know, General Jack," he said. "Man come by little bit ago and handed it to me. Can't read much, myself."

Casement snatched the paper from the man's hand, glared at it, and silently handed the flyer to Ted.

COMING TODAY!
Games of Chance!
Honest Tables!

The lettering was printed in bold block letters in a strong hand.

Liquor And Other
Gentlemanly Entertainments!

For The Enjoyment Of
Workers On the Great Road!

The signature on the paper was "Kilgore Yantis."

Ted groaned aloud, handing the paper back to Casement, who crumpled the flyer and hurled it to the ground.

"I thought we were finished with that bloodsucker!" Casement shouted. "It was bad enough with his crooked tables and fancy women and bad whiskey in Julesburg! By God, Ted, I'll bet he's already setting up shop!"

Casement spurred his black into a long lope. Ted followed, worry and anger growing at each step. The last thing they needed was a rolling saloon and whorehouse at rails' end.

Jack Casement was right. They found tents going up a half-mile past end of track. Directing the unloading of a half-dozen wagons was a thin, well-groomed man in a silk suit. Kilgore Yantis turned as Casement slid his horse to a stop and dismounted, his face twisted angrily above his bristling beard.

"Damn you, Yantis!" Casement stormed. "What the hell are you doing here?"

Yantis smiled smugly. "Just practicing the right of all Americans to do business, sir," he said in a mocking voice. "Your boys seemed to have had a good time with us in Julesburg, and it must get awfully lonely out here on these vast plains."

Casement shoved his face close to Yantis. "You take your crooked card games and whores back where they belong, Yantis! You're not going to pull this on railroad property! Clear out now!"

Yantis merely smiled. "Now, General Jack," he said, "you can't throw me off this land. The railroad doesn't own it." He pointed a manicured finger across the new grade along which rails would soon be laid. "I checked the survey. The railroad's deeded section is over there. I'm on public domain land—every other section along the track is still unclaimed country, sir."

Casement trembled in rage. For a moment Ted was sure the fiery little engineer was going to slug the bigger man. Secretly Ted hoped he would. Then Casement's shoulders slumped. "All right, Yantis," he said sharply, "if you're on public land I can't stop you. But by God, if you cause one minute's trouble for the Union Pacific, I'll be on you like a rooster on a grasshopper!"

Casement spun away and remounted. Ted reined Hellbender alongside.

"Welcome to Yantis-town, gentlemen!" came the sarcastic call from behind them.

"Yantis-town, my butt," Casement muttered. "Hell on Wheels is more like it."

"Anything we can do about it, Jack?" Ted asked.

"Not legally," Casement said bleakly. "That's the rub. As long as his bunch is on public land, I can't run them off. Dammit, we're really going to have our hands full now. I thought after Julesburg we'd left this sort of trash behind. I guess I've underestimated the drawing power of a big payroll where lice like Yantis are concerned."

News of the arrival of the rolling tent city swept the ranks of the railroad men like a prairie fire. Those who had money eagerly awaited the end of the day's labors. Those who had none and could not borrow any grumbled louder about the delayed payroll.

The arrival of Hell on Wheels brought a sneer of satisfaction to Bear Fallon's lips. For one reason, those who followed him would have money when the tents opened for business. That could recruit a few more men to his ranks. For another, the woman he had met at Julesburg would no doubt be in Yantis's group. Pittsburgh Rose was not one to stay behind when money was to be made.

And finally, if the payroll did not come through quickly, the Union Pacific would have a mob of mad workers on its hands.

Judy Hubbard listened with mounting concern to the rumblings of the growing crowd in the street outside the Laramie Hotel. Two teamsters—Monk Farler and Ed Gaither— and their cronies had been doing a lot of mean talk around town. It sounded like they had found some eager ears, too.

The two men and their group of hooligans had come galloping back into Laramie, scared and angry. Judy had not believed their tale of being ambushed by "two dozen damn heathens," as Gaither phrased it. But there were plenty of Indian-haters around Laramie, people who believed the only good Indian was a dead Indian.

Judy edged closer to the window. Her fears were confirmed. The crowd was growing rapidly, and it was turning unruly. Even through the glass she could clearly hear Ed Gaither's words.

"I tell you, boys, ain't but one thing to do! We gotta teach them redskins a lesson they won't never forgit! They jumped us outta the dark and plumb hacked up pore ol' Curly and my buddy Grits!"

An angry murmur swept the crowd. Judy wrinkled her brow as she recognized many of those in the mob. Some had reason to seek revenge on Indians, having lost property or relatives at the red man's hands during the previous Indian wars. But most were just idlers with nothing to do but drink and brawl.

There's going to be a massacre if someone doesn't stop this, she thought. *And no matter which side wins, we'll have a full-scale Indian war on our hands.*

As if in reply to her thoughts, she heard an authoritative voice raised above the crowd. "All right, what the devil's going on here?" The blocky form of Sergeant Major Albert Jonas was standing on the slightly elevated boardwalk at the edge of the street. Jonas carried a carbine in the crook of his arm.

Judy glanced around. There were no other soldiers in sight. She knew Abel and Major Wills were still out on patrol. And unless she badly misread the mob's intentions, Albert Jonas was going to need some help.

Automatically, Judy glanced at Albert's wife. A worried expression crossed the pleasant features of Sally Jonas. Judy walked quickly to Sally's side and placed a hand on her arm. "Don't worry, Sally," she said. "Albert knows what he's doing." She hoped she sounded more confident than she felt. One wrong move and Albert could be the mob's first victim. Judy reached behind the low counter and got the loaded shotgun she kept there.

"You boys are barkin' up the wrong tree," she heard Albert yell as she stepped outside. "The Cheyenne haven't caused any trouble and aren't likely to—unless someone else starts it!"

"What makes you such an authority on Injuns, boy?" a voice from the crowd challenged.

"In the first place," Jonas said evenly, "I've fought 'em a bunch. I know the Cheyenne. They gave their word for peace. And the Cheyenne don't ambush peaceable white parties at night."

"You a-callin' me a liar, you wooly-headed nigger?" demanded Ed Gaither, who was in the front line of the mob facing Jonas.

"I'm sayin' you may've been attacked, but not by Cheyenne," Jonas said. "And I'm a little choosy, Gaither, about who calls me a nigger!" The muzzle of Albert's rifle moved slightly, to point directly at Gaither's middle. "I'll not stand for any lynch mob goin' out after Cheyenne scalps," Jonas said. "I'll have no bunch of rowdies from Fort Laramie startin' an all-out Indian war—and that's exactly what would happen!"

"By God, boys," Gaither called, "I don't reckon I've ever seen no nigger Injun-lover before! Thought them redskins had more pride than that!"

A ripple of nervous laughter trickled through the gathering.

"I'll play like I didn't hear that for now, Gaither," Jonas said in a deadly calm voice. "I'll square my accounts with you later." He searched the ranks of the mob with his gaze, finally settling on one man at the edge of the front line. "Jonesy," he called, "you've traded with the Cheyenne. You ever know them to lie or cheat? Or cut down on a bunch of horsemen for no reason? And at night, to boot?"

The man called Jonesy shook his head, scuffing a toe in the dirt.

"Mark Hass!" Albert said with a sad shake of his head at another member of the group, "I never expected to see you in any mob of scalp hunters. You goin' to believe some wild story from a half-drunk teamster, or the word of Yellow Crow, a Cheyenne you've ridden with? You used to be a decent scout and a fair soldier until you took to the bottle. Use your head, man!"

Albert's gaze swept the mob in contempt, then returned to the former soldier. "Mark, you and I both know a handful of Cheyenne would cut this bunch to pieces and not even break into a sweat. Go home. You got a wife and a kid to think about. You want your kid growin' up knowin' his Pa was a sneak and a killer? You want your wife and kid dead in an Indian war?"

Judy could sense the determination of the mob wavering before Albert's steady gaze and the muzzle of his Spencer repeater.

"What you want us to do, Albert?" a voice called out. "Let them redskins get away with murder?"

Albert slowly shook his head. "I say we ask them."

A hoot of derision came from a round, bearded man in the front row. Judy recognized him as the teamster named Monk. "You gonna believe some damn lyin' redskin?"

"The Cheyenne don't lie," Jonas said. "And if it happened the way Gaither here claims, Yellow Crow will be the first to turn the guilty ones over to us."

Judy thought she detected a flash of panic in the face of the teamster Gaither. Odds were, she thought, he could not afford to have the truth known.

"You boys stop and think a minute," Jonas said. "Unless I don't remember so good, Gaither and Farler and Smith were brought in here by the Cheyenne for trespassing on their land. Could be they just want to get even—and get some of you fellows killed in the process."

Gaither, obviously feeling his control of the crowd was slipping, snarled, "We made up our minds, nigger! Now there's a bunch of us and just one of your black self. There's no way you could stop us if we decided to take you!"

Jonas remained calm. "There's some truth to that," he said. "Only question is, how many of you wouldn't make it past me? And you'd be the first to go, Gaither!"

"Come on, you cowards!" Monk yelled. "They's just one of 'im!"

At the edge of the throng near Judy, a raggedly dressed man reached toward the belt of his trousers.

"There's two!" Judy called out.

For an instant the crowd froze, startled at the sound of a woman's voice. To a man they turned, their eyes widening at the sight of the big bores of the sawed-off ten-gauge Greener in the blond woman's delicate hands. Judy shifted the muzzles toward the man who had reached toward his belt.

"You better be scratching yourself, mister," she said, her words clear in the stunned silence. "If you come out of there with a pistol in your hand, I'll pull this trigger!"

There was a sudden flurry of movement as men standing near the ragged one scrambled to get clear. A double load of buckshot from a Greener would cut a wide chunk from a crowd. Slowly, the red-faced drifter removed his hand, its empty fingers spread.

"You ain't gonna use that thing, ma'am," Gaither whined.

"Willing to bet your life on it, Mr. Gaither?" Judy let the silence hang heavy for a moment. "Now clear out, all of you! I'm getting nervous, and this thing's got hair triggers!"

A man at the back of the crowd began edging away from the rest. It was the crack in the dam. One by one, and then in groups, the mob began to dissolve.

"Gaither—you and Monk," Jonas yelled. "You two stay. I want to have a little man-to-man talk with you. Shuck out of those weapons you're carrying."

Gaither glanced about in panic as he saw his crowd disperse, leaving him and Monk alone to face the big black man with the carbine and the woman with the shotgun. For a tense moment, Judy thought the bearded man was going to reach for his own handgun tucked in his waistband.

"Mr. Gaither," she said calmly, "I think you should try to convince your friend here that you would like to live to see the sun rise."

"Come on, Monk," Gaither pleaded. "That gal means business. Do like the man says." Gaither dropped the rifle that had been in his hand, then gingerly slipped his revolver from the holster and tossed it aside. Grudgingly, Monk followed suit.

The portly Monk glowered first at Albert, then at Judy. "I'll get you for this, nigger—and you, too, you snippy bitch!"

Jonas stepped from the boardwalk and limped the three strides to the pair of teamsters. Without a word, he suddenly slammed the end of his rifle barrel into the pit of Monk's stomach. Monk gasped and went down, doubled over in agony. Jonas shifted the carbine to his left hand.

Gaither tried to step back, both hands held in front, pleading. "I—never—" The words ended in a solid *thump* as Albert's hamlike fist slammed into Gaither's mouth. The teamster tumbled back as though kicked by a mule and lay still in the street.

"That's for callin' me a nigger," Jonas said to the half-conscious Monk, who was holding his stomach and groaning. "I may be one, but I'm particular about who says it."

The sergeant major turned to Judy as she gently lowered the hammers of the shotgun.

"Judy Hubbard, you got more nerve than any five troopers I know," he said. "It was gettin' a mite touchy until you showed up with that scatter-gun. Reckon this old soldier owes you one."

Judy shifted the heavy shotgun to her left hand and placed her right on Albert's massive arm. "I'm just glad no one got hurt," she said, "except those two—they deserved that. What will you do with them, Albert?"

"Put them in the stockade for now. I intend to ask the Cheyenne what happened, like I said. If this pair was lyin', they'll be guests of Fort Laramie for quite a spell. Then we'll just apply a little push with a cavalry boot in the backside and invite them to leave town," he replied.

At the sound of rapidly approaching footsteps, Judy moved aside. Sally Jones swept to her husband's side. She held a revolver in one light-brown fist. After a brief embrace, she looked her husband straight in the eye. "You dumb nigger," she said fondly, "if you don't watch yourself you're never gonna get kids. I swear you gonna get yourself dead. You ever go up against a mob like that again, Albert Jonas, you gotta answer to *me*!"

Jonas grinned as he winked over Sally's shoulder at Judy. "Yes, ma'am," he said solemnly. "I'll sure watch my step from now on."

Judy left Albert and Sally and made her way back to the hotel, where she replaced the shotgun below the counter. She breathed a deep sigh of relief, then gradually became aware of someone watching her. She turned to face a wide-eyed Victoria Coulter.

Judy nodded calmly to the auburn-haired woman and thought Victoria might be a bit short of beautiful, but she was certainly attractive. The green eyes were expressive, their deep color a counterpoint to the rich shoulder-length hair. Her figure was full without being fleshy. Her shoulders were slightly more square than most women's.

Victoria's eyes were filled with awe as she looked at the blond wife of the post commander. "Judy, I've never seen anything like that. Where do you find such courage?" she asked incredulously.

"Albert Jonas was in trouble," Judy said with a shrug. "Someone had to help out. Besides, I don't think I was in any real danger. Few of those men would fire at a woman— especially when that woman is holding a ten-gauge Greener."

"Weren't you frightened?"

"Rather thoroughly, Victoria. I'm still a bit shaky, in fact. Join me for a sherry?"

Victoria shook her head. "I—had planned to go for a walk."

"I'd advise against it unless you have an escort. The streets of Laramie aren't all that safe for a woman alone anymore. Some of the rowdies around here wouldn't hesitate to grab you and drag you into an alley somewhere."

An involuntary shudder rippled through Victoria's body.

Judy stepped from behind the counter and placed a hand on the woman's shoulder. "Major Wills will be back from patrol soon," Judy said softly. "David would be delighted to escort you. Or perhaps one of the other men, a soldier or one of our regular customers here."

"No. I think I'll just go back to my room and read. Oh, Judy, I wish I had your strength," Victoria suddenly cried.

"The real strength comes from facing inner fears, not those from outside," Judy said softly. "Anyone can hold a gun."

Victoria slowly made her way to the staircase leading to the hotel's second-floor rooms. Judy felt sympathy for the other woman.

Victoria Coulter was a gentle, well-educated person who had lost her husband in an ambush at Fort Kearny during the recent Indian wars. After Colonel Coulter's death, Abel Hubbard had arrived on the scene with his crack troops that routed the Indians in the crucial battle that paved the way for the peace treaties. In the process Abel had saved Victoria's life.

Judy sighed. She suspected Victoria secretly loved Abel.

Once Judy would have flown into a jealous rage at the thought of another woman being interested in her husband. But after almost losing Abel twice, she had matured. She realized Victoria was a troubled, confused person, not a threat to her own marriage.

After the rescue at Fort Kearny, Victoria had accompanied Abel to Fort Laramie, attempting to sort out her life. She did not know whether to go back East, to stay on the frontier, or to continue west to the more refined regions of California.

Judy moved through the door separating the bar from the restaurant proper and ordered a small sherry. She sipped at the mild wine, her mind still on Victoria. Judy could sympathize with the woman's confused state since she had been there herself once.

She sighed. Victoria's future was apparent to all but Victoria herself. Major David Wills was obviously deeply in love with the widow though she was a few years his senior. Yet Victoria seemed to view David only as a friend. Her infatuation with Abel had blinded her to all other men. It was a shame, Judy thought, because Major Wills was a fine young man—and his lack of success in his courtship of Victoria was beginning to take its toll on him.

Finishing her sherry, Judy walked to the dining room. Silently she vowed not to interfere in Victoria Coulter's life. The woman would have to make her own decisions.

In the meantime Judy had other chores. The hotel's business had been booming. And as the railroad neared Fort Laramie, the community that had grown up around it would attract even more rough and unsavory types. It was even possible the Indian wars would break out once again.

Out there somewhere, Judy knew, the twin ribbons of metal were nearing the end of the Nebraska plains, coming ever closer to Wyoming.

Six

Taylor Elkins carefully folded the message from Ted Henderson and added it to the thick stack of documents in the bottom drawer of his desk. He locked the drawer, then stood and strode to the open window. There was little air moving in Washington City on the steamy summer afternoon.

Taylor wiped his brow with a handkerchief. For a moment he longed for the cool of the high country, where a man could escape any severe heat merely by stepping into the shade of a comforting pine. His stay in Wyoming had been relatively brief, but somehow the West had a way of grabbing a man.

At Vi's greeting he turned. It was remarkable how she could still look so cool and fresh despite the heat. Her white dress was unwrinkled. Only a single damp curl at the nape of her neck hinted at the weather. He crossed to her and took her in his arms.

"Reverend Miller asked about you, Taylor," Vi said. "I told him newsmen didn't always get Sundays off like most people. Would you care for some tea?"

Taylor kissed her on the forehead and followed as she headed toward the kitchen. The servants had the day off, which made Sundays special for the Elkins couple, since they had the whole house to themselves.

"Everyone at church was talking about how rapidly the railroad is progressing," Vi said as she set the teakettle on the stove. "Your readers are most impressed. Ted must be doing a good job out there."

"I would say so," Taylor replied. "They were averaging over a mile and a quarter of track a day until the Indian troubles started, and even now they haven't lost too much of that pace. The rails should be entering Wyoming by this fall.

That little table of railroad progress on page one of the *Globe* may be the most-read feature in the paper."

Vi led Taylor into the drawing room, where the heat would be less intense. She placed the silver tray on a low table in front of a divan and patted the cushion beside her.

"Taylor," she said, "I overheard something in church that was rather interesting. You know how Thelma Hutchings always likes to put on airs. I suppose she feels the need to impress people. Anyway, she said she and her husband were getting into the railroad business. I didn't hear the entire comment, but I'm almost sure she mentioned the Union Pacific."

Taylor's brows furrowed in thought. "That could be significant," he said. "Hutchings is mostly in the long-haul freight business. The railroad will be his biggest competitor." He did not add that he had a hunch Hutchings was a silent partner in a firm that had been quietly moving to acquire large blocks of railroad stock.

Ted had been right in his suspicions. On two occasions the Southern Overland company had come to the rescue of the money-troubled railroad with stock purchases and loans. Yet, the Southern Overland apparently had no business operation other than money. And its management and partnerships were proving hard to trace.

"Taylor?" Vi said, handing her husband his tea.

"Oh. Sorry, Vi. Just off woolgathering, I guess."

Vi put a hand on her husband's leg. "Don't you think you should take some time off, darling? This railroad thing has you all tied up in knots. You need a rest."

Taylor draped an arm around Vi's shoulders and tugged her close, kissing her gently on the neck. "You and an occasional Sunday are all the vacation I need, my dear," he said. "Besides, I can't waste any time now. I've gathered some pieces, and it's time to make them into a picture, like a puzzle."

He sighed and let his arm slip from Vi's shoulders. "I'm afraid I'll have to be out for a while this afternoon. I've a meeting with a man who could shed a little more light on the railroad situation."

Taylor placed a finger on her lips, silencing her protest. "It won't be for long. Lord knows I'd rather be with you, but can you forgive me for wasting a few hours of our rare time together?"

Vi stroked his clean-shaven cheek. "You've never wasted a minute in your life, Taylor Elkins. I know you wouldn't go unless it were absolutely necessary."

"Sometimes I wish you weren't quite so understanding," he said tenderly.

Taylor sipped his tea and stood. "If you will excuse me now, madame, I must see a man about a skunk. Or at least a stink." He tipped her chin up and kissed her. "Vi," he said solemnly, "while I'm gone, keep the doors locked."

He noted the alarm in her eyes and tried to reassure her. "Don't worry. It's probably just some crank, but I've gotten a couple of threatening notes. Apparently I'm getting close to something—I just wish I knew what. Every good newsman gets threatened several times during his career. Still, I'd like for you to be cautious when you're alone."

"Don't you tell me not to worry. It's a wife's God-given right to fret. I'll be careful, and I expect you to do the same," Vi said.

Outside the front door, Taylor waited until he heard the bolt slide home on the heavy oak door, then made his way to a small park a few blocks away. Finally he spotted a small, bespectacled man standing near a stone bench. The man glanced about nervously and seemed to grow even more agitated as the newsman drew near.

Taylor nodded a greeting, a nonchalant gesture as if he were acknowledging a stranger, then casually took a seat on the park bench. The thin man, a bookkeeper in one of Washington's bigger banks, fumbled nervously in a pocket of the dress jacket he wore, producing a sheet of plain paper.

"Here it is, Mr. Elkins," he said. "I copied it down from the ledger in a hurry. Hope you can read it." The small man glanced about furtively as Taylor took the paper. Taylor studied the scribbled notes for a few seconds, then reached in his pocket and produced a pair of bills. The bookkeeper thrust the currency deep into a pocket.

"Mr. Elkins, if the bank finds out what I did—"

"They won't," Taylor said calmly. "Thanks for your help."

The small man hurried from the scene. Watching him go, Taylor decided he was going to have to cultivate some new contacts at the bank. This one was entirely too scared to use again. He could turn into a liability too easily.

Taylor fought the impulse to study the notes on the spot. There would be time enough later. Walking casually he dallied in the small park for a time, watching children play. Satisfied that no one had followed either the little man or himself, he turned toward home.

Vi sighed with relief as she saw her husband turn onto the walk leading to their home. She swung the door wide as Taylor stepped onto the porch, mopping his brow with a handkerchief.

"Did everything go well, dear?" she asked.

"Everything's fine. Just give me a couple of minutes to see how well it really went," he said, "and I promise it will be back to Sunday afternoons as usual." At Vi's nod, Taylor went to his office, pulling the paper from his pocket as he sat behind the desk. He studied the nervous scrawls for a few minutes, then grunted in satisfaction. Another link. Now all he had to do was to find a chain it would fit.

He leaned back in his chair as Vi entered his cluttered office, carrying a decanter and a pair of wineglasses on a silver tray. She filled the glasses, handed one to Taylor, and then walked to the open window.

The afternoon sun streaming through the glass silhouetted her body. She had changed into a light green housedress, and Taylor could tell she wore little or nothing beneath it.

"All finished for the day, sir?" she asked with a knowing smile.

He grinned, trying his best to make his grin an evil leer. "With work, yes. But not with our Sunday."

Ted Henderson leaned against the side of the rail car for a moment, wanting nothing more than to climb into one of the bunks and sleep for a week. But Sundays were no time for rest. The construction gangs got the day off, but Indians did not observe the Sabbath. Besides, it was Sunday evening "roundup" time.

Ted glanced toward the tent city in the near distance, his expression sour. Hell on Wheels, as Jack Casement called it, had complicated Ted's already tough job. Twice the night before he and Kevin O'Reilly had been called to the portable town to put down disturbances before blood was spilled. Ted calculated last night's sleep at somewhere around three hours—about average for recent nights.

He rapped on the side of the car below Kevin's bunk. Through the open window he heard the groan of wood as Kevin heaved himself from his cot.

"Time again?" Kevin's voice was still slurred from his short nap. "God, what I wouldn't give for a full day's rest."

Moments later Kevin and several other supervisors had gathered, their handguns tucked in belts and with clubs the size of silver dollars clutched in their fists.

The Sunday night roundup was underway.

The group dispersed at the edge of Hell on Wheels. The routine was the same every Sunday and no instructions were needed. Several of the armed men spread out, prowling through tents where the women plied their trade. Soon the first of the bleary-eyed men inside were stumbling out, grousing at being rousted. Ted made his way to the big tent where Kilgore Yantis held court over various gaming tables.

The dim interior was heavy with stale smoke, sweaty bodies, and liquor. The odor assaulted Ted's nose as he stood quietly glaring about the tent.

Lanterns had been lit against the fading Sunday daylight. Railroad men crowded the bar, laughing and joking with the girls who hustled drinks. The gaming tables also were crowded. Men who still had money jockeyed for spots at the chemin de fer and blackjack tables.

At the far end of the tent, Yantis presided over a poker game. Ted thought wryly that it would take a head spiker only a half-hour to lose his month's pay. He shouldered his way through the crowd to the poker game.

Yantis had a considerable pile of money before him on the table, and a large amount of coin and currency in the middle of the table indicated some heavy betting was going on.

"Raise five," Yantis said expressionlessly. Ted saw that Yantis had a pair of eights showing in the seven-card stud hand. The gambler tossed a bill onto the table. At Yantis's left a bearded spiker studied his last card, which he held in his hand. Pain showed in the railroad man's eyes. There was no money before him on the table, only a pair of queens among the four up cards.

"I'm light," the spiker said.

Yantis leaned forward to rake in the pot. "If you can't call, you lose," he said calmly. Then the gambler straightened in surprise as Ted tossed a gold coin onto the stack.

"You're covered, Yantis, and raise five. Last raise, last hand. Looks like you'd best fold or call, gambler."

Yantis glared at Ted for a moment, then quietly tossed another five on the stack. "Call," he said.

The spiker's face brightened as he flipped his card on the table and turned over the two facedown cards. "Two pair, queens over sixes."

Yantis slipped one of the facedown cards from beneath the others and prepared to turn it over. He froze at the touch of a gun muzzle behind his ear. "Rest easy a minute, gambler," Ted said. He scooped the rest of the deck from beside Yantis's elbow and fanned them onto the center of the table. Two eights lay face up amid the undealt cards.

"I do believe we'll look at your own card now," Ted said in a calm, deadly voice. With his free hand he flipped it over. It was the eight of clubs, a mate to one in the fanned-out display.

"Why, you cheatin'—" the spiker started out of his chair in a rage.

"Sit down and shut up!" Ted snapped. "You play with snakes you deserve to get bit. Gather up that pot and head back to the bunk car—and don't forget to leave my ten on the table. I'll deal with this man."

An angry murmur rose from among the watchers who had been cleaned out earlier in the game. Ted raised his voice so that all might hear. "It appears Mr. Yantis has had the misfortune of being sold a faulty deck," he called out. "I'm sure he would be delighted to refund any and all losses"—Ted cocked the pistol nuzzled at Yantis's ear—"under the circumstances."

Ted nudged Yantis with the pistol barrel. It was not a gentle nudge. "I suggest, gambler, that you pay up what you stole from these men. And if I ever catch you with a loaded deck again, I'll burn this place to the ground. With you in it. Now hurry up. I'm tired and grouchy. When I get that way I twitchy—especially my trigger finger."

Yantis's features twisted in fear and anger. "I'll get you for this, Henderson," he said in a strangled voice.

"Any time you're ready."

The chill in Ted's words jolted Yantis into action. As the railroad men filed by to claim their refunds, Ted warned them, "Just because this man cheated you doesn't mean you can return the favor. Get back only what you lost. And remember what kind of games they run here."

Within a few minutes the refunds had been made. The glowering railroaders crowded around the poker table. "We oughta lynch this bastard!" someone yelled.

Ted pointed his big Dragoon in the direction of the speaker. "You'll do no such thing," he said. "Get on back to the train and sober up, the lot of you. We've got a lot of track to lay tomorrow."

Yantis glared at Ted as the group exited the tent. "You haven't heard the last of this, Henderson."

"I'd better have, Yantis," Ted said, then turned his back on the gambler and strode from the tent. Outside, the evening air still held the lingering heat of the day, but compared to the heavy smell inside the tent it seemed fresh and clean. He stood at the edge of the tent city and watched as the railroad workers filed past. Kevin stopped at Ted's side.

"Get them all?" Ted asked.

"Missing two by my count. Bear Fallon's one. The other's a back-iron man called Mike."

A passing worker, overhearing the conversation, stopped. "Fallon's with that high-priced whore called Pittsburgh Rose," he said. "Won't let nobody else near her. Ain't seen Mike."

"Forget Fallon," Ted said. "Let him stay where he wants. At least there we don't have to listen to him grousing. First day's work he misses, General Jack will have something to say to him." Ted sighed. "Okay. Let's see if we can locate Mike."

They found Mike in a greasewood clump a hundred yards outside Hell on Wheels. He had been stabbed to death.

"How many does this make, Kevin? Five, six?" Ted asked wearily.

Kevin shook his head. "I lost count, Ted. But it's too many. I'll send some of the boys back for him. Diggin' another grave will help them think, maybe." He kicked viciously at a stone underfoot. "You say the word, and some of us will clean that rat's nest out quicker'n a cow drops patties."

"The thought has occurred to me," Ted said, staring at the back-iron man's body. "Unfortunately, right now General Jack's got me on a tight legal rein. We'll just have to live with Hell on Wheels for a while. One day Jack Casement will get his fill of it—and that's the day I want to be around."

The next day the water carriers struggled through their usual harried Monday. Bad whiskey and ringing hangovers were not helped by the blistering sun and the jarring clang of maul on metal. Tongues parched by the poison of the night before clamored for water.

"Ye've had yer fun, me buckos," Kevin's mocking voice rang out over the groaning crews, "and now ye'll pay the price. I want a mile and a half of track today. And by all the saints I'll have it!"

Ted decided he would not bet against Kevin's reaching that goal. He reined his horse toward the northwest. He thought he had detected smoke in that direction, just after sunrise.

At midmorning Ted knelt and probed the ashes of the fire. They were still warm. A careful scout of the site confirmed his worst fears. It had been a meeting place. Some thirty unshod pony tracks approached from the west, joining about fifty that already had been in the temporary camp.

Ted swore softly. It seemed Long Walker was getting more and more reinforcements by the day. Ted mounted, slipping his carbine from its scabbard, and began following the tracks left by the combined Indian force. A mile from camp a dozen horses had turned south, toward the railroad's route. Ted reined his mount onto the trail of the twelve braves.

Soon Ted knew what the band had been up to: Every survey stake for miles had been pulled up. Grudgingly, he gave Long Walker credit. The blue-eyed half-breed knew the grading crews followed the stakes. Now the route of the rails would have to be marked once more. The delay could cost the railroad one lost day, possibly two.

Jack Casement would have to be informed as quickly as possible so the route could be restaked. Ted carefully studied the surrounding terrain, looking for signs of Indians or possible ambush sites. He saw nothing but was not reassured. He kneed his mount back toward rails' end.

He had covered only half the distance when he heard the faint sound of gunfire. Instantly he spurred his horse into a long lope.

The firing intensified as Ted pulled his blowing, lathered horse to a stop in a shallow draw a quarter of a mile from the forward grading crew's position. He ground-hitched the animal and clambered to the edge of the draw, rifle at the ready. The war cries of Sioux and Cheyenne sounded among the blasts of rifles and handguns.

Ted peered over the edge of the embankment, and his heart skidded. The grading crew were putting up a desperate fight against tremendous odds, but they were in danger of being overrun at any moment. Mounted Indians whirled their ponies in a circle around the supply wagon and the trapped men. In their midst was an Indian wearing the war bonnet of a Sioux chief—Long Walker! And the blue-eyed warrior was riding Ted's own horse, Buck!

A squad of infantry soldiers accompanying the armed graders had helped buy some time. Two railroad men were down, and a body in a blue uniform stretched unmoving beside the supply wagon. A few riderless ponies indicated that the besieged men had done some damage also.

Ted estimated that about sixty braves were on the attack— far too many for him to challenge alone. He glanced toward his horse, Hellbender. The animal stood with sides heaving. It would never stand up to a long ride for help. Frustration and helplessness swept over Ted. It appeared he would not be able to do anything but watch as Long Walker and his braves wiped out every railroad man and soldier below.

Suddenly the Indians broke off the attack. For a moment Ted could not figure out why. Then he saw the cloud of dust in the distance. Long Walker raised his rifle overhead and waved. The outer ranks of attackers turned their ponies and began racing away from the ambush—directly toward Ted!

Ted realized in an instant he was in grave danger. If the Indians kept their course, they would be on him in a flash. He sprinted to Hellbender and led the animal into a clump of scrub brush. Placing a hand on the horse's muzzle in the signal for quiet, Ted grimly raised his rifle. There was a time to hide and a time to fight. Unfortunately this was a time to hide. One man against a horde of braves would be suicidal. But he silently vowed if they spotted him and ran him down, at least some of them would pay a price. He held his breath as the braves raced toward him.

The lead Indians, intent on fleeing the approaching dust cloud, swept past Ted's hiding place. He breathed a silent sigh of relief as it became apparent the Indians would pass without noticing him. Then a shaft of fury pierced his body. Directly in front of Ted—no more than thirty yards away— rode Long Walker!

Instinctively, Ted raised his rifle. But common sense won out over his emotion. He did not squeeze the trigger, even though he knew he could not miss at such close range. The gunshot would have spelled Long Walker's death, but the Indians then would turn on Ted. With growing frustration he watched as the last of the braves quirted past, whooping and yelling. He cursed softly as the half-breed chief passed from view, urging Ted's own dun gelding to still more speed.

"Dammit, Buck," Ted muttered after the running horse, "you'll let anybody ride you!"

The dust cloud took shape as it neared the grading crew below, a wave of cavalrymen four abreast, handguns and carbines at the ready. The regimental flag of the Third Cavalry fluttered from a staff in the hands of one soldier. At the front of the line was Abel Hubbard.

Ted quickly mounted Hellbender and rode to the ambush site. Abel raised a hand in salute as he led his troops in pursuit of the fleeing Indians.

There was little Ted could do for the railroad men except keep a tally of the dead and injured. The two dead men would be buried at the site, their graves concealed so that Long Walker's bunch would be unable to return, dig up the bodies, and mutilate them. The seriously injured soldier from Fort Halleck was placed in the supply wagon for the trip back to railhead and the surgeon.

Ted scribbled in his small notebook as the grading crew chief recounted the events of the attack. "You did well," Ted said as the foreman concluded his report. "If your people and the infantry hadn't put up such a good fight, Long Walker would have had a major victory here. Will you be able to continue making grade?"

The shaken foreman nodded. "We'll put her down, sir. Just keep them rails a-chasin' us."

Ted mounted his exhausted horse to accompany the wagon and the injured soldier back to rails' end and to report the day's events to Jack Casement. "If Colonel Hubbard returns here, tell him I'd like to speak with him at railhead if he has time," he told the foreman.

The wounded soldier died a hundred yards from rails' end. He had been barely more than a boy.

Shortly before sundown a weary and dusty Abel Hubbard rode into rails' end at the head of his trail-worn company.

Ted greeted Abel with a handshake and a question.

"We never could catch up," Abel said disgustedly. "We've been on this patrol for eighteen days now, and our horses just were too tired."

Ted described his near meeting with Long Walker, and

admitted he was somewhat disgusted with himself for not taking the easy shot at the renegade.

Abel shook his head. "No soldier ever won a war by getting himself killed, Ted. You should know that better than anyone, it's what you hammered into my skull time after time."

Over coffee in Casement's office-living car, Abel recapped the chase. His company had been on patrol when they struck Indian sign headed toward the railroad. "We almost had them twice," he said. "But both times we were a little late. I don't have enough troops to protect this railroad the way it should be covered. I wish I could say reinforcements are coming, but I can't. I've asked for more people, but Washington's worried about balancing the postwar budget and won't come up with the funds for more seasoned troops."

"I understand, Abel," Jack Casement said. "Building a railroad scatters men along a lot of miles, from survey crews two hundred miles or more ahead to the supply trains behind. We appreciate your efforts, though, make no mistake about that."

The next few weeks ran together in a blur in Ted's life. An entire tie-cutting detail was wiped out on a remote stretch of a tributary of the South Platte River. Two survey crews were lost. The Overland Stage firm lost two employees and had coaches damaged in three separate incidents. And in the one assault that really spelled trouble, Long Walker's braves boldly attacked a lightly guarded army supply train. That raid netted the renegade's forces a fresh batch of new repeating rifles and plenty of ammunition.

Worse still, from Ted's point of view, was the frustration of being outguessed. Try as he might, he still could not seem to put himself in Long Walker's moccasins. When Ted expected a strike to the west of railhead, the Indians raided east. When all the signs pointed north, the strike came south.

He and the few troops Abel could spare from Fort Laramie or the commander at Fort Halleck sent had spent untold hours in the saddle chasing shadows. Between scouting forays and patrolling Hell on Wheels as best he could, Ted's working day averaged twenty hours. Although he was hardened to long hours and hard work, the heavy demands began to take their toll. He knew his temper was getting short, and that sometimes he was reacting with more vengeance than many situations merited. He also knew that his reflexes had slowed under the fatigue.

Adding to his aggravation was the fact he could find little time to tend to personal business. He had been trying for three days to finish a letter to Wilma.

He had just picked up a pen and the partially completed letter when the dreaded call came once more.

"Trouble at Hell on Wheels, Ted!" Kevin's voice sounded from the doorway.

Ted groaned aloud. He let the pen drop and heaved himself to his feet. "What is it this time? Some whore charging too much?"

Kevin's eyes were full of concern. "Much worse, I fear. It seems we're about to fight the Civil War all over again. The boys have been edgy of late—lots of baiting going on. The word is there's to be another showdown between North and South at the saloon tent."

Ted strapped his revolver around his waist. Kevin was armed and also carried a short, stout club. Together the two men set out for Hell on Wheels, a quarter-mile from rails' end.

"Any idea how the trouble started?" Ted asked.

Kevin snorted in disgust. "Simple little argument this afternoon over the Battle of Bull Run. A couple fellows discovered they were on opposite sides, and it built up from there. Also, a certain head spiker hasn't helped any, I hear. Bear Fallon's been baiting both sides."

Before they even reached the open flap of the tent, they could hear the angry words being exchanged. Near the door, a water carrier, a Confederate field cap pulled down defiantly over his eyes, was in a heated debate with a burly iron man about the relative fighting abilities of Generals Grant and Lee. Ted recognized the iron man as one of Fallon's gang of ruffians. He also realized that in the charged atmosphere of the saloon the dispute soon would degenerate to a discussion of the parentage of both generals.

Kevin went to a position flanking Ted. The drinkers had drifted to one side of the tent or the other and were hurling baleful glares and taunts back and forth in the stale air.

Suddenly a voice from the far side of the crowded tent began to sing.

We are a band of brothers, and native to the soil,
Fighting for our Liberty with treasure, blood and toil

The first verse of "The Bonnie Blue Flag," which had
been a patriotic song of the Confederacy, picked up considerable volume before the second line ended.

From the near side of the tent, voices were raised in an
attempt to drown out the Southerners.

Tramp, tramp, tramp, the boys are marching,
Cheer up, comrades, they will come

The chorus of the famed Northern marching song made
up in volume what it lacked in musical ability.

Ted lifted the handgun from its holster and cocked the
weapon, waiting for the baiting to stop and the brawl to
begin.

It turned out to be a short wait.

At the bar, one of the burly back-iron men suddenly
howled in rage and lunged at a nearby worker, reaching for
the man's throat. The crowds on each side of the tent surged
toward each other.

Ted's pistol shot blasted the room into silence. Men
headed for hand-to-hand combat froze at the blast. They
turned to stare at the smoking pistol.

"In case you boys haven't heard," Ted said, "the war's
been over for some time." He stared long and hard at the
square-jawed face of Bear Fallon. The hulking Irishman
clutched the neck of an empty whiskey bottle, his intent
plain. Fallon took a step toward Ted, his eyes glazed with
drink and fury. At the same time he cracked the bottle
against a table edge. The jagged edges of broken glass pointed
toward Ted.

"Put the bottle down like a good lad, Fallon, or I'll shoot
it out of your hand," Ted said grimly. "Half your belly will go
with it."

Fallon looked as if he wanted to defy Ted, but the bore
of the Dragoon was lined squarely on his belt buckle. "Put
down that cannon, scout, and I'll take you apart," Fallon
growled.

Ted returned the man's glare of hate. "If you couldn't do
it sober, you sure as hell can't do it half-drunk."

Fallon took another step in Ted's direction. Ted cocked

the handgun, the click of metal loud in the tense stillness. "Come on, Fallon," Ted said in a quiet, deadly tone. "Try it. I'd like nothing better than to drain some of that cheap whiskey out of you with a hunk of lead. Try me—please."

Suddenly Fallon realized through the fog of hatred and whiskey that the lean scout meant exactly what he said. With a weak show of defiance and a "We'll settle this later," the big man dropped the bottle.

"While I have your attention, Fallon," Ted said loudly, "I have a question for you. You've been stirring up this Yankee-Rebel brawl all day. Now tell us all—what side were you on in the war?"

Fallon stood for a moment, trembling with fury. Then he stalked from the tent.

A man standing near the canvas yelped in pain and grabbed at his wrist. Kevin's stick had cracked into the back of the man's hand. "No knives, boys!" Kevin called.

"No fists, either," Ted said. "I'm shutting this place down for the night, as of right now. If you idiots want to fight, go fight Indians or that rail bed! We may be short-handed, but I swear I'll kill the first man who makes a wrong move."

The once-angry faces before Ted suddenly became cautious. A man who was mad was dangerous, and Ted Henderson was thoroughly mad.

"The name of this road is the Union Pacific," Ted said in the deep silence, "and by God, we'll have union and peace on these tracks if I have to personally whip every single one of you. Now, clear out! Any man caught fighting for *any* reason over the next week is fined a month's pay."

The water carrier in the Rebel cap grinned sheepishly. "Reckon, fer a month's pay, I'll agree maybe ol' Gen'l Grant had a few smarts about 'im." He turned and extended a hand to the man he had been arguing with. "Want to say the same about Gen'l Lee? Before that feller off touches that cannon again?"

The iron man glanced toward the tent flap through which Fallon had passed. A grimace of disgust was on the laborer's lips. He studied the pistol in Ted's fist and the eyes of the man behind the gun. "Guess it won't hurt none, at that." The two shook hands. The simple act broke the tension, and the crowd began moving toward the exit of the tent.

"See here, now! You can't come in here and shut my business down like this!" a voice at Ted's side demanded.

Ted turned to the bartender. "I'll either shut you down or shut you up, dammit! The choice is yours!"

The bartender hesitated for a moment, then shrugged. "What the hell. A few dollars ain't worth gettin' shot over. You got the big pistol. Reckon that makes you the boss. Want a drink? Make you a special price on one just poured."

The weak joke was directed toward the wrong man. Ted's rage finally boiled over. He picked up a wooden chair and spun it toward the back of the bar. A dozen bottles of liquor smashed beneath the whirling chair. Slowly, the tension began to drain from Ted's body.

"You're lucky this time, mister," he said to the bartender. "The next time I hear of trouble like this, I'm walking in here with a big-bore shotgun and putting you completely out of business!"

The bartender swallowed hard. "Yes, sir, Mr. Henderson. I think you made your point."

Ted stalked from the tent and fell into step with Kevin, who had been waiting outside, encouraging a few stragglers. The two friends walked in silence for a dozen steps. Then Ted suddenly stopped and seized Kevin's arm.

"Kevin," he said earnestly, "I've just had a thought. That near civil war our friend Fallon tried to stir up reminded me of something. It just might be an answer to some of our Indian troubles. How would you like to be a soldier again?"

Kevin sighed in mock resignation. "When you get an idea, Colonel Henderson, it usually means more work for this ex-lieutenant. Where are you gonna get a battery of howitzers out here?"

Ted felt a fresh surge of energy as his enthusiasm for the plan grew. "I just realized something so obvious I feel stupid for not seeing it before. We've got at least two companies of infantry right here at our fingertips!"

"I haven't heard any bugles lately," Kevin said, intrigued.

"You saw back there how many ex-soldiers from both sides we have working on this railroad. Plus there are men who don't frequent Hell on Wheels too often. We've also got frontiersmen and farmers who know how to handle weapons. All we have to do is organize them into units, arm them to the teeth, and give them a little target practice! If Abel and the other cavalry troops can't be everywhere at once, why don't we build our own protection?"

Kevin slammed a fist into his palm in a burst of enthusiasm. "Damn me for a leprechaun! How could anything that obvious get by both of us this long? I'll bet one out of every two of these workers has seen action. If not against each other, at least in an Indian fight or three!"

"Right," Ted agreed. "And the next time Long Walker hits this railroad, he could be in for a rude shock. Come on, Kevin. Let's go wake up General Jack. He's already had his three hours sleep tonight."

Moments later, Jack Casement came awake in a hurry as Ted unfolded his plans. The wiry little engineer nodded in growing enthusiasm. "Ted, by God, you've hit on something! Give me a couple weeks and we'll have rifles, good ones, for every man in this outfit."

Casement suddenly stood, grabbed his hat, and headed for the door. "Help yourselves to the coffee, gents," he said in passing. "I'm going to wake up a telegraph operator! When Jack Casement doesn't sleep, by all the saints nobody else does either."

Meanwhile, not far away, Bear Fallon glared balefully at the partly empty bottle before him on a low table in the tent he shared with Pittsburgh Rose. The prostitute, her face puffy from the effects of long hours without sleep, tossed the light blanket back from her naked body.

"Come to bed, Bear," she pleaded. "It'll be daylight soon. Quit working yourself into a snit over it. Christ, the man had a pistol on you!"

Fallon took a long pull from the bottle and stared at the woman for a moment. He heaved himself from the low bench and stood, wavering slightly. "He won't always have that pistol, Rosie. And when I catch him without it, I'll grind that bastard Henderson into the dust," he said through clenched teeth. "I'll use the arms I rip off his pet Irish foreman to beat him into the ground! There won't be enough left of Henderson to use for fish bait!"

Rosie stretched her arms high over her head and arched her back. The motion tugged up her full breasts invitingly. She winked lewdly at the big Irishman standing by the bed. "You hush up about this Henderson fellow now, Bear," she said. "I got a problem I need some big strong man to help me with. I can't seem to put my knees together. And I know for a fact how good you are at fixin' that problem."

Later, as Bear Fallon snored at her side, Pittsburgh Rose

reached across the mountainous body and into the pocket of the pants Bear had thrown over the back of a chair. Her fingers clutched a handful of currency. She settled back, tucking the money beneath her pillow. She smiled in the darkness. *God,* she thought, *maybe I should have been an actress. But the pay for a night's work ain't near as good.*

A few hours later Bear awoke with the taste of bad whiskey coating his mouth. He reached for the water pitcher beside the bed and downed half its contents. He followed that with a substantial swig of whiskey, then leaned back against his pillow.

The water and alcohol gradually eased the pounding in his temples. He climbed from bed and dressed for the day's work. The dark shape of Rose's body on the bed helped cheer him. At the moment he had himself a gravy train. The Indian Long Walker was doing a fair enough job of hassling the railroad. The trackage rate had dropped a bunch of late. Fallon was getting paid well and regularly, taking credit for the delays caused by the Indians. If the folks back East were dumb enough to buy the story that Long Walker was on their payroll, too, so much the better. Fallon was on three payrolls—one from the Union Pacific, one from the Southern Overland, and on another the New York bosses thought was going to supply the Indians.

And when the day's work was over, he had Rosie. He would check his pockets later to see how much she had taken this time. He grinned. She did not know she was worth more—the best he'd ever had.

Fallon finished lacing a work shoe and took another drink from the water pitcher. The cool liquid gave him an idea.

He stepped into the growing dawn and made his way toward the meal car. A good breakfast would chase the rest of the fuzz from his brain. And he knew he need not fear any ribbing from the laborers about last night. All it took to shut them up was a mean look.

Maybe he was living like a pet hound, he decided, but finally he had one plan that would put Henderson down for good and another to knock the railroad's schedule into a deep ditch. In the meantime, he might as well toss out a few little nuisance tricks—just in case old Long Walker decided to ease the reins a bit.

*   *   *

Wilma Henderson glanced up at the sound of hoofbeats approaching at a slow trot. She wiped the perspiration from her face with a soggy bandanna, leaning against the garden hoe she had been using as Valdez Cabrillo rode up.

"All is well in the high pasture to the north, Miss Wilma," Valdez said, touching the brim of his sombrero in greeting. "But if we do not get rain soon, we must look elsewhere for grass or sell some stock." The aged vaquero glanced at the brassy sky. "I would not make a large wager on rain soon," he added solemnly.

Wilma knew what Valdez said was true. Still, the situation was not serious enough to trouble Ted.

She smiled as Wild Bill approached, a sawed-off hoe in his hands. The youngster was turning into a good helper. He had finished his daily chores, including the hated cleaning of the henhouse, with no complaints. Then without being asked, he had fetched his short-handled hoe to help out in the garden. He waved to Valdez as the man led his horse toward the corral.

A wisp of smoke drifted from the stovepipe of the ranch house despite the heat of the day. Wilma would not have traded places with Wind Flower. The garden was a hot place to work, but the kitchen would be even worse. The Navajo woman was busy putting up jars of jelly made from the wild berries she had gathered from the nearby hills and along the creek. They would be a tasty treat in the long winter months when no fresh fruits were available.

"Mom," Bill said, "if we don't get anything from the garden this year, will we go hungry?"

Wilma placed a reassuring hand on the boy's shoulder. "No, son," she said. "We have a well-stocked root cellar from last year's garden. But we need to save this one if we can. Otherwise we'll have to buy or trade for vegetables in the winter."

Bill nodded, then turned to weeding with a vengeance. Wilma watched her son work with quiet pride. The boy seemed to have inherited his father's drive and capacity for work, and the ever-busy Valdez was a good example as well.

"Mom," Bill called between swings of his hoe, "if we get through here, can I go with Valdez to tend the cows?"

"Of course, dear," Wilma said, turning back to her own work. Riding a pony was obviously more fun for a five-year-old than working in a garden.

Valdez Cabrillo walked to the end of a row and began loosening the sun-baked soil between plants with a spading fork.

"Valdez, you've already done a day's work," Wilma said. "You hired on to handle the stock, not tend the garden."

The Mexican merely smiled. "I am not too proud to work in such a manner. Around a ranch, one who would eat also must help provide his meals. A small amount of sweat has never been fatal to this old caballero."

The trio made good headway against the encroaching weeds. Valdez worked behind Wilma and Bill, breaking the soil they had just weeded.

Suddenly Wilma's heart leapt at a dry buzzing sound nearby. She glanced in Bill's direction. Coiled just beyond the child was a huge rattlesnake, poised to strike!

Before she could cry a warning, Valdez said firmly, "Do not move, Bill. Stand very still!"

The boy had turned at the warning sound of the rattler. Wilma could see his small body tense with fear as the child battled instincts that told him to run. But as Valdez ordered, Bill stood unmoving. Wilma was too far away to reach the snake with her hoe, and any movement might cause it to strike. She could only stare in terror.

A sudden explosion caused the snake's head to disappear, the coiled body twitching and writhing in its death throes. Wilma looked at Valdez. The old Mexican held a smoking revolver in his left hand.

Wilma dropped her hoe and dashed to her son's side, scooping up the trembling child. "Are you all right, Bill?" she asked anxiously. The boy stared wide eyed at the still-twisting body of the snake and nodded.

The back door of the house swung open and Wind Flower stood holding the old navy .36 in her hand. "It was only a snake, Wind Flower," Wilma called. "Valdez shot it."

Wind Flower walked to the garden. Valdez slowly approached the snake, his handgun still at the ready, and peered at the serpent for a moment. Then he turned to Bill. "You are very brave, *amigo pequeño*," he said. "To stand and face the snake is the true test of courage." The old man drew a knife and knelt over the still-squirming body of the snake. The knife blade flashed, and Valdez held the trophy high for Bill to see. The rattles were almost as broad as Valdez's work-hardened thumb and as long as his index finger.

"He was an old one, Bill," Valdez said, handing the boy the rattles. "Keep these. It is said that one who carries the rattler's warning will be safe from other snakes. But," he added with a smile, "do not believe all things that are said."

While Bill examined the rattles, Wilma gradually regained her composure. Bill glanced up at his mother. "I was afraid," he said. "I hate snakes."

"A wise man fears the snake. But he does not hate him," Wind Flower said to Bill. "It probably came to the garden only in search of shade, a place away from the heat of the sun. All creatures are placed upon the earth for a purpose. It is the nature of some creatures to be of danger to man. As you learn more of nature, Bill, you will see the wisdom in such creatures as even the rattlesnake." She shook her head sadly. "The only such creature lacking wisdom seems to be the one who walks erect on two feet."

Bill looked around carefully before resuming his hoeing.

"It is wise to be alert when a snake has been found," Valdez said with an approving nod. "Often they travel in pairs. It is a thing to remember."

After a couple of hours the work in the garden was finished. Valdez manned the crank at the well, while Wilma tipped the full buckets of water into a shallow trough, and Bill made small dikes to steer the water down the rows.

"Valdez," Bill said, "will you teach me to shoot like you did today?"

Wilma almost opened her mouth to protest, but stopped as Valdez calmly shook his head. "No, Bill," the old Mexican replied. "But do not be disappointed. It is not because I do not think you wise enough to use a gun. It is only that your hands are yet too small to grip the gun properly. Be patient. You will grow. Also, a son should learn such things from his father."

Bill thought about the explanation for a moment. "But can't a boy learn from a grandfather?" he asked.

"If he has one, of course."

"Aren't you my grandpa? In a special kind of way?" Bill asked.

Valdez placed an arm around Bill's shoulders and pulled him close. "Thank you, Bill," he said softly. "Never have I heard such a nice thing said to me. And I am honored to call you *nieto*—my grandson. Come now. We must saddle horses. There is much work yet to be done."

Wilma watched the two stroll toward the barn. She felt both friendship and gratitude to the aged Mexican. In Ted's absence, the old man had served as a father to Bill, always teaching and gently correcting, never scolding for inexperienced mistakes.

A sudden strong gust of wind set the bucket on the well rope swinging wildly. Wilma realized the howl of the wind had changed its tone. Some of the old-timers had told stories of winds strong enough to stagger a full-grown horse. This, she decided as she struggled back to the house, might be the beginning of just such a blow.

The hot wind sweeping across the southwest corner of Nebraska almost stopped the Union Pacific dead on its rails.

Ted Henderson held his hat in place with his free hand as he unsaddled his horse. An especially strong gust of wind caught the saddle blanket and sent it flying, spooking the horse. The animal lunged into Ted, almost knocking him down.

Cursing, he finally regained control of the horse and tethered the animal. He retrieved the wayward saddle blanket, which had flown almost forty yards despite being heavy with sweat from the horse. Ted then battled the gale toward Jack Casement's office car.

The wiry railroad man was glumly staring out the window as Ted entered the car and fought the door closed behind him. Placing his hat on the rack near the door, he felt the pounding in his temples and the sandy scrape of his eyelids. Fatigue and the pounding of the wind had left his vision blurred.

He nodded a greeting to Casement and stumbled to the water basin nearby, scooping a double handful of lukewarm water to his eyes.

"Dammit," Casement grumbled, "this blasted wind is like hitting an ocean. We won't make a hundred yards of track today. Find anything, Ted?"

"No. But that doesn't mean Long Walker's not out there. This wind can wipe out a trail in five minutes easily."

Casement grunted. "I might as well call the boys in," he said. "We're not accomplishing a thing. It's blowing so hard the tie men can't even bed wood, and there's a half-dozen places where the roadbed's been blown away."

"I've been through a couple of these blows," Ted said as

the rail car rocked at an especially strong blast of wind. "If it's any help, they usually don't last more than a couple or three days at the most."

"A couple of days means two miles of track," Casement snorted, "and here we sit, pinned down almost within shouting distance of the Wyoming line. This is going to throw us still more behind schedule, dammit!"

Ted dipped his bandanna in the water basin and gently held the damp cloth over his eyes for a moment. "I would suggest you call the crews in soon, Jack," he said. "This hot wind will sap the water from a man in a hurry. Not to mention drying out the eyeballs so bad he can't see. All we can do is ride it out, I'm afraid."

Casement snatched his hat from the rack and jammed it on. "I'll call 'em in. Ted, you better get some rest. You look awful," he said as he left.

Ted slumped onto a low stool, his head in his hands, and let the weariness take hold. He wanted nothing more than to crawl into a bunk and sleep until the blasted wind quit, but he knew that was out of the question. Casement's herd of Durhams, normally docile cattle, would be drifting and scattering, hunting shelter from the blasts of hot air.

Ted could only hope that he and a few rail hands who had handled cattle before could find the drovers and the livestock before Long Walker did. Ted arched his back and flexed aching shoulder muscles, then relaxed. He had not cut sign on the half-breed Indian but knew he was out there, and probably close. It was a feeling in his bones more than knowledge in his head. He had learned to trust the feeling.

Within the hour, Ted and his roundup crew were in the saddle, searching. They found a few head of Durhams huddled in a draw and a few more behind a bluff. It was a frustrating roundup. The cattle were unwilling to turn their faces to the wind, and as soon as a rider reined toward another group of cows the ones they had been pushing promptly started drifting again.

Slowly, the scattered bunches of stock melded into a single herd. Ted was grateful the cattle were not longhorns, who would have been half a territory away.

At Ted's side a Tennessee farm boy shifted in the uncomfortable McClellan saddle. "This is one helluva way to spend a Friday—and payday, too," the farm boy said.

Ted groaned. By Saturday midnight, Hell on Wheels

would be running wide open again. It had become even worse as word of the rolling saloon and houses of the evening spread. Teamsters, miners, and even folks from respectable towns were flocking to the cesspool run by Kilgore Yantis. It promised to be a long weekend, Ted thought.

Only a few hours remained before the Saturday dawn when he and his makeshift crew turned the herd over to a new pair of drovers. Ted dismissed his men with thanks and orders to catch a couple hours sleep, then dragged his own exhausted body toward Jack Casement's office. A light burned in the window despite the hour.

Ted found General Jack pacing the floor, angrily mouthing a big cigar.

"We got most of the cattle back," Ted reported. "As near as I could tell, we're missing maybe sixty head. The wind has shifted and it's dropped a bit. I think the blow is near an end."

Casement nodded. "About time we got some good news around here." He thrust a telegraph message in Ted's direction. Ted wiped his burning eyes on a shirtsleeve and read the message.

INDIANS DERAILED SUPPLY TRAIN EAST OF OGALLALA. CREW KILLED, BODIES MUTILATED. ALL SUPPLIES LOST EXCEPT RAIL IRON. SOME IRON DAMAGED.

With a bitter curse, Ted flung the message to the floor. "So that's what that bastard Long Walker's been up to," he said in disgust. "What does that mean to us?"

"It means we can't lay more than a mile of rails, because we don't have more than that!" Casement snapped. "That supply train was critical to our timetable. It could take as much as a week to replace those rails. And in the meantime we just sit here, stranded like a canoe on a sandbar!"

Ted sank into a sturdy chair. "I'll get up a salvage crew and see if any of the rails can be saved, Jack."

Casement eyed his scout critically. "You need rest. You can't be everywhere at once. I can get up a crew to handle that job without your help."

"Thanks, Jack, but I've got to go. There's a chance Long Walker and his bunch may be laying an ambush for a salvage crew. We can't risk losing any more men. You need Kevin here, and the two of us are the most experienced Indian fighters you have."

Ted heaved himself from the chair. "If you can have someone gather the crew and the wagons we need, I'll grab an hour's sleep and we'll leave at first light."

"Take my bunk," Casement said. "I don't expect to be using it anyway."

Monday's dawn brought the promise of a scorching day. Bear Fallon forced a scowl onto his face as he took his place on the construction line and glanced about. At least half the workers were nursing hangovers. His own head was clear. He had taken only two drinks at Rosie's over the whole weekend. Now he would simply watch and chuckle inwardly.

Within moments a back-tie man, sweating profusely from exertion and the furry tongue of bad whiskey, called for the water carrier. The man took a hefty swallow from the proffered dipper. Then he spat out the mouthful of water, his face contorted.

"Salt!" the back-tie worker snarled. He struck the water carrier with the back of his hand. "You little sonofabitch! I'll teach you how funny your joke is!"

A sudden crack split the morning air. General Jack Casement's bullwhip snapped within two inches of the tie-man's nose. "What the hell is going on here?" Casement demanded.

"That water ain't fit to drink, General Jack," the man grumbled. "It's plumb foul."

Casement motioned for the dipper. A small amount of water remained in the wooden bucket. The wiry engineer took a small sip, then spat it out.

"Salt, all right," he said blackly. "Kevin! Check the other buckets!"

Every container was heavily salted.

Casement whirled his black horse and raced the animal toward the supply cars. He returned a few minutes later, swearing fluently. "Every damn drop of drinking water we have is fouled," Casement declared as he rode up to Kevin. "I found three empty fifty-pound salt sacks outside the supply car."

"Jack, we can't work these men without water," Kevin said. "Even those without hangovers have to have water in this heat."

Casement nodded. "I know that, and it's twenty miles to

fresh water." Casement slammed his hat to the ground. "Dammit to hell! We've got only one mile of track left and we can't even lay *that!* If it's not the weather or the Indians it's horseshit like this! I wish to God I'd never seen a railroad!"

"What do we do?" Kevin asked.

Casement snorted. "What else can we do? Shut down construction until we can get more water. I'll start putting the water wagons together. In the meantime, Kevin, I want you and your boys to strip Hell on Wheels of every available drop of fresh water. Leave those gamblers and whores a pint each and no more!" Casement glared around the gathering of rail workers. "I'll find out who did this, mark my words! And when I do, that man will wish his mother had been barren!"

Bear Fallon watched the small man on the black horse ride away, shouting orders, and forced himself to hold back a grin. He had plenty of water—an entire cask stored in a hole he had dug beneath Rosie's bed. Only thirty minutes' work had brought the whole operation to a dead stop. Maybe it was only for one day, but every day was getting expensive for the Union Pacific. Before long he would fire his big guns. And Kevin O'Reilly would be standing right in front of the barrel.

In the days that followed, General Jack drove his men with a passion, and the Union Pacific finally crossed from Nebraska into Wyoming. The foothills of the Rockies were not far ahead. The mountains might pose problems for Casement, Ted thought as he returned from a patrol, but they would be a breath of fresh air for him.

"Jack, we're in Arapaho country now," Ted said as he entered the engineer's office. "By all rights Long Walker should have given up on us and stayed east. I visited the camps of a couple of Arapaho I know. They say Long Walker is not in their area, but I'm not buying that. I've cut sign on several trails, and though I haven't seen him, I would bet a month's pay that blue-eyed outlaw is right behind us. The big question is when will he strike—and where?"

Ted eased himself into a chair and accepted a cup of coffee with a nod of thanks. "I'm not really sure we won't have Arapaho trouble, either. Some of the young bucks have their backs up. Many of the younger braves I know personally wouldn't even talk to me."

"At least this time our boys will have a chance," Casement said. "You and Kevin have done a fine job organizing them into a fighting force." The engineer nodded toward rails' end a short distance away. Rifles were carefully stacked within reach of the work gangs. The guns were new repeaters, and each worker carried an extra twenty rounds of ammunition in a belt pouch. "They can drop shovels and turn into good, solid infantry at a moment's notice," Casement said. "I just wish we could give our surveyors the same chance. They're on their own out there, just like you and Jim Bridger and Kit Carson were in the old days."

Ted nodded. "They are vulnerable to attack. I've been in touch with Abel Hubbard at Fort Laramie and the officer in command at Fort Bridger. They're both doing all they can to protect the survey parties, but neither commander can spare troops to guard such small groups of men. Abel tells me other tribes, especially the Sioux and Cheyenne, are growing more and more belligerent. We can only hope Abel and the peace chiefs can keep those angry young bucks in line awhile longer."

Casement shook his head. "Sometimes hope is enough. Sometimes it isn't. When it isn't, we just have to make our own luck."

"We may have to do just that, Jack. Autumn is coming up on us fast. And if I know Long Walker, he prefers to fight hardest in the fall."

Ted's words proved to be agonizingly prophetic. A survey team, including Jeff Quarles, died in an ambush near the Laramie River. A wood detail was attacked, and only after a sharp battle were the men able to escape, leaving behind two severely wounded men. Following Ted's standing orders, the wounded who were left behind were handed a fully loaded pistol. The last round was for themselves.

Tie-cutting became one of the Union Pacific's most hazardous duties. Ted personally began to accompany the tie-cutters, his rifle always at the ready.

On one such outing shortly before the first frost of 1867, the tie-cutters were working on a ridge above the Laramie River. A flicker of movement among the trees along the river below caught Ted's eye. He hissed out a warning. The tie-cutters quietly went to retrieve weapons from the wood wagons as Ted ground-hitched his horse and crept forward silently, going down the slope and into the woods.

He came within a heartbeat of walking straight into the ambush. He was about to take a step when a grunt sounded only a few feet ahead of him and to his right. Holding his breath, Ted carefully studied a brush clump. A slight movement caught his eye, and he realized he was staring directly at the back of a Cheyenne Dog Soldier in full war paint!

The Cheyenne turned and muttered to an unseen companion. The Indians were beginning to wonder why the tie-cutters had stopped. Slowly, Ted looked about. More and more forms began to take shape in the deep brush. Ted could only guess at their number, but he was sure there were at least thirty braves. The cutters were outmanned and outgunned.

Scarcely allowing himself to breathe, Ted eased his way from his vantage point and began working his way back up the slope. The Indians, their attention focused on the workmen on the ridge above, did not notice him.

He returned breathless to the waiting men. "They're down there, boys," he said, "and we're getting the hell out of here. When I give the word, move! Turn around and go back to rails' head!" He gestured to the two best marksmen in the group. Unlike the others, the two were mounted. "You two stay with me. We'll put up a rear guard to buy some time, and with any luck get away ourselves. Keep hold of your horses. We may not have much time. Now the rest of you—go!"

The tie-cutting crew immediately retreated, the driver of the wagon team cursing his big draft horses into a sharp turn. At the same time a war cry rang from the timber below.

"Get set, boys," Ted told the marksmen beside him. "As soon as they can get to their ponies, they'll be coming right at us."

Ted had selected his rear-guard position carefully. The three riflemen were well protected on three sides by jumbles of boulders, and a deadfall in front provided a natural breastwork.

"Don't fire until I give the word," he cautioned. "Pick every target carefully—and for God's sake, hit it."

The Indians charged from the thicket, whooping in pursuit of the wagon that had gone back along the trail, dropping out of sight beyond the river canyon wall. Ted waited calmly until the first braves were only forty yards away, then picked his target.

"Now!" he shouted as he lined the sights of his Henry on a charging warrior's chest. The rifle bucked against his shoulder, and the slug tumbled the Indian from his pony. Then the other marksmen were firing, their shots measured. Another Indian fell. Ted recognized him as the Cheyenne Dog Soldier he had seen in the thicket.

The braves leading the charge whirled their mounts in confusion and began to retreat. A horse went down. Another warrior suddenly stiffened, grabbed at a leg, and dropped onto his pony's neck. Ted shot the wounded brave from his horse.

Suddenly, through the swirl of black powder smoke and dust, Ted spotted a familiar figure. Long Walker! The outlaw was again astride Ted's own horse, Buck. Ted levered a fresh cartridge into the Henry as Long Walker raised his own weapon. The two shots sounded almost as one. Ted felt the sting as wood splinters drove into his cheek, then his heart sank as he realized his own hurried shot had missed its mark.

As quickly as it appeared, the opportunity vanished. Long Walker wheeled Buck away from the unexpected and accurate fire. Ted snapped off another quick shot but knew even as he squeezed the trigger that the slug had gone wide.

With the Indians in retreat, Ted wasted no time. "Mount up!" he called to his two companions. "Let's get out of here before they figure out how few of us there are."

He did not breathe easily again until they had rejoined the tie-cutting detail, which was pushing hard back toward rails' end.

Ted wheeled his horse and sat for a moment, staring toward the river where the Indians had waited. "Long Walker," he cursed softly, "your medicine—or mine—will run out one day. We've traded shots twice now. The third time, one of us won't walk away."

Seven

Major David Wills cast a worried glance at the heavy, rain-filled clouds overhead. The dark cloud mass shrouded the tops of the mountains, hiding the late autumn blaze of golden aspen amid the pines and other evergreens.

The bleakness of the landscape matched David Wills's mood. Behind him the eighty cavalrymen of I Company slogged on, slumped in their saddles. For fifteen days they had combed the wide range between the Platte and Loup rivers. For ten of those days it had rained. And not once had they seen so much as a trace of Long Walker's band.

Wills turned to the sergeant riding at his stirrup. "No sense in getting wet again, Sergeant Turlock. Let's try to get home before this storm hits. At the trot, by twos."

Turlock grinned. "Glad to hear it, sir. Didn't look forward much to gettin' soaked again. Ain't dried out yet from the last one." The sergeant twisted in the saddle and shouted the commands. At the thought of hurrying home a fresh sense of energy surged through the column.

Touching spurs to his mount, David gently nudged the animal to the increased pace. Secretly he envied men like Turlock and Abel Hubbard with wives who anxiously awaited their return. To him, riding back into Fort Laramie was much the same as riding out. Each time there was the hope that Victoria Coulter would look at him—really look at him— and see in his eyes that friendship was not enough. But with the hope came fear that she would never do so. David Wills was not sure how much more he could take.

Dammit, he thought bitterly, *why don't I force her hand? An outright rejection beats hell out of being ignored.* But he knew he would not force the issue. Not while there was still a chance, no matter how slim, he could eventually win her.

Wills tried to keep Victoria out of his thoughts when he was afield. His personal troubles should not interfere with his abilities as an officer. But lately, his attention had wandered back to the woman with the auburn hair and green eyes when it should have been on military matters. He knew it could cost the scalps of a lot of good men, and it worried him.

I Company neared the gates of Fort Laramie just as the storm broke. Torrents of drenching rain swept the streets, slashed into the faces of man and beast, whipped through the smallest opening in ponchos, and dripped its chill over soaked horsemen. David glanced hopefully in the direction of the Laramie Hotel, but Victoria Coulter was nowhere to be seen.

Wills dismissed his men as rapidly as possible then headed to report to Abel Hubbard. Outside his commander's office, David removed his poncho and hat and shook the excess water from them, then dripped his way inside.

Abel waved the major to a seat by the fire and poured his junior officer a cup of hot coffee.

"Glad you made it back before the bottom fell out," Abel said. "Nothing is as miserable as a patrol in a driving rainstorm. Any luck?"

Wills shook his head. "No, sir. No sign of Long Walker's bunch. How in the dickens can he hide a camp of nearly a thousand warriors?"

Abel refilled his own cup. "Easy," he said, dropping his lanky form into the chair behind the cluttered desk. "He knows where he is, and where we are. Sometimes we don't know either one."

"Colonel, there's more," Wills said. "I made a couple of stops at the camps of friendly Indians along the way. Paints-His-Horses says many young Cheyenne have gone from the reservation. Big Nose, he said, has stopped trying to keep his young bucks home and is grumbling that he'd like to join them himself. Even Paints-His-Horses, one of the strongest peace talkers, is running short of patience. Even hinting at some thinly veiled war talk of his own." Wills sighed in frustration.

"One-Ear of the Brule Sioux all but kicked us off his range. And he says if a white man as much as said 'boo' to Sitting Bull, the chief would reach for a war ax. Colonel, if Sitting Bull and Big Nose explode on this country . . ." Wills let his voice trail away. He did not have to complete the sentence.

Abel stared into space for a moment. The only sound in the small office was the pounding of rain on window glass. "David," Abel finally said, "somehow we've got to find Long Walker and break his medicine once and for all. But here we are. We've worn down two companies of men and four hundred horses between us, and still we come up empty-handed."

Abel snorted in disgust, then drained his coffee cup and stood. "He'll make a mistake somewhere, David. He can't go on forever without one. And when he makes it, we'll be on him like a fox on a prairie hen. Now, go get yourself some rest while I think of a way to keep the fuse wet on some Indian tempers."

David rinsed his coffee cup and placed it in its niche in the office wall, leaving Abel deep in thought. A bath, a shave, and some dry clothes in the bachelor officers' quarters helped chase away some of his bleak outlook.

A few minutes later Judy Hubbard greeted David at the counter inside the Laramie Hotel door. "Tough patrol, Major?"

David nodded politely. "Tough enough, Mrs. Hubbard. I don't think I'll ever dry out." His gaze swept the dining room, then settled on a far corner. Victoria Coulter sat at the keyboard of a piano. The gentle notes of a Chopin nocturne filled the room.

"She's good, isn't she?" Judy said softly. "I'd much rather have two fewer tables and soft music, and Victoria enjoys playing so much. The piano may be one of the best improvements we've ever made here."

The nocturne slid gently to a conclusion, and the customers applauded in appreciation. Victoria smiled and nodded, then turned her attention back to the keyboard. The opening notes of a Bellini aria sprang to life beneath her fingers. David stood transfixed, wishing desperately he had paid more attention in the music appreciation class at the Point.

The ache in David's chest increased as Victoria began to sing the aria. Her rich soprano molded the phrases simply but exquisitely, the meaning behind the words becoming clear to the listeners, even if they did not understand the Italian words.

David excused himself and made his way to the piano. He stood by the instrument until she had finished the aria.

Victoria again acknowledged the applause, then glanced at David. The rich green gown she wore was almost the color of her eyes. He thought she had never looked more radiant or desirable.

"That was beautiful, Victoria," he said softly.

"Why, thank you, Major. Do you play?"

David shook his head. "Unfortunately, no. At the moment I'd sell my soul to the devil in exchange for such a talent."

Victoria's laugh was as musical as her playing. She placed a hand on his arm, her eyes sparkling. "I wouldn't go quite that far if I were you, David," she said.

"Victoria, I—will you have dinner with me tonight?" he blurted.

She shook her head. "I'm sorry, David," she said quietly, "but I've already made plans. Thank you for asking, though. It is most considerate of you." Without further comment, she returned to the piano.

David turned and slowly walked toward the door.

"You won't be eating with us tonight, Major?" Judy asked as David reached for his hat.

"I've just lost my appetite," he said sharply.

Judy held back the urge to offer encouragement to the young officer. She had vowed to stay out of other people's emotional lives. She watched from the window as the young major, his shoulders slumped, slogged through the driving rain toward his Spartan quarters.

"Darn you, David Wills," Judy said to herself, "don't give up. She's worth fighting for." Judy turned away from the window, her own spirits sagging. Young Wills had been showing signs of hiding his aches and disappointments in the bottle during his off-hours. It was such a short step from off-duty drinking to carrying a bottle in the saddlebag. And Judy hoped the troubled young man would not take that next step.

The prairie soil struggled valiantly against the onslaught of water, but still the rain pounded down. Lightning danced from the towering thunderstorms that built above the Rockies and rumbled across southern Wyoming and Nebraska before sweeping into Colorado and Kansas.

Finally the saturated ground and wind-whipped grass could hold no more. The flood began with a single trickle along the Plains watershed. The trickle became a stream pouring into Lodgepole Creek near the newly founded town of Cheyenne on the Union Pacific tracks. Muddy torrents charged into the stream, pouring water into Lodgepole faster than the creek could empty. The raging waters undercut a huge cottonwood tree, ripping the massive roots from the mud that had anchored them for decades. The tree spun into the mud-red waters. Lodgepole Creek released an angry ten-foot wall of water downstream.

The flash flood, capped by the tumbling trunk of the old cottonwood, slammed into the Union Pacific trestle over Lodgepole. The trestle shuddered at the impact, then sagged. With the ripping crack of splintering timber, the trestle vanished beneath the red water. Iron rails that could withstand the force of a locomotive twisted like limp ropes in the torrent.

Within seconds, the Union Pacific's crossing of Lodgepole Creek was no more.

Miles ahead, the raging Laramie River tore at the railroad's forward tracks, ripping great gaps in the roadbed. Where there was less drainage, floodwaters from the flatlands chewed support from beneath the rails.

At rails' end, General Jack Casement, Ted Henderson, and Kevin O'Reilly joined soaked and chilled laborers in the backbreaking, frequently futile task of laying bags of sand against threatened sections of track.

By morning the massive storm moved on. A single ray of sunlight slanted down, by chance focusing a strip two hundred yards long where only a few days ago new rails had been laid. Now there was only a mudflat.

Slipping and skidding in the ankle-deep mud, Ted made his way to Jack Casement's side.

"Looks bad, Jack," he said. "We won't know how extensive the damage was behind us until I can get out on scout. I wouldn't count on any supply trains getting through for a while."

"Ted, I can't ask you to do that." Ted saw the pain and disappointment in Casement's eyes. He understood full well how much the storm would cost Casement in terms of track laid. "You're driving yourself too hard," Casement said. "Both of us could use a rest."

Ted put a reassuring hand on Casement's shoulder. "What the hell, Jack," he said. "I got a few hours' sleep day before yesterday. I've been needing something to do in my spare time."

Within the hour Ted was mounted and on his way. As he rode he made notes on the storm damage encountered. By the time he reached Cheyenne he already had two pages full in the small notebook.

Cheyenne was soggy, but still intact. Already signs of permanence were appearing: wooden houses instead of tents, a general store that was fairly well stocked. He hoped Cheyenne would survive. So many railroad towns had not, once the rails were laid.

A half-day's ride beyond Cheyenne, Ted eased his horse to a stop on the edge of a bluff overlooking Lodgepole Creek. As he had expected, the trestle was gone. Flood debris was lodged high on the creek's walls, testimony to the ferocity of the floodwaters. Ted was no engineer, but he was sure the task of rebuilding the trestle could begin by the time a crew had been assembled and materials gathered.

He forded the swiftly flowing creek and rode for several miles. Only minor damage had occurred past Lodgepole. He was sure supply trains could get through once the trestle was rebuilt.

As the sun dropped low over his shoulder, Ted made his camp for the night. He located a reasonably dry spot, slipped a bag of grain over his horse's nose, and settled in. The stars were bright overhead, and the evening air was chilled with the deepening autumn.

A pinpoint of light just below a distant ridge caught his eye. It appeared to be a small campfire, possibly a lone traveler. But possibly it was more. Ted decided against building a fire of his own. Jerky and water would serve for supper. And if he could see that campfire, whoever was there could see his. He felt exhaustion tugging at him and rolled into his blankets. He would check on the campfire the next day.

Ted woke momentarily confused. Slowly it dawned on him why. The sun was well above the eastern horizon. For the first time in weeks he had slept beyond sunrise.

Remembering the campfire from the evening before, he saddled his horse and broke camp. On the ridge he found the remnants of the campfire—and around it the fresh tracks of five unshod ponies. The fire had been laid in the fashion of the Sioux. Ted traced the tracks for half a mile, rifle cocked and ready. The tracks joined a larger band, and among the prints were the familiar hoofmarks of his own dun, the horse stolen by Long Walker.

Ted followed, his nerves jangling an alert, until he had read the story of the crossing trails. He saw nothing moving in the bright sun-washed morning. At length, satisfied that he was not being followed or watched, he turned his horse back toward Cheyenne. He felt sure the Indians were watching the washed-out trestle. And there could be only one reason for that.

"Long Walker, you may have just stepped in it, clear up to the hocks, this time," he muttered. "I've got a little surprise ahead for you.

In Cheyenne, he discovered with relief that the telegraph lines were still open to Fort Laramie. He dictated a terse message to Abel Hubbard and waited until the key chattered in return a few minutes later.

The operator handed the message to Ted, who merely tucked it in a pocket. He had learned to understand Morse code coming off the wire since joining the railroad, and he was pleased with the clicking answer.

The telegrapher raised a quizzical eyebrow. "Strangest message I ever sent," he said. "Never heard of holdin' a surprise party in the middle of nowhere."

Ted grinned in anticipation. "Let's just hope that all the guests show up."

Major David Wills made his biggest command decision the moment the telegraph key fell silent. He nodded to the private operating the set.

"I heard. 'Surprise party for blue eyes set two days from now. You're invited. Lodgepole trestle.' Correct?"

"Yes, sir," the private said. "Reply?"

"'Invitation accepted. Don't start without us.' Signed 'Wills.'"

David Wills strode to the door. "Sergeant Jonas!"

The big black man appeared promptly, limping at top speed. "Sir?"

"Form up I Company. And all available members of Henderson's Scouts. Extra ammunition for every man. Fresh horses—two each. We may be in for a long, hard ride."

"Yes, sir," Jonas said, his eyes glittering. "Can I come along?"

"Sorry, Albert," Wills said quietly. "Abel hasn't released you for fighting duty yet—and someone has to tend the store. When Colonel Hubbard returns from patrol, tell him we're headed for Lodgepole trestle. Ted thinks we can catch Long Walker with his breechclout down."

"God, Major," Jonas said pleadingly, "I'd give a year's pay to be there."

"You stay here and run the army, Sergeant. We'll know Fort Laramie is in good hands. Be patient. You will be back in action soon. Now, Boots and Saddles, if you please."

Long Walker grunted in satisfaction. It was as he had planned. In the muddy bottom of Lodgepole Creek below, some thirty white men hauled timbers from wagons. He had known they would have to fix this bridge for the locomotives to carry supplies. Behind Long Walker waited some two hundred and fifty of his finest warriors. Sioux Crazy Dogs, Cheyenne Dog Soldiers, and the finest fighters from among the Arapaho and Ute.

He turned to the swarthy Two Thorns at his side. "It is as Long Walker dreamed," he said. "The red man shall pick the white eyes from the creek as the squaws gather berries." With exaggerated gestures, Long Walker plucked a ceremonial arrow from where it was tied by a thong to his white man's saddle. He mounted the dun gelding, held the medicine arrow high, then drove it into the ground.

At the signal the mounted braves behind him surged forward, fanning into a skirmish line. With war cries shattering the midmorning calm, they rode toward the railroad workers below.

"Here they come, boys!" Ted yelled. Already the workers were in motion, grabbing carbines from wagons or from stacks nearby. The railroad men dropped behind the heavy timbers that had been carefully placed to provide a solid rifle abutment. The well-trained laborers chambered cartridges and waited patiently for Ted's signal.

The charging Indians drew nearer, their ponies slowed somewhat by the mud of the creek bank. "Now!" Ted yelled, bringing his own weapon into line.

A blistering barrage from the rail workers ripped into the front ranks of the warriors. A half-dozen war ponies were left riderless in the first crash of rifle fire. The surprised Indians were expecting an easy kill and quickly realized they were in for a hard fight.

But there was no sign of wavering or hesitation among

the Indian ranks. They were veterans, hungry for scalps, and confident. A handful of white men could hardly slow them.

A second volley sounded on the heels of the first. Long Walker watched in disbelief from his post on the ridge as the concentrated, deadly fire raked the charging Indians. Never before had the white workers on the railroad fought so well. And now they had repeating rifles.

Indians whirled ponies about in sudden confusion, firing handguns and carbines toward the entrenched workers. The warriors' guns buried lead into heavy trestle beams or kicked mud from the creek, but the poorly aimed and hurried shots seldom came close to a live target.

Suddenly, above the smoke and noise, Long Walker heard a cavalry bugle sounding the charge from the opposite bank of the creek. His heart in his throat, the blue-eyed renegade watched a long line of soldiers sweep toward the Indians.

A young officer, handgun raised, whirled the pistol above his head. Above the rattle of gunfire, Long Walker heard the cries of surprised braves. The long knives had turned the Indians' left flank!

At a signal from the officer, the soldiers dismounted and shouldered their rifles. The Indians were trapped in a deadly, well-aimed cross fire between the soldiers and the rail workers. Long Walker cursed sharply. His elite corps of fighting men was being cut to pieces! Bodies of Indians littered the creek bed so thickly that ponies stumbled over them.

Finally, Two Thorns recognized the trap. The Ute tried desperately to organize an escape. But a soldier's rifle shot sent him spinning to the ground. The Ute managed to raise himself to one knee, and looked pleadingly in Long Walker's direction.

Long Walker ignored the call for rescue. Two Thorns's usefulness was at an end, anyway. The Ute's body jerked as a half-dozen slugs ripped his life away.

The remaining Indians, realizing they were about to be wiped out to a man, broke ranks and raced their ponies in a wild scramble toward the relative safety of the ridge over which they had so confidently ridden only moments before.

Long Walker knew the battle was lost, and he was no fool. This was no time for heroics. Still, he held his position until the first of the fleeing braves swept past. In a token show of bravado, intended more for the benefit of his warriors than an attempt to kill soldiers, Long Walker emptied his carbine in the direction of the white men. Then he wheeled the gelding and quirted the animal hard toward the northwest.

He twisted in the saddle to look back and saw the column of soldiers riding toward them in hot pursuit. The renegade settled down to flee for his life.

The battle raged for twenty miles as first one rear guard, then another, was overwhelmed by the seasoned, expert cavalrymen. A group of ten braves left behind to cover their comrades' retreat was simply bypassed and ignored. The harried Indians finally were forced to split up, scattering in all directions to avoid the relentless pursuit of the horse soldiers.

Long Walker had no idea how many braves were lost in the attack at Lodgepole. But he knew there were many. The elite band had been badly hammered. Long Walker cursed bitterly as he rode his horse hard. It would be easy to put it down to bad medicine. That was what he would have to do if he were to retain any fighting force at all. But what really galled the Seminole-turned-Sioux was that he had been outmaneuvered. He had been caught in the cardinal sin of warfare—underestimating his enemy. It would not happen again, he vowed. Ted Henderson would suffer many deaths before his end finally came.

At sunset the pursuing soldiers gave up the chase. There was little point in pushing tired horses any farther, and the scattered trails could not be followed in the dark.

Back at the battlefield, Ted walked slowly through the carnage. Long Walker's body was not among those in the creek bed. Ted counted more than fifty Indians dead or seriously wounded, and only David Wills would know how many more bodies were left in the wake of the chase. One thing was for sure—it was a defeat that would be difficult for Long Walker to explain, or to recover from.

The sounds of spike mauls and shovels rang over the battleground as workers returned to rebuilding the ruined trestle.

Ted mounted and rode to the highest point around, keeping alert for any Indians that might attempt to circle back and strike. There was little chance that would happen, but a little caution could save a lot of blood.

David Wills's tired troops returned in the early hours of

the new day. Their losses had been light. Two soldiers had been killed, a half-dozen had suffered minor wounds, and only ten horses were lost. Among the railroaders there was only one casualty, a shovel man who had taken a rifle ball through the leg.

"Colonel Henderson, in all, Long Walker probably lost a hundred braves," David said, concluding his report. "I think we may have cut his belly open. And I feel absolutely lousy. This was no great military victory. It was a massacre!"

Ted nodded solemnly. "It was, David. That's how we planned it. You and your men did a magnificent job here today. It's going to take that renegade a long time to build another powerful fighting force. His medicine shirt got soiled rather badly. And as long as you don't feel a sense of triumph at death, you'll be a fine officer."

One by one, the survivors of Long Walker's battered band trickled back into the secret camp along a remote stretch of the Niobrara River. Long Walker noted with growing disgust that many of those who had ridden on the trestle raid and escaped did not return. Several of those who did return began openly to challenge Long Walker's medicine. Among the Plains Indians, one who led an unsuccessful war party did not retain the right to order his followers into battle again by power of rank alone.

At first Long Walker made no attempt to answer the challenges, content merely to subdue the small rebellions with stoic, formidable stares and the power of his own personality.

Then one morning when the frosts lay heavy on the grass, Long Walker called a rare communal meeting of all braves. He had chosen his spot with care. He stood atop a low rock formation, knowing that those who looked up at a speaker viewed him as larger than the other people around.

"Warriors, listen!" Long Walker called. "For many days Long Walker's heart was troubled. Now he is at peace within himself, for Wakan-Tanka has shown him why his warriors were defeated in the battle at the bridge of the iron horse."

The renegade paused for dramatic effect, peering into the faces of his most vocal accusers. "There was bad medicine— but it was not Long Walker's. On the day before the raid, the Ute called Two Thorns saw an owl in the daytime. He did not speak of this bad omen. Thus it was Two Thorns who broke the medicine, not Long Walker! Was Two Thorns not among the first to fall, and was he not shot in the back?"

A low murmur of agreement rippled through the gathering of warriors. It was true that to see an owl in the daylight and say nothing could easily tear the delicate fabric of medicine. And Two Thorns had been killed. The fact that others had died as well began to lose importance. Now there was someone to blame.

"Wakan-Tanka has told Long Walker this to strengthen his heart and spirit. He also has told Long Walker that among our ponies is one who bears bad medicine." He turned and gestured. "Bring this animal to me!"

A stocky Arapaho appeared, leading a dun-colored horse. Long Walker took the hackamore rein and led the snorting, nervous animal onto a flat area among the rocks. From his belt he drew the sharp ceremonial knife.

"This was the horse ridden by the man called Henderson, the man who long has been Long Walker's enemy and the enemy of all who do not follow the white man's ways. In this horse is the bad spirit that tricked Long Walker and soured Two Thorns's vision. With its death this bad spirit shall be banished!"

Long Walker slashed out with the razor-edged knife, severing the dun's jugular vein. The horse sank to its knees, then toppled to its side and kicked its death throes as the blood gushed forth. Long Walker knelt and scooped the sticky fluid into a palm, then lifted it to his lips and drank. He held the bloodied hand high as he turned to face the assembled braves.

"Long Walker tastes the blood of his enemy! The bad spirit is gone from our midst! Now only great glories and many coups, much wealth, shall fall upon those who follow Long Walker!"

With the ceremonial knife, Long Walker sliced open his buckskin shirt. He bared his chest to the sharp wind which swept across the frosty grass. Then, with a studied deliberation, he placed his bloody hand over his heart.

"This shall be the symbol of death to the white man Henderson. It shall be the sign of death to the iron horses. The mark of the eternal darkness to all white men who tend the iron horses. Those who follow Long Walker will wear this mark and become great chiefs among all the people of the Plains!"

An excited whisper ran through the crowd. Such an oath and promise were medicine to be reckoned with. Slowly, Long Walker removed his hand from his chest. The bright red handprint stood in stark relief on his scarred, muscular breast. "Wakan-Tanka has shown Long Walker how to defeat the iron horses. This he will do. But now Long Walker must bring more warriors to his band, for it must be large. Those who would ride with Long Walker will go into winter camp at this place, to await his return. Long Walker goes to the land of the Cheyenne. When once more the grass grows green and rich, a long red line of Cheyenne braves will wear the bloodprint upon their breasts. They will join the Sioux, the Arapaho, and the Ute to cast the white man forever from Indian lands!"

With a sudden whoop of enthusiasm, the Arapaho who had led the horse forward leapt onto the flat rock, dipped his palm, and made the blood hand on his chest. "Strong Foot rides with Long Walker!" he yelled.

"And when the warm winds chase the snows, the Red Hands of Long Walker's great band shall once more touch blood," Long Walker promised. "It shall be the blood of the white man!"

Long Walker waited as a large number of braves filed past, dipping their palms in the horse's blood and making the Red Hand on their chests. Then he severed the buckskin's head from the body. He had a plan for the head.

Once more supplies were rolling on the Union Pacific. As the autumn of 1867 faded to winter, a new town called Laramie grew where the Laramie River met the Union Pacific tracks. The new town nestled along the river that fed the bustling fort of the same name to the north. Each day the rails edged forward, driving ever higher and deeper into the growing mountains.

The days grew shorter for the work crews, but not for Ted Henderson. Unable to convince himself that Long Walker would ever give up his assault on the railroad, Ted drove himself even harder. The daylight hours were devoted to scouting forays far afield, even into the high mountains where the snows already were stirrup deep. On such high-country scouts, Ted was forced to leave his horse below and trudge into the passes on makeshift snowshoes.

At night it was patrols of Hell on Wheels that drained

him physically and mentally. The rolling city had grown with
the advent of autumn. The tents swelled almost to the burst-
ing point as the freighting season ended. More tents went up
to accommodate the booming clientele. Teamsters with pockets full of pay flocked to the gaming tables and red-light
tents. Miners swarmed in as well, and it seemed to Ted that
every drifter west of the Mississippi began to turn up at rails'
end.

At least Kilgore Yantis had posed no major problems,
Ted thought wearily as he slogged through the mud in the
small hours one morning. Since Ted had caught him with the
shaved deck earlier, the gambler had been unable to run his
own table. Ted had heard Yantis was confining his actions to
counting the take.

Kevin O'Reilly and a husky iron man named Shaughnessy,
who were accompanying Ted on the night's patrol, entered
one of Yantis's tents with him. A roulette game was in progress, and Ted blinked against the smoke and the acrid smell of
unwashed bodies.

He leaned wearily against a tent support pole and glanced
around the crowd. A majority of those at or near the gaming
table were members of Fallon's circle of thugs. Fallon was
not among them so Ted paid them little mind. Fallon had
been doing his job, and Ted had to admit reluctantly the man
was one of the best head spikers in the crew. Still he wondered what Fallon was up to, if anything. He did not seem to
be a man to carry so much hate and yet take no action.

"Hey, bucko," he heard Shaughnessy mutter to Kevin,
"give a listen to that little ball a-spinnin'."

Kevin cocked an ear, then glanced at Ted. Amid the
chirr of the whirling ball a barely audible click could be
heard. At each click the roulette operator's hand was beneath
the table. The house seemed to be winning more often than
the odds suggested probable.

"Check it out, Shaughnessy," Ted said quietly.

The big Irishman shouldered his way through the crowd
and stood for a moment at the croupier's side. Then he
suddenly stabbed out a huge hand. The gambling table man
groaned in pain. There was a ripping sound, and Shaughnessy
held a small wooden box aloft. A ripple of angry voices began.

"Sure enough," Shaughnessy said, "table's rigged."

Ted nodded. "Bring that croupier here," he said, "then
bust it up."

The white-faced gambler winced as Shaughnessy and Kevin tipped the table over. Wood crunched beneath heavy work boots. "Your idea to rig the game?" Ted asked softly.

The croupier shook his head, the fear-sweat wet on his face. "No, sir. Mr. Yantis's orders, sir."

"And where is Mr. Yantis?"

"Went back to Omaha yesterday, sir. He he said he was running short of girls—"

Ted glanced about. The gamblers, faces dark in rage, had turned to glare at the croupier. Ted quietly and unobtrusively slipped his handgun from its holster and held the weapon alongside his leg. He nodded toward the angry crowd. "I would strongly suggest that you make a trip of your own to Omaha," he said to the croupier. "These gentlemen seem upset that the table was rigged. I can either escort you back to the construction train—a supply train is headed east tomorrow—or you can take your chances here, if you prefer."

The croupier swallowed nervously. "Under the circumstances, sir, I—I'd appreciate an escort."

Ted raised the handgun. "This man is in my custody," he called above the rumbling voices. "I am not a gambler myself, so I don't bluff. I'll shoot the first man who makes a wrong move."

No one in the crowd seemed inclined to challenge Ted. The four men made their way back to the construction train.

After settling down for the night, it seemed to Ted that he had scarcely closed his eyes when he felt a gentle shake on his shoulder. He dragged himself from deep sleep and groggily looked into the bearded face of Jack Casement. The railroad engineer's eyes were concerned.

"Ted, I'm sorry. I know how much you need rest. But we've got a problem. Just got a report from the forward grading crew. We sent a survey team out to double-check on the Bridger's Pass route. They were supposed to link up with a squad of cavalry from Fort Bridger. The word is that the surveyors never showed up. You're the only man I have who might be able to find them before they freeze to death, if they haven't already."

Ted shook the last bit of sleep from his mind, and began to struggle into his boots and greatcoat. "I'll find them, Jack," he said.

"I wish I could send some help along," Casement said apologetically, "but we're shorthanded now and have a big day coming up. We've got to make that first heavy cut west of the river. We'll be blasting and hauling all day. It'll take all hands and the cook to punch a grade through that rock."

Ted waved a hand. "Don't worry about it, Jack," he said. "I've been over these mountains enough on my own."

By the time the first gray smudge of daybreak streaked the eastern sky, Ted was three miles from end of track, headed deep into the rugged Rockies.

Kevin O'Reilly dumped a wheelbarrow full of rock fragments into a fill and wiped the sweat from his brow. Even in late autumn, warm days were not uncommon, and it did not take much work to turn a man's clothes soggy. He was not fond of wheelbarrow work, but the laborer who had slipped and broken a leg could not be replaced at the moment, so Kevin had pitched in.

Farther west, the powder monkeys plied their trade, placing black powder charges in strategic locations on the rock bluff. Then they touched cigars or torches to fuse ends and scrambled for safety with a warning cry.

The black powder blasted away at the side of the canyon, slowly chewing open a pathway for the grading crew. To save time, Jack Casement had split his forces, sending one crew ahead to work on ground that did not require blasting and keeping a crew in reserve to work with the powder monkeys on the cut.

Kevin glanced toward the nearby mountaintops, wondering if Ted had managed to find the surveyors yet. If not, he would not have long to search. A man would not last long up there unless he knew what he was doing.

Jack Casement reined his horse in alongside Kevin. "Might as well call 'em in for noon break," the bearded engineer said. "We're making some headway. I just hope we've got enough blasting powder for this cut. That's one tough chunk of rock out there."

"We have a full carload, Jack," Kevin said. "If that's not enough, I guess it's pick-and-shovel time until we can get a supply train in here."

Kevin gave the signal for the noon break, then fell into step with the laughing and joking workers heading back to the construction train. The crews were working well to the west of rails' end and had to pass through Hell on Wheels to reach the dining car and the rest of the construction train.

On the muddy main street of the sprawling tent city, Kevin suddenly checked his stride. He watched, curious, as an unfamiliar figure moved with gliding steps toward the big saloon tent nearby. The man was slender, and his dress marked him as neither bullwhacker nor prospector. The brim of the man's battered hat flopped in the light wind. He wore some sort of quilted jacket. From a brief glimpse, Kevin thought he looked Chinese. The man disappeared into the big tent. But Kevin's hunger was stronger than his curiosity so he continued to the dining car.

He took his meal on the first shift, then stood for a moment outside the dining car door, talking with friends and exchanging silent stares with Fallon's cohorts in the second meal shift. Soon Kevin moved a short distance from the linked rail cars. The construction train rested on a siding of temporary tracks that was connected with the newly laid rails by a Y-shaped switching track. Fifty yards away, near the apex of the Y, a small donkey engine chuffed idly, awaiting its call to move flatcars of supplies toward rails' end.

Laborers and powder monkeys who already had eaten lounged about on the sunny side of the sleeping cars, smoking and gossiping. Others went inside to grab a quick nap before being called back to work.

Kevin stretched and yawned, letting his muscles relax from the wear of the morning's work—then something slammed into his body, knocking him from his feet. A tremendous blast shattered the noontime quiet. Confused, Kevin stared for a split second at a sky that was suddenly filled with dark smoke and spinning debris. Then he whirled and huddled, facedown, as bits of wood and metal drove into the muddy earth around him.

The clatter of falling debris subsided and Kevin got to his knees. Where the powder car had stood, only smoking rubble remained. Someone or something had ignited the black powder stored in the wooden rail car!

Still momentarily dazed by the concussion, Kevin stared in dismay at the half-dozen bodies lying near the wreckage of the powder car. Screams and shouts came from the dozens of men trapped in the dining car. One end of the car was crumpled from the blast, and the shock apparently had jammed the exit doors. Wind-whipped flames from the rubble of the powder car licked at shattered wood just a few cars from the dining car. The fire caught hold and burst into a roaring blaze. In only moments, the entire construction train would become a raging inferno.

Without fully realizing what he was doing, Kevin sprinted toward the fire. From the corner of his eye he saw an engineer racing toward the donkey engine, while ahead Shaughnessy scrambled from the ground.

"Yank those linchpins!" Shaughnessy yelled, hurling himself almost beneath the wheels of a burning car. He struck upward with a heavy work boot, driving the coupling pin of an endangered car free of its flaming neighbor.

Other workmen raced for the water car, grabbing buckets. One slender spike peddler hefted a pickax and began bashing out windows on the dining car and sleeping cars, then began hammering away at the jammed door. Kevin dragged one injured man free as flames licked at his own sleeve. He brushed the fire from his burning shirt and joined Shaughnessy and others as they battled to separate the undamaged cars from the wreckage. Shaughnessy grabbed a fallen coupling pin and glanced at Kevin. "Come on, bucko! We get just one shot at this!" he shouted.

The two men raced toward the rear of the train. A bucket brigade had formed, pouring water on the cars threatened by the raging fire, but the flames continued to spread.

The door of the dining car finally yielded to the blows of the spike peddler's pickax. Coughing, soot-blackened men stumbled free of the car, gasping air into their lungs.

A long, mournful toot from the donkey engine made Kevin glance up. Instantly he understood what the engineer intended to do.

The engineer had put the donkey engine onto the siding and spun the wheels of the little locomotive as he closed on the exposed coupling unit of the last car on the construction train.

"Grab my waist!" Shaughnessy yelled. "If I miss this, yank me out quick! Otherwise it'll rip a hand off if I get caught!"

Shaughnessy jumped forward as the engine clanked into the coupling, then coolly dropped the pin in place before yanking his hand back. The wheels of the donkey engine screamed on the tracks as the engineer gave it full throttle in reverse.

For several heartbeats the little engine battled helplessly to move the enormous weight of the construction train. Then, as the burly rail workers realized what was being attempted, they all helped to shove it. Slowly, inch by inch, the construction train began to move.

The space between the blazing cars and those not yet burning grew to six inches, a foot, finally a yard, as the gallant little donkey engine pulled them to safety.

Rail workers armed with buckets of water, shovels, and soaked blankets clambered over the moving cars, extinguishing sparks before they could become flames, and snuffing out small fires before they caught hold.

Kevin sprinted back toward the shattered hulk of the powder car. Already, workers were moving among the dead and injured. Canvas covered perhaps a half-dozen huddled figures. The train surgeon, his own arm in a makeshift sling, moved among the wounded issuing instructions to his assistants. And everywhere, it seemed, was the wiry form of General Jack Casement—barking an order here, giving a reassuring word there.

Within the hour the grim figures were known. Seven men had died in the blast, another twenty had been hurt. Two of the injured were severely burned and given little chance of survival by the surgeon. The other injuries ranged from shattered eardrums to minor burns and cuts from flying debris.

Later, in Casement's office, Kevin downed a sorely needed shot of bourbon. He leaned back in the chair and winced from the sting of the small burns across his shoulders and lower back.

"I've given the crews the rest of the day off, Kevin," Casement said. "We'll have to reorganize. We lost a spike peddler, two back-tie men, a head spiker, a water carrier, and two laborers outright. Two others probably won't see the dawn."

Kevin sighed wearily. "Any idea what happened?"

"All we know right now is that somehow the powder car blew," Casement said. "Accident or otherwise, I can't say. It could have been worse. Those rail hands, your friend Shaughnessy and the donkey engineer in particular, staved off a complete disaster. If that whole construction train had gone up in smoke, the Union Pacific would be out of business, with two or three dozen fatalities to boot." Casement strode to a window.

"At any rate," he said, "we're going to be stuck here a

few more days. We can't cut through that canyon wall without blasting powder." Casement turned abruptly to face his foreman.

"Kevin, have you hired any new workers lately?"

The question caught Kevin by surprise. "No, sir. I don't hire anyone without checking with you. Why do you ask?"

Casement's brow furrowed. "Five men owe their lives to someone I don't think I've ever seen before. They were trapped under some wreckage and the fire was getting close. They said a skinny fellow in a floppy hat pulled them out. The smoke and confusion were so bad they didn't get a close look, but one of them said he looked Indian, sort of. Ring a bell with you?"

Kevin remembered the slender man in the quilted jacket on the street of Hell on Wheels. He had worn a floppy hat. "Maybe. Where is this fellow now?"

"We don't know. They said he just appeared, pulled them out of trouble, and vanished. Like a puff of wind, one of them said." Casement sighed. "Well, whoever and wherever he is, he did some people a big favor here today."

Bear Fallon slammed a fist into an open palm and swore bitterly. That Irish crony of Henderson's had more lives than a ship's cat and more luck than a gambler on a hot streak, he grumbled to himself.

He found slight consolation in the fact that the blast in the powder car had cost the Union Pacific a few days' work. But his plans for a double target had not panned out. *O'Reilly, damn his hide, would decide to take a walk just at the wrong time! He should have been standing right by the powder car when she blew*, Fallon thought.

At least Fallon knew he had covered his own tracks. The little whiner, Birch, had fired the fuse for him—and been blown over half the Laramie River in the process. A grin of satisfaction twisted Fallon's lips. The little man had not realized until too late that Fallon had switched fuses, replacing the slow-burning fuse with a hot one. He had probably fired the fuse and barely had time to blink before all the powder went off in his face. Now Fallon had covered his trail in the "accident" that killed Sean Grady as well. Birch had been the only man alive connected with that plan.

Fallon swept into Pittsburgh Rose's tent, shut off her questions with a dark glare, then poured himself a hefty slug of whiskey from the bottle on the bedside table. It was well past noon, and Rosie probably would still have been asleep if it had not been for the blast.

He downed the last of the drink and sat for a moment staring at his scarred knuckles. *Maybe his pet Irishman got away for now*, Fallon thought, *but, by God, Henderson won't be so lucky*. It was all set. All Fallon had to do was put out the word.

"Bear," Rosie said, her voice husky, "if you've got the day off . . ." She let the robe drop from her shoulders and sat naked on the bed, shivering in the slight chill inside the tent.

Fallon barely glanced at her. "Shut up, Rosie. Put your clothes on. I don't have the time to fool around with you."

Ted Henderson rode through Hell on Wheels shortly before sunset, the lost survey party in tow. From the shadows between two tents, Bear Fallon grinned. Henderson looked beat. It was just the way Fallon wanted him.

Fallon scraped a fingernail on the side of a tent. At the muffled question from inside Fallon said, "Get Minter, Pogue, and Gamblin. Four or five of our other boys. Murphy's saloon. Nine o'clock."

The huge Irishman stepped into the muddy street as Henderson and his charges passed the last tent of Hell on Wheels. "Tonight, Henderson, we settle up a bunch of accounts," Fallon muttered.

Ted eyed the blast wreckage critically as he delivered the rescued surveyors to the surgeon. "Might check them over, Doc," he said. "Could have some frostbite." He nodded toward the surgeon's arm in its sling. "Looks like you had some problems."

Ted listened carefully as the doctor outlined the events of the day while he worked on the surveyors. When he was satisfied that the men he had brought in from the high country would be all right, Ted went in search of Jack Casement.

"Got your surveyors home in one piece, Jack," he said as he sank, exhausted, into a chair in Casement's office. "Doc told me about the explosion. Think it was an accident?"

Casement frowned. "I don't know, Ted. Somehow I doubt it. I think we still have a skunk at this tent meeting. I can't see him, but the smell's pretty strong." He sighed in disgust. "It's as much my fault as anybody's. Only a damn fool would keep blasting powder in a car in the construction train. From now on, I'll keep it a hundred yards down track. In the meantime here we sit, stuck without any powder. When the boys start drifting into Hell on Wheels and slurping up rotgut, they're liable to take the roof off."

Casement glanced at Ted. The scout's chin had sunk to his chest. Casement shook his head in silent wonder. He was not surprised that Ted had fallen asleep. Not another man could crowd so many hours into a working day.

He placed a hand on Ted's shoulder. The scout came awake with a start. "Sorry, Jack. It's not that you're boring or anything."

Casement chuckled. "Some here might doubt that." He waved toward his own bunk. "Grab yourself a nap. Maybe then you'll be rested up enough to get a good night's sleep. I'd best go sit and stare at the telegraph key until it tells me when we'll get some more blasting powder."

It seemed to Ted his head had barely touched the bunk when someone was shaking him back to life. He blinked groggily, trying to focus his eyes on the face at his side.

"Mr. Henderson, you gotta come quick!" The speaker was a wiry spike peddler Ted knew by sight but not by name. "They's gonna be big trouble down at Hell on Wheels!"

Ted groaned and struggled to a sitting position on the edge of the cot. He could not seem to shake the cobwebs from his head. He looked at his boots at the side of the bunk and did not remember taking them off.

"What's the problem?"

"That big Shaughnessy feller. He's dead drunk, near out of his mind, and he's a-wavin' a pistol all around Murphy's place! I think that powder blast done shook his head up, Mr. Henderson. You best come quick afore he shoots a hole in somebody. He might listen to you."

Ted pulled on his boots, groaning aloud with the effort. "All right," he said. "I'll see what I can do. Doesn't sound like Shaughnessy's style, but he's too good a man to waste." He strapped on his belt gun, shrugged into his light jacket, and stepped outside. The spike peddler had disappeared into the darkness.

Outside Murphy's tent at the edge of Hell on Wheels, Ted paused for a moment to listen. He could hear nothing out of the ordinary from inside, only the muted murmur of conversations and clink of bottles. Shaughnessy must have calmed down some, or maybe passed out, Ted thought. Still, he had dragged his aching body this far, he might as well check it out.

He swung the tent flap aside and stepped into the dimly lighted saloon. Shaughnessy was nowhere to be seen.

An alarm bell suddenly went off in Ted's mind. Every one of the dozen or so men in the tent were Bear Fallon's cronies. And every man had a short club, a pick handle, or a shovel within reach.

Ted knew instantly he had walked into a trap. At a table a few feet from the bar, Bear Fallon sat, a massive hand wrapped around a bottle. The big head spiker's face twisted in a satisfied snarl. "Well, lookie here, boys," Fallon said mockingly, "seems our big mean scout's come to visit."

Fallon rose from the low spike keg on which he had been sitting and took a menacing step toward Ted. Quickly calculating the odds, Ted realized he only had one chance to avoid being stomped to death. He slipped the thong from the hammer of the Dragoon in its holster at his hip. His fingers closed on the butt of the weapon.

Then something slammed across the back of his shoulders, knocking him face first into the soggy sawdust on the saloon floor. The numbing blow shocked all the air from his lungs and sent the handgun flying from his weakened fingers.

Desperation gave Ted the strength to roll to one side. An ax handle grazed the back of his shoulder and thumped into the sawdust where his head had been. He twisted once more, gasping air back into his lungs. His hand bumped into a heavy shoe. He saw the man's other foot drawn back to kick his head. Ted cupped his hand behind the man's foot and yanked. With a cry of surprise, the big man crashed to the sawdust floor.

Ted lashed out with a bootheel, catching one man on the side of the knee. A club dropped beside Ted as the workman yelled in sudden pain. Ted scooped up the club, rose to a crouch, and lunged toward Fallon, dodging a wild swing from a nearby man.

But fatigue and the solid blow across his back had sapped Ted's small reservoir of strength. He never made it to Fallon. Big hands grabbed his clothing and he felt his arms pinned to his sides, the club ripped from his grasp.

Burly men on each side of him locked steel-trap grips on

Ted's arms, holding him perfectly still as Fallon approached. The big Irishman took his time, savoring each step.

"Not such a herd bull now, are you, scout?" Fallon smirked. Ted made no reply. He merely glared at Fallon and stood relaxed, hoping for just one chance to break free of the bruising grips on his arms.

Fallon was only a couple of strides away, the sneer on his lips reflected in the hate dancing in his eyes. The big man rubbed the knuckles of his right hand in anticipation.

Ted sensed his opportunity. With all the speed and power he could muster, he lifted a foot and stomped his heel into the instep of the man who held his right arm. Bones crumpled beneath the boot as the man gasped in agony. Ted tore his arm free, then spun and slammed a sweeping right fist into the face of the man holding his left arm. The blow caught the surprised laborer between the eyes. His left arm free as well, Ted cracked an elbow into the man's stomach. He folded and went down.

Then Fallon was on Ted, his big fist clanging into his opponent's temple. The blow snapped Ted's head back. In his blurred vision, the single lantern hanging from a pole almost flickered out. He felt his knees buckle, but he did not fall. Once again his arms were trapped in the powerful grip of two of Fallon's crew.

This time he was given no chance to escape. Fallon's fist plowed into his belly, driving the air from his lungs. Another heavy blow landed above his cheekbone. The skin split and the blood began to flow, but there was no pain. Ted tried weakly to kick Fallon in the groin, but the big Irishman slapped the boot aside. "Not this time," Fallon said with a smirk. "You're my meat now, Henderson."

Ted felt the jarring impact of Fallon's fists, again in his belly, then to his head, and back to his belly. The ringing in his ears grew to a roar. A dark curtain began to drop over his vision. Ted knew the only escape from the brutal beating was a short slide into unconsciousness—and he also knew he would never awaken.

A scuffling sound and a yell penetrated his fading sense of hearing. The first waves of pain from Fallon's hands lanced through his body. Suddenly the constant stream of blows on his body stopped abruptly. The confining arms fell away from his sides. Without that support, Ted began to slide toward the floor. Then strong hands were under his armpits, a broad face forming and then fading before his swollen eyes. Uncomprehending, Ted swung a weak fist toward the face. The blow was little more than a pat.

"Easy, my friend," the face said. "Give an old horse soldier a chance to repay a favor. It's Kevin."

Ted swayed in his friend's solid grip. He became aware of the sounds of a fight raging around him, shouts and screams of pain, the crack of wood against flesh and bone. He summoned all his strength and forced himself to speak through split and battered lips. "Kevin?"

"The same. Come on, Colonel. Let's get you out of the way while there's still time left for Kevin to play with the boys."

Ted let himself be half dragged, half carried, to the end of the bar where his back would be against the canvas wall. "Just sit easy now and watch the fun," Kevin said, lowering Ted gently onto a seat.

Ted's vision began to clear. Amid the struggling bodies and whirling clubs, he heard Kevin's whoop of pure delight as he leapt into the fray. Shaughnessy was there, too, cursing fluently, and with each cussword rapping a man's head into a tent upright. Slowly Ted began to recognize many of the men. Kevin had brought about a dozen friends.

In the middle of the swirling hand-to-hand fight, Bear Fallon hammered one of the O'Reilly crew to the ground, kicked the man in the ribs, then spun as a big hand clamped onto his shoulder. Kevin's fist landed squarely between Fallon's eyes. Fallon staggered and a second blow walloped into his belly. Then he took a sharp crack on the back of his head. Whiskey splashed from a bottle broken over his skull and poured into his eyes. He blinked at the sharp sting, his vision momentarily gone. Fallon instinctively reached for the knife at his belt, only to yelp in surprise and pain as an ax handle slammed into his hand.

"Finish up on him, Kevin," Shaughnessy yelled above the din of combat. "I spotted me one ain't been whupped yet!"

Kevin glanced at the groggy, whiskey-drenched Fallon, then swept a fallen club from the sawdust floor. With the same motion he cracked the weapon against Fallon's knee-caps. The thick club then flashed upward, rapping Fallon's temple. The blocky head spiker grunted and dropped to one knee.

"Not having near as much fun now, are you, Fallon?" Kevin asked in obvious glee. He measured the weaving Fallon with care, then swung a heavy boot into the kneeling man's jaw, sending him sprawling on his back. Kevin dropped onto the huge body and methodically began bouncing the club off first one side of Fallon's skull, then the other.

"Kevin!" Ted's voice was barely a croak. "Behind you!"

The ex-soldier reacted immediately. He rolled free of Fallon's body and jabbed upward with the end of the club. The weapon caught a laborer in the midsection, a short, powerful blow that *whooshed* the air from the body. A heavy hunting knife dropped from the man's grip. Kevin hammered a solid fist behind the man's ear and left him doubled over the club in his belly.

Suddenly one of Fallon's men, bleeding freely, bolted for the door. The rout was on. Kevin turned back toward the spot where Fallon had fallen. The man was not there. In a corner of the tent, a section of canvas fluttered back into place.

Kevin and Shaughnessy stood in the middle of the tent, grinning and bruised, and whooped in exuberance. Ted forced his trembling body into movement, plucked a bottle from beneath the bar, and tossed it to Kevin. The foreman twisted it open, lifted it, and drank deeply before handing it to Shaughnessy. When Shaughnessy lowered the bottle it was empty.

"Hot damn, my friends, that was a fun scrap!" Kevin called. "Now, where's old Murphy?"

One of Kevin's joint-tie men found the saloon keeper crouched beneath the far end of the bar and dragged the white-faced, trembling man to the center of the rough pine plank used as a serving counter. Kevin stuck a thick finger under Murphy's chin. The barkeep's eyes were wide with fear.

"Mr. Murphy," Kevin said, deliberately speaking in an exaggerated brogue, "it appears you have lost some customers. Now, since you obviously offered your small pub here to the pleasures of Fallon's men, methinks it only fair that you share the fruits of the field and orchard with us. Without charge, of course?"

The terrified Murphy could only nod. Kevin stepped behind the bar and began handing out bottles. Each of the grinning, sore-knuckled friends of Ted and Kevin soon had an armload of whiskey, rye, and rum.

"On your way out, drag one of Fallon's men with you," Kevin instructed his band. "The place sure is cluttered up."

Shaughnessy turned to Ted. "Mr. Henderson," he said, "you look plumb terrible. Anything busted?"

Ted shook his head. The effort seemed to set a crew of little railroad men with sharp mauls to pounding on the inside of his temples. "I—I'll be all right, boys. And thanks. They would have killed me in here. . . ."

"True, true," Shaughnessy said, "but still, I want to say thanks for the chance at that scrap. Damn, I ain't had so much fun since the brawl on the Boston docks two years ago."

Kevin chuckled. " 'Twas a fun fight, at that. Don't remember when I enjoyed myself that much. Old Bear's got some wounded troops in his den now." He glanced at Ted. "You sure you're okay, Ted?"

"I'll let you know tomorrow when I really start hurting," Ted said with a grimace. "How did you boys happen to wander by here just at the right time, anyway?"

"We been keepin' an eye on Murphy's place," Shaughnessy said. "It's been a hangout for Fallon's thugs for weeks. We seen that spike peddler come out and head for the rail cars, then come back. Pretty soon he ducks out and starts lookin' like a rabbit huntin' a hole." Shaughnessy rubbed a lacerated knuckle. "We found him 'fore he found his hole. He turned out to be a pretty talkative feller."

"Ted," Kevin said, "I'm sorry we didn't get here sooner. Took some time to round up enough boys to even the odds. It looks like you paid for that wait."

"If you hadn't shown up when you did, I wouldn't be alive right now. I'll trade a few bruises for my life anytime and swear I got a good deal." Ted tried to step from behind the bar and almost fell.

"Come on, Colonel," Kevin said, slipping a supporting arm around his friend. "Let's get you to bed. And this time you'll stay there if I have to sit on you."

"What do we do with this place?" Shaughnessy asked, surveying the wreckage from the fight and the empty liquor boxes.

Ted glared at the cowering, ashen-faced Murphy. "Burn

it," he said. "If Murphy gives you any trouble, work him over with a pick handle."

Shaughnessy grinned and reached for an oil-fired lantern. He waved the lamp toward Murphy. The saloon owner licked his lips and glanced longingly at the door. "Murphy, send the bill to Fallon," Shaughnessy said, hurling the lamp against the bar.

It was a quick, hot blaze. Murphy, wringing his hands and whining, could only stand and watch helplessly.

Meanwhile, inside Pittsburgh Rose's tent, Bear Fallon slumped on a chair as Rose dabbed at the blood smears on his face. Finally Fallon's rage overcame his physical pain. He swatted Rose's hand aside roughly and began probing through his travel bags.

"What you doing, Bear?" Rosie asked worriedly.

"Got—a gun in here—somewhere. I'll kill that damn O'Reilly—Henderson, too—tonight."

Rose bunched Fallon's shirt in her fist. "Bear, don't! Don't be foolish. They'll be looking for you to try something tonight. They'll shoot you on sight. Bide your time. Wait for the right chance," she pleaded.

Gradually, Fallon's fury subsided. He conceded that Rose was right. There was always another day. He sighed heavily and sat on the edge of the bed.

A few hours later on the far edge of Hell on Wheels, a bartender glanced up at a late arrival and frowned.

"You in the wrong place, boy," the bartender said quietly. "This here place is fer black folks like me. Don't serve nobody else."

The slender man in the floppy hat inclined his head respectfully. "I do not wish drink," he said. "If you would be so kind—I seek information. My name is Chin-Lu. I search for my sister, Ling-Tse. Do you know of her?"

The bartender shook his graying head. There was something about the slender Chinaman that made him want to help. "Don't reckon as to how I ever seen a China-girl here, but I'm new at Hell on Wheels. Been lookin' long?"

Chin-Lu nodded. Briefly, he told the bartender of his sister's abduction and subsequent sale into prostitution. "I traveled from San Francisco to the place called Omaha in Nebraska. There I learned that she had been seen at a town called North Platte. From there I went to the place named

Julesburg, and then I was sent here. She must be here, for the trail has followed the railroad. I will find her."

"I hope you do, Chin-Lu," the black bartender said solemnly. "My people know what it's like to be a slave. I'll ask around. Maybe somebody's seen her, even though us folks got our own women for hire. We don't get let in high-priced women-tents much."

"I would be in your debt," Chin-Lu said. He picked up his small bundle of belongings. "Do you know of a place where I might sleep?"

"Got any money?"

"A little. Enough, if I am careful," Chin-Lu replied.

"Out back there's a sleepin' tent. We get a few black folks through here what don't work for the railroad. You can stay there. Fifty cents a night, you don't mind the company."

"I have no reason to dislike a man for the color of his skin," Chin-Lu said. "It is such a small thing when weighed against the color of his heart." He counted out a few coins and placed them on the bar. "Your hospitality is most kind. I will stay a few days and continue the search for my sister."

Eight

The bitter north wind swept over the frozen Black Hills, rattling the stiff buffalo-hide covering of the Cheyenne senior warrior's lodge. But the wind was a warm breeze compared to the chill in the eyes of the peace chief standing just beyond Horse Catcher's cooking fire. Horse Catcher, who feared no man, was growing increasingly uncomfortable under the steady stare of Yellow Crow.

"Horse Catcher opened his lodge to the blue-eyed one named Long Walker," Yellow Crow said accusingly. "He has harbored an enemy, one who would destroy the Cheyenne people."

The senior warrior shrugged, outwardly indifferent. But his stomach fluttered. Yellow Crow's tongue could sting like the summer wasp when he was angry. Horse Catcher was ten summers younger than Yellow Crow, but he had no desire to further provoke his leader.

"Long Walker's arguments were strong," Horse Catcher said weakly. "Throughout the Cheyenne winter camps, he has brought promises of great victories when the grass greens. Many braves listen to his words—"

"Words," Yellow Crow interrupted contemptuously. "Words from one who kills babies. Words from one who wars on squaws and old men. Words from one who uses others to his own ends. Words from a coward." Yellow Crow stabbed a finger at Horse Catcher. "Does Horse Catcher of the Cheyenne believe these words? And what of Horse Catcher's own promise to keep the peace of the treaties signed with the white man? Do Horse Catcher's words no longer have meaning?"

The senior warrior felt the flush of anger in his own cheeks. "Horse Catcher will keep his word," he snapped. "None from his band will join Long Walker." Horse Catcher cocked an eyebrow at Yellow Crow. "And what of the peace chief of the Cheyenne? Will Yellow Crow stop his braves from hearing Long Walker? Or has he come to Horse Catcher's camp to avoid facing the blue-eyed one?"

For an instant Horse Catcher feared his temper might have pushed him too far. Yellow Crow's hand had dropped to the knife at his belt, and his eyes glittered in rage. "What does Horse Catcher mean?"

"Only that Long Walker is going from this place to the winter camp of Yellow Crow, there to recruit braves from beneath the peace chief's very nose," Horse Catcher replied cautiously. "Horse Catcher meant no slur on his brother's courage."

"When was the renegade Sioux last here?" Yellow Crow demanded.

"Two suns ago."

Even as Horse Catcher spoke, Yellow Crow hurled the lodge cover aside and mounted his lanky sorrel, slipping the Spencer carbine from its saddle boot. The dark rage built within him at each stride of the horse. Yellow Crow cursed vehemently and forced himself not to push the sorrel into a run. A long ride over treacherous, frozen ground lay ahead before he reached his own camp. There Long Walker would die—or be hunted down as the wounded wolf had been.

Yellow Crow found no comfort in the fact that his swing through a half-dozen winter camps had swayed many Cheyenne braves from joining the hated half-breed's group. At each stop he had hoped in vain to catch up with Long Walker and drive the special bullet through his heart. Now at last he knew where to find the outlaw.

On the rocky ledge of a hill overlooking the Cheyenne camp below, Long Walker rubbed his hands briskly to restore the warmth. His patience was wearing thin. For most of the night and nearly a day, he had watched and waited. Still, the target he sought had not appeared. Yellow Crow, the white man's pet who had so often stood in Long Walker's way, seemed not to be in his winter camp.

The flap of Yellow Crow's lodge fluttered open. A figure wrapped in a bulky buffalo robe stepped into the sharp wind, carrying a water pail. Long Walker realized it was the wife of Yellow Crow. A sinister smile touched his lips. If he could not ambush the hated Cheyenne chief, he could at least deal the coward a blow.

Long Walker lined the sights of his carbine on the small figure below and carefully squeezed the trigger. The rifle stabbed against his shoulder, and after what seemed at least two heartbeats the buffalo-robed figure staggered and fell. He grunted in satisfaction. The wife of Yellow Crow lay on the frozen ground.

Knowing pursuit would not be far behind, Long Walker sprinted to his horse concealed beyond the top of the hill. He swung into the saddle and yanked the animal toward the east. He knew the gaunt Indian ponies of the Cheyenne, weak from lack of grass, would be no match for his large, grain-fed mount. There was no need to fear capture.

A smile twisted Long Walker's lips. The death of Yellow Crow's wife helped salve some of the hate that burned in his scarred torso. Kicking his horse into a lope, Long Walker wished he could stay around to watch the Cheyenne peace chief mourn.

Talking Bird slowly regained consciousness and lay for a moment, confused. A great fire burned in her left shoulder above the breast, and a gray light hovered above her head. Then she recognized the light. It was the fading of day as seen through the smoke vent in the lodge roof. She reached toward the pain in her shoulder, remembering the blow that had slammed her to the earth. Her hand was clasped in a firm grip.

"Be still, little one," a calm and gentle voice said. "We are almost finished."

"What—what happened?" Talking Bird whispered.

"You have been shot. It is not a bad wound." Talking Bird recognized the voice. It was one of the most skilled of the Cheyenne medicine men.

"But why—who—?"

"Shush, be still. We do not know. This may cause some pain, but it will not last long. Do not move."

Talking Bird did as she was told, grateful that this Cheyenne medicine man saw nothing wrong with touching the female body, as some did.

Small, sharp flashes of pain continued as the Cheyenne surgeon carefully cleaned the wound. Then she felt a pressure that remained, and knew the healing poultice had been strapped into place. Gradually, the pain subsided to a more tolerable level.

She opened her eyes and looked into the knowing, kindly face of the medicine man, who smiled gently. "If the bad flesh does not come, you will be well again very soon, Talking Bird," the old one said. "You will have a scar and a story for the little ones who will one day nurse at your breast. Now you must rest."

Sometime later, Talking Bird awakened at the gentle touch of a calloused palm on her cheek. In the flickering light from the fire in the center of the lodge, she saw Yellow Crow kneeling at her side. She smiled weakly in greeting, then pulled him to her with her free hand. Her left arm and shoulder throbbed with the effort as she lifted herself for his embrace.

"Talking Bird—" Yellow Crow's voice was choked with emotion.

"Hush, husband," she said quietly. "It is nothing, little more than a scratch. The bullet was almost spent, and the heavy buffalo robe turned much of its power." She allowed Yellow Crow's strong arm to ease her back to the robes.

"Yellow Crow knows who did this thing," her husband said bitterly. "He has found the spot from where the shot was fired. He read the signs. This was the work of the Sioux coward Long Walker. It was a shot aimed not at Talking Bird as a person, but as someone Yellow Crow loves. For this Long Walker shall die!"

Talking Bird clutched at her husband's arm, her blood chilled at the tone of his voice. "Yellow Crow, what will you do?"

"Follow Long Walker—to the great sea, if necessary— and then he will die. Slowly. On this Yellow Crow vows the lives of his unborn sons!"

Talking Bird tightened her grip on his clothing. "Yellow Crow, listen. Do not leave this camp! For many moons this hatred of the blue-eyed one has been a blanket between man and wife. Even in Talking Bird's arms Yellow Crow's thoughts have not strayed from Long Walker. The bullet fired into Talking Bird's shoulder is but a bee sting compared to the hurt in her heart as she watches this hate destroy her husband."

She let her hand fall free and waved at the wall of the lodge, where pellets of sleet sounded a tiny drumbeat against the heavy hide covering. "Listen, already the small ice comes.

Soon there will be much snow. Yellow Crow is needed here by his people. He is needed here by his wife. All tribes need his tongue at the meeting with the white colonel of soldiers only a few days from now. At that meeting there will be talk of war and talk of peace. Who will speak for peace if Yellow Crow is not there? Do these things not mean more in his life than his hate for a crazy man?"

Talking Bird's heart sank still further as she realized her pleas had not reached Yellow Crow's ears. Already she could sense the plan of the hunt forming in her husband's mind. The muscles of his jaw bulged in determination.

"Yellow Crow will be but one man," Talking Bird pleaded desperately. "Long Walker has many warriors. They would kill Yellow Crow on sight, their hearts poisoned against him by Long Walker's tongue and Yellow Crow's work for peace with the whites. And should Yellow Crow find his enemy, might not Yellow Crow be killed anyway?"

She reached out, cupped a hand behind his shoulder, and pulled him to her. "Talking Bird begs—do not do this foolish thing. Stay here. Perhaps in these long winter nights husband and wife might make a fine son."

Abruptly, Yellow Crow pulled away. "Time rides past, Talking Bird. Each moment puts the coward who fires bullets at women farther from Yellow Crow's reach. Yellow Crow leaves with the first light of dawn and will not return until Long Walker is dead."

Then his voice softened as he turned to face her. "Yellow Crow does not wish to leave this lodge, to be gone from his wife's side, Talking Bird. But does his wife not see? Until Long Walker's scalp hangs from Yellow Crow's lance, the evil spirits that torment Yellow Crow—and his wife as well—shall not be chased from this body." He scowled as he fingered the leather pouch hanging about his neck. The outline of the single Spencer cartridge inside only heightened his resolve.

"In his dreams Yellow Crow sees the one with the blue eyes. He holds the body of a baby. It is covered with blood," Yellow Crow continued bitterly. "The baby is the son of Talking Bird and Yellow Crow. Thus the spirits speak. Long Walker must never have the chance to thrust his knives into children not yet born."

Talking Bird knew the argument was lost. Yellow Crow's hatred ran so deep the current could be turned only with death.

"Then may the spirits ride with Yellow Crow. Do nothing foolish. Live to return to Talking Bird's side. Her heart goes with her husband. When he returns, Talking Bird will be here to rejoice."

At the first pale wash of dawn, Yellow Crow, his face streaked with war paint, slipped the hackamore over the head of the palomino gelding he had ridden for many years. The horse, still strong and deep-chested, nuzzled Yellow Crow's side.

"Yellow Crow is sorry to interrupt the rest of the corn-colored horse," the Cheyenne said. "But for this hunt Yellow Crow shall need the best of all horses. He had promised the horse that no more would he have to take the trail. Yellow Crow must break that promise. Forgive him, and serve him well."

The palomino snuffled softly. It was as though the horse understood and agreed, Yellow Crow thought. He mounted the gelding, then leaned down and plucked his war lance from where its point dug into the frozen earth. The wind rippled the eagle feathers decorating the shaft of the lance. Yellow Crow raised the weapon high overhead. "Long Walker!" he called to the distant hills and prairies. "Yellow Crow takes up the hunt! The land of the red man holds no hiding place for Long Walker!"

Yellow Crow and the aging but eager palomino moved at an easy trot toward the east. It was the direction the tracks of Long Walker's pony had taken from the site of the ambush. By midmorning the sleet had changed to thick, wet, wind-driven snow. The faint set of tracks he followed disappeared beneath the growing layer of white.

At a ridge fifteen miles from the Cheyenne winter camp, the trail played out. Even the eyes of so fine a tracker could not see through three inches of fresh, heavy snow. Yellow Crow checked the palomino and let the horse catch its wind. He stroked the muscular neck.

"This hunt will be long, yellow horse," he said quietly. "May the spirits give both Yellow Crow and his horse the strength to find their game."

Bear Fallon slapped the eight of diamonds onto the nine of clubs, studied the layout, and then angrily swept the cards from the low table. He was bored with solitaire. As he glowered at the huddled form beneath a pile of blankets on the bed nearby, he realized he was getting a little bored with Rosie, too. *Slut don't do nothing that can't be done in bed*, he thought bitterly.

Fallon refused to admit that his growing dissatisfaction with Pittsburgh Rose was no fault of the prostitute. It was the pain in his face, still swollen and cut from the beating at Kevin O'Reilly's hands, that kept his mood sour. Abruptly he stood. *Damn that Irish hide of his—I'll settle his hash once and for all.* Fallon's fingers closed on the butt of the pistol in his travel bag.

He was checking the loads in the handgun when a quiet call came from beyond the flap of the tent.

"Bear? You in there?"

Fallon stomped the two strides to the door of Rose's living quarters and hurled the tent flap aside. The blast of cold air and wind-driven snow did not cool his anger. The man outside was bundled against the elements, but his face still carried the marks of the fists of O'Reilly's crew.

"Gamblin, you better have a damn good reason for bothering me!" Fallon said tersely, thrusting the revolver into his belt.

Gamblin held out a folded paper. "Message come for you, Bear. Tol' the telegraph operator I'd bring it."

"What's it say?"

Gamblin shrugged. "Beats me. I can't read."

Fallon unfolded the paper and stared at the block print letters.

MOM SICK. DAD MAD. GET HOME NOW.
BIG BROTHER.

Fallon stood for a moment, confused. Mom was the code word for Southern Overland. Dad was the board of directors, and Big Brother was Garth Pfister. Fallon did not understand why the chairman could be angry or the project in trouble. But the tone of the telegram left nothing to the imagination. When Pfister said "Get home now," he did not mean next spring.

"Gamblin, when's the next train headed back to Omaha?" Fallon crumpled the message and tossed it into a corner of the tent.

Gamblin scratched his stubbled chin. "Supply train loadin' right now, Bear. She'll pull out in fifteen minutes." Gamblin started to ask a question but thought the better of it. "Anything you need, Bear?"

Fallon already was stuffing personal items into the travel bag. He shook his head and waved a hand, sending Gamblin on his way. *Dammit,* Fallon thought, *I won't even have time to kill the Irishman or the scout. What the hell—they'll keep till I get back.*

"Bear?" Rose's voice was heavy with sleep. "What's going on? What are you doing?"

"What the hell's it look like I'm doing?" Fallon snapped. Then his voice softened a bit and he stroked her hip. "I'm going back East for a while, Rosie. New York. Then I'll be back. I'll bring you some fancy clothes like the rich ladies wear, okay?"

"Oh, Bear! Take me with you! I can be ready in five minutes, and it's been so long since I've been to New York!"

"Sorry, Rosie. This is strictly business," he said.

The hopeful smile faded from Rose's face. "But Bear, it's—so dreary out here. What am I supposed to do until you get back?"

"Just stay put, Rosie." Fallon counted out five hundred dollars and tossed it on the bed. "Here. Maybe this'll keep you company. And you won't be doing any work while I'm gone, will you?"

Pittsburgh Rose knew it was not a question, it was a threat. She tried to bunch her mouth into a pout and forced a smile. "All right, Bear," she said. "But don't be gone too long. It's going to get cold in this bed without you." She raised the covers and patted the bed beside her. "One for the road, Bear?"

Fallon winked at the invitation but shook his head. "No time, Rosie. Gotta sneak a ride on a supply train pulling out right quick." He crammed a final item into the travel bag. Then Fallon reached out and playfully—and painfully—pinched her exposed breast. "You save those things for me, Rosie," he said. "I'll be back for 'em soon."

Pittsburgh Rose watched the tent flap close behind the departing hulk. She stretched languidly. Fallon was a good meal ticket, she thought, but the four walls of the tent had been closing in on her. *Bear Fallon acts like he owns me,* she thought angrily. *Well, by God, I'll show him! I'm not about to sit here like some housewife while he's off partying in New York. Besides, it will be fun to get back in circulation again.*

There were other men out there with money. And maybe they would not play so rough as Fallon. Already, Pittsburgh Rose was planning what to wear for her prowls through Hell on Wheels. Bear Fallon could not keep her tied down to her tent if he was on the rails to New York.

Rosie giggled as she plucked the cash from the bed and tucked it into her bulging purse. That big Irish foreman that Fallon hated so much was a mighty handsome man, and he should have plenty of money in his pocket. None of the other girls had been able to arouse any interest from Kevin O'Reilly— and Rosie loved a challenge.

Kevin pushed himself away from the small table and paced the floor. "Ted, if Bear Fallon isn't our man, then by God the Pope's a Baptist!"

Ted thoughtfully touched the fresh cuts and bruises left from the fracas with Fallon. "It looks that way. But we have no proof. And it could be I'm just getting tired of Fallon pounding on me all the time."

Kevin turned and studied his friend. "Who else could be causing these delays? I didn't see Fallon anywhere before or after that powder car blew up. He was the only regular drinker not hung over on the day the water was salted. And the explosion that killed two powder monkeys last week came right after I saw a man who could have been Fallon running along the cut."

Ted nodded thoughtfully. "There's another thing, Kevin. I've been studying the accident that killed Sean Grady. The way those two were walking, the falling rails should have hit both men. But Fallon got free. Grady was right in the middle of the iron. I've been wondering how. The only answer I can come up with is that Fallon *knew ahead of time* that the iron would fall."

Kevin grunted in agreement. "Add this to the stew, Ted. Almost every man killed or maimed in Hell on Wheels was one we could ill afford to lose, shorthanded as we are. And not one of them was from Fallon's bunch."

"The big question is *why*," Ted said thoughtfully. "Fallon always seems to have plenty of money. One man wouldn't be trying to bedevil an entire railroad. My guess is he's working for somebody. Someone who doesn't like the Union Pacific. But who?"

Abruptly, Kevin reached for his hat and coat. " 'Tis time

we stopped wonderin' and went to searchin', me friend," he said. "I'm off to Hell on Wheels to see what this ol' Irish wolfhound can sniff out."

Ted rose and reached for his own coat. Kevin waved him back. "You're staying here, Ted. Folks get kind of close-mouthed when you're around."

Kevin tugged his hat down firmly against the icy wind and slogged his way through driving snow to the biggest saloon tent in Hell on Wheels.

"The luck of the Irish," he muttered as he stepped into the smoky interior, "if you want to call it that." Among the patrons of the combination bar and gaming hall were several men who were part of Fallon's group. Many of them bore fresh bruises and glowered darkly at Kevin. For a moment he thought they might be interested in continuing the battle they had lost at Murphy's, but one by one they returned to their drinking or card games.

Kevin grinned crookedly at one battered face, then weaved his way toward the bar. He made it a point to bump into one table and then jostle a drinker at the rough pine bar. "Sorry—friend," he said, slurring his words. "Reckon I'm a-losin' a battle with old demon rum. Time—fer another round. This Irishman ain't whupped yet." He clapped the drinker on the shoulder. "C'mon, Gamblin. Buy you a drink. Hot damn, that was one fine scrap in Murphy's. You tagged me a good one or two, you did."

Kevin soon realized his drunk act was working, and that Gamblin was not acting. The man had made a few runs through the rye already. A glass or two more might get the job done. Kevin made a bumbling show of peeling a bill from the roll he carried. He left the change on the bar, and produced another bill on the second round as though he had forgotten the change in a drunken haze.

"Hey, where's ol' Bear?" Kevin asked after the third drink. "Hope I din't—didn't—hit 'im too hard."

Suspicion flashed in Gamblin's bleary eyes, but Kevin's wide and boyish grin reassured him. "Been figgerin'," Kevin said, "ain't no use us a-carryin' on no fuss. Hell, ol' Bear ain't bad. Just cranky. Reckon he's mad 'cause I got the foreman's job. His place, I'd be mad, too. Wanna buy 'im a drink. No hard feelin's." Kevin let himself weave against the bar.

Gamblin belched noisily, and his eyes looked like they were about to go out of focus. "Tha—thass right white o' you,

O—O'Reilly. Hafta wait a spell though. Ol' Bear, he—he done lit out."

"Thassa durn shame," Kevin said. "Where'd a man find to light out to 'round here?"

Gamblin downed another shot of the rank whiskey and grinned crookedly. "He done—gone back—back East way of Omaha."

Kevin shook his head as if in awe. "Never seen the big—big town. Never hadda money." He sipped at his own drink. "Wunner where ol' Bear got his? Seems to me like he's allus loaded. He gam—gamblin' onna side?"

"Not ol' Bear," Gamblin said in bleary admiration. "Has his—hisself a gravy train. Big outfit back East sends 'im money."

"Could use—piece that pie myself," Kevin said. "Reckon they—they'd wanna hire—'nother one?"

"Not them shippin' folks," Gamblin said, tilting dangerously on the bar stool. Kevin propped the drunken man back into place.

"Any idee who he's workin' for?"

"Som—Sompin' Overland. Never catched the name." Gamblin turned to stare at Kevin, then his half-focused eyes settled on the tent entrance. "Well, I be—be damned," Gamblin muttered. "Never thought ol' Rosie'd have—nerve to be on prowl arreddy."

Kevin turned and took a long look at the woman who had just entered the saloon, shaking the snow from her heavy wrap and tossing it across an empty table. She was tall with ash-blond hair and a figure that turned every head in the place. She had to be Pittsburgh Rose, Kevin thought, Fallon's private stock. He could understand now why she had a reputation as being the highest-priced prostitute between St. Louis and San Francisco.

"Thass—thass Rosie?" Kevin muttered as though awe-stricken. "Man, I sure—like to have somma that."

Gamblin chuckled. "You got the price, you kin have it," he said with a leer. "Can't afford it myself. 'Sides, Fallon'd kill me when he gets back."

Kevin clapped his drinking partner on the shoulder. "Reckon I'll go check—check this one out, friend," he said.

Within minutes, Kevin was seated at a table, the woman on his lap. She wore a thin indigo gown, and she rested a firm, unsupported breast invitingly against Kevin's chest. Her hand rested behind his neck.

"Buy me another drink, honey?" Her voice was low and husky.

"You bet, girl," Kevin said, waving to the bartender. He fished out his hefty roll of bills again, and saw the look in the woman's eyes as she surveyed the wad with measured care.

"Tell you what, honey," she whispered in his ear. "Why don't you buy a bottle and let's go over to my place." As she spoke, Pittsburgh Rose lifted Kevin's free hand and placed it high on her scantily covered thigh. Despite himself, Kevin felt the strong urge that had been denied in the past months. He suddenly understood how many a happily married man could be unfaithful.

In Rosie's tent, Kevin placed the bottle on the table as the woman slipped out of her coat. He poured a drink and heard the rustle of cloth behind him. When he turned, Pittsburgh Rose had dropped the bodice of her dress, her breasts full and firm in the soft light of the oil lamp in the tent.

Kevin swallowed hard. He forced himself to recall Wind Flower's slender body and trusting face until the lush form before him no longer held such a powerful impact.

"You like what you see, honey?" Rose asked.

Kevin nodded.

"You can have all of it—for a hundred."

Kevin reached into a pocket, slipped a hundred dollar bill from his roll, and handed it to her. Rosie loosened a couple of buttons and hooked her thumbs in the waist of her dress, preparing to slip it down over her hips.

"Save yourself the trouble, Rosie," Kevin said, his voice soft, the slurred act dropped.

The prostitute looked up in surprise. "What the hell is this? Don't you like me, O'Reilly? And you're supposed to be drunk."

"Rosie, any sane man would want you," Kevin said. "But I'm not sane. I'm an Irishman with an Indian wife at home. No offense, but I'm taking her no unexpected souvenirs from this job." He waved a hand to shut off her protest. "You can still earn the money. I just want some information."

An hour later Kevin stepped from Rosie's tent. He admitted to himself he was a physical wreck, and that he had gotten out just in time. A man could stand just so much temptation from such well-shaped flesh. He took a deep breath of the icy night air. The snow had stopped and the wind seemed to be easing. It had been an expensive night but a profitable one, he thought, as he patted the crumpled paper from the corner of Rosie's tent, now safely tucked in his shirt pocket.

Kevin decided to take the shortest route back to the construction train and report his findings to Ted. The route led past the long row of tents with red lanterns burning in the windows.

He was nearing the last of the tents when he noticed a slender figure in a quilted coat framed for a moment in the light of an opened flap. It was the man he had seen earlier— the Chinaman. And possibly the man who had pulled five workers from beneath the wreckage of the railroad car. Instead of walking on past the tent, Kevin paused outside the canvas flap.

From his Sunday night roundups, he knew the layout of the interior. The tent was divided by canvas partitions into several compartments. The front was where the madam, a surly matron called "Miz Belle" by the railroaders, greeted her customers and collected. The remaining compartments each held a cot, a washbasin, and a girl.

Through the canvas wall Kevin heard the angry voice of a man called Moss, a big, powerful ex-coalminer who served as Miz Belle's bartender and bouncer.

"You ain't welcome in here, China-boy!" Moss warned. "We don't cater to your type! Now git out!"

Kevin tensed at the words. He knew Moss by reputation. The big man had beaten at least two men to death before leaving the coal mines, and even the burly Irishmen on the railroad wanted no part of a showdown with Moss.

Kevin heard the soft reply of the slender Chinese, but could not make out the words. Cautiously, he opened the tent flap a crack and peered inside. The Chinaman stood before the bar, his hat in his hands. The veins in Moss's neck swelled in rage. "Git out, I said!"

"I do not wish trouble," the Chinese said quietly, his tone respectful despite the challenge from Moss. "I wish only to find a woman—"

"I tol' you we got no women for no China-boy at any price," Moss said icily. "One more word outta you an' I'm comin' from behind this bar!"

The Chinese stood his ground, his face expressionless. "You are the proprietor?" he asked the bouncer.

"Awright! We'll do it the hard way!" Moss stomped around the end of the bar, fists clenched. An ominous grin of anticipation twisted the broad features. He approached the Chinaman. "You gonna go peaceable?"

The slender man smiled and shook his head. "I do not go until I have spoken with the person who runs this place," he said.

From a compartment nearby, a large woman, lumpy with fat, stepped into the receiving area. "What's the problem, Moss?" Miz Belle asked in an unfriendly tone.

"China-boy wants to talk to the boss."

"I'm the owner," Miz Belle said, "and I got nothin' to say to no slant-eyed runaway from some laundry. Throw him out, Moss!"

The bouncer cocked a big fist and reached with his other hand toward the Chinaman's collar. The watching Kevin crouched, prepared to spring into action and pull Moss from the smaller man before the Chinese was beaten to death.

Kevin could have saved his energy.

The Chinaman, still smiling politely, reached out and grasped Moss's extended wrist—and, standing flat-footed, kicked the much taller bouncer in the jaw with the heel of a foot. Moss's head snapped back as he grunted in surprise and pain.

The Chinaman slid his left hand past Moss's wrist, wrapped his arm beneath Moss's elbow, and grasped the big man's shirt, trapping the bouncer's elbow in a vicious arm bar. Then he ripped a short, choppy right fist into Moss's belly. Moss bent forward. The Chinaman crouched slightly, curled the fingers of his right hand back, and lashed upward with the heel of his hand.

The blow cracked into the point of Moss's chin with a force that the watching Kevin could scarcely believe. The bouncer's head popped back until his nose was pointed toward the ceiling.

Kevin saw Miz Belle's eyes widen in disbelief as the slender yellow man released his hold on the bouncer. Moss slid to the sawdust floor without a sound, unconscious.

The Chinaman turned and bowed politely to the big woman. "I am sorry if I injured your friend," he said. "But we must talk. I am Chin-Lu. I seek word of my sister, a woman named Ling-Tse. This is the last place I have to look. It is said that once a yellow-skinned woman was in your care." He took a slow, gliding step toward Miz Belle. The big woman, her eyes wide with fright, raised a hand as if to ward off the small man. Her chubby fingers trembled in terror.

"Please—don't hurt me!"

"I have no wish to injure a woman," Chin-Lu said politely, "as long as the woman speaks the truth. I must know of my sister. Is she here?"

The madam glanced at the still body of the bouncer, her face gray. Beads of sweat dotted her fat-swollen face.

"Your man will not help you," Chin-Lu said. "Now, what of my sister?"

"Please—I—"

"Answer."

"She—she was here. She's dead." The words came in a nervous rush. Miz Belle backed away, her bulbous body quaking.

The Chinaman dropped his eyes for a moment as though in sudden pain. Then he raised his gaze to the madam's face. "I have feared as much," he said. "Tell me of her death, and at whose hands."

"She—she killed herself. With a knife. It was when we—were traveling to this place. Please believe me! I had nothing to do with it!"

"Why should I believe your words? What proof do you have of her death?" Chin-Lu asked.

Miz Belle leaned heavily against the bar. Her breath came in short gasps. "I was—the one who found her." The watching Kevin thought she was near to fainting. "In—in my room," she gasped. "I have—her things."

Chin-Lu nodded calmly. "Get them."

The big woman staggered away and returned a moment later with a small bundle. Chin-Lu took it reverently, placed it on the bar, and unwrapped the covering. He picked a small object from the meager pile and held it aloft. It was a necklace bearing a crescent-shaped object of green. Chin-Lu replaced it, then unfolded a small square of parchment and studied the document.

Then, tenderly, he wrapped the items in the bundle again. "It is as you say," he said softly. "Ling-Tse is dead by her own hand. Yet the choice was not entirely hers. Someone must pay for her death."

Chin-Lu took a step toward Miz Belle. "No! Please!" the fat woman begged. "I—I didn't—even want her. Kilgore Yantis made me take her! Please—don't hurt me!"

"Who is this Kilgore Yantis?" Chin-Lu asked.

"The man who supplies—girls—to the brothels on the railroad," Miz Belle gasped, desperately trying to absolve herself. "He—said she was—fresh meat from California. She was—a beautiful girl. Yantis made me take her! I work only with professionals, not slave girls!" She reached out a pudgy hand and gripped Chin-Lu's arm. "You must believe me! Please."

Chin-Lu seemed oblivious to her pleas. "Where is this man? This Kilgore Yantis?" His voice was calm, but Kevin sensed a deadly intent behind the words and decided Yantis's days were definitely numbered.

"He—he's not here—gone back to Omaha. For more girls."

"And when will he return?"

"I don't know," Miz Belle said, her voice breaking into terrified sobs. "I don't know—please don't hurt me!"

Chin-Lu plucked her fat hand gently from his arm. "I do not hurt you, for you are a woman. The Chinese do not injure women. But if there are others like Ling-Tse in your employ, you would do well to release them. The keeping of slaves for sexual purposes is against the laws of man and nature."

"What—what will you do?" Miz Belle asked.

"I wait until the man named Yantis returns," Chin-Lu said, then abruptly swept up the small bundle from the bar, spun on a heel, and walked toward the opening of the tent.

Kevin stepped a few feet away from the entrance. As the slender man moved into the street, the foreman spoke. "Chin-Lu, I heard. I am sorry for your sister."

Chin-Lu turned to face the big Irishman. "Your expression of sympathy is genuine, and it provides comfort though you are a stranger," he said. "I had prepared myself for this moment. Yet perhaps one never truly prepares for such news."

The two men walked in silence for a few strides. "What are your plans now, Chin-Lu? I mean, your personal plans until Yantis returns?" Kevin asked.

"I do not know," Chin-Lu said.

"Have you money and a place to stay?"

"I have only a little money. The search for my sister has

been long and expensive, and care for my horses has used most of my funds."

Kevin suddenly stopped and turned to face the smaller man. "Chin-Lu, will you come with me?" he asked. "There is someone I want you to meet. A man named Ted Henderson. He is my friend, and a good man. A man of honor. I think he would like to talk with you."

"It would be refreshing to talk to a man of honor in this place," Chin-Lu said. "I sense you are such a man. May I know your name?"

"Kevin O'Reilly. Come, meet Ted."

They had covered only a hundred yards or so when Kevin suddenly became aware of an astonishing fact. While his own boots crunched audibly on the snow, the Chinaman moved without making a sound.

They found General Jack Casement in Ted's quarters, outlining one of the many problems that still lay ahead for the Union Pacific. The two men glanced up as Kevin and Chin-Lu entered the rail car, then Casement suddenly gazed with keen interest at the Chinaman's face, pointing a finger at him in surprise.

"You!" he said to Chin-Lu. "Are you the one who pulled some of my men from under a half-wrecked railroad car after the explosion?"

Chin-Lu inclined his head. "They were in grave danger. I did what was to be done."

"Well, I'll be damned for a Boston banker," the engineer said with a wide grin. "Looks like the Union Pacific owes you one, friend."

Kevin made the introductions and briefly detailed the encounter at Miz Belle's tent. As the short account ended, Casement offered a hand to Chin-Lu. "I'm really sorry to hear about your sister, sir," he said softly. "I know what it's like to lose someone you love. We'll see to it that Kilgore Yantis pays for this."

Chin-Lu bowed politely. "Thank you for your expression of sympathy, Mr. Casement. But, please—leave the matter of Mr. Yantis to me."

"Done," Casement said. "If any man has a right to revenge, you do."

"It is not a matter of revenge," Chin-Lu gently corrected. "It is but a matter of justice. In Chinese culture, taking one's own life is more honorable than to face degradation. Ling-Tse was a gentle and sensitive girl. To her, the peace of death was an escape from the torment of being repeatedly taken by strangers who had paid a fee, as if they were buying a meal or a bottle of liquor. In her note she said only death could cleanse her spirit and her body so dirtied."

In response to further questioning, Chin-Lu told of his travels through the West in search of his sister. Ted was astounded to discover that Chin-Lu had spent time in Yellow Crow's camp and had gained considerable mastery of the Cheyenne tongue. In reply to one of Ted's questions, Chin-Lu said sadly, "Your blood brother's body is once again strong, but his spirit is troubled. A shadow spreads over Indian lands. Yellow Crow faces a daily battle to keep peace among the Cheyenne. And above it all, the blood feud with the white Indian named Long Walker darkens his heart."

The three railroad men also learned why Chin-Lu had a penchant for learning new languages. "In my home country there are many dialects," Chin-Lu said. "The traveler must learn rapidly if he is to communicate with others. In some ways it is as though the Chinese are a people who cannot communicate with a common language."

That comment brought a chuckle from Jack Casement. "It's the same here, Chin-Lu," he said. "Just listen sometime to a man from Maine trying to carry on a conversation with a settler from Louisiana."

Soon it was decided that Chin-Lu would join the short-handed railroad crew. Until more laborers could be recruited, he would fill in as head spiker. "You won't get rich working for the Union Pacific," Casement concluded, "but you'll be well fed."

"As long as there is plenty of work, I will be satisfied," Chin-Lu replied.

Casement led the new employee to quarters in the crew cars, promising to fetch Chin-Lu's horses from the Hell on Wheels stable at first light and add the animals to the railroad herd.

As the two men left, Kevin briefed Ted on his discoveries at Hell on Wheels. "It looks like Fallon's out of our hair, at least for a while," he concluded. "Rosie said he was bound for New York. But we still don't know who he's working for. His buddy Gamblin said it was 'Somethin' Overland.' "

A thought flashed through Ted's mind. Southern Overland was the company that had bought up enough railroad stock to help the Union Pacific meet a payroll. He rose from his chair and stretched. "I'll feed the information you turned up to Taylor Elkins. If there's something there, he'll find it. Meantime, we'd best turn in. There's not much night left and we'll have a long day digging through that snow."

"Ted," Kevin sighed as he prepared to head for his own bunk, "I've discovered a weakness in me. For a while there I really wanted that woman."

Ted clapped his friend on the shoulder. "That was no weakness, Kevin. You may be Irish, big as a barn, and stubborn as a Missouri mule, but you're still human. I'm the last one around qualified to sound like a circuit preacher, but saying no took a lot more strength than most men have."

The annual New Year's Eve Ball at Fort Laramie seemed more festive than ever to most of those in attendance. Even the weather seemed to smile. A thaw had removed the snow except for shady spots, and the air had lost its bitterness.

Inside the Fort Laramie barracks, the soldiers of the Third Regiment had cleared away bunks and tables to create a large dance floor. On a raised platform, a fiddler, guitar player, and several semitalented Third Regiment musicians surrounded a piano carefully transported from the Laramie Hotel for the occasion. Farm and ranch families had come from miles around, the women in their best dresses and the men decked out in their Sunday finest.

At the barracks door, soldiers took turns making sure only the desirable guests gained entrance, quietly and efficiently turning away the drifters and riffraff who normally littered the Fort Laramie streets.

A hand-painted banner welcoming the year 1868 "with hopes it'll be better than '67" shared the walls and rafters with bright bunting and the tattered regimental flag that had been through the Civil War and more Indian fights than the veterans could count.

The mood of gaiety and celebration was heady inside the hall. Women and girls in bright calico and gingham, some in expensive evening gowns, swirled about the dance floor in the arms of husbands, friends, or any man lucky enough to find an open spot on some feminine dance card.

Among the celebrants was only one long face. Major David Wills was not a happy man.

The dashing young officer stood quietly in a corner,

oblivious to the flirting and giggling girls who kept glancing at him. The only pair of eyes David was interested in were directed elsewhere. Victoria Coulter concentrated on her keyboard, and when she did look up her gaze seemed to search out and settle on one lean figure in a lieutenant colonel's uniform. It seemed to David that those deep green eyes were meant only for Abel Hubbard.

David's misery had come first early in the evening when Victoria arrived. He had blown half a month's pay on a handmade necklace of gold and semiprecious stones for Victoria's Christmas present. It was not around her neck as she swept into the room, greeted David with a quick smile and wave, and headed straight for the piano.

Judy Hubbard was there, beautiful and composed in a rich wine-colored gown, her long blond hair swirling as she danced. David felt a touch of jealousy toward his commanding officer. *It just isn't fair*, he thought. *No man has the right to have a beautiful wife like that—and the way Victoria keeps looking at him, he could have a beautiful mistress, too.*

David pushed himself away from the wall as a lively tune ended. He crowded through the throng about the makeshift stage, finally shouldering his way to Victoria's side.

"Victoria?"

"Oh! Hi, David. Having a good time?" she asked casually.

"I would be, if you would favor me with a dance."

She placed a hand on his arm apologetically. "I'm sorry, David, but I'm here to play, and musicians almost never get to dance. But thank you, anyway."

He bowed slightly to hide the embarrassed flush of his cheeks. "Another time, perhaps."

"Certainly, Major," Victoria said, turning to listen to a request from a rancher.

David turned to his post in the corner, his heart heavy. "Happy New Year, Wills," he muttered bitterly. A moment later the first strains of "Greensleeves" danced from the piano. After a couple of false starts the guitar player found the right chords, and soon couples were drifting slowly around the dance floor.

Someone touched David's shoulder, and he glanced up at Sergeant Major Albert Jonas, who was leaning on a cane. "Major," Jonas said, "my woman's a mighty fine dancer and she does love to move them feet. I ain't up to dancin' the fast ones yet, and I was wonderin'—would you mind givin' her a whirl about the floor?"

"Sergeant, I would be honored and delighted," David said, feigning a lightness he did not feel.

The slow tune was winding down when David found Sally Jonas, who had just been escorted to a seat by a previous dancing partner. The fiddler struck up a lively song, the guitar player found the proper chord immediately, and David bowed low before Sally. "May I have the honor of this dance, ma'am?" he asked.

Sally smiled up at him, the flash of perfect white teeth glowing against her coffee-colored skin. She held out her hand and let David lead her to the dance floor. David waited until the proper time, and the pair began to whirl about the floor.

"Whoo-ee," Sally said after one particularly tricky turn step, "you dance mighty fine for a white man, Major Wills."

David flushed at the compliment. For the first time he took a good, long look into Sally's eyes. They were dark brown, flecked with gold, and sparkling with delight. Sally was not a small woman, but she was light-footed. And when it came to figures, she ranked a close second to Judy Hubbard. When the brisk number had ended, the winded David led Sally back to her seat realizing that Albert Jonas was a lucky man.

David ignored the smile and the obvious invitation in the eyes of an attractive young girl seated nearby as he made his way back to his corner. He did not want a young girl. He wanted a woman. He waited until the next dance began and, sure that no one was watching, filled his cup from the punch bowl and drank half of the warm, nonalcoholic liquid. Surreptitiously, he turned his back to the crowd and pulled a small flask from beneath his tunic. He tipped the flask, refilling the cup. It was his third such refill of the evening. The scarcely diluted liquor burned his throat and almost brought tears to his eyes. He drained the cup.

Moments later he saw Judy Hubbard coming his way, her full hips swiveling gracefully beneath a narrow waist. "Happy New Year, David," she said. "It may not be custom for the woman to ask, but I'm going to. Will you dance with me?"

The band had eased into a slow waltz as David took Judy in his arms on the floor. He began to relax as they moved gracefully to the three-quarter time of the waltz. Suddenly, over her shoulder, David saw something that jarred him to the core. Victoria Coulter was dancing with Abel Hubbard and quite obviously enjoying herself very much. David winced as Victoria suddenly tossed her head and laughed in that husky manner that held such promise. *So musicians don't get to dance, eh? What do you call that, Victoria? The changing of the guard?* he thought angrily.

"David?"

"Oh. I—I'm sorry, Judy. I was just—distracted for a moment." David felt his face redden, but did not know if it was from embarrassment or the effects of the liquor. He forced himself to concentrate on his dancing until the rhythm once more flowed naturally.

Finally the waltz ended. "Thank you, Judy," David said courteously. Over her shoulder he saw Victoria, led by Abel, making her way back toward the bandstand. The cinch across his chest seemed to tighten. He led Judy back to her seat and bowed as he released her hand.

"Excuse me, Judy. I—I think I'll call it a night. The poor fellow on office detail should have a chance to celebrate, too."

Looking neither to the left nor the right, Major David Wills strode through the door and into the brisk chill of the December air. It was not yet ten o'clock when he stepped into the office of the post commander.

The young corporal on duty as officer of the watch looked up in surprise. "Problem, Major?"

David shook his head. "No problem, Corporal," he said, trying to keep his tone light. "I'm just not the partying kind, I guess. I made my token officer's appearance. Why don't you go on over and have some fun? No use wasting a good dance on a bored major. And there's a little brunette in a white dress about your age, not half hard to look at, who could use some company."

The corporal's youthful face split in a wide smile. He snapped a salute. "Yes, sir, Major! And thank you, sir!"

The young man was gone before David had stowed his hat and coat on the rack by the fireplace. David dropped the mask, giving in to his dark mood. He crossed to a closet and groped in the far corner beneath a stack of old payroll records. His hand closed on the neck of the bottle he had stashed there.

He plopped into the chair behind the cluttered desk and

twisted the cork from the bottle. It was more than half full. He lifted the bottle and took a long swallow.

He paused, startled, the bottle in midair, as the office door suddenly burst open and slammed with a sharp thud. "Sally! What—"

Sally Jonas, her eyes flashing anger, strode to the desk and grabbed the bottle from David's hand. With a ferocity he had never seen in her before, she threw the bottle into the fireplace. It shattered, the blaze flaring briefly as it fed on the liquor.

Still stunned, David could only stare openmouthed as Sally doubled both fists and leaned toward him, her knuckles on the desk top.

"Now, you listen to me, you young whippersnapper!" Sally's voice cracked. "I may be just a plantation nigger woman, but by your soul, David Wills, you're gonna listen to me—and listen good!"

Sally thumped a fist into the scarred wood of the desk. "You've been moonin' around here like a lovesick calf for months, Major Wills! Now I'm not educated, but I'm not dumb, neither. I know what's eatin' you. But it seems to me you're not man enough to handle it!"

"But—but, Sally—"

"Don't you 'but, Sally' me till I've had my say! I don't hold with messin' around in a body's personal life without a reason. But I got a reason to mess in your life—a bunch of 'em! I've been watchin' you hit the jug like some dried-out prospector. I smelt it on your breath when we danced tonight. I figgered you were sneakin' off over here to hit the bottle again."

Sally jabbed a long finger under David's nose. "All you been doin', David Wills, is hidin' in a jug 'cause your feelin's are hurt! You sit around feelin' sorry for yourself, all on account of a woman! They're a bunch of good men on this post, Major, and whether you know it or not, you're one of 'em!"

The sergeant major's wife barely paused for a breath before she lit into Wills once more.

"How many people you gonna kill because your feelin's are hurt, Major? You for one, if you keep actin' like some dumb kid! You were a good officer—one of the best, my Albert says. Well, let me tell you somethin', *Major* Wills. You sit here a-killin' yourself, you're not doin' anybody any good! You gonna hit the bottle when you take men afield? My Albert's gonna be back in the saddle again soon. You gonna kill my Albert and a bunch of others 'cause your thinkin's all fuzzy with whiskey and a case of the 'pore Davids'? Well, I'm not gonna stand for it, Major! You get your head together, and you do it quick, or I'm gonna bust it open and stuff some sense in it myself!"

David noticed with surprise that despite her furious outburst, a single tear trickled down each of Sally Jonas's cheeks.

"Sally, I—"

"Shut up! I'm not through with you yet! Now you hear me and you remember good. You got the makin's of a good man. My Albert needs you. The army needs you. The only question I got is do *you* need you? You gonna throw away all the common sense and the talent God give you? Or you gonna stand up on your two hind feet and fight for what you want?"

Sally wiped the tears from her face with the back of a hand. "Don't let her kill you, David! I know it hurts, but if Victoria Coulter won't give you the time of day, that's *her* bein' stupid, not you! She's got problems of her own to get straight. You take care of yours while she's makin' up her mind what she wants. Then go after her and *make* her pay attention to you, boy!"

Sally suddenly sighed. "You gotta have faith, David. If the Creator meant it to be, you'll have your Victoria Coulter. If not, then He's savin' you for someone else. You sit here and study on it a spell. I said my piece, and now I'm goin'. Albert's back there at the New Year's party, prob'ly wonderin' why I took off. I'm not gonna tell him. This talk's between you, me, and that chair you're sittin' in. You're old enough to be a man, David. Start actin' like one!"

Abruptly, Sally turned and walked out, slamming the door behind her.

David slowly lowered his head into his hands. After a long moment he looked up at the door.

"Sally," he whispered, "I have a feeling you're right. I've got some heavy thinking to do." He glanced at the mantel clock ticking away the last hours of 1867. "At least I've got the rest of the year to do it in," he muttered.

The midmorning January sun touched the blue-white

mantle of freshly fallen snow, sending pinpoints of light dancing across the valley cradling the Henderson-O'Reilly ranch.
The light snowfall, barely two inches deep, had crept in
during the windless night and then moved on, leaving the
promise of a mild winter's day.

Inside the snug ranch home, Carl Keller curled his fingers about a warm coffee cup and listened to the chatter of
the women and children. The longtime member of Henderson's Scouts had brought his wife, Anna, and their adopted
daughter, Ellen, on this trip by wagon to deliver supplies.
Carl knew the trip would be safe, and Ellen had missed the
company of young Bill Henderson so much. The two were
almost inseparable in the rare times they had together.

The youngsters stood at a steamed window, their faces
pressed against the glass, peering out at the new snow. Wind
Flower's baby, nearly a year old, had been put down for a
nap, and adult talk was boring for active children—especially
when a fresh snow lay just waiting for them.

"Wilma, sometimes I envy you living out here on this
ranch," Anna Keller said. "It seems like there's more and
more bad types, real criminals, moving into Fort Laramie.
Why, it's got to where a decent woman's hardly safe anymore. I'd almost bet we get more robbers and thieves than
we get soldiers."

Wilma, busy slicing a hefty elk roast for the noon meal,
clucked her tongue in reproach. "I had guessed from talking
with Carl and the other scouts who drop by from time to time
that things were bad," she said. "It seems odd that the little
frontier village I grew to love could have changed so much."

She carved a chunk of the rich red meat and tossed it to
Toby. The solidly built dog, lying by the door of the room
where Patrick slept, looked at the meat and then at Wind
Flower. At the single Navajo word from his mistress, Toby
picked up the meat in powerful jaws and began to eat.

"Anna's dead right, Wilma," Carl said as he refilled his
pipe. "There's a shootin' or a knifin' most every night. And
any time you run across a horse or a cow track, you can bet
the man followin' it ain't the rightful owner."

"How is Judy making out at the hotel?" Wind Flower
asked, brushing the flour from her hands as she finished
rolling the crust for an apple pie.

"Judy's doing all right," Anna said with an emphatic nod.
"She's got real business sense. When the railroad went south

of Fort Laramie, she didn't let grass grow under her feet before she'd bought a chunk of the new town. Fort Laramie's days may be numbered since the rails went south. But if that happens the Laramie Hotel will just pack up and move— lock, stock, and kitchen knife—to the new town. Looks like the new Laramie will be as big as the old one in a few years."

Bill and Ellen turned from the window.

"Mom," Bill said, "may Ellen and I go outside? It's not cold, and all my chores are done."

Wilma glanced at Anna and received her nod of approval. "All right, Bill. But remember—stay near the house. We mustn't take any chances."

Moments later Bill and Ellen were laughing and giggling their way through a snowball fight. The intense battle raged past the barn and soon swept into the pasture north of the ranch house.

Bill, leaning down to scoop up a handful of snow, suddenly raised a hand to call the hostilities to a halt. He motioned Ellen forward and pointed toward a set of rabbit tracks in the white ground cover. "Cottontail," Bill said. "Big one, too."

Ellen peered at the tracks, then shook her head emphatically. "Not cottontail. See how the back feet lie flat? This was winter hare." She smiled teasingly at Bill. "White man not know how read tracks," she said in exaggerated pidgin English.

Bill scowled in mock indignation. "Girls bad trackers," he grumbled, playing the game. "Warrior bet two ponies, one squaw, three blankets he right. We follow tracks, catch up with rabbit. Then Arapaho woman know truth."

Wilma's warning to stay nearby was promptly forgotten as the two youngsters followed the tracks of the rabbit deeper into the pasture and through the tangle of vines along a small creek. The two moved rapidly except where the sign became tougher to read. Before they realized it, the youngsters were more than a mile from the house and were moving deeper into the foothills.

Bill was almost ready to concede that the animal was in fact a hare, for cottontails did not range this far afield. He turned to Ellen, preparing to speak, but she held a finger to her lips for silence and then pointed to her nose.

Bill took a deep sniff of the clear air and detected the scent that had caught Ellen's attention. It was the faintest whiff of wood smoke. He edged closer to Ellen. "What do you think?" he whispered. "Indians, maybe?"

Ellen shook her head. "I don't know. I think we should go and find out. It could be someone in trouble."

Bill suddenly realized how far they had strayed from the house. Still, his father and Valdez had told him many times to keep an eye peeled for anything that seemed strange on the ranch and tell them about it as soon as possible. And he did not want Ellen to know he was suddenly afraid. A warrior and tracker was not supposed to be scared. He nodded and motioned for her to follow.

The smell of wood smoke grew stronger as the two youngsters cautiously crept forward, deeper into the growth of timber. Then Bill heard something that set his heart to pounding even harder—the voices of white men.

After creeping another twenty yards, Bill and Ellen peered from beneath a tangle of fallen trees into a small clearing. A half-dozen dirty, unshaven, and tough-looking men sat around the fire. One of the men had a nose that had been badly broken; the bridge was crushed almost flat between his eyes. The men were passing a bottle back and forth as they talked.

"I tell ya, Gaither, it'd be like swipin' candy from a kid," one of the men said to the broken-nosed man. "Ain't nobody down there but them two women and the ol' Mex. Them cattle'd bring us a mighty pretty penny, not to mention the hosses."

Gaither took a long pull from the bottle and handed it to the speaker. "You sure 'bout that, Monk?"

Monk grinned wickedly and scratched his scraggly beard. "Shore 'nuff. All we gotta do is take care of the ol' Mex and one scraggly dog. Then we got all day to play with them two women. And they's lookers, too—damn if the Injun ain't near as well built as the white one. When we finish, we just cut their throats, bash out the papoose's brains, and kill the other kid. Then we gather the stock and ride off. Nobody's gonna find 'em out here in this godforsaken place fer a long time. We'll be in Mexico afore then."

Bill glanced at Ellen. Her eyes were wide with fright and alarm, but she did not move or make a sound.

Gaither belched. "Okay, Monk," he said, "I reckon it's just too good to pass up. I ain't had me a woman in so long I might's well be gelded. We'll ride in just afore suppertime. Might's well let 'em cook for us, too." Gaither grinned, the twisted mouth and battered face a picture of evil. "Boys, looks like this here rustlin' game just got to be more fun than we expected."

Bill felt Ellen's soft touch on his arm. She gestured back toward the ranch house. He nodded silently, and the two began worming their way back from the edge of the clearing.

For a hundred yards they concentrated on holding their fear in check, trying to move without making a sound. Then, when he was sure it was safe, Bill waved Ellen into a run. Gasping and stumbling, the pair raced back toward the house as fast as young legs would carry them.

They burst into the main room of the house, leaving the door ajar. "Some—men," Bill gasped, "out there—going to—"

"Easy, Bill," Wilma said gently. "Just catch your breath, then tell us about it as calmly as you can."

Slowly and haltingly, the story unfolded. Carl Keller's eyes narrowed. Valdez Cabrillo listened quietly, his weathered brown hands clenched into fists as Bill and Ellen repeated what they had overheard.

Even the dog, Toby, seemed to sense the approach of evil. Lying close by little Patrick, he rumbled a throaty warning.

"Bill, you and Ellen make fine scouts," Keller said as the story ended. "This one called Gaither, I know him. Albert Jonas busted his nose a while back. Monk's his right-hand man. Abel Hubbard and me both figger'd that bunch as the ones that's been raidin' livestock around this neck of the woods. Some bastards killed a ranch couple after rapin' the woman. Never could prove it was Gaither, though."

Keller stood and moved to a front window. The snow during the night had covered their wagon tracks. "Good thing we rode in here after dark. They don't know me and the missus is here."

The scout slipped his Colt Dragoon from its belt holster and placed it on the table before him. "Valdez, that bunch thinks you're nothin' but a dumb Mexican. Want to help change their minds?"

Valdez nodded, his expression grim. "It will be my pleasure. These outlaws will not harm my new family. And after today they will harm no others."

By early afternoon, everything was set. Ellen, Bill, and the baby had a safe hideout in the storeroom where Carl and

Anna had built a solid fort of bags of flour and grain. The heavy bags would stop any stray bullets.

"Toby will stay with the young ones," Wind Flower said. "He will be a comfort to them—and if somehow one of the bad men gets through to the children, Toby will tear his throat out."

Weapons were checked and rechecked. Wind Flower had her .36 navy tucked in the band of her skirt. Wilma kept one of Ted's spare Henry rifles nearby, the magazine filled. Beside the chair in which Anna sat, a wicked-looking twin-bore shotgun leaned, its chambers loaded with buckshot.

Carl Keller made one last check and grunted in satisfaction. "Valdez," he said, "I'd sure rather see you stay in the house. We've got us a fort here as solid as any you'll find."

"No, señor," Valdez answered. "They will be expecting me to be moving about outside, tending to chores. To do otherwise might tip them off that something is not as it appears." The side pocket of Valdez's chaps held a familiar bulge. "From the corner of the corral I will have a good field of fire. The back window will provide a position for a cross fire. The *bandidos* will come for me first, thinking I am the only one who stands between them and the women."

Reluctantly, Keller agreed that Valdez's plan was best. "Reckon that does it for now, then," Carl said. "Ever'body knows what to do. Now we just wait for the ball to open—and don't nobody be squeamish about pullin' a trigger. Them yahoos out there don't deserve no fair play."

At Toby's low growl, Wind Flower glanced out the window. "They come," she said quietly. She gathered the children and led them to the shelter of the storeroom, ordered Toby to stay and guard the youngsters, then returned to her post. She stood by the door, while Wilma and Anna moved to the front windows and Carl took up a vantage point at the rear window facing the corral.

Gaither and his gang were riding in just before suppertime, sticking to the plan Bill and Ellen had overheard. Gaither, Monk, and a tall, thin rider approached from the north toward the barn, while the other three reined their mounts to the front of the house.

Valdez Cabrillo, a partly filled bucket of horse feed in his right hand, leaned casually against the corner post of the corral and watched the trio approach. All three held rifles loosely across the pommels of their saddles. Valdez lifted the flap on the pocket of his chaps. He loosened the pistol, then waved lazily to the three horsemen.

"*Buenas tardes, señores,*" Valdez said with a broad, trusting grin.

Gaither returned the wave with a nod. "You speak American?"

"*No hablo inglés,*" Valdez replied, keeping the vacant grin on his face, hoping to project the image of the unarmed peon going about his usual ranch chores.

The two riders with Gaither casually reined mounts off to either side of Valdez, bracketing the old Mexican. Valdez looked from one to the other and selected his target. The thin man was between himself and the back window of the house, and the muzzle of the man's rifle pointed toward Valdez. He would have to be the first to die, Valdez decided.

At the front of the house the other three riders moved into position. "Hello!" one called out. Wind Flower swung the door open and stood in the doorway, her hands beneath the apron.

"Good afternoon," she said. "Is there something we can do for you gentlemen?"

One of the riders, a gap-toothed fat man, grinned wickedly. "Honey," he said, "I reckon there's a lot you could do for me." He dismounted and took two confident strides toward Wind Flower.

Wind Flower's hands whipped from beneath the apron. The navy .36, already at full cock, pointed at the gap-toothed man's chest. "I suggest you stop right there, sir," Wind Flower said sharply.

The man stopped in midstride, momentarily surprised. Then he grinned again. "Aw, c'mon, honey," he said, "you ain't gonna use that thing."

Wind Flower dropped the muzzle of the pistol and squeezed the trigger. The gap-toothed man yelped as the slug splattered snow between his feet. The sound of the shot sent all three horses plunging and rearing. "The next one goes between your eyes!" Wind Flower yelled.

One of the other riders who had come to the front of the house cursed sharply, swinging a revolver toward Wind Flower. Anna Keller's shotgun boomed, lifting the man from the saddle and tumbling him into the snow. The third rider suddenly wheeled his horse and slammed spurs into the animal's ribs. Wilma sighted down the barrel of the Henry

.44 from her post at another window and squeezed the trigger, sending the horseman on his way with three deliberate near misses.

Wind Flower still kept her revolver trained on the first man, the gap-toothed one, whose horse had bolted at the noise of the shotgun. "Drop your weapons—very carefully," Wind Flower said. The would-be rapist glanced about. The color drained from his face. The black bores of pistol, shotgun, and rifle barrels stared back at him from three directions. He swallowed, nodded, and reached for the buckle of his gunbelt.

As the first shot sounded from the front of the house, Gaither, back at the corral, yelled to one of his sidekicks, "Take him!" as he swung his rifle toward Valdez.

Valdez hurled the grain bucket toward Gaither's horse with his right hand, then whirled and crouched, swinging his revolver into line with his left. The thin man's rifle cracked, but the hurried shot went wild. Valdez's slug thumped into the thin man's chest.

Now Monk leveled his rifle at Valdez. As the weapon cracked, the Mexican dove from the corral post, rolled twice in the snow, and came to one knee as he fired. The slug caught Monk low in his ample belly. He shuddered, sagged over the saddle horn, and then fell heavily from his dancing mount.

Valdez threw himself to one side, expecting the impact of a bullet from Gaither's rifle. But from the corner window at the back of the house a pistol barked three times. Gaither's body jerked at the impact of the slugs from Carl Keller's Dragoon. Gaither's horse spun away, dumping his rider to the ground.

Monk, though shot through the stomach, struggled to reach his rifle. Valdez took careful aim and shot him between the eyes.

The barrage of gunfire had lasted only a few seconds. Valdez, his handgun cocked and ready, stuck a toe under Gaither's body and flipped the man over. He saw in an instant that Gaither was dead. Either of Carl Keller's two shots that connected would have done the job. He did not bother to check on Monk. There was no need.

The first horseman Valdez had downed, the thin man, clung to life, but barely. Pink fluid dribbled from the thin man's open mouth, the sure sign of a lung shot.

"Help—help me," the thin man pleaded weakly. Valdez merely stared at him. A moment later the man coughed, then his head dropped back into the snow, his eyes glazed in death.

Valdez made his way to the back door and peeked inside. "Is anyone hurt?"

"Nope, not in here," Carl replied as he reloaded the empty chambers of the Dragoon from a powder flask and rammed home the deadly round balls. "Some folks outside ain't feelin' too spunky though."

Valdez reloaded his own weapon, then went outside with Keller. Keller barely glanced at the man who had been hit by Anna's shotgun blast. A twelve-bore charge of buckshot made a considerable mess at twenty feet. The sixth outlaw, the only one to escape, was long gone. "Prob'ly halfway to Mexico right now," Keller said.

Moments later the gap-toothed man Wind Flower had captured pleaded frantically for his life, as Carl and Valdez tied him securely hand and foot. Almost casually, Valdez dropped a loop over the man's neck and tossed the free end of the braided lariat over an exposed rafter.

"You—can't—my God, no!" the captive babbled. "You wouldn't—hang a man! Please!"

Valdez raised an eyebrow at the women. Wilma, sensing the game to be played, nodded solemnly. Valdez tugged at the end of the rope, tightening the noose, and lifting the man onto his toes. "Please—" The voice was a strangled croak.

"Wait," Wilma said abruptly. "Maybe he'd rather tell us about those other raids. Work a trade, sort of."

Valdez shrugged as though it did not matter at all to him, then slacked the rope. The gap-toothed man's heels had barely settled onto the floor when he began babbling, naming the other outlaws and the places they had hit. Wilma wrote the man's words down, scribbling rapidly to keep pace.

"Colonel Hubbard will be delighted to get this information," Wilma said as the man concluded his statement. "Now, what do we do with him?"

Carl Keller's eyes narrowed. "I knowed some of them people he helped kill," the scout said. "Was it my decide, I'd hang 'im on the spot. Slow. But I reckon we best let the colonel take care of 'im."

In a far corner of the room Wind Flower gently rocked her child, waiting for his sobs to subside. "Hush, little one," she crooned, "it is all over now. There will be no more loud bangs to frighten you."

Toby laid his chin on Wind Flower's knee, trying in his own way to comfort the young boy—and his mistress, who obviously was still a bit shaken from the violence.

"Valdez," Carl said, "I've seen some handy men with a pistol before. But I never seen shootin' like you did today. I get the idea you been in a gun scrap or two before."

Valdez nodded slowly. "Yes. It is not something of which I am proud. I have killed before. It was twelve years ago. Some men came to my small ranch near Sonora. I was away hunting wild horses. There were three men. They killed my twenty-year-old son. Then they raped, tortured, and killed my wife and my young daughter-in-law."

The old man sighed. The pain that clouded his eyes was replaced by a surprising coldness. "I caught up with them in Sonora four days later. I killed them. They were the sons of powerful men in Sonora. I had to flee Mexico. I have not returned. I would not, even if I could."

Valdez glanced around the room. "I have a new family here. I will kill again if necessary to protect them. They are very brave, these women and young ones," he said, holding out his arms to Bill and Ellen.

Nine

The early weeks of 1868 looked as if they were destined to take their place in Plains Indian lore as "the time the gods of winter spoke with two tongues," Ted decided.

The relatively mild day that greeted the new year gave way overnight to a blue whistler, a bitter wind that ripped along with subzero temperatures. Rail laborers spent as much time trying to avoid frostbite as they did laying track. Many were not successful.

On the heels of the blue whistler came the chinook, a freak wind that poured warm air down the Laramie Basin. General Jack Casement, who had a thermometer outside his rail-car office window, watched in disbelief as the mercury jumped from twenty below zero to almost fifty degrees above in less than three hours.

Two days later it snowed.

The already shorthanded Union Pacific crew found its numbers depleted still more as frostbite and pneumonia claimed every third or fourth man. Snow, sleet, and freezing rain alternated with sunny days when the afternoon temperatures moved well above freezing.

Finally, the weather settled down—for the worse. Bitter cold sapped water from workmen's bodies, the problem compounded by the men's reluctance to drink from the nearly frozen pails of the water carriers.

Only Chin-Lu seemed oblivious to the effects of the weather. It had taken him just a few moments to grasp the rhythm of driving the spikes, and already the slender Oriental was earning a name for himself as one of the best head spikers to swing a maul on the Union Pacific tracks.

The railroad had turned north at the newly founded town of Laramie, followed the Laramie River for some fifty miles, and then turned west again. The crest of the Rockies—

Bridger's Pass on the Continental Divide—waited in a lofty challenge only eighty miles away.

"Ah, for the good old days when we made a mile of track a day," General Jack sighed to Ted. "We'll be lucky to make a quarter-mile a day until we break through the pass. What's it look like out ahead?"

Ted shrugged out of his heavy buffalo-skin coat. "Not too good," he said, making his way to the stove. He held his cold-stiffened fingers toward the welcome heat. "The roadbed's frozen solid between here and Bridger's Pass. There's a lot of snow to be moved before we can lay track, and the tie crews will have to chop the beds out with picks and axes. You may be optimistic at a quarter-mile a day."

He rubbed his hands briskly, then poured a cup of the strong, hot coffee. "What has me worried as much as the weather is just this side of Bridger's Pass. Tents and shacks are already going up at Rawlins. The town is drawing a rough crowd. Maybe one man out of ten has a legal job. And when Hell on Wheels moves into Rawlins we're going to have the devil's own time keeping men in condition to work."

Casement plucked a cigar from his pocket and lit it. "Between sickness and injuries we're so short of healthy workers we couldn't have a good poker game.

"I hate to dump this on you, Ted, but you and Kevin are going to have to run the railroad for a while. I've got to go back East and help Dan recruit more laborers. I'll be leaving within the week. Just don't kill yourself. Of course, we need all the track we can get, but I'll tell the bosses what we're up against."

Ted drained the last of his coffee, rinsed the cup, and reached for his coat. "We'll get you all the track we can, Jack," he said. "It will be slow going, though. January and February in Wyoming aren't something to look forward to."

The days that followed blurred one into the other as Ted and Kevin drove the work crews almost to the limit of human endurance. The Laramie Basin gave ground grudgingly, but slowly the rails inched forward and upward. Alternating ice storms, snows, and brief thaws left the workmen hacking at stone-hard roadbeds or slogging through mud, the constant threat of frostbite or "lung fever" always with them.

Near the end of February, Ted checked his horse and sat staring at the sprawling town of Rawlins only a mile or so ahead. The wagons that bore the rolling town of Hell on Wheels already were rolling into Rawlins's muddy streets.

"I don't know exactly why," Ted muttered to his horse, Hellbender, "but I've got a bad feeling about this place already. And we're coming up on another payday."

Ted's glum view of Rawlins turned out to be on the optimistic side.

As the rails drew near enough for wagon rides and walking, Rawlins drew railroad workers like moths attracted to a bright flame—and not only on Saturdays. The teeming settlement offered every vice known, and it was said a few new vices were even invented there. Teamsters, drifters, gamblers, ex-railroad workers, and dealers in firearms and whiskey all but crowded the few legitimate merchants from the town's streets. Each night was filled with the sound of gunfire and brawls.

Rawlins even drew a hefty number of railroad excursionists, people from towns as far away as the East Coast who were looking for excitement that was unobtainable in their more sedate hometowns. The Union Pacific frequently organized tours to rails' end in the hopes of generating new income from stock sales. Rawlins thrived on the excursionists.

Eastern money quickly found its way into harlots' garters, the pockets of Western gamblers, and the metal cash boxes of the saloons. Through news stories by visiting reporters Rawlins quickly acquired the reputation of "the wickedest town in the West." It proved to be great advertising for the boomtown.

Through it all, Ted and Kevin struggled to maintain some semblance of order among the rail workers. Each night, the two men took turns prowling through Rawlins, searching out straying laborers.

General Jack returned with a fresh crew of workers and tried posting notices that Rawlins was off limits to Union Pacific men. The notices were ignored. The laborers knew they were not likely to lose jobs by disobeying the order. The railroad needed them desperately, hung over or not.

Kevin had taken the second roundup shift one Wednesday night and was in the process of booting the backsides of a dozen workmen back toward sleeping cars when something caught his eye. The flap of one of the biggest tents in Rawlins swung open just as he passed, and presiding over a poker game near the entrance was the flashily dressed Kilgore Yantis, chuckling and smiling as he dealt a fresh hand.

Kevin resisted the impulse to enter the tent and bash Yantis's head in. That right, he decided, was no longer his or Ted's.

The Irish foreman delivered his charges to the sleeping car, cuffing one man behind the ear as a reminder to stay there, and went in search of Chin-Lu. He found the Chinaman asleep in another car.

"Chin-Lu?"

The slender Chinese came awake instantly at Kevin's soft call. "Yes?"

"He's back. The man you seek—Kilgore Yantis."

Chin-Lu swung from his cot in a fluid motion and reached for his quilted jacket. "Thank you for bringing this information, friend Kevin. I will go now to see justice served on this dealer in flesh."

"I'm going along," Kevin said. "I won't interfere in your dealings with Yantis. But I want to make sure no one else does, either."

Chin-Lu nodded calmly. "Your thoughts are well taken, Kevin. But I do not wish to place you in harm's way."

Kevin grunted sourly. "I'm tired and I'm angry. If it takes a healthy fight to get me back in a good mood, so be it."

The two men entered Yantis's tent quietly and unnoticed. Kevin stepped slightly to one side and stood along a canvas wall. Chin-Lu walked directly to the poker table.

"Pardon me," he said politely. "You are Mr. Kilgore Yantis, are you not?"

Yantis squinted through a curl of smoke from a thin cigar. "I'm Yantis. What do you want, Chinaman? I don't play cards with coolies!"

"I do not wish to play cards. Do you know of a woman named Ling-Tse?" Chin-Lu reached in his pocket and produced the necklace with the jade crescent. "She wore an ornament like this around her neck."

Yantis glanced briefly at the necklace, then grinned crookedly. "You're a little late, China," he sneered. "She's dead. Pity, too—she was one fine-looking woman. A real moneymaker. I had her myself, just to check it out. But she wasn't all that good in bed—just laid there." Yantis leered at one of his card-playing acquaintances. "Know something, boys? It ain't slanted like their eyes."

Chin-Lu waited patiently until the wave of laughter at the crude comment subsided. He looked deep into Yantis's eyes and stepped alongside the poker table. "Ling-Tse was my sister," he said softly. "Now you must face justice."

Alarm suddenly flashed in Yantis's eyes. His hand stabbed into a pocket and came out clutching a small two-barrel derringer. One of the card players yelped in surprise, and everyone dived clear of the table.

Kevin slid the Dragoon from his belt, ready to blast Yantis. There was no need.

Chin-Lu suddenly crouched and spun, pivoting on his left foot, and struck out with his right heel. The work boot he wore slammed into the back of Yantis's hand. Bones crumpled and the derringer thumped harmlessly to the top of the table. Almost casually, Chin-Lu picked up the deadly handgun and tossed it to the floor. Yantis's mouth opened in a silent scream of agony as he stared at the twisted, broken fingers of his right hand in disbelief.

An angry shout came from a nearby card player. The man reached for a handgun in his belt.

"Hold it!" Kevin yelled, cocking his Dragoon. "Touch that pistol and you're a dead man!"

The card player glared at Kevin, then at Chin-Lu. The crowd was growing more menacing by the second, not from any sense of loyalty to Kilgore Yantis, but because Chin-Lu was not white. Kevin waved the Dragoon from side to side. "The first man who makes a move to interfere files a six-foot-deep homestead! This is a private matter!"

"My God!" Yantis finally whimpered, still staring at his crushed fingers. "My—my hand—" Slowly the gambler looked up, his face pasty white. He saw something ominous in Chin-Lu's composed features. Frantically Yantis searched the faces in the crowd. "Somebody—do something!" he pleaded.

From the corner of his eye Kevin saw the bartender ease his hand beneath the rough countertop. Kevin turned and fired, the blast of the .45 rattling the canvas. Wood splintered beneath the impact of the ball just inches from the barkeep. The startled bartender jumped back. "Reach for that shotgun slow," Kevin said. "Pull it out with the stock pointed toward me and the barrels pointed at your belt. Then bring it here."

The barkeep did as he was told. Kevin hefted the sawed-off shotgun, tucked his revolver into his belt, and pointed the scattergun at the crowd. "Stay calm, boys, and maybe this thing won't go off," he said.

"What—what you going to do—China?" Yantis gasped.

"My name is not China. It is Chin-Lu. I have given much thought to how you should pay for what you did to my sister. And to so many others. Now I have found how justice might best be served."

Chin-Lu reached out, grasped the collar of Yantis's suit coat, and hauled the gambler to his feet. He spun the man about so that their faces were within inches of each other. "You—you're gonna kill me!" Yantis's voice climbed the scale of terror. "Somebody—stop him!"

No one in the crowd was willing to challenge both the shotgun in Kevin's hands and the almost supernatural power of the Oriental man.

"I will not kill you," Chin-Lu said softly. Hope and relief flashed in Yantis's eyes. "Death would be too merciful for such a man." Chin-Lu dropped to one knee at Yantis's side and scooped the gambler's legs from the floor with his free arm. For an instant the gambler seemed to hang suspended in midair. Then, with a sharp cry, Chin-Lu swung his free arm from behind Yantis's legs and clapped it across the gambler's thighs. He pushed down with controlled power, adding his own strength to the momentum of Yantis's falling body.

Yantis's lower back struck Chin-Lu's outstretched knee. The *pop* of a fractured backbone sounded loudly in the tense silence of the saloon tent. Yantis screamed.

Chin-Lu slid his knee from beneath Yantis's back and let the gambler flop to the floor. He stood over the fallen man. "From this day forward, Kilgore Yantis, you will never walk again. You never again will feel the touch of woman's thighs around your hips. The dealer in flesh has known the last of its pleasures. From your waist down you will feel nothing for the rest of your life. You will not be able to control your bowels or your bladder."

Yantis's mouth opened and closed silently, his vocal cords frozen in horror. A stain spread across the front of the gambler's expensive trousers.

Chin-Lu abruptly turned away. "Let us go, Kevin. Justice and honor have been served."

With Kevin's appropriated shotgun holding the crowd at bay, the two men backed from the tent and headed toward the construction train. After a few yards Kevin sighed in relief and lowered the hammers of the shotgun.

"Chin-Lu, I don't believe Hell on Wheels will be all that safe for you after today," he said. "If Yantis has any friends, they'll be after you. If he doesn't, there are always guns for hire."

Chin-Lu shrugged. "I have taken from this place that for which I came. I have no further reason to return."

Ted listened attentively to the account of the incident with Kilgore Yantis, then nodded his agreement. "To civilized people, your crippling of Yantis might seem harsh, Chin-Lu," he said. "But Rawlins is not civilized. Nor was Yantis. The old adage, 'let the punishment fit the crime,' has much merit. What are your plans now?"

"I wish to continue work on the railroad," Chin-Lu said. "I have need of funds."

"To return to your homeland?" Ted asked.

"To buy horses. I would tie them before a certain lodge in the camp of Paints-His-Horses."

Ted grinned. "I approve. I've known Little Fern since she was a child. She's a fine young woman. I wish you good fortune on your quest."

After a brief discussion, it was decided Chin-Lu would be too exposed to retaliation from Yantis if he stayed with the rail gang. With his talent for languages and his remarkable physical abilities, the Oriental would be a more valuable asset as a scout at Ted's right hand.

In the following days, Chin-Lu quickly picked up a working vocabulary of the Sioux language. With his knowledge of Cheyenne, the slender scout could understand most of the tongues native to the area. He was an adequate, if unspectacular, horseman. But afoot Chin-Lu seemed to vanish into shadows, to walk silently through crusted snow or fallen leaves, and then suddenly reappear. In a way it was an almost frightening talent, Ted mused.

By the end of the first week in March, Ted decided he finally had had his fill of Rawlins. The clincher came late one day as he wearily made his way back through the red-light district, herding a half-dozen drunken railroad workers. As the group passed a clapboard shack, an overweight prostitute stepped from a door and grinned at Ted. She hoisted her skirt to her waist. There was nothing under the skirt but bulbous thighs.

"Wanna good time, mister?" the whore asked, swaying her hips lewdly. "Just five dollars is all it takes."

Ted glared balefully at the prostitute. Several customers had been beaten and robbed at her place.

He found Kevin O'Reilly nursing a light whiskey in Jack Casement's office.

"Jack, Kevin, I want to put this hellhole behind us," Ted said firmly. "We're losing more men to Rawlins than to anything else so far. It's a disgrace to the people of the Plains. Kevin, I want those rail gangs pushed to the limit. When they get through with a day's work I want them so tired they don't even think about women and whiskey!"

Kevin nodded. In the next two days the track crews put down more than a mile of rails. Jack Casement's whip and Kevin's tongue kept them working at a frantic pace.

Then, on the morning of the third day, an ominous rumble sounded off to the north.

"What would that be?" General Jack asked with a puzzled frown.

Ted swung into the saddle and waved for Chin-Lu to follow. "One thing it's not is thunder," Ted said as he wheeled his mount.

The two riders were back in a half-hour. "Get the men off railhead!" Ted yelled. "We've got the biggest herd of buffalo I've seen in years headed straight toward us!"

The buffalo poured over the northern horizon, a long brown line of shaggy beasts moving at a quick trot. Ted climbed to the top of a railroad car for a better look. The ocean of hides and horns stretched as far as his eye could see.

The first wave swept past just as the last worker scrambled to the relative safety of the rail cars. The carefully prepared rail bed vanished beneath the hooves as the stupid, heavy-headed, humpbacked beasts spilled around the construction train. Some bumped their thick skulls against the rail cars before giving way. Within fifteen minutes the construction train was isolated in a driving, pulsing ocean of buffalo.

A rifle shot cracked, then another and yet another. Ted cursed sharply.

Two cars away, a half-dozen new workers were blasting away at the sea of brown bodies. Jumping from car to car, Ted raced to the spot where the first rifleman knelt. He grabbed the rifle from the man's hand and jarred the worker with a solid backhand blow.

The shooter's companion glanced up, startled. One by

one the other gunners fell silent, staring at the lean figure crouched atop the car. Ted's face was a study in fury.

"You idiots! What gives you the right to pull a stunt like this? I should skin every one of you alive!"

"Aw, hell, Henderson," one of the riflemen grumbled, "they's just buffalo."

Ted glared at the man until the worker dropped his gaze. "Just buffalo? I'll tell you what these are! These are Indian lives. You're killing the food of an entire race of people—and for sport!"

Ted's voice cracked in contempt. "Do you fools know what would happen if the Indians found out the Union Pacific was killing buffalo for the hell of it while their people go hungry? They'd be down on your heads like lice on a dog, and I'd be tempted to help them myself!"

He took a deep breath and willed himself to calm down. It did not help much. He glowered at the handful of riflemen atop the rail car. "Any of you ever hold a baby that was dying of starvation? With its belly swollen and arms no bigger than a man's thumb? By God, I have. And I'll tell you dumb asses something—a baby's a baby regardless of its color!"

He waved a hand toward the dead buffalo as the herd parted, leaving the downed buffalo untrampled. "When this herd passes, you fearless hunters are going to skin out and butcher every dead buffalo," Ted said. "Then you're going with me, to deliver the meat and the hides to a Cheyenne camp south of here."

One of the marksmen started to protest but fell silent under Ted's stare. "The next man who pulls a trigger on these animals will find out firsthand what it's like to be shot! Do I make myself clear?"

The red-faced railroaders grudgingly nodded their understanding. One by one they clambered from the top of the car. Ted made his way back to Casement's car.

"Dammit, Jack," he said morosely sinking into a chair, "am I going too far this time? Am I just taking my bad temper out on some men who simply don't understand?"

General Jack studied his chief scout for several moments. "You did what you thought was right. I agree with you. The Union Pacific has tried hard to get supplies to Abel Hubbard for the needy Indians. A wholesale buffalo slaughter by our men for no good reason would turn the tribes even more violently against us."

Casement lit a fresh cigar. "I'll see that those guilty do their share to make things as right as possible. You can have all the teams, men, and wagons you need."

At midafternoon of the next day, the last of the migrating buffalo passed railhead. In their wake was almost two miles of flattened roadbed that would have to be rebuilt before tracks could be laid.

Under Ted's watchful eye, the railroaders who had fired into the buffalo herd skinned and quartered the downed animals and loaded the meat into wagons for the trip south to the Cheyenne camp.

Ted sniffed the brisk north wind. He knew the meat would not spoil during the long haul. All the signs pointed toward an extended cold spell. Staring at the buffalo meat, Ted wondered how many times he would see a great buffalo herd again. Deep inside he knew the huge herds were a symbol of a vanishing way of life—a symbol that time was passing and he could do nothing to stop the West he loved so much from vanishing forever.

Taylor Elkins slipped the confidential dispatch from its envelope and carefully studied each handwritten page, his brows furrowed in concentration. Finally he refolded the report and stood gazing out the window. He was not seeing the hacks and pedestrians who were slogging through the light March rain in the street below. In his mind, he saw a spider's web of financial intrigue with New York as the lair of the builder.

Taylor idly tapped the folded dispatch against the palm of his hand. His contact in a major financial house in New York had provided yet another link to the still-incomplete chain—a name, Garth Pfister, chairman of the Southern Overland. And where Pfister went, Taylor knew something was afoot. It might be just on the hazy side of the law or simply unethical, but the fat man had a wide streak of larceny.

Tucking the paper into a pocket Taylor continued his daily routine, approving the final rough layouts of the national news section of the next morning's edition of the *Washington Globe*. Then he asked his assistant editor to take over for a few days. "Another trip to New York," he explained. "Incidentally, if you get wind of any big stock buys involving the Union Pacific while I'm gone, please wire me in care of the financial desk at the *New York News*."

Later, as Taylor shared an after-dinner brandy with Vi, the two compared notes on the Union Pacific project.

"I've done the best I could to draw some of the wives out," Vi said. "So far all I've managed to do is be bored to death and waste some awfully nice wine. I did get Thelma Hutchings alone and sherried up enough that she admitted they were buying into the Union Pacific. But she stopped short of telling me how. I suppose she was afraid we might cut a slice from their pie."

"You've been more help than you realize, Vi," Taylor said. He swirled the brandy in the snifter, smiling over the rim at his wife. "The names you turned up from those incessant sherry and dinner parties helped give me a place to start. Darling, I know how much you hate playing the role of a social climber and snob, but if you ever want a full-time job as a spy, just let me know. We'll put you on the payroll."

Vi lowered her glass and stood behind her husband, idly massaging his neck. "You're all the full-time job I can handle, Mr. Elkins. And it's been a comfortable life here for a woman who used to think clean water for a bath once a week at a Pony Express relay station was a luxury."

Abruptly, her tone became concerned. "Are you sure you have to make this trip to New York, darling? Call it superstition or a sixth sense, but I feel all crawly inside when I think about it."

Taylor reached up and patted her hand reassuringly. "I have to go, dear. I'm so close to putting it all together. All those hours looking through records of stock sales, all the blind alleys, and using all my friends and contacts here and in New York is very near to paying off."

Taylor entwined his fingers in hers. "I think I've found the pattern, Vi. There are too many coincidences in the way the Southern Overland is structured. The same people keep showing up, or at least sending their money, from companies that will be hurt by the railroad. There have been funds from several overland freight companies, sailing vessel owners, and monied businessmen filtered through Southern. All I need now is two more links—how it works and why. I'm sure that information is in New York. So I have to go."

He steered her around the chair into his lap. "Maybe I can wrap it all up on this trip and start doing some research at home. It's time I stopped being a government agent and started being a husband full-time. Incidentally," he added, "if

you see two tough-looking gents wearing brown bowler hats
lounging on the porch across the street while I'm gone, don't
shoot them. They're not sizing up the place for a robbery.
They're special agents assigned to protect you."

"Some of your contacts are pretty rough people, Taylor.
Can you be sure they aren't working both sides of the street,
like your prostitute friends?" Vi asked.

Her husband could not suppress a smile. "Do I detect a
tinge of jealousy in your voice, my dear? After all, it *is* all in
the line of duty—"

He yelped in mock pain as she lightly cuffed his ear.
"Joke if you want, sir, but don't touch," she warned. "Come
on. If you're determined to go to the big city, I'll help you
pack. You might forget your socks. Or, heaven forbid, your
morals."

Garth Pfister stabbed the half-smoked cigar into a heavy
glass ashtray where a half-dozen other stubs lay crushed.
Pfister glared long and hard at Jack Fallon, who was seated
across the desk. Three of Pfister's men stood around the big
Irishman. Pfister was not taking any chances.

"Dammit, Fallon," Pfister snapped, "when I hire somebody to do a job I expect to see it done!"

"You want to explain that, Pfister?" Fallon demanded
angrily.

"Isn't it obvious to you? We sent you to the Union
Pacific railhead to delay construction. So what happens? In a
year's time, the railroad lays track across half of Nebraska and
damn near half of Wyoming. We're way behind schedule in
our takeover plan, Fallon, and I think I'm looking at the
reason for it!"

Fallon's knuckles turned white as he squeezed the arms
of his chair, his fury building. "I did my job, Pfister. I bought
you as many delays as any man could! It ain't my fault if
you're behind schedule—"

"Shut up!" Pfister's small eyes almost disappeared in the
pudgy, anger-flushed face. "I don't pay for excuses, I pay for
results! And what the hell's this high-priced half-breed we've
been paying done lately? I haven't seen any results from him
in some time!"

Suddenly Fallon became cautious. If the chairman found
out his money was not going to Long Walker as he thought it
was, there would be hell to pay.

"We're waitin' for the best time, Pfister," Fallon grumbled. "Long Walker and I figured to stop the Union Pacific dead in its tracks in the pass through the mountains."

Pfister snorted in disdain. "We've paid you and the half-breed a hell of a lot of money, and the company doesn't think it's getting its money's worth." He leaned back in his chair, his hands folded across his huge girth. "You know what happens when somebody doesn't deliver what we pay for, Bear."

"Damn you, Pfister! Don't you threaten me!" Fallon knew he might be letting his temper get the best of him, but he did not care. "All I had to work with out there was a bunch of dumb Irishmen, worn-out soldiers, and niggers with nothing on their minds but women and whiskey! Some damned fine organization you built. No wonder you had me do Sean Grady in. At least that put the blame on somebody!"

"I'm not threatening you, Fallon. I'm stating a fact. If there's any blame, maybe it's on my head. I thought you could do the job. I guess I was wrong."

"You fat bastard," Fallon snapped. "You sit here and smoke your cigars while I'm out there fighting the whole damn Third Cavalry with a handful of Indians! I'd have the goddamn railroad shut down if I'd had my way! You didn't tell me there'd be two men at railhead near as tough as me. *You* go up against Ted Henderson and that damn O'Reilly pet of his all by your lonesome! You'll find out in a hurry that it's no easy job!"

"Watch it, Fallon," Pfister said ominously. "You're walking on thin ice. One more wrong step and you might find yourself at the bottom of the Hudson River with a rock around your feet."

The veins in Fallon's neck bulged under his building fury. "You give me another six months, Pfister, and I'll stop the Union Pacific. I'll stop the railroad and I'll kill Henderson and O'Reilly! Then you and the Southern can step in and take the whole damn thing over."

Garth Pfister's voice was ominously quiet. "You've had your chance, Fallon, and you screwed it up. I've got a six-year-old nephew who could have done the job as well as you did."

With a howl of rage, Fallon jumped from his chair, obsessed with wrapping his hands around Pfister's fat neck. A hand clamped on his shoulder.

Fallon twisted away, kicked the chair back, and slammed a fist into the guard's jaw. Something cracked into the back of his skull, staggering him. He turned, half groggy from the blow, and swung a wild right at a man holding a short club. The blow connected, knocking the man against the wall. Then an arm of iron locked around Fallon's neck and dragged him to the floor. For a moment Fallon held his own against the three guards. The struggle was matched evenly enough to send Garth Pfister scrabbling in the desk for his gun before his bodyguards gained the upper hand.

Pfister grinned as the trio pounded Fallon with their fists and feet for a few moments. "Enough!" he finally called.

Fallon was hauled to his feet, facing Pfister.

"Have you learned your lesson, Bear? Now, you may not realize it, but you owe me one. The committee wanted you killed, no excuses, no questions. I talked them out of it—*this* time."

Fallon, one eye beginning to swell and a trickle of blood oozing from his mouth, tried his best to glare defiantly at the chairman.

"I have a job that needs to be done. I think you might be able to handle this one," Pfister added sarcastically. "Get this done right, you'll get one more shot at the railroad. But from this point forward, Fallon, you get paid when the job is done and you carry your own expenses. The only other option you have is to wake up one morning and find yourself dead. Do I make myself clear?"

Fallon nodded glumly. The promise of another crack at Henderson and O'Reilly was enough to partly soothe his pride. "All right. What's the job?" he asked.

Pfister reached inside the desk, pulled out a bottle, and poured himself a glass of rye whiskey. He did not offer one to Fallon. Pfister took a sip, then looked over the rim of the glass at the big Irishman. "There's a nosy newsman who's getting too close to the Southern Overland," Pfister said. "He's in New York now. His name is Taylor Elkins. Find him and kill him. Then jump a freight and head west." Pfister downed the rest of the rye. "I warn you once more, Fallon— screw this up and you'll be feeding the fish."

Taylor Elkins pushed his chair back from the table in the library of the *New York News* and rubbed a hand across his tired eyes. He closed the small notebook in which he had been scribbling and tucked it into a shirt pocket.

Returning the half-dozen binders that held back issues of the *News* and other national papers to their proper place among the racks, he reflected wryly that newsmen had been accurate when they tagged newspaper libraries as morgues.

Ah, Taylor thought, climbing the steps from the morgue to the newsroom, *the glamorous life of the secret agent— three more days of reading and talking to whores and heads of corporations.*

He stepped into the bustling newsroom where reporters and editors prepared the next day's edition of the *News*.

"Find anything useful?" asked the financial editor of the *News,* a man Taylor totally trusted.

"I think so, Abe," Taylor replied. "I'm much in your debt. If you ever need a favor . . ."

The thin, stooped man with the mustache and an uncanny knack for breaking stories that escaped other writers grinned. "What's the chance I could have your story the same day you run it in the *Globe?* With byline credit, of course."

Taylor smiled back. "You have it, Abe. And we'll share the byline. You've put me on all the right leads, and your help has given me details I could never have gotten on my own. I'll wire it to you when we're ready. Same-day publication. And if you ever decide to leave the *News,* you've got a desk at the *Globe.*"

"Thanks. I'll keep that offer in mind." The thin man turned back to his work, glancing up to wave a hand in farewell as Taylor lifted his overcoat from the rack nearby.

Outside, the streets of New York City were all but deserted at the late hour. Theaters had closed, and the chilly north wind had chased the city's residents indoors and sent the drifters into alleys or deserted buildings to seek shelter.

Taylor pulled his coat tighter as he stepped onto the breezy street. He was glad that he had donned the special vest Vi had slipped into his suitcase. Its weight was a nuisance, but it did provide some warmth. For years the military had been attempting to devise a lightweight garment that would stop a bullet. Since President Lincoln's death the research had intensified. The vest Taylor wore was the latest design, thin metal mesh quilted over tightly packed shredded canvas and strips of an experimental material of some sort.

He paused at the bottom of the steps of the *News* building, trying to decide whether to return directly to his hotel room or attempt to find a restaurant that was open.

Taylor saw the muzzle flash from a dark alley across the street just a split second before something slammed into his chest just above the heart. The impact twisted his body and sent him skidding to the cobblestones of the street. He lay stunned, the gaslight on the post above fading in and out of focus. Suddenly he realized he had been shot.

He turned his head just in time to glimpse a chunky body sprinting down the alley. A stray beam of light from a window glinted on metal in the figure's hand.

Taylor stumbled to his feet and thrust his hand beneath his coat. His fingers closed on the butt of the specially made .44 revolver. Slipping it from the shoulder holster, he sprinted across the street toward the alley.

He reached the end of the alley in time to glimpse the blocky figure running down the street fifty yards away. Taylor thumbed the hammer of his revolver and brought the sights into line—then cursed as a nightshirted fat man waddled from a door directly into his line of fire.

The opportunity for a clear shot lost, Taylor forced himself into a shambling run. Twice he glimpsed the big man running through the streets, but each time the man turned a corner before Taylor could aim, and Taylor knew he was losing ground.

He finally gave up the chase. He leaned against the corner of a building and slid the revolver back into the shoulder holster. His fingers probed his chest beneath the protective vest, and he winced in pain. The skin was sore and he would have a deep bruise. But there was no blood. The experimental vest had stopped the pistol slug, spreading the effects of the impact over a wider area.

Taylor offered a silent prayer of thanks for the cold that had led him to don the vest that morning. Had the weather been more pleasant, he could well be a dead man.

Wearily, he looked around, collected his bearings, and began walking toward his hotel, his senses tuned for any strange sound or movement in the night. But New York City seemed to be asleep once more. He decided he would not report the incident to the New York police. That would raise questions he did not care to answer until his investigation was complete.

Taylor suddenly stopped, struck by a thought—the ambusher no doubt thought he was dead, for the impact of the bullet had knocked him to the ground. His attacker had not caught sight of him during the chase, or he would have turned and waited in another ambush.

One thing was reasonably certain, Taylor concluded. The shot had not been a random attack. It appeared the Southern Overland was getting very nervous.

A blizzard that blanketed the Plains with swirling snow and bitter cold caught Yellow Crow as he continued tracking the renegade Long Walker. Though he was reluctant to interrupt his search for his hated enemy, the Cheyenne knew it would be fatal not to take shelter and wait until the storm blew itself out. Finally, along the Republican River, he found a cave that was large enough to protect both him and his horse. Yellow Crow stumbled inside and wearily closed his eyes for some much needed rest.

A warning snuffle from the rear of the cave brought him fully alert. The palomino gelding many times had sensed danger even before the sharp-eyed Cheyenne warrior. When the yellow horse spoke, his owner listened.

"Quiet, friend," Yellow Crow muttered in Cheyenne. "Your voice is heard. Now be still."

Yellow Crow could see or hear little in the raging blizzard outside the cave. He squinted into the blowing snow, and cocked the scarred Spencer .56, fully aware that he was alone in enemy lands. The outlaw band that followed Long Walker controlled this territory.

Yellow Crow realistically appraised his situation. The cave was adequate protection from the elements, with a small fire guttering at the rear near a spring of clear, cold water. It was a good place to defend, with only one entrance and that partially shielded by boulders and small scrub trees, but with a good field of fire. But his supplies were running low. The sack of grain he had carried for the palomino was almost empty, and the horse was gaunt from lack of filling dried-grass fodder.

If necessary, Yellow Crow decided, he could hold out for two days, perhaps three, before his ammunition was gone and exhaustion and hunger dulled his fighting ability.

Through a sudden break in the white curtain, he spotted a dark form. He raised the muzzle of the Spencer, prepared to fire if the shape drew nearer the cave. His finger tightened on the trigger—and suddenly the shadowy form seemed to stumble and sink into the deep snow. Yellow Crow watched for several moments, his rifle at the ready, but the figure did not move.

Cautiously, Yellow Crow made his way from the cave, keeping the weapon trained on the still form. It was only a few feet to the figure in the snow, but the Cheyenne took his time. One did not rush to the unknown if one wished a long life.

Finally he knelt beside the downed man. Already, snow had begun to form a small drift behind the body. Yellow Crow saw at a glance the man was a Sioux of the Santee tribe. He was near death. The craggy features were pale, and the fingernails were tinged with blue. The Santee appeared to be unarmed, and there was no horse in sight.

Yellow Crow placed a cautious hand on the Santee's shoulder. The Sioux stirred reflexively, trying to draw away from the grip of death. "Brother, do not be alarmed," the Cheyenne said. "This is the hand of friendship, and shelter. Can the Sioux stand?"

The Santee tried to rise, but his strength was near its end. Yellow Crow slipped an arm about the Indian's waist. After what seemed a long time, he eased the Santee into the relative warmth of the cave. The palomino snorted nervously in the background as Yellow Crow half carried the Santee to the fire. Ice crystals and snow had stiffened the man's blanket. Yellow Crow had to pry the frozen hands from their grip on the blanket. As he peeled the thin, tattered blanket away, he noticed the dried blood crusting a large spot on the cloth.

Working quickly, the Cheyenne draped his own blanket about the man's thin shoulders. From a single cooking pot resting by the fire he dipped a gourd of warm water and held it to the Santee's lips. The Sioux, half conscious, sipped it slowly. When the warm liquid gradually filtered through his body, the Santee's eyes opened, his wavering gaze focused on Yellow Crow's face.

"Where—where is this place?" The Santee's voice was barely a croak. Blood from the cracks in his lips had frozen on his mouth and chin.

"It is a cave near the Republican River. Yellow Crow of the Cheyenne welcomes you to it."

The Santee nodded. "Yellow Crow's name is well known. Crooked Leg of the Sioux thanks Yellow Crow."

The Cheyenne refilled the gourd with warm water. "Drink, Crooked Leg. The warm waters will help chase the cold from the bones. How does Crooked Leg come to be alone in the storm? And injured as well?"

Crooked Leg drank deeply from the gourd, then placed it beside him and held both hands toward the small fire. "When Yellow Crow learns of these things, the Cheyenne will kill Crooked Leg. That is as it should be. It is known that Yellow Crow and Long Walker have sworn the blood oath each against the other. Crooked Leg rode with Long Walker."

Yellow Crow studied the weather-ravaged face. Crooked Leg squared his shoulders, preparing to meet his death with dignity and pride. "Crooked Leg says he rode with Long Walker," Yellow Crow said quietly. "Does he no longer?"

Crooked Leg shook his head. A shudder racked his body. "Long Walker left Crooked Leg to die several suns ago. There was a fight at a ranch house during a raid. Crooked Leg was hit and could not keep up. Long Walker took Crooked Leg's horse and left him afoot."

Yellow Crow snorted in disgust. "It is Long Walker's way. Where is the blue-eyed one now?"

"Far from here. After the fight with the soldiers at the place called Lodgepole, Long Walker gathered his band. They were moving to winter camp along the Sweetwater River when the fight came at the ranch house. Long Walker's plan is to strike the white man's iron horses and builders of iron trails when the grass comes."

The Santee's voice gained strength. "Deep in the mountains, Long Walker waits now in camp. Many white men will die when Long Walker sounds the war cry."

"Does Crooked Leg know the location of this camp?" Yellow Crow asked.

The Santee shook his head. "Only that it was to be in the Sweetwater range. This is all Crooked Leg can say, for it is all he knows." The Sioux nodded toward the rifle resting on Yellow Crow's lap. "When Yellow Crow kills Crooked Leg, he should aim his shot well."

Yellow Crow pondered the situation. He had the right to kill the Santee, but not the wish. Even though Crooked Leg had ridden with Long Walker, Yellow Crow's quarrel was with the blue-eyed one—not those who had been deceived into following him.

He stood. "Crooked Leg will not die at Yellow Crow's

hand," he said firmly. "There is but little in this cave. Crooked Leg will have his share. Yellow Crow will treat the Santee's wounds as best he can. When the storm stops, both will go to a Cheyenne camp two days' travel away. There medicine men will treat Crooked Leg's wounds. When he is well again, he will be given a horse and a choice."

As he spoke, Yellow Crow took slices of dried meat from his rapidly dwindling supply. "Should Crooked Leg decide to ride again with Long Walker, he will die the next time he meets Yellow Crow," the Cheyenne warned. "Should Crooked Leg decide to join the Sioux who do not war on the white man, he will be free to enter the land of his own people."

Crooked Leg studied the Cheyenne's face for a long moment. "It is said that to spare the life of an enemy is a weakness," the Sioux said.

Yellow Crow merely shrugged. "At the moment Crooked Leg and Yellow Crow are not enemies," he replied logically, "so there is no shame in being spared and no weakness in the sparing. Crooked Leg and Yellow Crow are but two lone red men trying to survive in a blizzard. No more, no less."

The aroma of jerky stew drifted from the pot. "One day, perhaps, Crooked Leg and Yellow Crow will fight each other, perhaps one day fight side by side as brothers. For now, though, Crooked Leg and Yellow Crow eat."

By mid-April Ted Henderson began to relax for the first time in months. Frequent letters from Wilma exerted a strong pull on him now that the ranch was not that far away from railhead. The ranch stock had come through the hard winter in good shape, thanks to the competent efforts of Valdez and Wilma.

Jack Casement looked up from his work on a daily progress report as Ted folded Wilma's last letter and returned it to a pocket.

"Getting a little homesick, Ted? That's the fourth time today you've read that letter," Casement observed.

"Yes, I guess I am," Ted said. "There's not enough to keep me busy all of a sudden." He grinned at Casement. "You're slipping, Jack. I've gotten six or seven hours' sleep every night for almost a week now."

"Don't blame me," Casement replied, scribbling his initials on the report and closing his daybook. "You've just done too good a job. Took all the fun and excitement out of building a railroad." Casement tossed the book into a desk drawer, then looked thoughtfully at Ted. "How long has it been since you've had a day off?"

"Sixteen months, give or take a couple of weeks."

"God! Has it really been that long? And what about Kevin?" he asked.

Ted realized with a start that over a year had passed since Kevin had joined him on the Union Pacific. "He left a week-old baby behind," Ted said, "and the youngster's already had a birthday."

Casement clucked his tongue in mock disgust. "You two should be ashamed of yourselves, neglecting your families that way! Your wife may have taken up with a traveling salesman by now, Henderson. Tell you what—I think you and O'Reilly should take a couple of weeks off."

Casement waved away Ted's objection. "We can spare you around here for a while. The boys are working well together, and we finally have a full crew. Shaughnessy is as much a foreman now as Kevin is. There's no Indian trouble that we know about. And I'm not sure I can put up with you two when there's no action going on; you'd drive me out of my head. Like a couple school kids looking for mischief, you are."

Casement pointed toward the door, his face stern. "Go, Ted Henderson. Take your Irishman with you. Get thee from my sight for two weeks. Give your tired ol' pappy a rest!"

Ted grinned. "You won't have to say that twice, Jack. But I want you to know I've been run off from better outfits than this before." He started toward the door.

"By the way," Casement said, "Chin-Lu asked for a bit of time off. Said he'd saved enough to buy some horses. Something about tying 'em up in front of a lodge. I figure any man dumb enough to take a wife, let alone buy one, deserves his fate. He rode out at daylight with a handful of lead rope and a smile."

"I wish him well," Ted said solemnly, "but old Paints-His-Horses will be a tough nut to crack where Little Fern is concerned. Don't let anyone tell you the Cheyenne trade their daughters for just anybody's horses, and Little Fern is that old chief's favorite." Ted paused at the door. "Jack, you're not going to have any scouts if Chin-Lu and I are gone at the same time."

Casement shrugged. "We'll get by. But don't be gone

too long. We'll need you when we start putting rail beds through Bridger's Pass."

Ted found Kevin with the track gang, sweating profusely and singing an off-color Irish pub song. After the final chorus, he told Kevin about their vacation.

"Been havin' me a cravin' to see me wee urchin," Kevin said, exaggerating his Irish act. "And if the lad's mother should happen to be nearby, 'twould not be too great a disappointment."

Atop a low hill overlooking the camp of Paints-His-Horses, Chin-Lu sat quietly, waiting as the first light of the new day painted a tinge of pink across wispy clouds in the eastern sky.

Below, three fine horses stood before a certain lodge. Tied to one hackamore was a small pouch that contained exquisitely carved jade figurines.

Chin-Lu held his breath as the flap of the lodge swung open and Paints-His-Horses stepped stiffly into the morning light. Hope stirred in the Chinese man's breast as the old chief studied the animals with a critical eye and examined the contents of the pouch. Then came the moment Chin-Lu both welcomed and dreaded. Little Fern's father slowly untied the three horses and stood for a long moment staring toward the hill where Chin-Lu waited. If the chief turned the animals into the Cheyenne pony herd, Little Fern was Chin-Lu's bride.

The Chinese man's heart skidded as Paints-His-Horses took the reins and led the three animals toward the hill, not toward the pony herd. The slender Chinaman willed his spirit to be calm as the old man approached.

Paints-His-Horses limped painfully up the slight rise and handed the reins to Chin-Lu.

"It is with sadness that Paints-His-Horses returns the ponies to the warrior Chin-Lu," the old chief said. "Chin-Lu is a noble and fearless man and would be a fine husband and son. Little Fern has pleaded with her father to accept the gifts, for Chin-Lu stands tall and straight in her eyes."

"Please," Chin-Lu said, "if it is not a violation of the Cheyenne custom, may Chin-Lu know the reason his request for the hand of Little Fern has been rejected?"

The old chief sighed wearily. "It is not the custom to ask," he said, "but Paints-His-Horses feels Chin-Lu deserves an answer. It is a simple reason and has nothing to do with

Chin-Lu's worthiness. It is that Little Fern, as the last surviving child of her family, may not marry outside the tribe of her birth. And Chin-Lu is not of the Cheyenne."

The crestfallen Chin-Lu tried not to let his disappointment show. He squared his shoulders and faced the aging chief. "Then this Cheyenne law shall be honored and respected," he said calmly. "But will the chief Paints-His-Horses answer another question?"

"Chin-Lu deserves this courtesy."

"How does one become a Cheyenne?" Chin-Lu asked solemnly.

The chief's eyes sparkled in obvious delight at the question. "Paints-His-Horses believed the warrior Chin-Lu would not surrender easily. A man may earn acceptance into the Cheyenne tribe by performing a great feat of courage to the benefit of the Cheyenne or other Indian tribes allied with the Cheyenne."

"Then, if fate so ordains and the spirits smile, Chin-Lu might yet gain the right to tie ponies before the lodge of Little Fern?"

"If the spirits so decide," Paints-His-Horses said.

"And where is Chin-Lu to find such deeds to perform?"

"Do not go in search of these adventures. If it is to be, they will come to Chin-Lu. Now go. At this moment it would but cause pain were Chin-Lu and Little Fern to meet. Ride with calm heart and faith. The spirits of Paints-His-Horses and Little Fern ride with Chin-Lu." The old Indian suddenly smiled. "Little Fern has eyes for no other warrior bearing ponies. Chin-Lu shall have time to perform these deeds."

The old chief watched in silence until Chin-Lu and the horses were but a distant image against the prairie. He felt an ache in his own breast. He knew that such pains pierced the heart of his daughter and troubled the soul of the man riding away. "Chin-Lu will return. Then laughter will once more touch Paints-His-Horses's lodge."

A day and a half from rails' end, Ted and Kevin rode in tense silence through the rugged, narrow canyon in the wild Rattlesnake Range. Both men had spare pistols tucked into waistbands and both held their carbines cocked and ready.

Ted's gaze constantly swept the country ahead. From time to time Kevin would turn in the saddle and study their back trail. For the last two hours the pair had been stalked by

Indians. Ted was not sure how many warriors there were in the group. There could have been as few as four or as many as twenty. A glimpse here, a sound there, a bird call that was a bit off-key, had been the only indications of their presence. To the two veteran Indian fighters, the warriors might as well have stood on top of a hill and waved a red blanket.

"Got him spotted yet?" Kevin asked quietly.

"Yes. Only there's four of them. About two hundred yards ahead, two on each side of the trail. One behind a scrub cedar, one in the rocks by the dry wash on our left. The other two are straight across from their friends."

"Got 'em," Kevin said. "Damn Indians, don't they know there aren't supposed to be any hostiles around? It's getting so a man can't even depend on his enemies anymore."

"It's time to start getting twitchy," Ted warned. "As far as they know, we're riding along as innocent as pilgrims who've never seen an Indian. The way they're set up, they'll be expecting us to ride into the trap between those four afoot. Then the rest of them will come after us from behind."

Kevin tightened his grip on the handle of his Henry. "Can you make out the tribe?"

"Not yet. But I expect we'll get close enough to check their teeth before this is over," Ted replied.

"We can't go back," Kevin muttered. "We can't go around. There are mountains straight up on both sides of the trail. So that leaves just one direction, right?"

Ted slowly nodded. "Through the middle. Can you take the two on the left?"

"I reckon that I damn well better," Kevin said dryly.

The two men held their horses to a casual walk for another hundred yards. "I haven't been this spooked since we rode into the Canyon de Chelly against the Navajo," Kevin muttered softly.

"If it's any consolation, I know exactly how you feel. Well, let's get on with it."

With a ringing Cheyenne war whoop, Ted slammed his spurs into his horse's ribs. The animal leaped, startled at the sound and the sharp jab, then was moving at a dead run through the narrow trail. Kevin's mount was only a stride behind.

Ted heard the *splat* of a lead slug against a rock by the trail, and a split second later the crack of a carbine rattled the mountain walls. The concealed Indian, startled at the sudden

dash by the horsemen, had rushed his shot and was far wide
of the mark.

The trail widened slightly. Ted kneed his horse aside,
making room for Kevin to ride abreast. At Ted's yell they
pulled their mounts to a skidding stop, taking cover. Ted
crouched in a tangle of fallen trees while Kevin tucked his big
bulk into a niche between two boulders.

Their rifles blasted together. The Indian Ted had in his
sights yelped and sagged against a rock. Kevin's shot struck
one of the braves on the left side of the trail in the neck.

A hundred yards down range, an Indian stood for a
better field of fire. Ted cut him down, levering three quick
shots. Kevin cursed as a rifle ball ripped the air near his
head, then took careful aim and fired. The rifle slug thumped
into the brave's exposed knee. The Indian jerked, and his
head came into view above the rocks. Kevin's quick shot took
him between the eyes.

The two veterans turned, rifles pointed down the back
trail as echoes of the shots tumbled one upon the other along
the narrow trail. The rumble of hooves grew loud, then a
half-dozen warriors swept into view around a slight bend in
the trail.

For a moment Ted was surprised that the Indians so
readily exposed themselves. Then it dawned on him that the
braves in the rocks had carried Henry rifles. The pursuing
Indians no doubt expected the white men to be the ones
downed.

Their expectations quickly faded beneath the accurate
and deadly fire of the two white men. While Kevin blasted
away at the riders, Ted dropped his sights and, reluctantly,
dropped two Indian ponies with four shots. The dying horses
fell heavily into the narrow trail, their riders tumbling. A
third pony, unable to stop, charged into the mass of flailing
hooves, stumbled, and went down.

A fourth rider clung to the mane of his pony as the
animal leaped high, clearing the tangled mass of bodies, and
charged down the trail toward Ted. The Indian, his face
streaked with paint and a red handprint across his bare breast,
leveled his handgun at Ted. The warrior was a better horseman than marksman, and firing from the back of a running
pony was one of the trickiest bits of shooting a man could be
called upon to do. The slugs sailed wide.

Ted swung his rifle barrel toward the Indian, lined the

sights, and squeezed. Only a dull click sounded as the hammer fell on a faulty cartridge. He braced himself for the impact of a pistol ball as the Indian skidded his horse to a stop almost within arm's length. Then the brave suddenly tossed both hands skyward and slumped over the neck of his horse. Ted glanced across the trail and saw Kevin's smoking rifle barrel turn back toward the remaining Indians.

The surprise counterattack broke the spirit of the pursuing Indians. After milling about for a moment and firing a few harmless rounds, they turned their mounts from the scene and fled back down the canyon trail.

Ted worked the action of his Henry, ejecting the dud cartridge and chambering another. He stood, his ears ringing from the muzzle blasts, and surveyed the scene. He moved cautiously from one huddled form to another. Kevin joined him, probing the bodies with the barrel of his carbine. All the braves wore the strange red palm-and-fingers print on their breasts. Most of the attackers had been Sioux, with a couple of Cheyenne.

Ted slipped a toe under one red body and flipped the Indian over. "I know this one, Kevin," he said. "Teton Sioux. He's been riding with Long Walker since the beginning."

"Uh, oh," his friend said. "I thought we had maybe seen the last of that outlaw."

Ted shook his head. "It appears that once we clear Long Walker's range, he just changes ranges. He's in these mountains somewhere nearby. It's my guess he plans to hit the Union Pacific as the rails cross the mountains. What a determined cuss." He pointed to the blood-red handprint on a dead warrior's chest. "Looks like he's gotten himself a brand-new war society to work with, too."

Concern clouded Kevin's features. "There's dozens of places in the mountains he could hide out," he said, "and even more where he could stage little surprises for our men." Kevin sighed. "So what now, Ted? Back to railhead to sound a warning?"

Ted stared briefly into the distance. The longing for his family weighed heavily in his heart.

He forced away the image of Wilma snuggling near in the darkness of their bedroom. *Damn you, Long Walker,* he thought bitterly, *you won't even let a man visit his wife and son, will you?* But Ted knew more was at stake than his own desires. Lives hung in the balance, and each passing hour placed those lives in deeper jeopardy.

He sighed heavily. "No, Kevin. It looks as if my vacation will have to be forgotten for now. We'll split up. You ride on to the ranch—our families must be warned of Long Walker's presence. I'll sneak my way over to Fort Laramie and see if we can't get a few equalizers from Abel Hubbard."

"Ted," Kevin said, "you've been away longer than I have. I'll ride to the fort—"

"You'll do no such thing, Kevin O'Reilly," Ted interrupted. "You'll go to the ranch and stay there until you feel it's safe to return to railhead—not a minute before! Railroads we can rebuild. Wives and children we can't."

Ted toed the stirrup and swung aboard his snorting horse. "Let's get moving now, before we find out we're up to our butts in mad Indians. And, Kevin—"

"Yes?"

"Explain to Wilma and Bill why I couldn't come. And—give them my love." Abruptly, Ted wheeled his horse. Two hundred yards away he reined the animal onto a faint trace that led toward Fort Laramie. He twisted in the saddle and lifted a hand in a farewell salute to Kevin. His friend returned the wave, then kneed his own horse into a ground-eating trot toward the ranch.

Lieutenant Colonel Abel Hubbard leaned back in his chair and studied the drawn, weary face across the desk. Ted looked like he had used up a lot of miles in the last few months, Abel thought. His temples were heavily grayed and the rugged face, brown from the sun and wind, wore new wrinkles. But the sharp eyes remained alert and active.

Abel took his time digesting the information Ted had brought. His gaze shifted from Major David Wills to Sergeant Major Albert Jonas. The latter had just returned from leading a long patrol on a sweep to the north and west of Fort Laramie.

"Well, Sergeant," Abel finally said, "you've heard what Ted had to say. Long Walker's in the mountains, probably in force. What's our status elsewhere with the Indians?"

"Still peaceful for the most part, Colonel," Jonas replied. "Helpin' the poorer bands make it through the winter bought us some time, if nothin' else. They still ain't happy about the railroad, but I didn't find nobody puttin' on war paint."

David Wills suddenly rose and walked to a map on the wall behind Abel's desk. For a moment he studied the pencil track that marked the progress of the Union Pacific rails.

"Colonel," he said firmly, "I can have two companies at Boots and Saddles by dawn, my own I Company and Sergeant Jonas's R Company. If the Union Pacific can feed us, we can travel light. Without supply wagons to slow us down we can be in position to back the railroad in three days. Those two companies are the best in the army. We'll hold the Union Pacific's hand all the way across Wyoming if need be."

Abel raised an eyebrow in Albert Jonas's direction. "How about it, Sergeant? Do you feel physically up to leading R Company on what could be a long and tough campaign?"

Jonas's answering smile was grim. "Colonel, for another crack at that damn blue-eyed renegade and his bunch I'll walk barefoot through the biggest cactus patch in Arizona," he said flatly. "Now I ain't the smartest man that ever come down the pike, but it looks to me like we got a chance to put ol' Long Walker in a deep pit full o' mad rattlers. And if you don't give me this crack at that red bastard, I'll quit your army quicker'n a hawk hits a rabbit."

Abel glanced at Ted. Both men knew that the loss of several close friends in the long-ago fight with Long Walker had left a deep scar on Jonas's soul.

Ted shifted in the rawhide chair. "There's not a man alive I'd rather have beside me than that hulk of a sergeant over there," he said. "And Albert's right. We have a chance to bury this Long Walker threat for all time. All we need are good men, seasoned Indian fighters, and a little luck. R Company and I Company are the best in the business. If necessary, we'll make our own luck."

Within the hour preparations were under-way to field the force of almost two hundred men. Six of the more experienced Indian fighters among the crack Henderson's Scouts unit were saddling up for the trip to the Henderson-O'Reilly ranch, with four squads of mounted infantry to follow. The solid ranch house would serve as a temporary fort to protect settlers in the vicinity until the Indian threat had passed.

"Ted, I'm beginning to have some doubts about young Wills," Abel said when the two friends finally were alone. "He has personal problems—woman trouble. For a time it looked as if he might throw himself into a bottle and stay there, but for weeks now he's been dry. Still, I wonder how long it will last. Do you think his personal problems will interfere with his ability to command in the field?"

Ted smiled. "I seem to remember another young officer who went afield with some personal demons," he said quietly. "That young man came through just fine. Abel, if you could handle your problems at that time, Wills must be given the opportunity to prove he can wrestle with his own and still be a competent officer. Besides, if he starts to foul things up, how long do you think it will take Albert Jonas to set him straight?"

Abel nodded in agreement. "I can't argue with that. For all practical purposes, though, you're in command."

In the post stable tackroom, David Wills applied fresh neat's-foot oil to the stirrup leathers of his saddle, rubbing the conditioner into the leather with a vengeance. Since the confrontation with Sally Jonas, David had tried on several occasions to gain Victoria Coulter's attention. He had come away still feeling that she saw him as a younger brother. She only had eyes for Abel Hubbard, who did not even seem to realize it.

"All right, Victoria," Wills muttered as he snapped a stirrup leather taut. "When I get back from this campaign, we're going to have this out once and for all."

In the meantime, he welcomed the danger of going against Long Walker's braves. It would keep his mind busy on something besides auburn hair and green eyes.

Ten

A weary Ted Henderson led the Third Regiment's two crack companies into rails' end in the dark of night. Jack Casement greeted Ted and the well-armed contingent, noting each man carried a new repeating rifle and a brace of revolvers—one in a saddle holster, another in a belt rig.

"Damn, am I glad to see you boys," Casement said as Ted introduced David Wills and Albert Jonas. "Ted, we've got big troubles. Two days ago Indians wiped out a survey crew. Yesterday they hit a team of tie-cutters. If it hadn't been for some sharpshooting by the workers, every man would have been killed. As it was we lost one cutter and two more are laid up with injuries."

Ted frowned. "These Indians—were they wearing a red handprint on their chests, about here?" He touched a hand to his shirt over the heart.

Casement nodded, surprised. "That's what the survivors said. How'd you know that?"

Ted briefly told Casement of the clash with the Red Hands in the narrow pass. "There's no doubt in my mind that we're dealing with Long Walker," he concluded.

"Think any Indians saw you and the troops ride in?" Casement asked.

"We can't be sure one way or the other," Ted replied, "but Long Walker will know soon enough if he doesn't already."

"I'm sorry about your lost vacation. We'll make it up to you," General Jack promised. "I know how much it must have hurt to ride back without seeing your family."

Ted sighed wistfully. "This new development seemed to take priority, Jack. Any word from Chin-Lu?"

Casement plucked a cigar from his pocket. "He rode back in last night. He didn't say much, but I don't think he had any luck with his offer for the Cheyenne girl. He brought back the same horses he rode out with. He's out on scout now. Didn't waste much time getting back into action." Casement lit the cigar and studied its tip worriedly. "Chin-Lu must have found something, Ted—or else something found him. He was due back in before dark."

A faint sliver of moon rode low over Chin-Lu's shoulder in the springtime sky as the slender Chinaman neared the end of his careful stalk. He had cut sign on the two Indian scouts just before sunset. The trail had led to a pinpoint of light from a campfire in a steep, secluded ravine in the mountains barely five miles from rails' end.

The Indian camp nestled in the center of a towering grove of aspen. Chin-Lu tethered his horse a safe distance from the camp and crept toward the camp on moccasined feet.

He stopped only twenty feet from the fire, resting quietly behind the trunk of an aspen. Had he wished, he could have reached out and almost touched the nearest warrior. He counted thirty-four braves in the small camp, the majority of them in the war paint of the Cheyenne Dog Soldiers. An Indian in the war bonnet of a Sioux chief squatted near the edge of the fire, addressing the braves. The flickering light of the small fire touched the dark handprint on the Sioux's breast.

Chin-Lu listened for ten minutes, then quietly slipped away, mounted his horse, and kneed the animal toward railhead. Jack Casement would be most eager to hear of the Sioux chief's plans.

In the light of the early April morning, Long Walker grunted in satisfaction as he watched the woodcutters with their two wagons enter the mouth of the canyon. There were only six men with the wagons—six easy scalps, and perhaps some valuable plunder beneath the canvas covers of the wagons. Within another fifty yards, they would be entering his carefully planned ambush. The lead wagon neared the wedge-shaped boulder that had been chosen as the landmark for the attack to begin.

Long Walker wheeled his mount into the open, waving his shield overhead in the signal to attack. Whooping and yelling, half his force opened fire from their hiding places in the trees and behind the boulders. The other half anxiously held their ponies in check behind the riflemen, ready to rush forward and overwhelm the teamsters once the firing warriors had pinned down the victims.

Long Walker yanked his horse to a stop in astonishment as the canvas covers were suddenly whipped from the two wagons. In each wagon, a half-dozen soldiers leaned over the sides, their carbines cracking. A bullet buzzed past Long Walker's ear, barely missing its mark and jarring him into action. He whirled his pony and urged it toward the protective cover of the nearby trees at a dead run.

Glancing over his shoulder, Long Walker grimaced. The warriors in the trees and behind the boulders were trapped.

The Indians on horseback charged into the battle, racing toward the wagons a hundred yards away. Suddenly, from behind the mounted attackers, fifty cavalrymen spurred horses toward the braves exposed below. Long Walker cursed bitterly. Instead of catching the wagons in an indefensible position, the Indians themselves were trapped between the blistering rifle fire from the wagons and the handguns of the mounted troops!

The cavalrymen ripped into the surprised ranks of the mounted Indians. Dust and powder smoke mingled with the cries of wounded warriors and ponies. Through the melee, Long Walker saw a hated figure in buckskins in the thick of the cavalry charge—Ted Henderson!

The renegade Indian leveled his Henry toward the man and touched off two quick shots. Both slugs fell short of the mark. Bullets cracked the air around Long Walker as soldiers trained their weapons on the Sioux in the war bonnet. Long Walker's pony shuddered and stumbled. The half-breed barely had time to prepare for the fall before the horse went down, shot through the lungs. The slug that killed the horse had taken a chunk of flesh from Long Walker's thigh, but he scarcely felt the pain.

Desperate to escape the deadly rifles, Long Walker sprinted to a cluster of boulders. From the cover of the rocks he turned to look back. Racing toward him on a pony was a Cheyenne brave. Long Walker raised his rifle and shot the Indian from the back of the horse. Timing his moves carefully, he lunged from the rocks and grabbed the trailing hackamore rein as the pony sped by. The rein ripped skin from his palm, but the pony whirled about and stopped after two jerking lunges. Within moments Long Walker was aboard the horse, quirting the animal to top speed away from the ambush site.

Leaning low over the withers of the lathered horse, Long Walker knew his losses would be heavy. He cursed bitterly in English. Once again his authority, his medicine, would face a challenge from among the ranks of his warriors.

"How did they know?" he muttered, ducking beneath an overhanging limb while the horse plunged into the trees. "What spirits could have led them into Long Walker's thoughts?"

A quarter-mile behind the fleeing Long Walker, Chin-Lu swung aboard his rangy bay. Soon the Oriental had mapped in his mind the route the half-breed had taken. It would not be difficult to pick up the tracks. By the time Long Walker had made camp, Chin-Lu would be watching from the darkness once more.

Two days later Long Walker tried again, sending fifty of his wild Sioux Crazy Dogs against a forward grading crew from the railroad. And once more the soldiers seemed to spring from the earth itself, routing the Red Hands with heavy losses. Again the despised Henderson was among the first to ride into battle.

Watching the destruction of his elite fighting force from a safe distance, Long Walker used every epithet he knew in four languages. Pain from the gash in his thigh fed his raging fury.

The next few days were the most difficult Long Walker had ever faced. His leg healed slowly, but the greatest wound of all was the one that nearly broke his control over the disgusted braves—the possibility that among the glowering faces of his band might be one who was in league with the white man. Long Walker could think of no other reason that the hated Henderson seemed to know where and when the next strike would come. The renegade slept sparingly. He took no warrior into his confidence. He spent many hours staring into the campfire, hatred growing in his heart.

Finally he reached his decision. Ted Henderson would be taken alive, his spirit and medicine broken in the ordeal by fire. Long Walker's warriors would watch and laugh as the white man screamed in agony and begged for death. They would watch as, near the end of Henderson's ordeal, Long Walker carved the captive's still-beating heart from his body. From it he would squeeze a dipper of blood, so he could drink the power of his enemy.

Then and only then would Long Walker's hate be stilled. The half-breed limped from his lodge to a shallow cave a few hundred yards from camp. There he pulled a canvas-wrapped bundle from the snow he had piled in the rear of the cave during the winter. He had carried the head of the buckskin horse for many months, waiting for just such an occasion. The stench of decaying flesh was the bittersweet odor of challenge and victory to the blue-eyed Indian. Long Walker had come to know his adversary well, and he had an idea where Henderson might soon be found. Henderson was a man who loved the land. And a man who loved the land always returned to a treasured place. That was where Long Walker would use the severed head of his enemy's favorite horse to trap the white man.

An uneasy peace settled over the Union Pacific railhead as April faded toward May. David Wills was almost constantly in the saddle, leading patrols into the mountains or escorting railroad work crews. Wills drove himself and his men hard. Being constantly on the alert for danger dominated his waking hours. When he slept it was the deep sleep of exhaustion, rarely interrupted by dreams of an auburn-haired widow.

Ted more than matched the hours Wills put in, but to no avail. Long Walker's band was nowhere to be found.

Chin-Lu returned to rails' end. "I am sorry, Ted," he said. "I have lost them. Your student is not as good as the master at reading the sign of Indian passage. For many days I was almost part of their camp. Then one day many trails appeared where one had been, and the blue-eyed one vanished as a wisp of smoke in the forest leaves."

Ted placed a hand on his scout's shoulder. "Don't blame yourself, Chin-Lu," he said gently. "It's a big country out here. A man could ride within a couple of hundred yards of an Indian camp and never see anything suspicious. If I had a dollar for every time I've lost a trail, I would be a wealthy man."

He turned away and swung into his saddle. "Don't fret. Long Walker's still out there—and we'll find him. You've already done a major service to the Union Pacific and to the people of the West, both red and white. That renegade is hurting now because of your sneaking into his camps and eavesdropping on his plans. He's been hit hard a couple of times, thanks to you and the men of the Third. The word from Abel is that few new recruits are joining Long Walker. Their enthusiasm for the war lance has been a bit dulled lately."

Then Ted reined his horse toward Bridger's Pass, only a few miles distant. The grading crews were deep into the pass, laying roadbed that soon would carry the Union Pacific across the Continental Divide, down the west slope of the Rockies, and into the vast sweep of desert beyond.

He rode slowly along the rail bed, feeling himself drift toward melancholy as he moved deeper into Bridger's Pass. Familiar landmarks, trails he had ridden many times, were vanishing beneath the picks and shovels of Union Pacific laborers. Never again would Bridger's Pass hold its magic for him. The gateway to the West, where Jim Bridger, Kit Carson, and Ted once rode, was losing its majesty as the sloping roadbed gobbled up the famous passage. What had once been a test of man's determination to find freedom would soon be only a few minutes' ride in a comfortable chair pulled by a smoke-belching locomotive.

"Hellbender," Ted said quietly to his horse, "I think you and I were born about twenty years too late."

Yellow Crow probed the ashes of a cooking fire on the banks of the Sweetwater River. The ashes were cold, as he had expected, yet they told a story. Not long ago, many warriors had camped here for several days. At the edge of the campsite the Cheyenne discovered a discarded fragment of an arrow shaft. It bore the markings of the Sioux Crazy Dogs.

He tossed the shattered arrow aside. The trail that had so long eluded him took shape in his mind. The hated half-breed Long Walker had passed this way.

The Cheyenne stroked the neck of the trail-worn palomino as the gelding dropped its head to crop at the fresh green grass at the edge of the campsite. "Soon the search will end," Yellow Crow said softly. "Then peace will once more come to the heart of Yellow Crow, and your days beneath the saddle shall end forever."

Yellow Crow probed among his belongings until his fingers touched the small wooden box. He carried it to the clear waters of a stream fed by melting snow. He stroked the water, then touched the fine powders in the box. When he finally finished, the angular features of the peace chief were streaked with color.

The Cheyenne Yellow Crow was painted for war.

He squatted for a long time, letting the palomino graze, and tried to ease his way into the thoughts of the man he sought. Finally he stood. "Below South Pass, Yellow Horse," he said firmly. "It is there, in the Canyon of the Wolves, that Yellow Crow shall make his kill."

Ted Henderson shook his head doggedly. "Jack, you and David can fuss all you want. My mind is made up. I'm going to South Pass, and I'm going alone. If Long Walker's there, one man will have a better chance of finding him than a patrol. I know every foot of that country." Ted swung into the saddle of a spirited, new horse from the railroad's herd and rode from rails' end without looking back.

Jack Casement stood alongside David Wills and watched his chief scout ride away. "I don't like this one bit, Major," Casement said. "If Ted rides into hostiles and we don't know where they are . . ." The engineer's voice trailed away.

"Leave him be, General Jack," Wills said softly. "I think I know why he has this burr under his blanket. A man can love a special spot on this earth as much as he loves a woman. Besides," he said with a grin, "Chin-Lu will give Ted a couple hours' head start, then follow. Just in case."

The days still were short in the high country in early May, yet the mountains sparkled with wildflowers of many shades. On the higher peaks the snows still sparkled white against the bright blue of the sky.

Familiar landmarks from Ted's past appeared: the small meadow where livestock grazed and horses rested after the climb over the spine of the Rockies, the spot where an ambusher's rifle slug had ripped into Ted's back but had not stopped him from completing his famed Pony Express ride. And on the left was a grove of quaking aspens where he and Wilma had shared a carefree blanket nearly a decade before, acting like kids in their teens.

Beyond the pass would be the western slope. At the base of the range waited the Pony Express station where a strong, lonely woman named Vi had fed and housed the men and horses who carried the mail some eighteen hundred miles in ten days. Idly, Ted wondered if its walls might still be standing, or at least if the foundation stones would be in place.

It seemed to Ted that each rock, every tree, even the wandering game trails of South Pass, held powerful memories for him. Looking back, he realized that even the painful memories now were cherished.

Suddenly, as he rounded a sharp bend in the trail, he saw a stake in the center of the trail with a burlap-draped object on it. Flies buzzed about the covering.

Sliding his rifle from its scabbard, Ted cautiously approached the strange object. The horse between his knees snorted and sidled away nervously. Gently Ted edged the animal closer. Gingerly he leaned out and lifted the burlap—and almost vomited in horror and revulsion.

A severed neck was jammed onto the top of the stake. It was the partly decomposed head of the buckskin that had been Ted's favorite mount—the horse called Buck, which Long Walker had stolen! The decaying skin pulled away from the dead horse's teeth. The sight and odor of rotting flesh momentarily froze Ted's reflexes. He did not see the glint of sunlight on metal as a blue eye sighted down the barrel of a rifle and a finger smoothly eased the slack from the trigger.

Ted heard the solid *whock* of lead against flesh at the same instant his horse went down. He tried to kick free of the stirrups, but the fall was quick and hard. The earth tilted crazily and slammed into the side of his head. Then there was darkness.

Consciousness returned slowly and painfully. First Ted became aware of a pounding in his temples. For a moment he could not understand why he was unable to raise a hand to his aching head. Then he realized he was bound hand and foot. He had been tied securely to the back of an Indian pony.

Gingerly he tested the bonds. He knew instantly there could be no escape. The bindings were strong rawhide, pulled deeply into his flesh and twisted tight with a determined cruelty. Cautiously he raised his head—and almost screamed in anger and frustration. Leading the pony to which Ted was tied was Long Walker!

A half-dozen Indians rode beside him. One of the Sioux realized Ted had regained consciousness and lashed out with a quirt. The flick of the leather thong cut Ted's cheek. He forced himself to stare straight ahead, showing no response as the Indian quirted him once more. Others took up the game.

Bleeding from a dozen cuts, the captive struggled to retain consciousness. Ted was determined not to give them the satisfaction of seeing him try to avoid the beating. His patience and endurance finally paid off as the braves tired of tormenting the unresponsive prisoner. Instead they turned to verbal abuse, cursing and taunting him. Ted ignored the tirade.

He concentrated on determining where he was. Familiar landmarks began to surface as the group turned into the wide mouth of a canyon. It was the place known as the Canyon of the Wolves. Tucked away in an obscure corner of the mountain wilderness, it was visited by few white men and not many more Indians. Even before he saw the lodges or smelled the smoke, Ted knew he was in Long Walker's stronghold.

The hoots and taunts of scores of warriors swirled about him as he was led into the camp. Strong hands untied the rawhide strips that held him in place, then yanked him from the back of the pony. He was dragged roughly to an open space in the center of the camp where a sturdy pine tree had been stripped of its branches.

Once again Ted felt the bite of rawhide as his hands and feet were bound to the oversized stake. Another strip of the rough leather was passed across his forehead, squeezing his head painfully against the post.

Only then did the blue-eyed outlaw approach his captive. Ted stared defiantly at Long Walker's twisted, grinning features.

"Behold the great war chief of the long knives, brothers!" the Indian cried. "Without his guns and his soldiers he is but a squaw! Speak, white man. Beg for your life!"

"The white man will speak, but not to beg," Ted said in fluent Sioux, his voice strong, carrying clearly to all the Indians. "Once more Ted Henderson meets the half-breed who makes war on women and children. Long Walker desires to be a great chief, but his medicine is weak and his courage that of a rabbit."

Long Walker's eyes narrowed in fury. Ted pressed home his desperate gamble.

"Will the leader of the Red Hands prove his courage? Will Long Walker meet his enemy in single combat—the *mano-y-mano*—to the death? Or will he hide like a coward behind the braves he has used and deceived to his own gain?"

For a tense moment, the half-breed's hand gripped the knife at his belt. Then, slowly, Long Walker's fingers released the weapon. Ted's heart sank. He had lost his one chance to survive or at least to die quickly—and his last opportunity to kill the only Indian he truly had grown to hate.

"It will not work, Henderson," Long Walker said. "The white man will not trick Long Walker into giving him a quick and easy death! To kill the white in combat would be an easy thing. But Long Walker will not deprive his people of their just revenge! Before Ted Henderson dies, he will whimper like the rabbit in the jaws of the fox and plead for the bullet or the knife!"

Long Walker's lips lifted in a sneer as he savored the moment of his triumph. "Ted Henderson, hear now your fate! When the sun touches the canyon floor tomorrow, the trial by fire begins!"

Ted shuddered inwardly. The Sioux were masters of torture, of keeping a man alive and in agony for hours and even days. The trial by fire was the most horrible of deaths. Still, his gaze did not waver and his voice was calm.

"Then Ted Henderson shall speak no more," he said. "His spirit is at peace. No longer will his words be wasted on the ears of a liar and coward doomed to forever walk in the darkness of the Place Between Worlds."

The taunts and curses of Long Walker's braves continued throughout the long afternoon. Ted's thirst grew steadily until the desire for water became more painful than his wounds or bonds. Yet he remained expressionless and outwardly uninterested when one Ute held a dipper of water almost to his lips, then pulled it away and spilled the clear liquid at Ted's feet. The Ute laughed gleefully at his great joke, but his amusement faded rapidly under Ted's level stare. From time to time an Indian would approach and jab Ted with a stick or nick his skin with the point of a knife.

Each blow and cut seemed more agonizing than the one before. And Ted knew full well that the worst remained several hours ahead. *Lord,* he pleaded silently, *I've never asked much from You. Grant me one last wish. Give me the strength to die like a man. And if You see fit, send a sign of my love to Wilma and Bill.*

The physical pain inflicted on his body was small compared to the agony in Ted's mind as the hours dragged toward sundown. By force of will he held the faces of his wife and son in sharp focus, drawing strength from Wilma's gentle violet eyes and Bill's impish grin.

*   *   *

Chin-Lu was concerned when he found Ted's horse dead in the South Pass. His worst fears were confirmed as he watched the scene taking place before him in the canyon.

His first instinct was to wait until nightfall, slip through the Indian ranks, and free his friend. But the bulk of the Red Hands camp lay between him and Ted. There were too many Indians for even his abilities as shadow-walker and fighter. And if the rescue was successful, Long Walker's band might flee. The opportunity to wipe out the Red Hands threat once and for all would be lost.

The slender Chinese looked once more at the lone figure tied to the stake in the Indian camp. "Forgive me, Ted," he said softly, "but the lives of many weigh more heavily on the scales than a single life. Your death will not be in vain. I will bring soldiers to end for all time the outrages of the Red Hands."

His decision made, there was no time to waste. Quickly he committed the layout of the camp to memory, noting paths through which the canyon might best be entered by a large attacking force and through which horsemen might flee. Then he gathered the reins of his horse and led the animal for several hundred yards in silence before vaulting into the saddle.

Chin-Lu's heart was heavy as he touched heels to the rangy bay. He did not know how long his friend Ted had to live. Perhaps until dawn, perhaps not. Even if he lived, he would surely be put to the lance when the soldiers attacked. Yet Chin-Lu knew Ted would understand and approve. The Red Hands led by Long Walker must be wiped out, and the half-breed had carelessly established his camp in a spot vulnerable to attack.

Almost fifty miles to the southeast waited the fine soldiers Ted himself had once commanded—the elite fighters known as R Company. They must be brought to this place quickly, Chin-Lu knew, before Long Walker could break camp and move from the canyon to another spot. The Oriental settled in for a long, desperate race against time.

From a grove of pines on the north side of the Canyon of Wolves, Yellow Crow studied the Indian camp below. His guess had been accurate. The camp was that of his sworn enemy, Long Walker. But Yellow Crow found no satisfaction in the fact that the long chase had neared its end. There was a more pressing problem.

The war-painted Cheyenne had instantly recognized the figure tied to a stake in the center of the camp. Somehow, the half-breed had captured Yellow Crow's blood brother. The Cheyenne must find a way to rescue Ted.

Yellow Crow knew it would not be easy. The camp was heavily guarded, and there were almost two hundred braves milling about. The attempt must be made in silence, the lance and knife his only weapons. Long Walker's life would be spared, for the moment, in exchange for Ted's. The bonds of blood brother went deeper than the Cheyenne's seething hate. It would be a fair trade. Once Ted was free and safe, the hunt would resume. As Yellow Crow carefully surveyed the surrounding terrain, he thought there might be a way. . . .

He began his search. In an hour the route of approach and escape was fresh in his mind. He willed part of his strength toward the lean body tied to the stake below. "Be strong, my brother," Yellow Crow whispered. "When the stars are at their brightest in the hour before the dawn, I will come. Together we will live, or together we will die."

As the stars wheeled slowly overhead an almost overwhelming sense of loss engulfed Ted. It was not for himself. He had long lived with danger and the idea of his own death. The loss he felt was for his wife and son, and for that last visit that had never been. *Don't grieve for me, Wilma*, he pleaded across the miles. *Grieve only for yourself and our son and for what might have been. Then go on with your life.*

A faint sound cut through Ted's thoughts. At first he thought it was a random noise. Moments later, the sound came again. This time Ted realized it was a lethal sound—a choked, gurgling noise he had heard before—the death gasps of a man whose throat had been cut.

Suddenly, out of the corner of his eye, Ted detected a movement in the black shadows of the moonless night, a barely seen flutter in the faint starlight. The movement disappeared behind a lodge. Ted realized he had been holding his breath and let the air out very slowly.

Then he heard the soft shuffle of a moccasin on sand behind him. A familiar voice whispered, "Be still, my brother. Make no noise. The sentries are dead and the camp sleeps." Ted's head sagged forward involuntarily as the rawhide brow band was cut.

"Yellow Crow?" Ted whispered in disbelief.

"Yes, brother. Silence now. Nod if you are strong enough to slip quietly from this place of evil." Ted inclined his head twice. He felt the touch of cold steel against the inside of his wrists, and then his hands were free. His knees buckled and he almost went down before a strong arm slipped around his waist.

"Come now. We go," Yellow Crow whispered. Ted managed a few stiff steps with Yellow Crow's strength supporting him. Then the knowledge that he was free seemed to fuel his strength. His steps became lighter, and he felt a measure of power flow back into his body.

"Wait here," Yellow Crow suddenly muttered. The Cheyenne slipped silently to Long Walker's lodge nearby, a weathered war lance in his hand. Yellow Crow knelt and cut a small gash in the heavy buffalo hide of Long Walker's shield that stood beside the entrance of the lodge. The Cheyenne thrust the lance through the hole, burying the sharp steel tip deep into the soil. "The challenge is made. We go now—quickly," Yellow Crow said.

By the time they had passed the dead sentry at the northern edge of the camp, Ted was moving freely and matching Yellow Crow's long, silent stride. He realized the sensation was a false strength, the body's way of coping with sudden and unexpected events. Later the exhaustion and pain would return.

Deep in the covering aspens above the camp, the two men stopped to catch their breath. Ted grasped his blood brother's shoulder.

"Once again Yellow Crow has saved his brother's life," Ted said. "Wise-One-Above has led Yellow Crow to his brother's silent cry in the night."

Yellow Crow shrugged. "Ted would do the same for Yellow Crow. The blood of brothers runs thick. My horse is but a few yards from here. He is old and tired, but he will carry us to the place I have chosen."

Ted discovered how much he had overestimated his strength as he tried to rise. Yellow Crow reached down, wrapped a strong hand around Ted's arm, picked him up, and swung him into place behind the saddle. They rode in silence for almost a mile.

Abruptly, the Cheyenne pulled the horse to a stop at the edge of a clearing that Ted judged to be about fifty feet wide. Yellow Crow dismounted, handing Ted the reins.

"Go, my brother. Yellow Crow stay. Soon the blue-eyed one comes. He will know the lance that pierces his shield and cuts his war medicine. He will follow. Here we fight. Only one will leave."

Ted shook his head firmly. "I'm not going. I will stay to watch my blood brother kill his sworn enemy."

"And should Long Walker kill Yellow Crow?"

"Then," Ted said grimly, "I will kill Long Walker myself."

Long Walker woke from a deep sleep as the gray light of early dawn touched the patch of sky visible through the smoke vent in the top of his lodge. He stretched luxuriously, savoring thoughts of the events to come that day. Finally the scalp of Ted Henderson would hang from his belt.

A sudden, startled cry from outside brought Long Walker to his feet. He whipped aside the flap of the lodge and stood frozen for a second, uncomprehending. The pole stood alone in the center of camp. Henderson had escaped!

One of his lieutenants sprinted to his side. "The sentries are dead, their throats cut," the Indian said. "Someone came during the night, killed them, and released the captive. The tracks lead there," he said, pointing north.

Long Walker swore bitterly, his fists clenched in rage. Then he saw the Cheyenne war lance piercing his own shield, the tattered eagle feathers fluttering a challenge. Long Walker reached inside his lodge and scooped up his rifle. Before the furor over the captive's escape had fully awakened the camp, he was astride his swift war pony, quirting the horse along the trail left in the dirt of the canyon floor. Cold rage boiled in the half-breed's chest. This time, he silently vowed, the Cheyenne Yellow Crow had pushed his medicine too far. The challenge would be answered. There would then be time to recapture the former cavalry colonel. *This day will bring a double victory,* he vowed silently.

Long Walker's pony was more than a quarter of a mile away before the first few Red Hands had gathered weapons and mounted to prepare for the chase.

At the mouth of the canyon, Major David Wills sat his horse, flanked by Sergeant Major Albert Jonas on the one hand and Chin-Lu on the other. Chin-Lu held the bow and arrow quiver given him by Paints-His-Horses. Behind the three men a skirmish line of cavalry waited, their revolvers ready. The tension seemed to revive the cavalry horses, blowing and sweating after the long forced march at a pace that would have killed lesser animals.

Wills peered through his field glass.

"Something seems to have them stirred up. Chin-Lu, did you say Ted was staked out in the middle of the camp?"

"Yes. It was there that I saw him."

"Well, I can make out the pole, and there's nobody on it. Either they've already done Ted in, or he's gotten away somehow. By the way they're acting, I'd guess the latter. The Indians appear to be forming up a pursuit." Wills clapped the glass back into its leather carrying case and turned to Jonas.

"Sergeant, do we have one good charge left in these horses?"

Jonas's face was grim. "Sir, you've got more than one. Every man in this company's ready to kill a horse if need be to tear those bastards up. And if anything has happened to Colonel Henderson, I'd hate to be a red man this morning."

"Very well, Sergeant. Let's get this party started." Wills raised a hand and motioned R Company forward at a trot. He felt no mercy toward the outlaw Indians, and he knew R Company would show no quarter. There was not a man among them who did not respect Ted Henderson.

"At the canter," Wills called. "Use the red hands for targets! I'm not interested in prisoners from this bunch!"

On the edge of the Indian camp, an Arapaho suddenly stood, staring in astonishment toward the mouth of the canyon. A line of mounted men stretched across the canyon entrance. "Soldiers!" the Arapaho cried in warning.

The Indians had no time to organize. R Company's horses swept over the hastily formed rear guard. Then the soldiers were in the camp, firing handguns at point-blank range into the Red Hands. Two Indians went down with Cheyenne arrow shafts quivering in their breasts from Chin-Lu's bow.

The leaderless Red Hands had superior numbers, but the attack was so swift and so effective that the first pass of the soldiers through camp equalized the fighting forces. Some Indians broke and ran, only to be cut down by the deadly Dragoon pistols of the cavalry.

The soldiers wheeled their horses and charged back through the camp. The second charge was more devastating than the first. Within moments only small clusters of organized Indian resistance remained. Several troopers and Indians clashed in hand-to-hand combat. David Wills clubbed one Arapaho down with the butt of his handgun. A second Indian, lying on the ground, pointed his rifle at Wills but suddenly jerked and slumped back, an arrow protruding from his neck. Wills waved his thanks at Chin-Lu, then yanked his spare revolver from its saddle holster and charged into the fray once again.

Soon, only sporadic firing could be heard in the Canyon of the Wolves. The defeat of the Indians had been swift and brutally efficient. Almost fifty braves had died; another score injured and thirty had surrendered. The other survivors, many on foot, had scattered.

Major Wills stood in the center of the battlefield, surrounded on all sides by bodies of the Red Hands band, and glanced at the sweat-streaked face of Albert Jonas.

"Pursuit, Major?" Jonas asked.

"No, Sergeant," Wills replied. "Our horses are worn out, and I doubt we would catch enough Indians to make it worth our while. How many casualties did we have?"

Jonas's grin partially answered the question. "Sir, this bunch of bluecoats knows how to whip Indians without losin' their own hair. We got three boys shot, none serious. Touch of whiskey, a clean bandage, and a day or two off, they'll be ready to go again."

Wills arched an eyebrow. "You mean with all that shooting we only had three men hit?" He glanced at the sky. "It's unlikely that any deity takes sides in a war," he said, "but it looks like we had some help from somewhere today, for which I offer my sincere thanks." David removed his hat, wiped the perspiration from the sweatband, and slapped the dust free. "Any sign of Ted or Long Walker?"

"No, sir," Jonas answered.

"Ted's resourceful," Wills said hopefully. "If he's still alive, I think he'll show up sooner or later. At any rate, we've broken Long Walker's back, even if we don't have his scalp on a pole. It'll be a cold day in hell before any more Indians cast their lot with that half-breed."

Meanwhile, in a clearing about a mile away, Ted watched in tense silence as two warriors circled each other, each awaiting an opening. Neither Yellow Crow nor Long Walker had spoken. They had simply stripped to the waist, gripped a knife in one hand and a war ax in the other, and stepped forward. One—or both—would not leave the mountain clearing.

Yellow Crow's revolver was tucked in Ted's belt, loaded and ready. Ted silently vowed not to interfere. He owed his blood brother that much. But if Long Walker managed to kill the Cheyenne, Ted would blast the half-breed.

The two men continued to circle warily, the sound of distant, sporadic gunshots ignored. Sensing an opening, Long Walker lunged forward, feinted a blow with the war ax, and slashed with the knife in his left hand. Yellow Crow spun away, partially parrying the knife thrust. The tip of Long Walker's blade left a shallow cut along the Cheyenne's forearm. Yellow Crow lashed out with his tomahawk, catching Long Walker a glancing blow that opened a gash alongside the blue-eyed Indian's ear.

Yellow Crow suddenly dropped to his side, a foot sweeping into the back of Long Walker's heel. The Sioux staggered and fell, but almost instantly rolled to the side. Yellow Crow's war ax ripped into the pine-needle carpet where Long Walker's head had been. Both men bounced to their feet and stood, silently staring into each other's eyes.

Again it was Long Walker who struck first, his war ax descending in a blur toward Yellow Crow's head. The Cheyenne swept the blow aside with an arm and in the same motion whipped his knife across Long Walker's shoulder and chest. The renegade grunted in pain and surprise, blood from the deep cut flowing across his torso. Long Walker attacked furiously.

Ted saw in growing concern that the blood from Yellow Crow's cut arm was flowing down over his hand, making the handle of his tomahawk slippery.

Even as Ted realized the danger, a wild swing of Long Walker's ax cracked into the head of Yellow Crow's tomahawk, sending the weapon spinning. Yellow Crow danced backward, fending off the knife and dodging the rapid whirling of the Sioux's ax. Abruptly Long Walker changed tactics. He leapt backward and whipped his knife in an underhand throw. The weapon struck Yellow Crow in the side. The Cheyenne stumbled at the impact but quickly regained his balance. Long Walker, sensing a quick end to the battle, swept his tomahawk forward. The flat side of the weapon landed a glancing blow to Yellow Crow's head. The Cheyenne staggered backward and went down heavily, stunned. Still, his hand gripped the haft of his knife.

Long Walker charged, his war ax raised for the final

blow. Ted's heart leapt in dismay as the tomahawk arced toward his blood brother's head. But at the last instant, Yellow Crow twisted aside. The war ax nicked his shoulder as he grasped the Sioux's wrist. At the same time he rammed a knee upward, catching Long Walker in the belly. A powerful pull sent the renegade tumbling overhead. Long Walker struck the ground with such force that the tomahawk flew away from his numbed fingers.

Ted sensed the strength slipping from his blood brother as the two Indians grappled desperately. Long Walker closed a powerful hand across Yellow Crow's throat, his other hand locked on the Cheyenne's knife wrist. For several heartbeats it was power against power, Yellow Crow's smooth muscles straining against the strength in the broad shoulders of the Sioux.

Yellow Crow's breath began to come in ragged gasps as Long Walker tightened his choke hold with all the hate and desperation he could muster.

Suddenly, Yellow Crow twisted his knife hand sharply against Long Walker's grip on his wrist. The sudden reversal of pressure broke Long Walker's grasp. The Cheyenne's knife flashed and buried itself to the hilt in the renegade's side. Long Walker stiffened, his mouth open in a silent cry of shock. Then his hand slowly slid away from Yellow Crow's throat.

Yellow Crow struggled to his feet. Exhausted and covered in blood, he stumbled to the palomino gelding and pulled the Spencer .56 from its saddle scabbard. He opened the deerskin bag around his neck. Holding the single cartridge in his hand, he turned to face the disabled Sioux. For the first time, Yellow Crow spoke, panting.

"This medicine bullet—Yellow Crow has carried—many moons. It is from the long-ago fight in the canyon—when Long Walker stole the children. Now it stills two hearts. It rips the life from Long Walker and the hate from Yellow Crow."

Deliberately, Yellow Crow opened the action of the Spencer and removed the cartridge that had been chambered. He put the special bullet into its place and snapped the action closed.

Long Walker's blue eyes followed Yellow Crow's movements with no expression of fear. Instead, they sparkled with hate. The half-breed faced his death with the same rage with which his life had been lived.

Yellow Crow aimed with care and squeezed the trigger. The slug slammed through Long Walker's breast and shattered his heart. The renegade shuddered once, then lay still. As Yellow Crow lowered the weapon Ted started toward him, but something in the Cheyenne's eyes stopped him in his tracks.

For a moment the Cheyenne sagged against his palomino. Then, from somewhere deep inside, an awesome strength welled up. Yellow Crow slowly made his way to Long Walker's body and pulled his knife from the dead man's side.

Deliberately Yellow Crow wrapped his left hand in Long Walker's hair. There was a ripping sound, then an audible *pop*. At last Yellow Crow held the gory scalp of his sworn enemy in his blood-streaked hand.

After a few moments of silence the Cheyenne turned to face Ted.

"It is ended. Now Yellow Crow is free of the darkness that has so long stalked his spirit. Many moons have passed since Yellow Crow took a scalp. Now the blue-eyed one forever walks the darkness of the Place Between Worlds. The evil spirit of Long Walker can never return to the land of Wise-One-Above."

Ted nodded solemnly.

Yellow Crow tied the scalp to a thong on the skirt of his saddle. Seemingly oblivious to his wounds, the Cheyenne mounted his horse.

"Go now, my brother," Yellow Crow said as he gathered the reins. "Your soldiers wait in the canyon below. They will worry."

"And what of you, Yellow Crow?"

"I have been too long from my lodge. I return now." A hint of a smile creased his face, the war paint smeared by sweat. "The woman Talking Bird has her heart set on a son. Perhaps we shall make one."

Ted placed a hand on the neck of the aging palomino and studied Yellow Crow for a moment. "And the two brothers— one red, one white—will they meet again?" he asked.

"If it is the wish of Wise-One-Above, they will meet again." The Cheyenne worked the lever of the Spencer, and the empty hull of the cartridge that had taken Long Walker's life flipped from the chamber. Yellow Crow caught it deftly in midair. He solemnly handed the still-warm brass case to Ted.

"Let this cartridge, which can never again be fired, remain a symbol of our brotherhood," the Cheyenne said. "It is now useless for the taking of a life. When the peace between red man and white ends, only such silent weapons will be drawn if brother meets brother on the field of battle. The spirit of Yellow Crow rides with you in this hollow cylinder of brass. Go now, Ted Henderson. Teach my godson well."

The peace chief abruptly kneed his horse into motion. He did not look back as the palomino lifted into a ground-covering trot, headed for home.

Ted closed his fist over the spent cartridge. His eyes began to sting as he watched his blood brother ride away, perhaps for the last time. "I will carry it always, Yellow Crow," he said softly, "and I will remember."

Word of Long Walker's death and the defeat of the Red Hands swept the Rockies and the Great Plains, spread by Shoshone scouts serving with the Third Regiment. In camps throughout the region, Indian leaders who sought the path of peace breathed a sigh of relief. For the moment, at least, a crisis had passed.

A few days after the battle a solitary Cheyenne appeared at railhead. Deer Stalker, from the camp of the chief Paints-His-Horses, sought Chin-Lu.

"Paints-His-Horses summons the warrior Chin-Lu to his camp," Deer Stalker said. "Chin-Lu is to bring three ponies and the strange stones of green. Chin-Lu has twice counted coup, once on the enemies of Paints-His-Horses and now on the enemy of the Cheyenne council of peace chiefs. If he wishes, Chin-Lu will be welcomed into the Cheyenne tribe."

Chin-Lu nodded solemnly, his heart racing at his good fortune. "Chin-Lu is greatly honored. He will leave soon."

Ted was delighted at the news and sent Chin-Lu off with hearty congratulations and a message of respect for Paints-His-Horses. "You have done well," Ted told the Oriental. "Little Fern is all that a man needs in a companion, a friend, and a wife."

Chin-Lu inclined his head. "I go for now, Ted," he said, "but I will not forget my duties. Before many days have passed, I return. My job with the Union Pacific will be completed. This I owe to my friends and to myself, for a task once pledged must be finished."

"Take your time, Chin-Lu. With Long Walker crushed, the Indian threat is all but over. There shouldn't be any trouble that one scout can't handle for quite some time to come."

Word of R Company's destruction of the Indian Red Hands band was not universally welcomed. In a hotel room at the growing settlement of Ogallala, Nebraska, Bear Fallon crumpled the weekly newspaper in a big fist and angrily hurled it into a corner.

"By God," he muttered darkly, "Henderson better enjoy his days as a hero—'cause he and that bastard O'Reilly are livin' on borrowed time right now." Fallon tossed his few belongings back into a battered bag, paid his bill, and stalked toward the rail station. A westbound train would take him to Rawlins, where he would make his headquarters while scouting out the Union Pacific's progress.

And when the time and the place were right, Bear Fallon would strike.

On a mild spring day in 1868, the Union Pacific laid the final stretch of iron going up to the Continental Divide. The next section to be laid had an almost imperceptible downward slope. The Rocky Mountains had been crossed. Wild cheers and whoops rang out as the workers stood at the crest of the mountain range. Two bottles of ale were opened. One bottle, poured on the uphill side of the last fishplate, dribbled its contents to the east. Four inches away ale from the other bottle flowed along the rail to the west.

"By God, boys!" General Jack yelled. "We've whipped the mountains! It's all downhill from here! Now let's beat the Central Pacific plumb past Salt Lake!"

The crews flung themselves into their work with a renewed vigor. And watching them, Casement had an idea.

Back in the rail car that contained the telegraph office, Casement hastily wrote out a message: "To Charlie Crocker, Central Pacific. Rockies penetrated. We'll beat you to Salt Lake. What stakes on bet? Casement, Union Pacific."

In a few minutes the reply came: "Broke through Sierras. Locomotives, grade headed east. Have five hundred personal dollars ready when my coolies run by you. Central Pacific adds ten thousand bet our Irish iron men and coolies put down ten miles of track one day. We pick day and place. Crocker, Central Pacific."

"Challenge and wagers accepted," Casement wired back. "Be waiting for you west of Salt Lake."

Jack Casement grinned at the telegrapher as the key fell silent. "It looks as though you have just played a role in starting the biggest construction race in the history of the world," he said gleefully.

"Kevin O'Reilly, you've been back at rails' end for almost a week. In that time me and the boys have given you lots o' track. And I tell you this—if you'll cease this constant braggin' on this son o' yours, we'll give you even more track! Have heart, man! The ears can't stand any more of the proud father!" Shaughnessy grumbled.

Kevin squared his broad shoulders and grinned. "I can't help it if I have but the best son the world has ever seen"—he raised a hand in mock pleading for mercy as Shaughnessy balled a fist—"but I'll make you a deal. I'll not speak of my fine, strong young son on those days when you lay a mile of track a day. Fall behind, boys, and you lose the next day's bragging rights to me!"

Shaughnessy turned to the other workers near him and turned on a thick brogue. "Well, me paddies? Why is it that ye stand about so? Let us give this man his mile of track, that we might work in peace and quiet. Hit the rails, lads, and let's earn our ears a rest."

As the rails rushed down the western slope of the Rockies, Kevin found himself losing bragging days more and more frequently. Watching the rapid progress of the tracks despite the rough terrain, Jack Casement shook his head in amazement. He knew no amount of money or threats could have inspired the tremendous labor that Kevin's simple joking challenge had. And Kevin kept his word. When the rails gained a mile a day, no amount of coaxing could bring the grinning Irishman to boast of his young son. When the crews fell short, they were put through an unmerciful period of Kevin's bragging about the tremendous feats of strength and mental agility of his almost eighteen-month-old boy.

As the Union Pacific's rails moved steadily to the west, Ted recovered from his ordeal in the canyon and once again began riding far ahead of rails' end on scouting missions. One day while on a mission he looked up at the sound of hoofbeats to see Jack Casement riding toward him. The engineer's face was grim.

"Ted, I have some sad news," Casement said. "Josefa Carson has died, and your old friend Kit Carson is in deteriorating health. He seems to have lost his will to live after his wife's death."

Ted swallowed against a sudden tightness in his throat. "Josefa was a remarkable woman," he said softly. "Kit was totally devoted to her. He was ill before. Losing her may be the final straw for that fine old man."

Casement nodded. "You served with Kit a long time, Ted, and he has spoken highly of you. Things are moving smoothly here. Why don't you go and see him?"

"Thanks, Jack. I owe him that much," Ted said quietly. "I'll be leaving at first light."

The trip to Boggsville in southeastern Colorado, where Carson had built a new white house, was a long one. Ted thought he had steeled himself for the meeting, but he was shocked at the appearance of his old friend.

Kit Carson sat slumped in a rocking chair near a window, his gray hair falling tangled below his ears. The once-alert eyes were sunken and dull. The lines on his face seemed deeper. The weathered skin had paled. For an awkward moment Ted feared Carson would not remember him.

Then the aging frontiersman held out a thin hand. "Hello, Ted. I'd hoped one of my favorite officers might come by for a visit."

Ted took the once-strong hand, and the frail, tenuous grip sent a stab of pain through his heart. "Kit—I'm sorry to hear about Josefa. All of your friends at Fort Laramie send their condolences."

Carson lifted his gaze to Ted's face. "We were together almost twenty-five years," he said. "And I think we'll be together again soon."

The remark sent Ted's spirits to an even lower ebb. "What does the surgeon say?" he asked.

Carson waved a feeble hand. "Doctor doesn't know anything about a sickness of the spirit, Ted. I don't bother taking his medicine. I haven't known hunger in weeks. By God, I used to be a free man. Now I've got people hanging around fretting over me like some hen with a single chick." The frontiersman sighed heavily. "I'm an old man now. But I've had a good life, at least up until a few months ago." He waved a hand at a box on a table in the corner of the room. "Hand me that, will you?"

Ted got the box and handed it to Kit Carson. His fingers trembling with fatigue and illness, the older man opened the box and for a brief moment stared inside. Then he lifted out a small revolver.

"I won't be needing this any longer," Carson said. "I'd like for you to have it, Ted. It's the thirty-two rimfire Smith & Wesson I was carrying when those two outlaws jumped us in Laramie." For an instant, life flared in the bleary eyes of the ex-scout. "We had some good times together. Here," he said, holding out the weapon, "take it. As a favor to me. I'll know the gun is in good hands."

Ted carefully lifted the small revolver from the weathered hand. "Thanks, Kit," he said, his voice cracking slightly. "I'll see that it's well cared for."

"You always did take good care of your weapons and your men," Carson said. "And your enemies, too, one way or another." Suddenly a curtain of deep gloom settled on the legendary scout's shoulders. Nothing Ted said in the next two hours brought the old man from his shell. Finally, Carson waved a hand.

"Go, Ted. I know what you're trying to do, and I appreciate the effort. But even though you're one of my best friends, I'd like to spend these last days alone. At least as alone as I can get, what with the blasted doctor and his helpers puttering around all the time. Go back to your family and build your railroad. I've outlived my usefulness anyway. There are no more mountains to climb or rivers to ride."

Kit Carson held out his hand. Ted took it, realizing they both knew it would be their last handshake.

Outside, Ted carefully wrapped the .32 revolver in a piece of soft deerskin and stowed it in a saddlebag where rain and dust could not reach it. Without looking back he swung aboard his horse and nudged it into a slow trot toward railhead.

He had been back at rails' head only a few days when the word came over the telegraph. Kit Carson had died just before dawn on May 28, 1868, in his own bed. He was fifty-eight years old.

Late into the evening, Ted sat alone beneath a stately pine tree overlooking a canyon a hundred yards from the construction train.

"I feel I should go to him, say something," Jack Casement said to Kevin as they stood and stared at the lone figure. "It's so painful to lose a close friend."

"There's nothing you can say," Kevin replied. "Something more than just a friend or a fellow soldier passed from Ted's life when Kit died. Another bit of the frontier Ted loves so well has been eroded. Leave him be. Let him grieve in his own way. He'll find his peace in the canyon walls, not in the words of a man."

Bear Fallon rubbed his aching backside as he studied the lay of the land before him. The long ride from Rawlins had been grueling to a man unaccustomed to saddles and horseback riding. His head still ached from the homecoming at Pittsburgh Rose's the previous night. The combination of bad whiskey and a frenzied night in Rose's bed left him feeling used up and sluggish.

But he decided the ride had been worth it. He had found the perfect spot for his revenge. Rails' end was rapidly nearing the river known as Black's Fork in western Wyoming. Already grade had been laid and a trestle built over the riverbed. The east side of the trestle, where timbers touched the high bank of the roadbed, was the ideal place.

In his mind's eye, Fallon saw the scene unfold in sharp detail. The Irish bastard, O'Reilly, would lead his rail crew atop the roadbed onto the edge of the trestle. As they dropped the first iron rails onto the bridge, a string of powder charges would blow O'Reilly and his bunch straight into hell. If he were lucky, that damned Ted Henderson would be with the crew also. If not, Fallon knew the blast would bring the scout on the run—and straight into the sights of his rifle.

"Nobody bests Jack Fallon and lives to grin about it," he muttered through clenched teeth. "Within the week the buzzards will pick the bones of O'Reilly and Henderson. And I'll have the last laugh."

Ted was growing bored. With Long Walker dead and the Red Hands finished, a sort of quiet had settled over the Union Pacific railhead. In the absence of any Indian threat the soldiers of the Third were back in Fort Laramie. It seemed to Ted there was almost nothing for a scout to do.

It was restlessness that had driven him to saddle up and set out on a late-afternoon scout along Black's Fork.

All at once the boredom came to a swift end. Ted quickly checked his horse and swung from the saddle, studying a single set of footprints. A big man in work shoes had passed this way early in the day when the dew was still on the soil. Ted was sure no railroad workers would have wandered more than a hundred yards from the rail bed. But the tracks were no mirage.

He cautiously slipped his new rifle from the scabbard and tethered his horse in a nearby clump of cedars. Then he began a careful stalk along the route of the footprints. They led toward the heavy earth fill at the end of the trestle spanning the narrow river.

As he examined the fill, Ted's nerves suddenly went taut. A long, slender hump of sand snaked toward the base of the earth fill. Carefully he brushed the sand away, exposing a length of fuse. The fuse branched twice. Within moments, Ted had traced the fuses to bundles of stick-shaped objects buried beneath the rail bed. The main fuse led to a cluster of bushes below a large outcrop of boulders.

Ted recognized the bundles instantly. They were the new, powerful "patent blasting powder" that had been used with tragic results on both the Union Pacific and the Central Pacific. It appeared someone had prepared a little surprise for the Union Pacific. A big man wearing work shoes. Ted studied the surrounding terrain for a long time, but nothing moved.

Ted knew the next morning Kevin's track-laying crew would be working on the trestle directly above the explosives.

Working quickly, he unsheathed his knife and cut a two-foot section from each length of fuse. Then he carefully piled sand along the removed sections, shaping the sand into its original pattern. When he had finished and brushed away his tracks, he studied the area carefully and was satisfied. The fuse track looked perfectly natural. But when the burning fuse hit the gap it would go out. The only explosion would come when he jumped the culprit from the rocks overhead.

The next morning Ted was in position well before dawn. Kevin had been warned but also advised not to tell his crew. Nothing outwardly suspicious must spring the trap set for the trapper.

Ted's senses snapped to full alert as the first gray light trickled into the riverbed of Black's Fork. A big, blocky form appeared from the shadows upstream, working its way toward the brush clump and the exposed end of the main fuse. Ted recognized the man instantly. Bear Fallon! Ted fought back the urge to kill Fallon on the spot. He needed to catch the man in the act. Then he would have the proof he needed.

It seemed to Ted that an eternity passed as he crouched, his handgun ready, only six feet from the hulking figure. At last he heard the laughing and joking of workmen approaching along the rail bed. Then came the clang of spike mauls as the crew dropped a length of iron, then moved onto the east end of the trestle.

Kevin stood directly over the explosive canisters, calmly leading the crew in an Irish pub song. Ted held his breath. Below, Fallon touched a match to the main fuse. For one horrifying moment, Ted wondered if he might have missed a fuse in his search the day before. Then he banished the thought. He had been painstakingly thorough. The fuse caught and sputtered, fiery sparks rushing toward the earth bank and then burning beneath the light covering of sand.

Ted launched himself feet-first toward the man below. His bootheels slammed into Fallon's shoulder, knocking the big man down. Before Fallon could recover, Ted rapped him hard above the eyebrow with the butt of the heavy Dragoon. Stunned, Fallon tried to lift his hands to ward off the blows, but Ted grimly whipped the Dragoon back and forth, hammering Fallon's features again and again.

Then he felt strong hands beneath his arms, and he was rudely yanked from the prone, bleeding body of the big Irishman.

"Easy, friend," Kevin's voice said. "Don't kill him right away. Remember, we need some information."

Gradually, Ted regained control.

Kevin and Shaughnessy hauled the barely conscious Fallon to his feet. An angry crowd of rail workers surged around the battered man.

"Somebody get a rope!" a worker yelled when the group understood what Fallon had tried to do. "Hang him to the trestle!"

"Hold on!" Kevin yelled. "Not even this dog will be lynched. Shaughnessy, get these men to work uncovering those blasting sticks. And be careful—one of them could still go off. Ted and I will take care of this one."

Grudgingly, the workers began carrying out Kevin's orders.

Fallon regained consciousness a short time later to find himself bound hand and foot. Ted was idly whetting the edge of a skinning knife on his leather leggings.

"Go ahead, Henderson," Fallon croaked, "kill me."

Ted shook his head grimly. "No way, Fallon. You don't get off that lightly—not this time." The knife point flicked out. Fallon's belt parted, along with a thin layer of skin. Terror flashed through Fallon's eyes. "What—you—gonna do?"

Kevin grinned. He reached out a big hand, grabbed Fallon's pants, and yanked. The material gave way with a ripping sound. "Reckon as to how we're going to make a steer out of you, Fallon," Kevin said softly. "Poor ol' Rosie. I guess she'll have to get hers someplace else now."

"My God—you can't—" Fallon was near the breaking point. A threat of death meant nothing. But the thought of losing his manhood was more than he could bear.

"The hell we can't," Ted said, moving the knife point closer. "I've cut four-year-old stud horses. The only difference is that I didn't really enjoy gelding them."

"Stop—for God's sake—what do you want—money? I've got money—" Fallon's eyes were riveted to the knife point.

"There is *one* thing," Ted said. Hope flashed in the big man's eyes. "Tell us who you work for and why. We want names. The whole story, Fallon. From the beginning. Maybe then you can keep your private parts."

Ted realized that for what was probably the first time in Bear Fallon's whole life, the man truly was terrified. Haltingly at first, then more rapidly, the story tumbled out—how the Southern Overland operated, the names of several men involved with Garth Pfister, the stock grabs set up by sabotage and construction delays. Fallon even detailed the death of Sean Grady and the killing of "that newspaper fellow Taylor Elkins."

"You didn't get that job done either, Fallon," Ted interrupted. "You hit him all right, but he's far from dead. I got a wire from him just two days ago. Pfister hired you to kill him, eh?"

Fallon nodded numbly, then continued his story. Kevin scribbled rapidly in a small notebook as the man poured out everything he knew. "So what are you going to do with me now, Henderson?"

Ted slowly replaced the knife in its sheath. "You're

headed for the lockup at Fort Laramie. When the time is right, you'll be tried for murder, attempted murder, and anything else we can come up with. After that, it's back East for more trials. I think you'll be seeing the inside of prison walls for a long time."

Before noon, Bear Fallon had been placed under armed guard and sent on his way by rail handcar to the new city of Laramie. From there another guard would take over for the wagon ride into Fort Laramie and the post stockade. At the same time, Ted was writing a long telegram to Taylor Elkins.

In the telegraph room at the *Washington Globe*, Taylor read the final line of the message from Ted, then leaned back in his chair and smiled.

"Reply, sir?" the newspaper's telegrapher asked.

"Just 'Well done and thanks.' "

Taylor rubbed the deep bruise on his chest as he sorted the new information, adding it to what he already knew. All the links finally were in place. The network of financial intrigue made sense. And the names Fallon had supplied jibed with Taylor's own hunches and research. He reached for his coat and summoned his private coach. The White House would be eager to hear the latest developments.

Two days later, agents of the federal government quietly knocked on doors of plush homes and offices in New York, Boston, Washington, Omaha, Chicago, San Francisco, and New Orleans. The scandal was broken in banner headlines in both the *Washington Globe* and the *New York News*. The story would be picked up by every newspaper from frontier weeklies to the foreign press, Taylor knew. The Southern Overland was crushed, and the holding company broken.

Eleven

The wagon carrying Bear Fallon jounced over the rocks and ruts of the new road connecting the city of Laramie with its namesake fort to the north. Fallon, his wrists manacled around a sturdy stave of the wagon, muttered a curse at the driver. The driver merely spat a stream of snuff over the wheel. The wind whipped some of the spittle into Fallon's battered face.

At his side the driver carried a scarred Starr revolver nestled deep in a belt holster. Fallon's eyes kept drifting to the revolver. Getting just one guard had been a real stroke of luck. Now it was only a matter of picking the right place and time. Ever since he had been chained to the wagon stave, Fallon had been working on the wood. Now one sharp yank would tear it free.

The first scattered buildings on the southern outskirts of the community around Fort Laramie lay only a mile away when Bear Fallon acted. A quick, powerful jerk of his massive shoulders ripped the wooden stave from the wagon box. At the sound, the driver started to turn. He never made it. The chain dangling between Fallon's wrists whipped around the man's neck. Fallon gave a tremendous yank as the team bolted in sudden panic, and the driver died instantly, his neck broken.

Fallon scooped up the reins and brought the frightened team to a halt, then probed in the man's pockets until he found the key. Within seconds his hands were free. He stripped the driver's gunbelt, hefted the awkward Starr revolver, then casually put a foot against the dead man and shoved him from the wagon. The horses had run no more than a hundred yards during the swift, brutal attack.

Fallon's split and bruised lips twisted in a sneer as he set the team back into motion with a tap of the reins. "By damn, Bear Fallon's not done yet," he gloated aloud. "I'll get me a kit together in Laramie, steal me a horse—and the next time I see O'Reilly and Henderson it'll be over the sights of a rifle."

But first there was the matter of a hideout, a place where he could recover from the pistol-whipping for a couple of days and accumulate the supplies he needed. That should not be a problem, Fallon realized. In a run-down house at the edge of the Fort Laramie settlement were two of his old cronies from the early days with the Union Pacific. Ted had fired them for drinking on the job, and Fallon had been sending them some money from time to time. They should be happy to hide him for a spell—or at least afraid not to do what he wanted.

They would have food, a place to sleep, maybe some women, and whiskey. Fallon needed the whiskey worst of all.

A few hours later Bear Fallon wrapped a hairy fist around the nearly empty bottle and cursed bitterly. Killing the guard had merely whetted his appetite for violence.

Cheap whiskey added its sting to the cuts around his mouth as he lifted the bottle and drained its contents. Fallon's head still pounded from the pistol-whipping Ted had given him, and the pain was a constant source of fuel for the hate that twisted in his belly like an angry rattlesnake. He thumped the empty bottle onto the tabletop.

"Dammit, Quint! Ain't you got any decent whiskey in this house?"

Quint, a broad-shouldered, unshaven man, heard the menace behind the slurred words. Quint knew Fallon was only a word or a look from breaking a few bones, and Quint wanted no part of that explosion when it came. He shook his head. "Sorry, Bear," he said. "That there bottle's the last of the bunch."

Fallon hurled the bottle into a wall. Shards of broken glass tinkled to the floor. Quint sat quietly as Fallon heaved himself to his feet. The big man had finished off two bottles during the past three hours, and with each drink his mood had darkened.

"Gonna go get some more," Fallon said, weaving slightly as he made his way to the door of the shack. "Good stuff this time."

Fallon blinked in the afternoon sun, a swollen eye watering slightly at the sudden change from the dim interior to the brightness of the day. He swiped angrily at the watery eye, then winced at the stab of pain from a deep bruise. The fury boiling in him peaked as a dog darted from a nearby shack, yapping furiously at Fallon's heel. Fallon spun and lashed out a heavy shoe with all his power. The shoe slammed into the cur's head. The dog fell lifeless into the dust, its skull crushed.

Fallon kicked the dog's lifeless body from the street and stood glowering toward the main business section of the Fort Laramie community. His hand drifted to the butt of the Starr revolver thrust into his waistband. One day soon, he vowed silently, he would crush Henderson and O'Reilly—stomp them into the dirt like the cur dog.

"Might's well start right now," he grumbled to himself. "Get a jug, rifle, powder and lead, steal a horse. Hell, they can't be lucky forever."

Lieutenant Colonel Abel Hubbard closed the ledger on his desk and glanced at the clock on the office wall. The afternoon was fading rapidly, and he still had to make his rounds before joining Judy for dinner. Abel rose and crossed to the rack that held his gun belt. He strapped it about his waist and called to the corporal of the guard.

"Keep an eye on the place, will you, Myers?" Abel said. "I've got to go see if I can keep Fort Laramie's streets safe for women and children."

"Will do, sir," the corporal replied. "Wonder why the town doesn't get itself a proper sheriff?"

Abel smiled wryly. "Why spend good money for law enforcement when the government pays the army to do it? Anyway, it's been quiet enough lately. We've only had two killings this week." He reached for the doorknob. "I'll send some relief for you after supper."

Abel strode rapidly through the compound, letting his long stride exercise the stiffness from his body. Sitting in a chair was a lot more tiring than riding a cavalry horse.

He paused for a moment outside the Fort Laramie gates and surveyed the main street of the settlement. All seemed relatively quiet. Farmers and ranchers went about their business as usual, while the drunks and drifters slept off their hobbies in the sun or in alleys. There was little traffic in the saloon areas. The early drinkers were inside and the serious elbow bending would not start until sundown.

Abel sighed. Sometimes being a stand-in sheriff was not so bad. But it was not a job he wanted full-time. It would be a toss-up whether the boredom or a bullet would do him in first.

A hundred yards down the street he saw Major David Wills leaning against the doorway of the Laramie Hotel, talking earnestly with Victoria Coulter. Abel smiled. David, fresh from the successful campaign against the Red Hands of Long Walker, was now launching his drive toward his major objective. Abel silently wished the young man luck as he strode toward the pair.

Thirty yards from the two, Abel waved and was about to call out a greeting when out of the corner of his eye a movement caught his attention. Weaving down an alley toward the main street was a man who obviously had been drinking. Despite the distance between them, Abel immediately sensed something evil about the intruder. The man was huge, his features battered and bruised as though he had been involved in a recent brawl. More menacing, however, was the exposed butt of a pistol shoved into his waistband. A gun in the hands of a drunk was a dangerous matter.

Abel changed his direction to intercept the burly man. The small detour would take only a moment, and Abel would feel better knowing the drunk had been disarmed.

At her counter near the doorway of the Laramie Hotel, Judy Hubbard did not have to eavesdrop to catch the conversation between David Wills and Victoria Coulter. Judy shook her head as Victoria's words reached her.

"Thank you, David," the young widow said, "but I'll not be attending the Saturday dance."

"Victoria," Wills replied calmly, "you can turn me down this time, and I'll just keep coming back. You're going to have plenty of practice at saying no, and one day I'll catch you at an off moment and you'll say yes. My mind is made up, Victoria. You're going to have to physically run me off now that—"

Victoria's eyes widened as she looked over David's shoulder. She lifted a hand to her cheek in alarm. "David, there's a big man out there with a gun—and Abel's walking right up to him!"

David turned, his hand drifting toward the flap of the military holster at his belt. He instantly recognized the man from Ted Henderson's detailed description. It was Bear Fallon—drunk and armed!

"Hold it, mister," Abel said, stopping a few feet from the big man. "No guns are allowed in this part of town. Hand it over, then go off someplace to sober up."

Bear Fallon stood swaying slightly in the street, glaring at Abel for a brief second. Then he placed his hand on the pistol butt and slowly withdrew the weapon as though to surrender it. Suddenly, Fallon whipped the revolver up and fired point-blank into Abel. The cavalry officer spun and fell into the street.

At the sound of the shot, David Wills hurled himself in front of Victoria, pressing her body against the wall of the hotel with his own as he shot at Fallon. A slug hammered into the door frame as Fallon fired back—again and again, bellowing in rage. Victoria felt David's body jerk against her own.

Stunned and shocked at the sudden violence, Victoria could only stare wide-eyed at the downed figure of Abel Hubbard in the street. A shot from the pistol shattered a window somewhere on the street—and then a shotgun boomed twice in rapid succession from the doorway of the hotel almost at Victoria's elbow.

Bear Fallon stumbled backward, the pistol spinning from his hand. He fell heavily onto his back. From the corner of her eye Victoria saw Judy drop the shotgun and dash to the side of her husband, her face white with fear.

Judy cradled Abel's head in her lap and looked at him. Blood soaked his shirt and pants. "Get the surgeon!" she called, almost calmly. "Abel's been hit!"

At the hotel door, David Wills moved away from Victoria. "Are—are you all right—Victoria?"

David's voice sounded strange, she thought. She nodded silently, her eyes riveted on the man in the street, fear and shock freezing her against the hotel wall. Then David turned away, stumbled once, caught his balance, and walked haltingly toward his commanding officer.

Only then did Victoria notice the dark stain spreading across David's left shoulder. She realized with a start the young major had been hit, that he had shielded her body with his own, and the slug would have struck her but for David's action.

The street erupted in bedlam as the echoes of the shots died away. The post surgeon shoved his way through the growing throng around the two army officers and the woman in the street. He glanced at Abel's side and began barking orders. Then he ripped away part of David Wills's tunic and stared for an instant at the blood-soaked shoulder. Dr. Mason looked up as Sergeant Major Albert Jonas hurled a man aside and stood looking down at the wounded officers.

"Get a litter detail on the double, Sergeant," the surgeon said, "and give me a hand with Major Wills. We've got to get these men to the hospital immediately."

"Who did this?" Jonas said as he slipped an arm around Wills's waist and helped the officer to his feet.

"Big man—name of Fallon," Wills gasped, his voice weak from shock. "Judy Hubbard—shotgunned him—across the street—"

Only a smear of blood and a fallen revolver marked the spot where Judy's shotgun blasts had downed Fallon. Somehow, incredibly, the big man had crawled from the street, into an alley, and staggered away. The search for the attacker was in full swing when a dozen strong hands gently lifted the unconscious Abel Hubbard onto a litter.

Judy Hubbard sat on a bench near the door to the operating room for what seemed like hours as she awaited word from the surgeon. Her fingers, which tightly grasped Albert Jonas's hand, were cold and clammy. Both rose as the door finally swung open.

Wiping his hands on a clean towel, the surgeon pulled no punches.

"Judy, your husband suffered a nasty wound to the side. I don't have to tell you how difficult it is to treat abdominal wounds. We won't know just how serious it really is until I can get in there with a knife and check it out. Young Major Wills isn't hit too badly. I've turned his case over to my assistant.

"I'm sorry I can't spend more time with you right now, Judy—but it's going to get busy in there." The surgeon turned to Albert Jonas. "Sergeant," he said, "I'm going to need some fancy stitchwork done if I'm to save Colonel Hubbard. Get Sally over here. Sewing delicate human tissue is no more difficult than stitching fine cloth. Ask her for me. If she won't come, beg!" Then Dr. Mason rushed back into the operating room.

Within minutes Sally Jonas stood at the physician's side. "I don't know medicine, Doc," she said. "I'm not even sure I can help. But Abel's a good man, a friend of mine. You just point me in the right direction and tell me what needs to be sewed. If I stitch somethin' wrong, yell at me."

Dr. Mason smiled at the young woman. "Thanks for coming, Sally. I need your talents badly."

A series of instruments were laid out on metal trays alongside the operating table. As he snipped away with shears at the ragged edges of the wound, the doctor briefed Sally on which instruments would be used. Then he nodded toward two shallow pans nearby.

"Wash your hands in the one on the left," the doctor said, "and dip the needles, thread, and surgical instruments in the other. It's something I read about just a few days ago. Mixture of one part carbolic acid, four parts almost pure distilled alcohol, and five parts water. With that and a lot of luck, maybe we can keep blood poisoning from setting in."

Beads of perspiration formed on Dr. Mason's brow as he completed the preliminary cleaning of the wound. Sally dabbed at his forehead with a clean cloth. "Okay, Sally, hand me that knife, and let's see how much trouble this man is in," the surgeon said.

On the hard bench outside the surgery, Judy Hubbard interrupted her silent prayer as Victoria Coulter entered the room. The auburn-haired woman's face was pale and her fingers trembled as she walked unsteadily to Judy.

"How—how is Abel?"

"We won't know for a while, Victoria," Judy said, surprised that her voice sounded as calm as it did. "It doesn't look good. But Dr. Mason is an excellent surgeon. David Wills is on the operating table, too," she said pointedly. "The doctor says the slug hit his shoulder blade at an angle and deflected. A lot of muscle was torn and he's in severe pain, but he should make it."

For a moment Victoria merely stared, as though she did not comprehend the statement. Then she nodded, trembling fingers stroking her throat as though searching for a necklace that was not there. Tears welled in the corners of her deep green eyes, and Judy wondered if the woman was on the verge of an emotional collapse.

Judy took Victoria's elbow and eased her onto the bench, then sat beside her.

"Judy, I—I've been—such a damn fool," Victoria said after a long silence. "I've—a confession to make. I—I love your husband. Or at least I thought I did. Ever since he saved my life—at Fort Kearny—"

Judy placed a reassuring hand on Victoria's arm. "I know," she said. "I've known it ever since you arrived at Fort Laramie."

"You—you knew? And you never said anything?"

"There was no need," Judy said. "I know Abel and trust him. I feel no resentment that you fell in love with him. How could I fault you for loving someone like Abel?" Judy sighed. "Victoria, I never felt you were a threat to my marriage. The bonds between Abel and me are so strong I don't think they can be broken by anything—anything except death."

Victoria buried her face in her hands. Her shoulders shook as the tears flowed freely. Judy put a comforting arm around the woman's shoulders and waited patiently until the sobbing subsided.

"Judy, I realized something this afternoon," Victoria said. "David Wills threw himself into the path of a bullet headed straight for me—after the way I've treated him, ignored him. My—my feeling, my infatuation, with Abel has blinded me to everything else."

"Now you're getting smart," Judy said. "David would lay his life on the line for you anytime. He loves you deeply. If it takes a senseless tragedy like this to make you realize it, perhaps it's worth it."

"Is it—too late, Judy? Will you and David ever forgive me?" the young widow asked anxiously.

"For my part, Victoria, there's nothing to forgive. And I feel sure David has room for no one else in his heart," Judy said reassuringly.

The minutes dragged on as each woman sat wrapped in her own thoughts. Without speaking, Victoria suddenly rose and walked from the hospital. She returned a short time later, wearing the necklace David had given her for Christmas.

It was after midnight when Dr. Mason emerged from the operating room. Instantly Judy was on her feet, afraid to ask the question.

Dr. Mason smiled. "He's going to make it, Judy. With Sally's help we were able to tie off the damaged blood vessels and clean out the wreckage. He'll be laid up for some time, but you'll have your man back before you know it."

Judy sagged into the doctor's arms, letting the tears flow for the first time.

By noon the next day both injured officers were awake, if somewhat groggy from the effects of morphine. Abel looked long and deep into his wife's eyes. "Now I know where angels are. But Fort Laramie's a damn strange place to find one," he said weakly.

Across the small room, Victoria Coulter sat at David Wills's bedside. The major was wrapped in bandages from the waist up, his left arm strapped firmly to his side. A heavy cloth padding covered the torn muscles and new stitches ran along his shoulder blade and back.

"Now I know I'm not going to that Saturday dance," Victoria said, her husky voice touched with deep emotion. "And the next time I put on dancing shoes, there's only going to be one name on my card—David Wills."

With his free hand David tightly squeezed Victoria's fingers. "Do you mean that?" he asked.

The young widow nodded, tears in her eyes.

"God," Wills muttered, "if I'd known it would work this way I'd have shot myself." His eyes closed, and the young man drifted into a peaceful doze.

Watching David sleep, Victoria realized for the first time that he was an unusually handsome man. And for the first time she also discovered that she could never again look upon him as a younger brother. The stirrings in her breast were anything but maternal or sisterly.

At midnight Albert and Sally Jonas relieved Judy at Abel's bedside. "You need rest too, Judy," the sergeant major said firmly. "I'll watch him."

"Any sign of the man who shot him?" Judy asked.

"No, blast the luck. We combed this place high, low, and sideways and come up empty," Jonas grumbled. "But anyways, I reckon you nailed him pretty good with that scattergun. If he ain't dead, he's in bad enough shape not to cause no trouble."

Dr. Mason interrupted the conversation to check on his patient and clucked his tongue in satisfaction. "Prettiest piece of work I ever saw, if I did do it mostly myself," he said. "Sergeant, your wife is the best natural-born surgical nurse I've ever seen. She's not squeamish, and she has quite a touch with a needle."

The surgeon winked at Albert. "I'll warn you up front, Sergeant. I'm trying to take your woman away. I can't let that much talent in the operating room go to waste."

Jonas smiled with genuine pride, hugging his tired wife firmly against his side. "Doc, I ain't gonna tell this gal what to do. Just be wastin' my breath if I did, anyhow."

The sergeant major gently kissed Sally's cheek, then released her. "You go get yourself some rest now, woman," he said tenderly. "With the colonel and the major laid up and the other officer out on patrol, it looks like your old man's gonna be the commander of Fort Laramie for a spell. I always wondered what it'd be like to have sergeants jump when I hollered. And there's a few little announcements I'm gonna make right off."

By midmorning notices had been nailed to any flat surface available throughout the Fort Laramie community. The lettering was crude but left no room for doubt.

> WARNING!
> ALL DRIFTERS, THIEVES, ROBBERS,
> AND CARD CHEATS ARE HEREBY
> INVITED TO LEAVE THIS PLACE
> IN ONE HELLUVA HURRY. THEM
> WHO STAYS DEALS WITH R COMPANY.
> ALBERT JONAS, SGT.
> ACTING COMMANDER
> FORT LARAMIE

Judy Hubbard had to grin as she made her way back toward the hotel after spending most of the day at Abel's bedside. "This may be the first time I've ever seen so much dust on the trails leading *out* of Fort Laramie," she muttered to herself.

True to his word, Albert Jonas led R Company in a sweep through Fort Laramie, the surrounding shacks, and even the grounds of homes owned by leading merchants and citizens. A few hours later the post stockade bulged with the unsavory characters who thought the notice was a bluff—or couldn't read.

But one man had escaped the dragnet.

Bear Fallon, his teeth clenched in agony, dragged himself from the hayrick of the post livery stable and staggered into the night. Fallon knew he had been hit hard by the shotgun blast. The pain in his left arm and shoulder removed any doubt about that. But there was one safe place where he could hole up and heal for a while, a lonely dugout on the banks of the Laramie River only a mile from the fort. He had friends there, people who owed him.

Gasping from the searing pain, Fallon staggered down the faint trail toward the hideout. "By God," he muttered bitterly, "I ain't gonna die. This country ain't seen the last of Jack Fallon. And one day, I'll pop the heads plumb off Ted Henderson and Kevin O'Reilly. By all the saints I swear it!"

By the end of the week, a number of individual decisions had been made in Fort Laramie.

Victoria Coulter, her spirits rising by the day as David Wills recovered, used her remaining money to buy Sally Jonas's share of the Laramie Hotel.

"Judy, I've decided there may be things in life more important than operas and fine wine," Victoria said. "This country is raw and violent, but it has something I'm going to need—a certain major in the United States Army's Third Cavalry. I've always been served, never a server, but I think I can learn."

Sally Jonas had no qualms about selling. The price was fair, but that was almost an afterthought.

"Judy, this plantation gal's finally found her true callin', I reckon," Sally said, beaming. "Doc Mason needs a good hand in surgery. I've got a talent give me by the good Lawd, and it's no use wastin' it. Maybe I can help some of these sojer boys live."

Abel's condition improved daily, and within another week the crisis had passed. There were no signs of blood poisoning or sepsis. The surgeon's carbolic acid and alcohol mix, coupled with Sally Jonas's deft stitching, had conquered the terrors that normally proved fatal in abdominal wounds. Dr. Mason's report of the techniques used was published in a medical journal and created an excited stir in the hospitals and physicians' offices around the country.

And finally, a lieutenant returned from patrol to assume temporary command of the Third Cavalry—much to Albert Jonas's relief.

"Reckon I ain't officer material," Jonas admitted. "Spent more time fillin' out reports than gettin' things done." But he proudly accepted the commendation recommended by the recuperating Abel.

Judy was more than satisfied as she watched one-time socialite Victoria Coulter efficiently wait tables and sweat over a hot laundry tub. Her new partner was learning rapidly. And physical labor seemed to bring a new and appealing blush to Victoria's cheeks. Of course, Judy admitted, young Major Wills might have something to do with that also.

As 1868 drew to a close, the Union Pacific steadily moved west. Despite the peace that had come with the destruction of Long Walker's Red Hands, there was still plenty to keep Ted busy. As work gangs battled the worst snows of winter, Ted spent most of his time in the saddle, scouting for fresh water and dry-grass graze for the Casement animal herds.

The friendly rivalry between the Central Pacific and the Union Pacific threatened to turn vicious as the two railroads grew closer together. No meeting point between the two lines had been agreed upon, and neither company would give in to the other's wishes. Finally it took President Grant himself to force the railroads into a rather reluctant cooperation. They were ordered to meet at Promontory Point, Utah.

With the settlement of the junction question, both the Central Pacific and Union Pacific stepped up the rail-laying pace in the heated competition to be the first line at the Promontory connection.

Telegraph messages bounced back and forth between the Central's Charlie Crocker and the Union Pacific's General Jack Casement. When Crocker reported a mile of track laid one day, Casement's crews attacked the high desert with a vengeance to put down even more track the following day. The competition between railroads shifted from violent confrontation to a healthy sprint.

On April 26, 1869, the Central Pacific railhead had pushed to within fourteen miles of Promontory—and Charlie Crocker issued his famous "ten miles in a day" command. Reading Crocker's telegram that the feat would occur on the following day, Jack Casement merely shook his head.

"Can't be done," Casement grumbled to Kevin O'Reilly.

"Most of the grade is winding and uphill. Still," he added tugging at an ear, "I'd not underrate old Charlie's determination, and Jim Strobridge is as good as any foreman I've seen work. We'll just sort of wander over and see if Crocker and his gang can pull it off. Think I'll place a few bets that they can't."

More than just a handful of curious people were on hand at first light on April 27 at rails' end of the Central Pacific. "There must be over a thousand people here," Casement muttered as the sun started to peek over the eastern horizon.

Charlie Crocker's massive bulk suddenly loomed at Casement's side. "Ready to pay off, General Jack?" the Central Pacific engineer asked with a grin. The rail gang, called "Crocker's Pets," stood alongside the rail truck and waited calmly for the signal to begin.

Jack Casement's eyes narrowed as he gazed along the railbed. "What's this?" he demanded. "The ties are already down!"

Crocker laughed heartily. "Remember the bet, Jack? I was to lay track. That's all—just lay track. Nobody said we couldn't bed the ties early."

Casement snorted. "Well, maybe it's a touch on the shady side of the cottonwood tree, Charlie, but the bet still stands. *Nobody's* crew lays ten miles of track a day!"

Crocker's Pets did.

Eleven hours later, the last spike was driven for the day. Workers slumped in exhausted pride alongside the tracks. For one herculean day's work they were to receive four days pay—and, Casement said repeatedly as he moved among the rival railroad gang, they had earned it.

If he had not seen it himself, Casement knew he would not have believed it. The day's count totaled 3,520 rails spiked down, each thirty feet long and weighing 560 pounds. The eight Irish rail lifters in the crew had handled 11.2 short tons of iron per man per hour—with no mechanical help! Just over ten miles of Central Pacific rails had been laid in one day.

Casement offered his congratulations to Crocker and Strobridge and went in search of his own foreman. He found Kevin O'Reilly casually counting out a hefty sheaf of bills. Kevin finished counting and tucked the currency into his pocket.

"Come into an inheritance?" Casement asked.

Kevin grinned broadly. "Sort of. I talked to Chin-Lu about these coolies, and I know what a stubborn Irishman can do when he wants, so I bet on Crocker's boys. Loyalty to the Union Pacific is one thing, but cash money for the taking's quite another."

On the way back to the Union Pacific railhead, Casement was more reserved than usual. Finally, Kevin asked what was bothering the engineer.

"With that sprint today," Casement said, "the Central Pacific is less than four miles from Promontory. We're six miles away over tough ground. It's going to be embarrassing if they are standing there waiting for us to bed the last chunk of track."

"There's a way to get around that," Kevin said with a grin. "Let's start laying track *east* from Promontory."

A grin spread slowly over Jack Casement's features. "An astute suggestion, my Irish friend," he said. "Maybe they'll beat us in terms of finished trackage, but in the history books we'll be at Promontory first! Think your boys can cover the rest of the ground in a week or so?"

Kevin yawned lustily. "Just keep us supplied with rails, General, and we'll get you there on time," he said.

It seemed to Ted Henderson that dignitaries, railroad officials, and representatives of the government began arriving at Promontory even before the rails were laid down. From East Coast and West Coast they came. News reporters. Politicians. The social set determined to see history made on the bleak and chilly Utah range. The town officials of Promontory made the most of their time in the sun. Promontory sprouted such colors and flags as were available in a settlement made up mostly of tents.

The growing population began to grate on Ted's nerves. It seemed that no matter where he turned, someone was asking him some silly question about Indians or railroads or the nearest "comfort facility."

Ted was within only a few hours of saddling a horse and heading home—when home suddenly came to him on May 10, 1869.

A Union Pacific engine pulling three special cars softly chuffed its way onto the siding at Promontory. Idly, Ted watched the brakeman place the portable steps before the door and wondered why Jack Casement had asked him to meet this particular train.

He soon had his answer. Standing in the doorway was a full-figured beauty with violet eyes and a tousle-haired youth at her side. A surge of warmth chased the lingering chill from Ted's bones as he jumped a puddle of water and skidded his way over the mud to the rail car.

Ted embraced Wilma for a long, silent moment. Then he pushed himself back and offered a hand to his son. In the many months since he had last seen Bill, the boy seemed to have grown enormously. There was a quiet confidence in his son's eyes that had not been there before.

"Come in, Dad," Bill said. "There's lots of our friends here with us."

Ted grinned as he glanced about the plush interior of the car, calling greetings. Judy Hubbard, a blond vision in a rich blue dress, greeted Ted with a hug and a light kiss on the cheek. Abel stood, favoring his wounded side, and offered his hand. Ted took it, surprised that Abel was still feeling some effects from the fight with Bear Fallon.

Wind Flower and her active son, Patrick, were also on board, eagerly awaiting Kevin's arrival. Major David Wills tossed a cheery greeting to Ted from his seat at Victoria Coulter's side. The auburn-haired widow smiled rather protectively at the young officer even though he had completely recovered from the shooting.

"Looks like all of Fort Laramie is on board," Ted said with a contented smile. "Who's minding the store?"

Wills chuckled. "It's in good hands," he said. "Sergeant Major Albert Jonas is training a lieutenant while we're gone."

"How are you, Abel?" Ted asked his friend.

"Coming along. It's just that sometimes if I turn in a certain direction or try to reach very far I get a twinge in my side," Abel replied. "Dr. Mason says most of it should go away eventually. But then I'm lucky to be alive at all, so I don't mind it when a bit of pain reminds me I'm still kicking."

"If Abel is still bothered all this time after the shooting, can you imagine what Bear Fallon feels like?" Judy asked.

"That man beats all," Ted grumbled, shaking his head with grudging admiration. "He's absorbed more physical punishment than I would have thought any human being could take and still live. Did any trace of his whereabouts ever surface?"

Major Wills frowned. "None. Absolutely none. Henderson's Scouts combed not only Laramie but the whole territory for miles. Everyone in the Third Cavalry questioned all the residents and anyone who passed through for months. But Fallon just disappeared."

"He must be dead," Victoria insisted. "No one could survive a shotgun wound like that without medical attention, and he didn't see a doctor in Laramie. He must have died and been buried by an accomplice who then disappeared."

"I don't know," Ted said. "I have a funny feeling that Fallon is still alive. At least I'm not going to rest easy as far as he's concerned until I see that man lying cold in his coffin."

Ted now turned to Little Fern, who was sitting next to Wind Flower.

Little Fern, her eyes wide with wonder at her strange ride in the belly of the iron horse, exchanged a quiet, respectful greeting with Ted in Cheyenne. Ted had forgotten how beautiful she truly was. He would make it a point to congratulate Chin-Lu, who had recently ridden out to Promontory ahead of his bride, in order to offer his help in the last stages of railroad construction.

"How was Little Fern's trip?" Ted asked.

The young woman shook her head in amazement. "It goes fast, but it is most noisy. Little Fern does not think she likes this thing called a train. It is better to walk or ride horseback, where one can smell the flowers and sage and feel the wind in one's face." She glanced around anxiously. "Will the iron horse let Little Fern go from its belly? She would see her husband."

Helping the young woman down the steps, Ted felt a strong admiration for Little Fern's courage. She had entered the belly of the iron horse despite her fears, because it would bring her to her husband's side more quickly. Within moments he had located Chin-Lu, who greeted his wife with a gentle word and dancing eyes.

Jack Casement stopped alongside the car as the other passengers began to descend.

"Quite a setup, eh, Ted? The Union Pacific's sending you off first-class after the final spike ceremony. Plush seats, the best of food, fine wines, and good friends." Casement glanced at his pocket watch. "Should be another surprise along any minute."

In the distance a black smudge soiled the sky and soon yet another locomotive chugged onto the siding. Ted watched in growing curiosity as the door of the single car swung open. At his side, Wilma gave a sudden squeal of delight. Standing in the doorway was Vi Elkins, her husband grinning broadly over her shoulder.

The two women embraced as Ted warmly shook hands with the newsman. "After all the blood and sweat we've invested in this railroad," Taylor Elkins told Ted, "I wouldn't miss this for the world. Besides, it isn't often a man gets to witness an incident of such historic importance. And in the company of friends, as well."

Ted nodded toward the single car in which the couple had arrived. "Traveling in high style, aren't you, Taylor?"

Elkins chuckled softly. "A little expense-paid vacation trip from our friends in high places in Washington." He reached inside a coat pocket for a packet, then handed it to Ted. "A bit of a bonus for your efforts, my friend, and everyone knows you've earned it."

Ted opened the flap of the packet and peered inside at the hundred-dollar bills.

By midmorning the last of the guests had arrived. The bad weather had ended, the temperature edged into the sixties, and two bands lustily entertained the growing crowd. Counting the military bands and soldiers of the Twenty-First Infantry Regiment, about one thousand people waited patiently beneath the United States flag fluttering from a telegraph pole that stood between the track ends at the crest of the pass between the North and South Promontory Mountains.

As noon neared, a growing sense of excitement swept through the crowd. Reporters from several newspapers and a wire service jostled for interviews with railroad officials as well as common laborers and dignitaries. Twice Ted graciously refused interviews, telling reporters he had had little to do with the progress of the railroad. Instead, he sent the reporters toward the talkative Kevin O'Reilly and pointed out the Central Pacific's Jim Strobridge.

"They're the men who built the railroad," Ted said. "They would make a much better story for you."

The best story of all he did not mention. Chin-Lu and his new bride had earned their privacy. He watched as the Chinese man and the Cheyenne woman stood quietly, holding hands and watching, as preparations continued for the placement of the final spike. For Chin-Lu, perhaps there would be a sense of progress for his native country, as the new rails brought the China trade to all of the United States. But it meant something entirely different to his adopted culture, the Cheyenne. Ted wondered if Chin-Lu held the same ambivalent feelings toward his part in the construction of the railroad as Ted did.

His musings were interrupted by shouts. The great ceremony was about to begin.

The opening prayer droned on and on until Ted began to wonder if the grass beneath his feet would grow to his boot tops before the preacher shut up. He almost chuckled aloud as, at his side, young Bill whispered, "Dad, reckon he's going to bless the bugs, too?"

Finally the verbose preacher yielded to the politicians, and the words flowed in torrents of praise for the builders, the workers, the financiers, the government, Manifest Destiny—and, of course, the politicians themselves. Words tumbled upon words as everyone except those who had actually been involved in the hazardous and bold task took the podium.

At last the final politician spoke, and bowed in recognition of the roar of applause that followed, unaware that the outburst was not for the content of his oration, but a celebration that at last it had ended.

Then came the real moment of excitement.

Iron men from both Union Pacific and Central Pacific crews hefted the final lengths of rail and carried them forward, preparing to complete the link between West Coast and East.

The elaborate final tie—a gift from the states of California, Nevada, Idaho, Arizona, and Montana—was brought out. It was of California laurel, eight feet long, eight inches wide, and six inches thick, ornamented with silver and polished to a soft, lustrous sheen. Holes had been drilled in the final tie so that the soft metal of the spikes would not be damaged.

California Governor Leland Stanford stepped up to the final tie, holding a silver-headed maul specially made for the occasion. *Now*, Ted thought with relief, *we'll get on with the business.*

He had forgotten the propensity of preachers. There was another long prayer, then mercifully brief speeches by railroad officials.

At last, Governor Stanford struck the first blow to symbolically seat the Golden Spike and link the two coasts. His stroke with the maul missed the spike and hit the rail, but no matter. The gathered throng exploded in a lusty, lingering cheer.

The transcontinental railway was now a fact!

Jack Casement and Charlie Crocker each had a turn at gently tapping home the ceremonial Golden Spike, along with other railroad officials.

"The last rail is laid! The last spike is driven! The Pacific Railroad is completed!" A telegraph operator at the site sent the news to a waiting nation.

To complete the ceremony, two locomotives sounded whistles. Disconnected from the cars that they had brought to the scene, the engines chuffed gently forward. The Union Pacific's burly No. 119, with its tall, straight stack, and the Central Pacific's funnel-stacked Jupiter touched cowcatchers.

The most ambitious construction undertaking in the history of the nation was now complete!

After another wild celebration, the symbolic touch of the locomotive cowcatchers was broken. Soon the magnificent laurel tie would be removed, along with its Golden Spike, and ordinary railroad materials substituted.

Ted was not among those who so lustily cheered the completion of the railway. Chin-Lu and Little Fern were also reserved, he noted.

Across the United States, cities exploded in huge celebrations even more intense than those that had followed the end of the War Between the States. Church bells rang, bands played, throngs cheered the accomplishment. Even the Liberty Bell was sounded in exaltation. Newspapers across the country rushed out special editions, flamboyant reports of the magnificent feat. Only the *Washington Globe*, with Taylor Elkins's byline, played the story as straight news.

At Promontory, Ted and his friends prepared to board the special cars for the ride to Cheyenne, where stagecoaches would be waiting to carry the party to Fort Laramie. There, away from the reporters and the fanfare, an extended celebration was planned. The entire Laramie Hotel had been reserved for the occasion, with the exception of rooms occupied by permanent guests.

Ted turned to Chin-Lu and Little Fern. "Will you join us? We would be most honored," he said.

Chin-Lu shook his head sadly. "No, my friend," the slender Chinese said. "From here we travel by horseback to the camp of Paints-His-Horses. It is a time for contemplation, a time for being together. I am now a Cheyenne. Already I begin to think as one. Little Fern and I will never forget you—but we must go now to our own people."

"I understand, Chin-Lu. May the spirits ride with you." Ted extended a hand, felt his fingers gripped firmly, and then watched as Chin-Lu and his bride mounted and rode away, the lowering sun at their backs.

As his family settled into the rail car, Ted said a quick farewell to Shaughnessy and to Jack Casement.

"Take good care of old Hellbender for me, General Jack," Ted said. "I'm going to miss that horse."

Casement, who was no better at good-byes than Ted, merely nodded and offered a hand. "Take care of yourself, Ted Henderson—and thank you."

The sun was almost at the western rim of the desert as the posh rail car floated along the iron ribbons. Wineglasses clinked and eating utensils clattered as Ted sat at a window seat, his young son dozing beside him.

Ted's fingers toyed with a chunk of metal, the fired cartridge from Yellow Crow's .56 Spencer rifle.

"Something wrong, dear?" Wilma's voice was quiet but concerned. "You seem preoccupied, almost depressed despite all the celebration going on."

Ted gestured out the window. On a distant ridge a dozen mounted Indians stood in sharp relief against the blood-red sunset. A hunting party, he supposed. None of the Indians seemed to move. They merely sat on their horses and stared at the iron horse passing below.

"They aren't celebrating either, Wilma," Ted said softly. "The land they have called home for so long has been wounded. The injury was inflicted by two long strips of iron. I share their pain, darling. In my heart I resent this so-called progress." Ted sighed heavily. "Honey, I don't want to dampen anyone's party. Go ahead and have fun. Let this old frontiersman sit and think and listen to his son snore." He patted her shoulder gently. "And Wilma—thank you for all you've put up with. For all you've meant to me."

Wilma, a tear in the corner of a violet eye, leaned

forward and kissed her husband gently on the cheek. Then, respecting his wishes, she turned to join the others at the bar of the special train car.

The locomotive whistle wailed out the day and ushered in the night. The sound was a death song for a way of life, Ted realized. *Am I feeling genuine sympathy for the Indian,* he wondered, *or am I feeling sorry for myself because there is no more frontier? No place still out of reach of man's machines?*

The one-time Pony Express rider, former soldier, rancher, and now ex-railroad scout, stared out the dark window, but he saw scenes. Scenes brought by the twin iron rails. Plows digging into prairie sod that had protected the earth against the sweeping wind for centuries. Herds of cattle grazing on vast grasslands. The success of the Henderson-O'Reilly ranch proved livestock could live year round in the Plains, thriving in warm weather and surviving the rough winters. The Great Plains could become a stockman's heaven.

Ted was still haunted by the buffalo-shooting incident on the railroad. Was he seeing the beginning of the end for the great, shaggy beasts? How would the red man's culture survive without them? How long would the Indian tolerate the white intrusion into their ancestral lands?

There were so many questions. And no place to find the answers except in the future.

His fingers drifted once more to the spent rim-fire cartridge in his shirt pocket, the symbol of a renewed vow of brotherhood with the Cheyenne chief Yellow Crow.

Somewhere out there, in the shrinking vastness of the Plains, perhaps Yellow Crow sat asking himself the same questions. And now, a new Cheyenne friend—a small man called Chin-Lu by the whites and Shadow-Man by the Indians—probably was settling down to spend the first night on a long trail home, nestled in the arms of a beautiful young Indian woman.

Ted clicked a thumbnail across the crimp in the rim of the spent cartridge where the firing pin had struck it.

"Wise-One-Above," he whispered quietly, "if the peace between red man and white should end, lead the white man called Henderson on a separate path from his brother's."

Ted became conscious of a presence in the seat next to his softly snoring son.

"Feeling better, dear?" Wilma said, reaching across to stroke his cheek.

Ted smiled. "I suppose so. I was just wondering what the future might hold for Bill," he said, gesturing toward the sleeping youth between them.

"A long and happy life, we pray," Wilma answered. "The child has a better chance than you did, Ted. The West is getting tame now."

Ted arched an eyebrow. "Are you sure 'tame' is the right word? It may be open to settlement, but I'm not sure this magnificent country will ever be completely tame."

★ WAGONS WEST ★

A series of unforgettable books that trace the lives of a dauntless band of pioneering men, women, and children as they brave the hazards of an untamed land in their trek across America. This legendary caravan of people forge a new link in the wilderness. They are Americans from the North and the South, alongside immigrants, Blacks, and Indians, who wage fierce daily battles for survival on this uncompromising journey—each to their private destinies as they fulfill their greatest dreams.

☐	26822	**INDEPENDENCE!** #1	$4.50
☐	26162	**NEBRASKA!** #2	$4.50
☐	26242	**WYOMING!** #3	$4.50
☐	26072	**OREGON!** #4	$4.50
☐	26070	**TEXAS!** #5	$4.50
☐	26377	**CALIFORNIA!** #6	$4.50
☐	26546	**COLORADO!** #7	$4.50
☐	26069	**NEVADA!** #8	$4.50
☐	26163	**WASHINGTON!** #9	$4.50
☐	26073	**MONTANA!** #10	$4.50
☐	26183	**DAKOTA!** #11	$4.50
☐	26521	**UTAH!** #12	$4.50
☐	26071	**IDAHO!** #13	$4.50
☐	26367	**MISSOURI!** #14	$4.50
☐	27141	**MISSISSIPPI!** #15	$4.50
☐	25247	**LOUISIANA!** #16	$4.50
☐	25622	**TENNESSEE!** #17	$4.50
☐	26022	**ILLINOIS!** #18	$4.50
☐	26533	**WISCONSIN!** #19	$4.50
☐	26849	**KENTUCKY!** #20	$4.50

Prices and availability subject to change without notice.